TRUST

CHARLES EPPING

TRUST

A NOVEL

GREENLEAF
BOOK GROUP PRESS

Austin, Texas

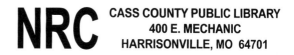

Published by Greenleaf Book Group Press
4425 Mopac South, Suite 600, Longhorn Building, 3rd Floor, Austin, TX 78735

Distributed by Greenleaf Book Group LP

For ordering information or special discounts for bulk purchases, please contact Greenleaf Book Group LP at: 4425 Mopac South, Suite 600, Longhorn Building, 3rd Floor, Austin, TX 78735, (512) 891-6100

Design and composition by Greenleaf Book Group LP
Cover design by Greenleaf Book Group LP

Library of Congress Control Number: 2006920563

ISBN 10: 1-92977438-9
ISBN 13: 978-19297743-8-8

Printed in the United States of America on acid-free paper

09 08 07 06   10 9 8 7 6 5 4 3 2 1

First Edition

For Elemér—and Roswitha.

Tout m'est suspect: je crains que je ne sois séduit.
Je crains Néron; je crains le malheur qui me suit
D'un noir pressentiment, malgré moi prévenue.

I fear that everyone, including myself, can be corrupted.
I fear Nero, and the dark star that follows me.
Haunted by a black presentiment, despite myself.

—Jean Racine, *Britannicus*, act 5, scene 1

TRUST

PROLOGUE

Keleti Pályaudvar Station, Budapest
May 21, 1938

"They can't do anything to me, darling. I'm a Hungarian citizen, after all. I have every right to pass through Austria, Nazi-occupied or not."

"Figyelem! The Orient Express to Vienna, Zurich, Basel, and Paris is now boarding. Track nine."

Aladár Kohen peered through the thick cigar smoke filling the wood-paneled telephone cabin. The first-class waiting room was emptying rapidly.

"I have to go now, darling. That's the third time they've—. Yes, I'll call you when I get there." He quickly gathered up his newspapers. "Don't worry, I'll make sure your money's safe—that *our* money's safe."

"Attention, please! The Orient Express is about to depart. Track nine."

"I really have to go now. Give my kisses to István and Magda. Goodbye now. *Csókolom.* Yes dear, my suit is fine. We saw each other two hours ago, remember?"

Aladár snuffed out his cigar, grabbed his newspapers, and headed to the station's main floor, his leather suitcase in hand.

When he stopped to get his hat from the rack, he glanced into the large gilded mirror to the left of the waiting room door and smiled. With his pinstriped suit, Eden hat, and dark tie, he thought he looked just like a banker—a Swiss banker even.

"Attention please. The Orient Express is about to depart."

He rushed out the door, not noticing that his shirt and tie were sprinkled with drops of soup and small crumbs from his quickly eaten meal in the station restaurant.

"Attention, please. Last call."

As he hurried through the crowded station, several sections of his newspapers fell to the ground. He didn't stop to pick them up. It didn't matter; the news was all the same. From the local *Pesti Napló* and the German-language *Pester Lloyd* to the *Neue Zürcher Zeitung* and the *Manchester Guardian*, it was clear that Hitler's *Anschluss*, his annexation of Austria, was only the beginning.

He got to the train just as the porter was removing the small wooden steps to the sleeping car. "*Kérem a jegyét!*" The porter held out his hand for the tickets.

Aladár searched frantically through his pockets. "I know they're here somewhere . . ." He opened his leather wallet and several bills and pieces of paper fell to the ground. As he knelt down to pick them up, he felt the hot steam coming from under the dark blue Compagnie des Wagon-Lits sleeping car.

A shrill whistle blew from the far end of the station. Aladár looked up sheepishly. "I don't know where they are. I had them just an hour ago." As he stood up, the conductor spotted the tickets sticking out of Aladár's left vest pocket. He quickly helped Aladár onto the train, and then blew his whistle. Within seconds the train began to move.

Inside his compartment, Aladár set his suitcase on the bed and got out the toiletry case his father-in-law had given him before he died, just two years before.

Aladár ran his fingers over the soft brown leather—some of the best the Blauer factory had produced. He could still hear his father-in-law's voice telling him about the Swiss. "*Akármi is lesz*—whatever happens, you can always trust them with your money. They're honest, they know how to keep a secret, and above all, they know how to stay out of wars."

Mr. Blauer often said that his decision to keep the Blauer money in Switzerland during the Great War had allowed him—and the leather factory—to survive the chaos and inflation of the *après guerre.* Now it was Aladár's turn to make sure the Blauer fortune survived the coming conflagration.

He heard footsteps in the corridor. A beautiful dark-haired woman was walking by. He smiled. The woman paused, then walked on. Aladár leaned out his compartment and saw her disappear into the second-class sleeping car next door. A hint of Chanel No. 3—one of his favorites—lingered in the passageway.

He sat back on the bed and stared out the window as the expansive fields of wheat and barley glided by. At one point, he reached into his pants pocket and ran his fingers over three small keys. He thought of the call he had received from the Blauer family banker in Vienna last week. "We've only been part of the Third Reich for a month," the normally stoic banker had whispered, "and they've already started seizing accounts with Jewish names. Thank God you transferred everything to Switzerland *before* the Anschluss. How did you know?"

"Actually, it was Katalin's idea . . ."

The train screeched to a halt. Aladár leaned out the window and saw a large flag billowing over the border crossing. The black swastika in the center of the red and white banner sent a shiver down his spine. He sat back to wait.

He opened his passport and stared at the name on the first page: *Kohen.* The name his father had been so proud of. So proud that he hadn't changed it at the beginning of the century when most of the Jewish families in Budapest were changing theirs.

Perhaps that was why his father remained a lowly professor, while Jewish families with German-sounding names like the Blauers' headed up the social and economic ladder.

Aladár heard shouting from down the tracks. He turned to see three border guards in green uniforms leading a woman from the train. The lining of her coat trailed on the ground behind her. It was the woman he had seen passing through the corridor earlier. He watched as the guards pushed her into a one-room building with the word Hegyeshalom written above the door. Apparently the Hungarians were on the lookout for capital flight, arresting anyone trying to take valuables out of the country.

When they got to Aladár's compartment, they made only a cursory look through his things, obviously having learned from experience that passengers traveling first class had more ingenious ways of getting their money and jewels out of the country than sewing them into the linings of their coats.

A few minutes later, the Nazi border guards arrived. "Heil Hitler!" They gave Aladár a quick salute and told him to open his suitcase.

One of the guards—a young, blond man with a strong Austrian accent—asked for his passport. Aladár handed it to him without a word. His heart was pounding.

He watched as the guard read the name carefully, then handed the passport to a man in the corridor wearing a black suit and a Nazi armband. The man carefully copied Aladár's name and address into a small, leather-bound book, and then handed back the passport and moved on.

Once they had gone, Aladár locked his door and kept it locked for the entire journey across Austria—Ostmark, as it was now called. Österreich, the "Empire of the East," had become part of the Nazi Reich. How long would it be before the same thing happened to Hungary?

Aladár lay back and closed his eyes. He tried to sleep, but ended up counting the hours as they headed toward the Alps—and the Swiss border.

You could have taken the southern route, he told himself, even though that would have meant traveling through Zagreb, Trieste, and Milan, and then over the Alps through the St. Gotthard Pass to Zurich. *But would it have made any difference? Would the Italian Fascists have been less menacing to someone with a name like Kohen?*

At dawn, he opened his curtains and revealed the Alps glowing pastel orange in the dark blue morning sky. The sight of these impressive peaks always moved him.

The untouched, snow-capped mountains made him feel weightless somehow, as if they could pull him up to their level, away from the worries of life, away from everything.

At Buchs, the Nazi border guards were much more thorough than when Aladár had entered Austria.

They went through everything, including his shaving kit. Finding nothing of importance, they left his belongings in disarray and moved on.

The Swiss border guards, on the other hand, were exceedingly polite. Bringing money or gold into or out of Switzerland had never been restricted. They simply asked Aladár the purpose of his visit.

"I have to meet with my banker in Zurich," he told them in English.

"Welcome to Switzerland."

They handed back his passport without any further questions.

"The Hotel St. Gotthard, please." Aladár climbed into a shiny black taxi waiting outside Zürich-Enge station. "Um . . . could we please drive along the lake's edge? It's such a beautiful morning, no?"

Although he spoke fluent German, Aladár always used English or French when he was in Switzerland, afraid that his High German accent would type him as a *Dütsche*, a German national, something he wanted to avoid at all costs.

He opened the window of the gleaming Buick sedan and breathed deeply. The air smelled of freshly mown hay and the faint odor of cow manure. He leaned out. The lakeshore was lined with green fields and sprawling villas. It looked so clean and fresh, and the houses and boats looked perfectly placed, like carefully constructed miniatures on an elaborate toy train set.

"Do you know which mountain that is?" Aladár squinted at a snow-covered peak rising through the mist at the end of the lake. "Over there. See?" He pointed excitedly. "That one. Above the lake steamer. Is it the Titlis? How high do you think it is?"

"About three thousand meters, I guess," the driver answered laconically. His English was almost as heavily accented as Aladár's.

"Oh, but it has to be more than that." Aladár leaned closer to the driver. "The Claridenstock is 3,270 meters, and that mountain is much higher than—"

"If you knew, then why ask?" The driver kept his eyes fixed on the road.

"Well, actually I wasn't sure." Aladár sat back. "My father would have known, though," he muttered. "God bless his soul." They turned up the Bahnhofstrasse and Aladár stared at the people walking along Zurich's main thoroughfare. Instead of the bright clothes and stylish hats he was used to seeing on Budapest's Váci Utca or Vienna's Ringstrasse, it seemed everyone here wore black.

He wondered why they looked so unhappy, so bored. Didn't they know how lucky they were to be living here?

"How do you feel about the Anschluss?" he asked the driver.

"Why do you ask?"

"I mean, how does it feel having the Nazis on your eastern border?"

The driver shrugged. "What difference does it make? They've been on our *northern* border for years."

"Yes, but . . . doesn't it bother you what's happening?" He remembered the guard writing his name into the small leather notebook. "The Nazis are starting to take—"

"The Austrians got what they wanted. Didn't you see them welcoming Hitler into Vienna with open arms? Flowers, music, Nazi salutes. Didn't you see? The referendum was 100 percent in favor of—"

"Actually, it was 99.7 percent." Aladár put his head through the window of the partition that separated him from the driver. "But the referendum only took place after the Nazi troops had already marched in . . . it was hardly a fair election."

The driver shrugged again. "The Fascists are taking over everywhere. What can you do?" He parked under a low awning next to the Hotel St. Gotthard, and a bellhop came to open the door.

"But now that they have Austria, who's going to be next?" Aladár asked.

The driver pulled on the brake and pointed to the meter. "Nine francs please."

As he checked into the hotel, Aladár noticed that his room cost much less than it had when he was here last winter with Katalin to take charge of the Blauer family accounts after her mother passed away. His room at the St. Gotthard, one of Zurich's finest hotels, now cost only twelve Swiss francs—twenty peng, less than three U.S. dollars.

Dinner was even more of a bargain. For eight francs he was able to enjoy a three-course meal of consommé, veal in a cream sauce with Rösti potatoes, and sabayon for dessert.

After dinner, Aladár sat down in the hotel lobby to read the local newspapers. He noticed that a new Jeanette MacDonald movie, *Tarantella—Die Spionin von Madrid* (*Tarantella—The Spy from Madrid*) was playing nearby at the Alba, just across the Limmat.

His meeting at the bank was not until ten the next morning. Why not go? Maybe a movie would relax him.

It didn't. The newsreel before the film chronicled a recent meeting between Hitler and Mussolini in Rome. Aladár watched in horror as thousands of Fascist supporters crowded into the Piazza Venezia shouting, "Duce! Führer!"

The image of the crowd and the goose-stepping soldiers marching through Rome took his thoughts beyond the film, beyond the calm Zurich night. He thought about what would happen if war came to Europe. He wondered what would happen to Katalin, to his children, to himself.

When the film ended, the crowd calmly filed out of the cinema. In Zurich, everything seemed in order, whereas the rest of the world seemed to be spinning out of control.

The ocean liner was docked in Venice. It was trying to head out to sea, but it couldn't move. It was firmly attached to the wharf with long, powerful ropes. People on board were running around, confused and panicked, looking for life rafts and putting on safety vests.

Aladár held his daughter's hand tightly. A sailor, a blond youth who looked like the Nazi border guard, was dragging away his wife and son. "Katalin! István!" Aladár called. He started to run after them, but Magda pulled him back. "Papi! Papi!" she shouted. "Don't leave me!" A pregnant woman ran toward him, screaming, "Save my child! Please! Save your child!" It was the woman from the train.

He woke up in a sweat. It was still dark outside. He glanced at the phone by the bed. "Don't panic," he whispered. "It was only a dream. Things will be better in the morning."

They weren't. He walked down the Bahnhofstrasse in a daze, looking for his bank among the dozens lining the elegant boulevard. *What am I doing here?* he asked himself. *Is this the place I should be putting all of our money?*

He read the names as he passed the austere buildings: Bank Leu, Swiss Bank Corporation, Credit Suisse, Union Bank of Switzerland, Julius Bäer.

All these banks, all so full of money. People must come here for a reason, Aladár told himself. *Switzerland, the land of peace and prosperity—in the middle of the maelstrom.*

He spotted his bank through a line of emerald green Linden trees. Helvetia Bank Zurich was spelled out in large gold letters—in English, French, and German—on a solid granite wall.

He looked around for Herr Tobler, his private fund manager. Tobler had said he'd be waiting for Aladár at the Bahnhofstrasse entrance to HBZ.

Rudolph Tobler, like his father, had been in charge of all the Blauer family accounts in Switzerland since well before the Great War, and now that the older Tobler had passed away, it was his son who was in charge.

Aladár finally spotted him standing next to a column to the right of the front door. He was wearing a pin-striped suit, shiny black shoes, and an Eden hat, just like Aladár's.

When Tobler saw Aladár, he calmly put out his cigarette and walked inside without saying a word. Aladár reminded himself that Tobler was only respecting the cardinal rule of Swiss banking: Never acknowledge your clients in public. In 1935, Clause 47B of the Swiss Federal Banking Act had even made it a crime to divulge the name of any client of any Swiss bank—to anyone.

As he walked through the front door, Aladár noticed two nude cherubs carved into the stone lintel watching, smiling, and protecting the clients of one of Zurich's premier private banks.

Tobler was standing in front of the elevator on the far side of the long marble hall. To his right, a long line of men waited at a counter marked GOLD/OR. Aladár wondered if they were buying or selling. Buying probably. Gold was the only thing that was holding its value these days. Not bonds, not commodities, and definitely not stocks.

Aladár followed Tobler into the wooden elevator. Tobler still didn't acknowledge him. Without a word, he pushed the button for the second floor marked PRIVATKUNDEN — PRIVATE CLIENTS. Only when the doors closed did Tobler hold out his hand. "How nice to see you again, Mr. Kohen." His handshake was firm, warm. "Did you have a nice trip?"

"It was the first time I've passed through Nazi territory. A harrowing experience for someone with a name like mine."

"Why? Did they give you any problems?"

"No, not me . . . fortunately." Aladár remembered the woman being led away by the border guards at Hegyes Halom. "Thank God Katalin had the foresight to send our valuables ahead of me. Did everything arrive?"

Tobler nodded. "Three suitcases. Is that correct?"

Aladár nodded.

"They're downstairs—in a temporary storage room inside the bank's vaults. They're just waiting for you to decide where to put them."

"Excellent."

"They can't stay there for long, though. We should probably rent a safe for you—as soon as we're finished up here."

"Fine." Aladár began searching his pockets. "I have the keys here somewhere—"

"Don't worry." Tobler put his hand on Aladár's shoulder. "We can take care of that later, once we've arranged for the new account to be opened. First things first."

The elevator stopped with a jolt and opened onto a large, wood-paneled room. The concierge directed them to a group of leather chairs in the far corner. Light poured in from a long row of windows overlooking an interior courtyard. Aladár noticed that there were no windows on the side of the building that faced the street. *Discretion oblige.*

After they sat down, Tobler got out two cigars and offered one to Aladár. "How is Mrs. Kohen?" he asked.

"Not good. Ever since the Anschluss, the Hungarian Fascists are making things extremely difficult for anyone with a Jewish name. They've gotten especially severe now that the Nazis are so close."

"Don't forget," Tobler lit Aladár's cigar, "they're right on our border, too."

"Yes, but you have your neutrality to protect you."

"Apparently." Tobler lit his own cigar and leaned back. "And how are your children? Magda and István? Is that correct?"

"Yes." Aladár took several short puffs. "István is almost as tall as me now. He should be starting university soon, if they let him." He sat back and stared out the window. "And Magda's as fresh and irreverent as only a ten-year-old can be. She's so innocent. She has no idea of what's in store."

A waiter appeared from a side door carrying a silver tray with two glasses of water and two coffees. He served Aladár and Tobler silently, and then went back through the door and closed it firmly behind him.

"I'm afraid." Aladár took a sip of water. "I'm afraid it won't be long before Hungary is absorbed by the Third Reich. And it will be, one way or another.

That's why I've come here. We want to make sure our money and valuables are safe. We want to put everything in a new account, an account that no one else knows about. No secretaries, no accountants back in Budapest—no one." He leaned forward. "Only myself and Katalin. And you, of course."

"And the bank." Tobler took a sip of his water.

"Yes, of course." Aladár nodded. "And I want it to be a secret account. So no one knows where the money went."

"A good idea." He paused. "But the bank will still need to know your name and address."

"No problem. Swiss bankers are required by law to keep all account information a secret, right?"

"Yes." Tobler looked around the room carefully. "If you apply *Swiss* law they are."

"But what other kind of law could there be?"

"It's just . . ." Tobler began looking through his papers. "I mean, if Switzerland were ever to be invaded. . ."

"But how could *that* happen? Switzerland is neutral, and has been for hundreds of years." Aladár stared at Tobler. "Switzerland was able to survive the last war unscathed. Why would things be different this time?"

Tobler looked up. "Who knows what Hitler and his cronies are capable of?"

"But the Swiss would *never* allow the Germans to come marching in. This isn't Austria, after all."

Tobler nodded. "We *have* mined all the mountain passes. And we've agreed to cooperate with all sides in the event of war. That's part of being neutral, of course."

"But still," he looked into Aladár's eyes, "you never know what the Nazis may do. They're calling for a thousand-year Reich, don't forget. A German Reich." He paused. "And now they have Austria. Who do you think will be next? The Sudetenland? Then what? How many more German-speaking countries are there?" He took another sip of his water.

"You may be right." Aladár sat back, remembering last night's dream of the Nazi soldier, of losing his family on the ship. "But where else could I put the family's money? I can't take it back to Budapest or Vienna. And Amsterdam or London would be even more vulnerable to Nazi attack, wouldn't they?"

Tobler put his hand on Aladár's shoulder. "I'm sorry to have frightened you. I'm sure everything will be fine." He started to stand up. "I'll go see what's keeping the banker who's supposed to be meeting us."

"No, wait!" Aladár reached over and pulled him back down. "Is there any way to be certain that our money never falls into Hitler's hands?"

Tobler took a deep breath. "Several of my clients have opted for another solution—my clients with Jewish names, that is."

"What is it?"

"Many of them have opened *Treuhandkonten*, trustee accounts. They're Swiss bank accounts like all the others, it's just that," Tobler lowered his voice, "the account is put in someone else's name—a non-Jewish name. That way, if Hitler were ever to decide to invade . . ."

Aladár waited for him to finish. He didn't.

"But even if the Nazis *did* take over Switzerland, what would stop them from forcing the banks to tell them about *all* the Jewish accounts, just like they did in Austria?"

"Because the banks wouldn't *know*." Tobler leaned closer. He put his hand on Aladár's shoulder. "The thing about these trustee accounts is that the banks are never told whom they really belong to. We don't even say that they *are* trustee accounts."

"But . . ." Aladár glanced across the room at the concierge. He was sitting quietly at his desk, reading a newspaper. "But if I opened a trustee account . . . and if no one at the bank is told, if no one knows that *I'm* the real owner of the account . . . what recourse would I have if there were a problem?"

Tobler took a long puff of his cigar. "That's why you need to choose someone you can trust. Someone without a Jewish name, of course."

"But Katalin's father's name doesn't sound Jewish. Why can't we put the account in the name of Blauer?"

"You don't think they'd know about the Blauers being Jewish? They've been doing business in Germany since before the Great War. There's no way the Nazis wouldn't know—Aryan name or not."

Tobler took another puff of his cigar, then placed it carefully in the silver-plated ashtray. "You don't have to choose *me*, by the way. You could choose anyone: a lawyer, a banker, whomever you want. If there's someone else you feel you could trust more than me—"

"Actually, there's no one in Switzerland I trust more than you. And you know I promised Mr. Blauer that I would continue to use you and your father to manage their money here in Switzerland. It's just that—" Aladár pushed back a long strand of hair that had fallen into his eyes. "I just don't know."

"Fine." Tobler stood up. "Then open a normal account as you originally requested." He seemed angry. "But remember that even though I manage the funds in your accounts in Switzerland, someone from each bank has to be *nominally* responsible—and that means knowing the name and address of the account owner."

"And if we opened a new trustee account, they'd only know about *you*."

Tobler nodded. "As a matter of courtesy, we're supposed to tell the bank every time we open a trustee account. But we're not required to. Not by law." He stared down at Aladár. "It's your decision, Mr. Kohen, but you have to make it *before* we meet the banker." He glanced toward the heavy wooden door at the far end of the waiting room. "You can't change your mind once we tell him whose account it really is. Just tell me what you want to do."

Aladár shook his head slowly. "I don't know. It's not easy to make a decision like this."

"If you want, we could start putting your things in the safe downstairs. That would give you time to think."

"It's just . . . how can I put all of my money, my wife's family money, into someone else's hands?" Aladár stared down at the intricate designs of an oriental carpet on the floor in front of him. "I don't know what to do."

"Then I'll go over and see if they'll let us delay our meeting."

After Tobler left, Aladár continued to stare at the carpet.

I can't afford to make a mistake, he told himself. *Not now. Not with war about to explode across Europe.*

His eyes were drawn to a small design on the edge of the rug. It looked like tiny swastikas had been woven into the intricate pattern. A common symbol in India, he reminded himself. But it made him uneasy, seeing this hated sign of Nazi power in the heart of Switzerland.

Tobler's polished shoes suddenly appeared next to the design. "Have you made a decision?" he asked calmly.

Aladár looked up. He shook his head slowly.

"So let's go down and start putting your things into the safe." He helped Aladár up and led him to the concierge's desk. "But remember, you have to decide what kind of account you want before you leave the bank. Every safe has to be linked to an account of one kind or another." Tobler turned and began speaking in Swiss German to the concierge.

He looked so comfortable, so assured, so calm, Aladár thought. It was all so easy for him. Of course, why wouldn't it be? He was a Swiss citizen—with a good Aryan name.

The basement vaults of the Helvetia Bank of Zurich were hot and stuffy. Aladár felt claustrophobic—and the decor didn't help a bit. Thousands of painted papyrus leaves and lotus blossoms covered the columns and beams. It looked as though the bank had hired a second-rate Hollywood moviemaker to come in and cover the vault's walls with intricate Egyptian motifs to give the place a feeling of timelessness, but it simply made the room feel even more cluttered.

Tobler led Aladár to a half-open steel door. Above the door, the words Tresor—Sammelraum were etched in gold. Aladár peered inside. The room was full of trunks, paintings, and suitcases of all sizes. "Where did all this stuff come from?" Aladár whispered.

"A sign of the troubled times we're now living in, I'm afraid." Tobler led Aladár through the door and down an improvised aisle of wooden crates, suitcases, and paintings stacked on wooden racks. "This place has been full ever since the Anschluss."

"Is that a Picasso?" Aladár pointed excitedly to a painting leaning against a storage rack to his right. "And over there, that's a Kandinsky!" Many other paintings were stacked along the walls, neatly wrapped in paper and string. Many of them had names written on them. Aladár noticed that almost all of the names were Jewish.

He tried to push aside a leather suitcase that was blocking his way through the shelves, but it wouldn't budge. He tried to lift it to move it out of the way, but it was too heavy. *Only one thing could be that heavy*, Aladár told himself. *Gold*.

"*Nein! Hände weg!*" the guard shouted. "Don't touch!"

"I'm sorry," Aladár muttered. "I didn't know . . ."

Tobler put his hand on his shoulder. "Your things are over there." He led Aladár across the room to an overladen shelf.

Like most of the other boxes and crates in the room, Aladár's three suitcases were tagged for identification with a tiny lead seal attached to the handle with dark brown twine. The guard put the cases on a small wooden cart and wheeled them out of the musty room. Aladár and Tobler followed silently into a large, well-lit room marked Tresor.

The walls were covered with hundreds of metal doors with dark, wooden molding. Some of the safes were as small as shoe boxes, others were as big as coffins. Tobler led the way to one of the largest, at the far end of the room.

The guard handed Tobler a small silver key. He put an identical one into one of the two keyholes and waited for Tobler to insert his. They turned the keys at the same time. The guard then opened the door to reveal a closetlike vault lined with light-brown wooden shelves. He pulled out his key and muttered something in unintelligible Swiss German before leaving.

"What did he say?" Aladár asked.

"Just to call him when we're ready to leave. We have to have both keys to lock the safe. That way, no one can open it without the bank's knowledge."

Tobler got down to open the first suitcase on the cart. "Do you have the keys to open these?" he asked.

Aladár had to look through his pockets twice before finding the keys Katalin had given him in Budapest.

After inserting the key, Tobler quickly opened the faded leather suitcase, breaking open the small Hungarian seal melted onto the front flap. He lifted the lid gently. "You're lucky to have your contacts at the embassy. Diplomatic couriers are the only ones who can get things across borders these days." Tobler pulled out several carefully wrapped packages, each one numbered and tied with string.

"It was all done by the people at the factory. They used the old Blauer contacts at the embassy to get it here. I had nothing to do with it." Aladár sat down on the cold stone floor and watched Tobler open the first package.

The contents of these suitcases, Aladár realized, had, in fact, already been put into someone else's hands, and everything seemed to have arrived intact.

"Look at this." Tobler handed Aladár a small wooden box inlaid with ivory and mother-of-pearl. "It's so heavy."

"I'll check what's inside." Aladár clipped open the gold clasp. "Kati will surely ask if everything arrived safely." As he opened the lid, several gold ingots fell out onto the floor. "Oh dear!"

"Don't worry." Tobler reached down to pick them up. "They don't break." He looked up and smiled. "And even if they did, it wouldn't matter. Gold is sold by weight, in whatever form it is."

He laid the ingots on the top pine shelf and began opening the second package.

Meanwhile, Aladár opened a drawer in the bottom of the box and found four antique watches. Two had hand-painted enamel covers, one in engraved silver, and one in gold. He picked out the gold watch and examined it carefully. It had a glass backing that displayed the clockworks inside. "I never knew the Blauers had so many things. All of this must have been stored at the factory. I never saw any of it at home."

"Look!" Tobler held out a blue felt bag and motioned for Aladár to reach inside. "Napoléons."

Aladár pulled out a fistful of gold coins.

"Do you know them?" Tobler took one out of Aladár's hand and held it up to the light. "See? That's Marianne. *Symbole de la France*," he said in perfect French. "There must be several hundred in here."

"I wonder how much they're worth." Aladár put his hand back into the bag and ran his fingers through the coins.

"Several hundred thousand francs, I'm sure—*Swiss* francs, of course." Tobler opened another package. "At today's deflated property prices, the coins in that one bag would be enough to buy a villa along the lake." He pulled out a small velvet-covered box and handed it to Aladár. "This looks important."

Aladár opened the box to reveal an exquisite diamond *collier*. Even in the dim light of the vault, it sparkled spectacularly. "I know this." He took it out and held it up to see it better. Three pendants hung on each side of the necklace, each one holding a large pear-shaped diamond.

"Katalin wore this to the Opera-bál in 1922." Aladár ran his fingers over the cold stones. "Budapest high society was trying to outdo Vienna in elegance. On that night, I think they succeeded." He held the collier up to the light. "The Blauers let me accompany their daughter—just that once, or so they thought.

I'm sure they never imagined their little princess would fall in love with a poor college professor's son."

Aladár stared at the collier, remembering how these diamonds had glittered around Katalin's neck that night, how happy she was, how happy they both were. It had all seemed so natural, as if it would never end. And now, less than sixteen years later, Mr. and Mrs. Blauer were both dead, and their prize possessions were being hidden in a stuffy vault under the streets of Zurich. It was now up to Aladár to make sure their wealth was preserved for the next generation, and the one after that.

He watched Tobler open the second suitcase. It was full of stocks and bonds, carefully stacked and tied with dark burgundy ribbons. Tobler set them gently on the floor beside the cart.

Aladár knelt down and read the title of the first certificate. It was in English: "State Loan of the Kingdom of Hungary, 1924." Underneath the seal of St. Stephen was written "Issue in the United States of America of 7.5 percent sinking fund gold bonds. Nominal value: $1,000."

"How many of these are there?" Aladár asked.

"Several hundred, I suppose." Tobler ran his fingers along the edge of the bonds. "That means there's several hundred thousand dollars worth of bonds in this one stack . . . if they ever get paid back." He set more bundles of stocks and bonds off to the side.

"Amazing." Aladár knelt down and read some of the names aloud. "Société Métallurgique de l'Oural Volga, Railway Lines of the Kingdom of Romania, Government of Czechoslovakia. Why aren't you putting them in the safe?" Aladár asked.

"Because you should sell them." Tobler had begun filling the safe with jewelry and gold bars from the third suitcase. "And I think you should sell them immediately. We'll be lucky to get their full value as it is."

"But they sent these things here for safekeeping, not to get rid of." Aladár looked through the remaining certificates. "There must be close to a million dollars worth of securities here—the bulk of the Blauer fortune."

"Which is why you should sell them." Tobler stood up and brushed off his hands. "You must realize that if war comes, these securities will be worthless."

"How so?" Aladár pointed to a line under the Hungarian state seal on the first stack of bonds. "It says these are backed by gold. In the United States, in fact."

"Exactly. If war comes, Hungary will almost certainly be on the side of the Germans, which means that if the United States ever decides to stand up to the Nazis, the gold backing these bonds will be seized as enemy property." He pointed his finger down at Aladár. "And you, as a Hungarian citizen, would be an enemy national. Your assets in the United States would all be seized."

"But I'm Jewish!"

"That doesn't matter. You're still a Hungarian citizen."

Aladár looked around the vaults, bewildered. "So what you're saying is that I'd be persona non grata on both sides?"

"I'm afraid so." Tobler wiped his hands with his handkerchief. "Now, if your assets were in *my* name, since Switzerland is a neutral country, there would be no problem." He stacked the empty suitcases on the cart and pushed it over by the door. "But it's your decision."

"I know." Aladár reached into the vault and picked up one of the gold bars lying on top and read the inscription: UBS/SBG 1 KILO FINE GOLD 999.9 ESSAYEUR FONDEUR. Underneath was an eight-digit serial number. The last four digits, he noticed, were 2499, the exact altitude of Mt. Rysy, one of his favorite peaks in the Tatras.

He placed the bar carefully back on the shelf and turned to Tobler. "But if I were to open one of these trustee accounts, what would happen, if . . . if something were to happen to *you*?"

"If I were to die, you mean?" He wiped his forehead with his handkerchief. "With my other clients, we prepared a document describing the trustee account, outlining the exact details of what would happen in any and every eventuality. Essentially, my successors would be required to keep your assets in trust for you, or your family, just like I would do if I were still alive."

He put the handkerchief back into this pocket. "The document is then kept in my own personal vault, along with my will and my other private papers."

"And your other clients are comfortable with this?"

Tobler nodded. "They know that the reason for this whole exercise is to keep any and all documents relating to the trustee accounts away from the banks— as far away as possible, in fact. That way, if the Nazis were ever to invade Switzerland, the only thing they would find at HBZ would be an account in my name. Nothing more."

"And what if something were to happen to me and Katalin?" Aladár asked.

"The account would *always* belong to you and your heirs, no matter what. Under Swiss law—as well as Hungarian law, I believe—your estate would then be divided between your children."

"Does that mean I would have to tell them about this account?"

"That is up to you, Mr. Kohen."

"Of course, István should know," Aladár muttered. "But I couldn't tell Magda. Not yet. She's too young. If she were ever to be interrogated by the Nazis—"

"You have to decide what's best."

Tobler reached into the safe and began lining up the gold bars in neat rows. "If you decide to open a trustee account, I will have to go upstairs and fill out an account-opening card. That's all. Since the account's in my name, all I have to do is sign the card, and they give me a number. No questions asked."

He turned to Aladár. "You could then transfer everything into the new account from all your other accounts. If you do, I suggest you use an anonymous intermediate account at another bank, so no money goes directly into the trustee account. That way, no one is able to trace where the assets from your old accounts ended up."

"Typical Swiss efficiency."

Tobler turned back to the safe and continued stacking. "You should keep at least one small account open, however, in your own name. Put a small amount of cash and securities in it—just enough to keep it active. That way, if anyone should ever come looking for your money, they would find *something*. It would be unrealistic to think that someone of your family's means would not have *any* account in Switzerland."

"You've thought of everything, haven't you?"

"By the way, the small account should be kept totally separate from the trustee account. You can also give the members of your family a power of attorney for the dummy account so they could have access to it at any time, like any normal Swiss bank account."

"And if my family wanted access to the actual trustee account?"

Tobler put his arm around Aladár's shoulder. "All they would have to do is come and see me." He walked toward the entrance. "I'm going to get the guard. And when I come back, you're going to have to decide what kind of account you want to open. We'll need the account to rent the new safe. Every deposit box in the bank has to be linked to some sort of account."

"But what happens if war *does* come," Aladár asked, "and we're trapped inside Hungary?"

"In that case . . ." Tobler walked back to Aladár. "You wouldn't need to do anything. I'd be here. I'd be in charge of the account. I would take care of everything for you."

"But if I'm trapped in Hungary, how would you get paid?"

Tobler smiled. "Don't worry. If you give me your permission, I could just deduct my usual half-percent annual fee from the account." He stared into Aladár's eyes. "But most of my other trustee account clients have opted for a simpler solution: they chose to pay me a lump sum fee of 5 percent—but only when the account is safely back in their hands. After all of this is over."

"And if the war lasts longer than ten years?"

"Then I end up working for free." Tobler forced a smile. "But I doubt any war will last that long. I'm sure the English and the French and the Russians will stand up to Hitler at some point. And if America joins in . . ." He clasped Aladár's hand tightly. "Don't worry. As long as I'm alive—indeed, even after I'm gone—your account will always be here, waiting for you."

He left the vault and Aladár walked over to the suitcases. He felt tired, confused, alone. How could he just hand over his entire fortune—his father-in-law's entire estate—to another man? How could he trust someone he hardly knew? But if he couldn't trust Tobler, whom could he trust?

He took off his jacket, got out his handkerchief, and wiped his forehead. The room had begun to smell of damp wool.

Aladár sat down on the cart, next to the suitcases. *Maybe I should call Katalin,* he told himself. *But what would she say? Do whatever you think best, my darling.*

But he knew in his heart that if something went wrong, she'd never forgive him.

He looked down and noticed that the diamond collier was still clenched in his left hand. He walked over to the safe and laid the collier on top of the gold bars, carefully placing the large center diamond on the identification number of the bar ending with the number 2499, the altitude of Mt. Rysy.

That way, if anyone got in while he was gone, he'd know.

CHAPTER 1

The thin line of code glowed cobalt blue in Alex Payton's dark eyes. On the surface it looked innocent, innocuous. But something was wrong. She just didn't know what.

It looked too perfect somehow—as if it had been put in there to look as innocent and innocuous as possible.

Just like that morning Alex had been called in to "say her goodbyes." Her mother's body had looked so peaceful lying there, her head flat on the mattress, her mouth partially open. She looked so calm—as if she were still asleep, as if nothing had happened to her.

"What's up? You look like you've seen a ghost." Eric Andersen walked around the low wall separating their workstations. He put his hand on Alex's shoulder. "What is it?"

Alex touched a lacquered nail to the highlighted code at the top of her screen. "It's an old millennium bug, and I can't figure out why it's here."

"Let me see." He put his hand on Alex's shoulder and leaned in for a closer look. She could feel his body's warmth. It felt good. Their basement office in the main building of the Helvetia Bank of Zurich was kept cold, allegedly to keep the computers from overheating.

Thompson Information Systems required its women consultants to wear business suits or skirts at all times: "Assume the client could come walking in at any time," they'd told her when she started three months before. "It's important to always be prepared."

As if Jean-Jacques Crissier would ever come in unannounced. The Swiss IT consultant HBZ had hired to oversee the project hardly ever came down to see what they were doing. But Alex had to dress up every day just in case. Fortunately, Thompson allowed its newly hired "green bean" consultants an advance on their salaries to buy new clothes, whatever it took to look the part of well-off professionals—even though their student loans would keep them in debt for the next ten years.

"Here's why it got flagged." Eric pointed to the 87 in the short line of digits labeled DATE. "Although it doesn't really matter anymore. If it didn't surface in the year 2K it's not going to—"

"Actually, this one *could* activate—in the year 2087 in fact." Alex touched her fingernail to the numbers just after the name RUDOLPH TOBLER. "But only on that one day, October 19."

"Who cares?" He stood back and stretched. "Just remove it and let's call it a day."

"But I can't figure out why they put it in here in the first place." She moved the cursor to the words RUDOLPH TOBLER in the middle of the highlighted text. "If all they wanted to do was change the names on this guy's account statements, why go through all the trouble and change the code to do it? Especially back in the eighties when space was at a premium."

"You're not supposed to say eighties, you know." Eric sat on the table next to Alex's computer. "Remember what they told us when we started here? 'Now that we're in the twenty-first century, it's important to refer to years with their complete—'"

"Whatever." Alex moved the cursor to the end of the code. "It still makes no sense why they put this in here—in the nineteen eighties or any other time."

"So let's delete it." Eric reached for her mouse. "It's almost quitting time. Let's get out of here."

"Wait a minute." She held onto her mouse tightly. "I want to see something."

She moved the cursor to the end of the code and double-clicked the words TOBLER & CIE at the end of the text. "It looks like they wanted to have this name on the sale statements—but only on that one particular day. Why?"

"What difference does it make? It's probably the same guy anyway. That's probably his company." Eric touched his finger to the letters CIE. "Those are the initials they used to use for companies back then. You still see it sometimes on old buildings." Eric sat back on the table and stretched his legs out and around the base of Alex's chair.

"But if it's the same guy we're talking about, why change the names?" Alex sat back and crossed her hands behind her head. "And why use the code to do it when it would have been a lot more efficient to—"

"So what? The account itself wouldn't have changed, only the name on the account statement."

"Hold on." Alex grabbed her mouse and highlighted the entire string of code. "Let me try something."

She quickly copied the text onto a word-processing document on the lower half of her screen and broke the long line of code down into five discrete elements.

```
1014102 IF T31-TRAN-ACCT-NUMBER=249588
IF T31-TRAN-ACCT-PRI-NAME="RUDOLPH TOBLER"
IF T31-TRAN-EXECUTE-DATE=871019
IF T31-TRAN-TYPE-CODE="SALE"
MOVE "TOBLER & CIE" TO P22-PRT-CONF-PRI-NAME
```

"Look at that account number." Eric pointed to the end of first segment. "It only has six digits. I wonder if it's even *at* HBZ. Didn't the one they gave you when we started working here have a lot more? Plus a few letters? Mine did."

"Mine had twelve numbers. But maybe the account numbers have grown since 1987."

"Like telephone numbers? I remember how the one we had when I was growing up in Copenhagen started out with letters, then five numbers. They replaced the letters with numbers and kept adding new ones—but the original number was still in there."

Alex sat back. "I wonder if someone was trying to cheat that guy."

"How? Why?"

"I don't know. Maybe someone should ask him." Alex pushed the speaker button on her phone to get a dial tone and then started dialing.

"What the hell are you doing?" Eric reached over and grabbed her hand. "You know what the bank would do if they found out you contacted one of their clients?"

"Relax." Alex smiled. "I'm just calling Crissier. We're supposed to show him any two-digit references to dates before we delete them, remember? Or has it been so long since you've found one?" She sat back and waited for the phone to ring. "Good thing we're not paid on commission."

"Very funny." Eric crossed his arms and leaned against the wall of Alex's cubicle. "Did you ever wonder how Crissier gets away with not even having an office in the bank? I mean, why did they hire him at all? He doesn't do anything that we couldn't do."

"I'm sure there's some rule about having a Swiss oversee foreigners who may have access to client information. You know how fanatic they are about—" Crissier's voice mail came on. She held up her hand.

"Grüezi, hier Jean-Jacques Crissier . . ."

Alex left a message telling him about the code and asked him to come down to the computer room as soon as possible. While she spoke, Eric got out his pack of cigarettes.

"Don't you remember," she asked once she hung up, "what they told us when we first started working here?"

"I don't remember Crissier saying *anything* about smoking." Eric lit up casually. "I just remember him telling us to ignore all the client information." He smiled. "And, of course, to immediately report any two-digit references to dates." He held his cigarette between his thumb and index finger and began speaking with an exaggerated German accent. "You are to show me every-sing you find. Especially references to code in years of ze nineteen eighties, yes? And remember to ignore all ze names you may see."

He then switched back to his regular voice. "As if we were computers—as if we could just push Delete and forget whatever we'd seen."

CHAPTER 2

Zurich
Thursday Evening

"Where *is* everyone?" Eric shoved the empty champagne bottle, top down, into the ice bucket. He looked around the semi-deserted restaurant. "Did you ever notice that Swiss waiters are never there when you need them?"

Alex finished off her glass and set it on the table next to the ice bucket. "Are you sure you want to order another bottle?"

"Of course, if I can find someone to come out here and *take* my order." He looked around again. "All this talk about the fine art of Swiss service, but when it comes right down to it, they're much more concerned about making sure the kitchen's clean. It's like they're more interested in the process than the people."

"Like at the bank?"

"What do you mean?"

"Like what Crissier said when we showed him the code manipulation." Alex held up her fingers and counted the words aloud. "'Just delete it.'" She sat back. "After making us wait for over an hour, that's all he has to say?"

"Why should he care anyway? It was a long time ago. Why should anyone care?"

"It doesn't make sense. That code was used to make an alteration on a client's account statement." She looked into Eric's eyes. "You'd think there'd be alarm bells going off all over the place."

"Maybe there are," he smiled, "and we just can't hear them." He looked around for a waiter again.

"Did you notice that Crissier didn't even make a copy of the code before we deleted it?" Alex asked.

"So?" Eric drained his glass. "Ours is not to reason why, ours is but to do or die."

"So that's it?" Alex asked. "We just go on as if nothing happened?"

"What else can we do?"

"I think someone should look into what happened."

"Why? That guy's probably dead by now."

"What was his name again?"

"Tobler. A good Swiss name if I've ever heard one." Eric smiled. "I thought you had a photographic memory?"

"For numbers, not names." Alex shrugged. "The account number, if you're interested, is 495880. Or was. As you said, it's probably grown a bit since 1987."

"What? The account, or the number?"

She smiled. "Both, probably."

Eric stood up. "I'm going to see if I can find a waiter."

"Maybe you'll find one back there," Alex pointed to the alcove marked WC–Telefon, "cleaning something instead of taking care of us."

"Hey!" Eric's eyes brightened. "I bet they have a telephone book back there. Do you want me to see if there's an entry for Rudolph Tobler? With a name like that, and with an account at the main branch of HBZ, there's a good chance he lived in Zurich, or still does."

"What makes you think he'd still be in Zurich?"

"Use this then." He handed Alex his cell phone. "Directory assistance gives you numbers for the whole country. The number, by the way, is three fives. Want me to dial it for you?"

"Very funny." Alex took the phone. "Just because I don't use a cell phone in Europe doesn't mean I don't know how to use one."

"I never understood how you can live without a cell phone."

"Who needs 'em? I use my computer to make all the calls I want. And with VoiP, I avoid the roaming charges."

"So that's it. You want to save money."

"Maybe." She started dialing.

"It's amazing how all you American MBAs have to live like paupers until you pay off your student loans. You pay a fortune to go to the best business schools, and then you spend the first ten years of your career paying it all off."

Alex looked up. "Well, that's the way it works. We don't have free universities like you Europeans." Alex smiled. "Hey, I bet I find him before you do."

Eric smiled. "If you do, I'll pay for another bottle of champagne for us. Back at the hotel." He turned to walk away. "What do you think of that?"

"Sounds good." Alex pushed the green button to send. "You better hurry, I'm almost there."

She watched Eric jog over to the WC–Telefon alcove. He looked great. Lean, sexy.

How do these Europeans get such nice bodies? Alex sat back and waited for directory assistance to answer. *They never work out, they smoke, they drink, but they still manage to look great.*

The operator finally answered. *"Auskunft."*

"Um . . . *Ich möchte* . . ." Alex quickly switched to English. "I'd like a number for Rudolph Tobler, please." She spelled the name carefully.

"Für welche Stadt?"

"I'm not sure. Can you try all of Switzerland?"

"Yes, please hold."

After a few seconds, the operator came back. "There is only one listing for that name. Please hold for the number." An automated voice came on and gave Alex a number with the Zurich prefix.

"Bingo!" Alex saw Eric walking toward her from the alcove. She pressed a small button at the top of the phone to hang up, sat back, and smiled.

"What did you find out?" he asked. "There was no phone book back there. And no waiters, of course, either."

"You owe me a bottle of champagne." Alex smiled proudly. "I just found out that Rudolph Tobler is alive and well and living in Zurich." She set the phone on the table in front of Eric.

"But how do we know if he's the one who had the bank account in 1987?"

"We don't. But that wasn't what we bet, is it?"

"You're right." Eric got out his wallet. "Let me pay the bill and let's get out of here. Then let's go back to the hotel and have some fun."

"Sounds great." Alex's heart raced. "Your room or mine?"

Eric looked shocked. "What do you mean?"

"I thought you wanted to go back to the hotel."

"I meant drink a bottle of champagne in the hotel bar."

"I'm sorry. I—"

"Look Alex," Eric put his hand on her shoulder. "You're a beautiful woman. One of the most beautiful women I've ever worked with, in fact." He stared into her eyes. "But it just isn't going to happen."

Alex shrugged. "I know the rules forbidding fraternizing while on assignment. I just thought . . ." She tried to make it sound innocuous. "I was just joking. Let's get some champagne back at the hotel then."

"Great. I'll be right back."

She could see the look of shock on his face as he turned to walk away.

You idiot, Alex thought. *What were you thinking?* She glanced up at decorated arches full of Germanic coats of arms lining the walls. *Coming on to your manager—after nine weeks on the job? What a fool.*

She heard a voice coming from Eric's phone and picked it up to listen. "Halo?" It was a man's voice. He sounded angry.

"Who's this?" Alex asked.

"Who's *this*?" the man asked angrily.

"I've already got the number. Thank you."

"What number?"

"The number for Rudolph Tobler. Thank you, I already—"

"But this *is* Rudolph Tobler."

Alex searched for the button to hang up. There were several on the top of the phone. She pushed one.

The voice continued. "Halo? Are you there?"

She found a button marked with a red circle on the side of the phone, pushed it once, and the voice stopped.

She looked across the room. Eric was talking with the waitress at the door to the kitchen. "Shit!"

Alex put the phone back on the table. She decided to act as if nothing happened. After all, nothing had happened.

The phone rang. She quickly read the ten-digit number that appeared on the screen. It was the number they'd just given her—Rudolph Tobler's number. She reached for the red button to turn off the phone but paused.

If you don't answer this call, she told herself, *Eric will see the "missed incoming call" message when he comes back. Or even worse, he'll find that he has a message from Tobler telling him I've used his phone to break the cardinal rule of Swiss banking.*

The bank had even made her sign a form when she began working at HBZ pointing out that it was a criminal offense to divulge the name of any of the bank's clients. What would they do if they found out Alex had actually called one of them?

She pushed the green button and held the phone tightly to her ear. "Mr. Tobler, I'm sorry for calling you, but you have to understand. It was all a mistake. The phone company—"

"Why did you say that before?"

"I'm sorry, I didn't know that directory assistance connected you automatically and—"

"You said, 'Rudolph Tobler is alive and living.' Why?"

"It doesn't mean anything. It was just a stupid bet." She looked over at Eric. He was getting a receipt from the waitress. "I'm going to hang up now. Please don't call back. This isn't my phone."

"I also heard something about a bank account in 1987."

"It doesn't mean anything. Just a stupid bet." Alex's heart was racing. "I've got to go now. Goodbye."

"If you hang up, I'll call back and keep calling back until I get an answer."

"I'm sorry." She glanced up. Eric was on his way back to the table. "I have to go."

"Rudolph Tobler was my father's name. He was killed in Tunisia in October 1987."

CHAPTER 3

Zurich
Friday, Early Morning

Alex squinted at the alarm clock. 06:00. It was still dark. The LED clicked over to 06:01, then 06:02. She buried her throbbing head under the pillow. She'd hardly slept all night. She had gotten up several times to go the bathroom, to get a drink of water, or to pop another Advil.

Rudolph Tobler's number came ticking back into her brain, followed by his words: "If you can't talk to me now, then I must insist you call me in the morning. Otherwise I'm going to call back and speak to your friend if I have to."

Alex pulled the comforter around her. 06:06. What was Eric doing now? Sleeping probably, without a clue about what had happened last night. Not yet.

With one phone call, Tobler could end her career before it even got started. Once Eric found out what she'd done, he'd have to report her to Thompson— and to the bank.

She threw back the comforter. Her whole body ached.

Would they really put her in jail? Maybe not, but at the minimum she'd lose her job. After getting fired nine weeks into her first job out of business school, she'd never be able to find work in consulting again.

"What a fool I was!" she muttered to herself. "I'm never going to drink that much again."

The bells outside her window rang once. Six-fifteen.

She stood up, pulled off her T-shirt and panties, and headed into the shower. The hot water poured over her body for several minutes as she decided she would have to convince Tobler to give up and make sure he didn't talk to Eric. She had to keep him from telling anyone.

As she dressed, Rudolph Tobler's number kept going over and over in her head. 044-252-4726.

She sat down to put on her shoes and glanced at the telephone on the table next to her. You have to call him before Eric wakes up. Before he turns on his phone.

She reached over and picked up the phone. She would convince him that it was all a mistake, that it didn't mean anything. She dialed zero to get an outside line, then the number. The phone rang several times.

She glanced over at the clock. 06:47. Was it too early? Tobler said to call first thing in the morning. And she had to do it now.

"Tobler." He answered with his last name only, the same way Crissier did.

"Good morning, Mr. Tobler. This is the woman who—"

"I know who you are. I've been waiting for your call." He sounded tired, angry. "Can you tell me what this is all about?"

"I told you. It's . . . not about anything. I made a bet with my friend that I'd be able to find the numbers of various people and—"

"What did you mean when you said that Rudolph Tobler was still alive?" He spoke as if he were reading his lines, as if he'd been practicing these words all night. "If you don't tell me, I promise you I'll contact your friend."

"I've told you, Mr. Tobler, this really has nothing to do with me, with any of us."

"But if it has something to do with my father's death, I must know."

"But I don't *know* anything. You have to believe me."

"Then why did you call me back this morning?"

"Because you threatened to call my friend. You said you'd keep calling until—"

"I think you have something to hide."

"I don't have *anything* to hide."

"Then meet me and tell me everything you know."

"I can't meet you. I don't even know you."

"Of course you know me. You know my name. All you have to do is look in the phone book and you'll know where I live—*and* what I do."

Alex glanced down at the *Zürich Stadt* telephone book lying on the shelf next to her bed.

"Mr. Tobler, I'm sure you're a perfectly respectable person, but I really can't meet you." She opened the book and flipped to the *T* section. There was only one entry for Tobler: "Rudolph. Filmproduzent. Nägelistrasse 8." *In a country that prides itself on secrecy,* Alex wondered, *why would they put people's professions and work addresses in the public phone book?* There was a second address: "Filmbüro, Limmatquai 31." She recognized the street. It was just up the river from her apartment.

"All I'm asking is for you to meet me for a coffee. It won't take but a few minutes. Look, there's a café in the center of the old town called Schober." He spelled it. "Everyone knows it. Meet me there at eight, all right?"

"And if I say no?"

"Then I may have to call your friend and have *him* meet me."

CHAPTER 4

Zurich
Friday Morning

Alex pulled her coat tightly around her as she headed up the Limmat, her laptop bag banging against her hip. She had brought her own computer in case things went badly and she needed to download her personal files from the computer at work.

To her right, she felt cold rising from the river. It was an alpine cold—a mineral-green, fresh-from-the-mountains cold. She looked down into the current and saw a small whirlpool starting to form. A maelstrom—isn't that what Eric would call it? She imagined being sucked under, pulled down into the river, like that time up in the Cascades near Seattle when she'd been fishing with her father and fell into the rushing mountain stream.

All she could remember were the thousands of bubbles rushing upward as she grasped an underwater branch to keep from being swept away by the current. She held on like that until her father pulled her to safety. She couldn't have been more than seven—it was well before the divorce, before he walked out of her life.

Images of those rushing bubbles and fighting the raging current by holding onto that underwater branch ran through her mind as she climbed the Marktgasse toward the bright orange awning of the Café Conditorei Schober.

She pushed open the heavy glass door and walked inside. Smells of chocolate and roasted coffee filled the narrow wood-paneled entry. Hundreds of different types of chocolate were displayed on trays throughout the room, as if the shop itself were one big box of chocolates.

Alex made her way to the "tearoom" at the rear of the shop. No one was there.

She sat down at a table for two and waited. Strangely, she felt invigorated, alive. Her hangover seemed to have disappeared completely. She checked her watch. Five minutes to eight.

On the wall to her right, she noticed a framed black-and-white photograph of the café at the end of the nineteenth century: women in black dresses and white aprons stood stiffly in front of the main entrance. The photo reminded Alex of the many years she had waited tables at Tully's in Seattle before she went to business school, before she began her career at one of the most prestigious systems management firms in the world. Thompson—her first real job.

Don't lose it now, she told herself. *Do whatever you have to. Tell Tobler whatever he wants to hear. Then get back to work and pretend nothing ever happened.*

The door opened and a lean, tanned man came over to her and held out his hand. He must have been about fifty; he had a full head of hair and a rugged face. "Hello. I'm Ruedi Tobler." He seemed nervous. "Pleased to meet you." His handshake was firm, but his hand was cold.

He looked anxious—frightened somehow. Not at all the bully on the phone. "Have you been waiting long?" he asked.

Alex shook her head no.

"That's good." Tobler sat down and pulled his chair close to the table. "Have you ordered yet? The coffee here is excellent. They grind the beans themselves. And the hot chocolate is said to be the best in the world."

"I'll just have a coffee, thank you."

Tobler called into the kitchen, "Zwei Espresso. Und au äs par Gipfeli." He turned back to Alex. "Thank you for coming. I'm excited to hear what you have to tell me. To find out what happened to my father."

"But I don't have anything to tell you, Mr. Tobler. I told you on the phone that I don't have any idea what—"

"Please. Call me Ruedi. It's short for Rudolph, the same name as my father's." He took off his tweed jacket and hung it on the back of the chair. "Would you prefer to speak English or German? I see by your accent that you're American."

"I prefer English. I studied some German in college, but it's kind of rusty. And when people start speaking Swiss German, it's impossible for me to—"

"No problem. We'll speak English then. I spend a lot of time in the States. LA mostly. I'm in the film business, as you know." He folded his hands on the table in front of him. "So, where would you like to start?"

"What do you mean? I told you I have nothing to tell you, nothing to add."

He stared at her for several seconds, his blue eyes large and expressive. "In October 1987, my father was killed in Tunisia. No one knows what he was doing there, but . . ." He bit his lip, then continued, "I mean, we used to go there on holiday, when I was a boy. But we hadn't been back in a long time."

The waitress came over to serve the coffee. She placed a small basket of croissants in the middle of the table and disappeared back into the kitchen with a slight bow.

"The Tunisian police called us one morning," Tobler continued, "to say that my father's body had been found in the main square, in Sousse, at the base of the fortress tower. His death was never *geklärt*, never explained."

Ruedi took a sip of his coffee. The cup rattled in its saucer. "That's why I want you to tell me everything you know."

"But I told you, I don't know anything about your father."

"Then how did you get his name?"

Alex started speaking, softly. "It's just . . . the name *Rudolph Tobler* was in some code at the place where I work. That's all."

"And what was that about a bank account in 1987?"

"There was a date in the code. October 19, 1987. That's all."

"That was four days before my father was killed." He stared into her eyes. "Was there anything else?"

"Nothing." She took a sip of her coffee. It was burning hot.

"Could you write down the code for me?" Ruedi asked.

"Why?" Alex shrugged. "It wouldn't do you any good."

"Please." He pushed his napkin over in front of her. "Just write it down there. I want to have *something* to take with me."

"Why? It's meaningless."

"Just do it for me. Please." He pulled a gold-plated pen out of his jacket pocket. "That's all I ask. Then you can go."

"And you'll never bother me again?"

"I promise. I can't ask for more than you know, right?" He handed her the pen. "Please. That's all I want."

"And you promise you'll never call my friend's number again?" Alex took the pen. "That you'll never tell anyone else about this meeting?"

"I promise." Ruedi dropped the cap to the pen on the floor and leaned far under the table to pick it up.

Alex started writing.

"Actually . . ." Ruedi returned to his chair and took a sip from his coffee. "Do you mind if I ask you a question?"

Alex looked up. "What is it?"

"Why were you so worried about someone finding out about your phone call to me?"

"I just want to make sure." She took a deep breath. "It's my job. We're not supposed to have any contact with people outside." Alex looked into Ruedi's eyes. They were deep blue, just like Eric's. "If they ever found out that I met with you I could get fired."

"Don't worry," Ruedi said softly. "I promise I won't tell anyone about the call—or about this meeting."

"Thank you." She handed him the pen and the napkin with the long line of code. "Here it is. I don't know what good this will do. I'm sure it won't make any sense." She pushed her chair back to leave.

"Wait a minute. What are these numbers after the word DATE?" Tobler pointed to the digits 871019.

"That's the date I told you about," Alex explained. "October 19, 1987. That's how they wrote it, with only two digits for the year. That's why it got flagged in the first place."

"But . . ." Ruedi pointed excitedly to the end of the code. "That's the name of my father's old company." He held his finger over the words, TOBLER & CIE. "But the thing is: he sold it *before* he died. To his partner, Georg Ochsner. Do you know what that means?"

"No I don't." Alex picked up her laptop case and held out her hand to say goodbye. "I'm sorry, I have to go now."

"Wait." Ruedi grabbed her wrist. "I have to figure this out before you leave. Please, it will only take a minute." He let go of her wrist and began dialing. He motioned for her to stay seated while he dialed.

Alex considered walking out. She had fulfilled her part of the bargain, and he promised he'd let her go.

"This will only take a minute." He pointed to his phone—the one he could use to call Eric if he wanted, Alex realized. "Just stay here until I call," he added.

Tobler spoke on the phone for several minutes in gutteral, unintelligible Swiss German. Alex couldn't understand a word he said.

She glanced up at the clock next to the photograph of the waitresses. Would Eric be at work by now and wondering where she was?

Tobler's eyes flashed at her several times during the conversation. He seemed to be getting increasingly agitated as he spoke.

A mother with twins, a boy and a girl, sat down at a table on the far side of the café. The children were speaking excitedly in French. The mother seemed so content, so happy.

Suddenly, Tobler slammed the phone on the table. "You lied to me."

"What are you talking about?" Alex pulled back. "I gave you the code exactly as it appeared in the—"

"But you didn't tell me that the account was at the Helvetia Bank of Zurich!"

Alex didn't reply.

"You knew the name of the bank, didn't you!"

Alex shrugged. "You never asked me about the name of the bank." She started to stand up. "I'm sorry, but I have to go now."

"Please. Sit down." He placed his hand on hers. "I only want to find out what this all means. Just a few more minutes."

She glanced around the restaurant. No one seemed to have noticed them.

"Please," Ruedi said softly.

Alex sat back down.

"I don't understand." He shrugged. "Why didn't you tell me everything as you promised?"

"I told you I could lose my job. Just for contacting you."

"But I promised you that I wouldn't tell anyone." Ruedi looked hurt, disappointed at her lack of confidence. "The fact that the account is at the Helvetia Bank of Zurich is very important. It could help me find out why my father was killed. Don't you understand?"

"I'm sorry, but I don't know anything about what happened to your father." Alex glanced up at the clock. "I really have to go back to work now."

"Just a minute." Ruedi picked up his phone and pressed the redial button. "I want you to explain to Georg Ochsner, my father's old partner, exactly what the code means. He's the one who told me where the account was."

Alex shook her head. "There's no way I—"

"Please." Ruedi waited for the phone to ring. "I just want you to explain to him in your own words what this code is about."

"I told you, I don't have any idea what it's about."

"Then tell him that. At lunch. Today. It'll just take an hour or so of your time." Ruedi kept the phone pressed to his ear.

Alex leaned close and whispered. "Don't you understand? I *can't* get involved in the affairs of a client of the bank."

"But I *am* the client," Ruedi answered confidently. "And it's *my* account. Or my father's, which is the same thing since I'm his sole heir."

"All I'm asking you to do is meet my father's old partner. Just have lunch with us, and then you're free."

Alex shook her head slowly. "I'm sorry. I can't."

He pointed to his phone. "Then maybe we should call your colleague. I'm sure he'll be more cooperative." He stared into her eyes. "I assume he works at the Helvetia Bank of Zurich, too?"

CHAPTER 5

Zurich
Friday, Noon

"Wo ist das Restaurant, bitte?"

The concierge of the Hotel zum Storchen pointed to the elevator with his pudgy index finger. "Upstairs," he muttered to Alex in English, then went back to reading an Italian-language newspaper.

Alex sat at a table on the terrace overlooking the river. Across the rooftops of the Zurich *Altstadt* she could see the Alps breaking through the haze. She ordered a mineral water and waited.

To her left, next to a wide concrete pedestrian bridge, was a tall neoclassical building with the sculpture of a fallen angel on the pediment. She noticed the word KRIMINALPOLIZEI engraved over the door.

Maybe I should go there, she told herself. *Tell the police that Rudolph Tobler is stalking me. But what good would that do? The bank would be brought into it, and then what?* Not only would she lose her job, but the police would know she had broken the law regarding bank secrecy.

Do what Tobler wants, she told herself. *Then go back to HBZ and act as if nothing is wrong.* That morning in the office she hadn't mentioned anything to Eric about last night, and he hadn't said anything to her.

Maybe he'd forgotten. Or pretended to forget.

She shuffled through the sugar packets on the table in front of her. Each one had a sign of the zodiac. She found hers. *Jungfrau*—Virgo. She read the description: "Virgo is a determined, orderly person with intelligent behavior at all levels."

"Yeah, right," Alex muttered. How orderly was it to screw up and allow that call to go through? How intelligent was it to be caught lying? How determined was it to let Tobler talk her into coming here today?

She looked up and saw Ruedi leading a well-dressed older man around a table of Japanese businessmen smoking cigarettes. They slowly made their way to the terrace.

Her heart began pounding. *Relax*, she told herself. *In two hours it'll all be over.*

"Nice to see you again." Ruedi shook her hand as if they were old friends. "I'd like you to meet Georg Ochsner."

Alex noticed how Tobler deftly avoided bringing up her name.

Ochsner shook her hand and smiled. "A pleasure, dear Fraulein." He was wearing a sport jacket, like Ruedi, but the rest of his clothes were much more formal: a blue monogrammed shirt, Hermès tie, and dark slacks. A burgundy silk *pochette* was sticking out of his left breast pocket. Ochsner sat down across from her.

Ruedi sat at Alex's side, between her and the door. "Thank you for meeting with us today." He smiled. "And for agreeing to explain what you found in the computer."

"I can't . . ." she turned to Ochsner. "I don't know anything other than the information I gave to Mr. Tobler this morning."

"That's all right." Ochsner nodded. "I'm sure your insight will be very helpful. I don't know if Ruedi told you, but I am his father's executor."

"I already told her." Ruedi got out the Café Schober napkin and laid it in the middle of the table. "I need to understand what this is all about."

"Don't worry, young lady," Ochsner said softly, "anything you say here today will be kept strictly confidential. I'm a Swiss banker—well, a former banker, but a banker nonetheless."

A waitress wearing a dirndl walked over to take their order. "The fish here is quite excellent," Ochsner said authoritatively.

Alex glanced at the menu. The prices were astronomical.

"I suggest I order a sea bass for everyone." Ochsner's accent sounded more upper-class English than Swiss German. "And may I suggest some wine?" he added. "A St. Saphorin, maybe?" He didn't wait for anyone to agree or disagree, but ordered for everyone.

As soon as the waitress was gone, Ochsner turned to Alex and took up where he had left off. "As I was saying, we simply would like to know more about what the code means."

Alex touched a fingertip to the edge of the napkin. "All I know is that it mentions an account number and some names. That's all."

"But would you be so kind," Ochsner looked through the lines of text written on the napkin and pushed it over to Alex, "and tell us what this could have been meant for?"

"It just tells the computer to change the names on all that account's statements, on one particular day in 1987. October 19th." She pushed it back to the center of the table. "I don't know why they put it in there, though. It made no sense."

"Did you notice the date?" Ruedi asked Ochsner excitedly. "Exactly four days before my father died. That has to have something to do with—"

Ochsner motioned for Ruedi to wait while the waitress poured their wine.

Once she left, Ochsner turned back to Alex. "What do you *think* it means?"

He slipped a gold cigarette case out of his jacket pocket and opened it calmly. "Surely you must have an idea why someone would want to change the names on an account statement."

"I have no idea. I'm a computer analyst, not a banker."

"I can see that." He took a long sip of wine.

Alex took a sip of wine as well. It was cool, fruity, sweet. Would this be all they wanted? Was it over? Was it that easy?

"What do *you* think it means?" Ruedi asked Ochsner.

"Frankly, I don't know." He pulled out a thin, gold-tipped cigarette and lit it slowly. "I'm a banker, not a computer expert."

"But you knew that this account existed," Ruedi continued. "You told me on the phone that—"

"Of course I knew about this account. It belonged to your father. And I, as his executor, am in charge of it—like everything else in his estate."

"But why didn't you tell me about it?" Ruedi persisted. "After Mother died, I became Father's sole heir. Aren't you, as his executor, required to tell me about *all* of his assets?"

Ochsner blew the smoke out slowly, "The only thing I am required to tell you is that this account at the Helvetia Bank of Zurich does exist."

"But if this account's in my name, in my father's name, then it must belong to me, right?"

Ochsner took a series of quick puffs and snuffed out his cigarette, then said, "*Ja-ein.*"

"And what does that mean?" Alex asked.

"It means yes and no." Ochsner leaned toward her, his elbows on the table, his hands clasped. "The account *is* in Ruedi's name. But it doesn't belong to him."

"But he's his father's sole heir." Alex took another sip of wine. "What belonged to his father must belong to him."

"Do you know what a *Treuhand* account is, young lady?"

"No." Alex shook her head. "I don't."

Ochsner held out his hands, palms up. "It comes from the words *trust* and *hand*. You have a similar expression in English, I believe."

"You mean the word *trustee*?" Alex asked. "Or *fiduciary*?"

"Correct." Ochsner smiled stiffly. His teeth were stained yellow. "And until recently, it was perfectly legal in Switzerland for people from other countries to have as many trustee accounts as they wanted. These anonymous accounts were meant to protect clients' assets from unwanted attention." His eyes narrowed. "You may not know, but in many parts of the world it is a crime to have money in banks outside your home country—even legally earned money."

"So?" Alex asked.

Ochsner glared at her. "I see by your accent that you're American."

Alex shrugged. "So?"

"You may find this hard to understand," he lit another cigarette, "but people from many countries around the world have come to rely on Swiss banks to preserve their families' assets from one generation to another. There are many cases, even today, in which countries put strict limits on the amount of money one is allowed to take out or spend abroad. This is especially true in Latin America, Africa, and Asia, but it's true even in Europe. For example, in France under the Mitterrand regime. And of course, in Germany before World War II." Alex noticed that he was holding his cigarette exactly as Eric had done when he was imitating Crissier. "You may not be aware of this, but it was when the Germans began confiscating Jewish bank accounts in the 1930s that the Swiss enacted the Bank Secrecy Act."

"But that was just a pretext, wasn't it?" Ruedi interrupted. "The Swiss bankers had been trying to get that law for a long time—for their *own* benefit. It had nothing to do with what the Nazis were doing."

"Of course the Swiss banks wanted that law," Ochsner answered angrily. "Banking is a business, just like any other."

"But why take advantage of others' misfortunes?" Ruedi asked.

"They *didn't* take advantage," Ochsner answered. "They were providing a useful service."

"I don't buy it." Ruedi shook his head disgustedly.

Alex took another sip of wine and leaned back to watch them spar.

"Don't forget," Ochsner continued, "your father was a *Treuhänder*, and like many Swiss fiduciaries, he helped his clients safeguard money that otherwise would have been confiscated by the authorities at home."

"So?"

The waiters arrived, set the fish on a side table, and began to debone them carefully.

Ruedi turned to Ochsner as soon as the waiters left and said, "I still want to know why I was never told about this account."

"I told you. Because it's not your account," Ochsner answered testily. "It's a *trustee* account. It is only in your name, it's only yours unofficially."

"Whose is it officially?" Alex asked.

Ochsner looked up. His eyes flashed. "That's not your concern." He began eating.

"It's *my* concern, though." Ruedi interjected. "And I want to know who this account really belongs to."

"I'm sorry. I can't tell you that." Ochsner took another bite and stared out over the river as a glass-covered tourist boat pulled up to the dock and picked up the group of Japanese businessmen who'd been inside the restaurant earlier. "It's none of your business."

"But since the account is in my name—don't I have the right to know?"

"Technically, you do, but I—"

"So then *tell* me." He glanced over at Alex. "Tell us. Who does this account belong to?"

Ochsner put down his knife and fork and wiped his mouth with his napkin. "The truth is, this account was opened by your father in 1938 for someone from another country. My instructions as his executor were to *not* inform anyone of its existence. You were only to be told about this account upon my death."

"And what if I had died before you?" Ruedi asked.

"Then I would have left instructions to turn over the account to your heirs."

"But I have no children," Ruedi persevered. "Who would have gotten the account then?"

"Whomever you had chosen as your heir. But, like your father, they would have held it in trust—for the true owners."

"Do you know who the true owners are?" Alex asked Ochsner.

"I . . . I can't really say."

"You *can't*?" Ruedi asked. "Or you won't?"

Ochsner stared at Ruedi for several seconds. "The truth is your father made an agreement with the account's real owner, the beneficial owner as we call him, to keep their name a secret—even from any future trustee. It's in a sealed envelope, in my safe at home."

"It's been sitting there ever since my father's death?" Ruedi asked.

Ochsner nodded.

"And you've never told me about it?"

"Swiss banking practice requires me to do nothing until the beneficial owner shows up."

"You've never thought to open the letter?" Alex asked. "To see who it belonged to? To see if maybe they could be contacted?"

Ochsner shrugged. "I had no right."

"What about the dormant-account scandal back in the nineties? Why didn't you tell someone about it then?"

"I couldn't."

"Why not?" Alex persisted.

"Because it wasn't a dormant account. It was a trustee account."

"What's the difference?"

"The dormant-account scandal you refer to only involved those accounts that hadn't been touched since World War II. Most of them were only worth a few thousand dollars—the money was placed in noninterest-bearing accounts. Only a few had more than a hundred thousand, if I remember correctly." He turned to Ruedi. "And do you know why?"

Ruedi shook his head. "No."

"Because they were 'dormant accounts.' Other than deducting their fees, the banks didn't do anything with them. By the time the Americans forced the Swiss banks to disclose the accounts, there was hardly anything left—after all the fees and commissions had been deducted." He started eating again. "It certainly wasn't enough to warrant the worldwide scandal."

"So why didn't the banks disclose these trustee accounts?" Alex asked.

"They couldn't," Ochsner replied.

"Why not?" Ruedi asked.

"Because the banks were never *told* about them. That was the whole point. It was the *trustees* who knew who the accounts really belonged to."

"So why didn't the trustees report them to the authorities?" Alex continued.

"Because no one has asked them to." Ochsner sat back. "And until they do, we have no legal right to disclose them." He pushed his plate aside. "Swiss banking secrecy. I'm sure you understand what that entails."

"This is ridiculous." Ruedi interjected. "If no one has come to claim these trustee accounts by now, they *never* will."

"You never know." Ochsner sat back and lit another cigarette. "And until someone forces me to do something otherwise, my responsibility as your father's executor is to make sure the assets are wisely invested." He took a long puff. "And wait for someone to claim them."

"And in the meantime you've been investing the money?" Alex asked.

"Yes. I personally managed the money in this account until I retired in the early nineties. Then I gave the mandate to a man at a fund management company in Zurich named FINACORP." He turned to Ruedi. "But I still keep a keen eye on the balance. I check it every three months, in fact. And I must say, it's doing quite well."

"So why hasn't anyone from FINACORP ever contacted me?" Ruedi asked. "The account is in my name, someone should have—"

"As far as the fund manager knows, the account belongs to your father's estate," Ochsner shook his head. "I, as your father's executor, am the *only* person they're legally required to report to."

"Until when?" Ruedi asked.

"For as long as I'm alive." Ochsner replied. "You know I transferred all your father's other assets to you years ago, but this account is still part of your father's estate and as his sole executor, *I'm* responsible for it, not you."

"Ruedi's father died in 1987 and the estate is still open?" Alex asked. She remembered how her mother's executor had taken all of three weeks to get rid of her mother's assets.

"You may not be aware of this, but in Switzerland," Ochsner told Alex tersely, "an estate can remain open for as long as the executor deems necessary. Years. Decades, if necessary." He stared at her defiantly. "That's the way it works here."

"So *you* were managing the account in 1987?" Alex asked.

Ochsner's eyes flashed. "I resent your insinuation, young lady." He snuffed out his cigarette angrily. "Although I bought Tobler & Cie when Ruedi's father retired in the early eighties, he insisted on managing this account personally until he died—four days *after* the code was entered into the bank's computer."

"It's a bit of a coincidence, isn't it?" Ruedi asked. "My father was murdered just four days after the computer manipulation mentioning this account that *he* was managing?"

"Murdered?" Ochsner looked puzzled. "You know very well your father committed suicide."

Ruedi's face flushed. "But . . . that's never been proven for sure."

"What are you saying, Ruedi?" Ochsner scowled. "There was a suicide note."

Ruedi glanced back over at Alex. "Okay, there *was* a note, but all it said was 'Ruedi, I'm depending on you to take care of your mother.'" He shrugged. "They found it in his hotel room—in Sousse."

Ochsner reached over and put his hand on Ruedi's arm. "Ruedi, everyone has accepted that your father committed suicide. Me. The police. Even your mother. Why can't you accept the fact that—"

"But why was his suicide note addressed to *me*, and not to my mother?"

"He probably knew you would have the most trouble accepting his death." Ochsner sat back. "I have to tell you something, Ruedi. When your father told me about this account in 1987, the day before he went to Tunisia, he talked like someone who wasn't going to be coming back."

"Then why didn't you stop him?" Ruedi's voice cracked. "If it was so obvious what was going to happen?"

"What could I have done?" Ochsner looked shocked, insulted. "Anyway, no one knew for sure *what* he was going to do."

"Then how can you be so sure now that he did commit suicide?"

Ochsner shook his head. "I'm sorry, Ruedi." He put his hands on the table, palms down. "In hindsight, it's clear he knew what he was going to do."

Ruedi stared into Ochsner's eyes. "If you'd only *done* something, said something, to me or to my mother."

"There was nothing I could do." Ochsner shook his head slowly. "It was none of my business."

"Oh really?" Alex pushed her plate aside. "Just like with that account?"

"I told you, there was nothing I could do," Ochsner answered defiantly.

"There was a lot you could have done. You were executor. You had every right, if not the obligation, to do something."

Ochsner took a deep breath. "I know it is hard for you Americans to understand this." He stared into her eyes. "But it's *not* the job of Swiss bankers to go around the world sticking their noses into clients' private matters. Our job is to hold their assets responsibly until the owner, or the owner's heirs, come to us. That's what Swiss bank secrecy is all about." This was obviously not the first time he'd given this speech. "*American* banking secrecy, if you pardon my saying so, is an oxymoron. You Americans want everyone to know everything about everyone. You want people to tell everything about themselves, which is one of the reasons clients put their money in Switzerland. They know we're not going to go around talking about it."

"But look what's happened here," Alex insisted. "This account's been sitting since World War II, and nobody even knows about it. Maybe not even the account owners. Or their heirs. Just because of your cherished 'bank secrecy.'"

Ochsner got out his handkerchief and wiped his forehead. "I happen to know for a fact that Ruedi's father made quite diligent efforts to find the owners of all of his trustee accounts after the war. But for many of them, there was just no trace." He turned to Ruedi and continued. "And it's not as if your father didn't have an incentive. If I understand correctly, the agreement on this account, like many of the others, was that 5 percent was to be paid to your father as a management fee—but only when the account was returned to the original owner."

"Five percent of what?" Alex asked.

Ochsner sighed. "Five percent of the account's total value."

"And how much *is* that?" Alex asked.

"I *can't* tell you. But I will say this: any account that was consistently invested in stocks over the past century would have done quite well." He got out his credit card and handed it to the waitress, then turned back to Alex. "Are you aware that just a thousand dollars invested in the Standard & Poor's 500 at the end of World War II would have risen to more than a million dollars today? Do you know what the term *exponential growth* means?"

"Of course I do," Alex answered.

"Then you should know that by reinvesting dividends and interest any long-term investment in stocks would have grown more than most people would ever imagine."

"So how much are we talking about here?" Alex asked.

He didn't answer.

"A million dollars?"

He still didn't answer.

"More? How much is it?" Alex stared into Ochsner's eyes.

He blinked several times. "It's not really any of your business, is it?"

"That's what I've been telling you all along." Alex replied tensely.

CHAPTER 6

Zurich
Friday Afternoon

"What a piece of work, huh?" Ruedi stood next to Alex as she watched Ochsner's black Daimler sedan roar down the narrow cobblestone street behind the Storchen.

"I think if he'd said the words *Swiss banking secrecy* one more time, I would have screamed." Alex turned to Ruedi. "Was he always like that?"

"He used to be so nice to me when I was young. I remember when I'd go to my father's office, Georg would always set me on his lap, tell me stories, let me help him work. But after my father's death, he seemed to change." He stared into Alex's eyes. "I always wondered why my father named him executor and not *me*. Just think, if he'd named me, I'd have known about this account since 1987."

"Well, for whatever it's worth, my mother didn't name me executor either. Not that there was anything like a Swiss bank account involved in her estate."

She took a deep breath. "Sometimes you just have to move on." She looked at her watch. "I should get back to work now. It's almost two."

"But what am *I* supposed to do?" Ruedi asked.

"Don't you have to go to work, too?"

"I want to find out what happened to my father."

"Wasn't it clear in there that—"

"I'll never believe my father committed suicide—not until I know for sure what happened. And I'm not going to stop asking questions until then." Ruedi looked like a disappointed little boy, standing in front of the hotel.

"Hey! I just had an idea!" He grabbed her arm. "Let's go to the bank. I can go in and see the account firsthand."

"Not with me. I—"

"Then I'll do it alone if I have to. That account, theoretically, belongs to *me*. Ochsner said so. Right? They have to tell me everything."

"Whatever you do, you have to keep me out of it." Alex stared into Ruedi's eyes. "Do you understand? I could lose my job if—"

"Don't worry. I promised I'd keep you out of it if you helped me." He slipped his arm around Alex's lower back. "And you did help, you know. Thank you."

He started walking. "If the bank asks me how I found out about the account, I'll just say Ochsner told me. And he *can't* divulge your name." Ruedi turned to her and smiled. "That's just one example of how Swiss bank secrecy can be used to our advantage."

He led her down the narrow lane behind the Storchen and then up toward the Bahnhofstrasse. "I wonder how much money really is in that account now. Although I have to say, I remember looking at those lists of dormant accounts when they were released back in the nineties. Unfortunately, Ochsner was right. Most only had a few thousand dollars. A hundred thousand max." He squeezed her arm slightly. "But just think, if this account has been wisely managed over all these years, it should have a lot more. Maybe even a million!"

"Well, all you have to do is go in and ask." Alex pointed across Bahnhofstrasse to the main entrance of HBZ. "There it is." Two stone cupids, naked little boys in worn granite, were guarding the door.

"Unfortunately, my entrance is around the back." She held out her hand to say goodbye.

"Just think. All that money in there," Ruedi's eyes widened. "Just waiting for me to come in and claim it."

"But it isn't really your account, is it."

"Well, at least the management fee is. Isn't that what Ochsner said, that 5 percent of the account belongs to my father, which means it belongs to me?" He nodded. "And 5 percent of a million dollars would be—"

"Fifty thousand dollars."

"Hey!" Ruedi gripped Alex's outstretched hand. "What do you say we split it? I'll give half of it to you."

"Why would you do that?"

"For helping me."

"But I didn't do anything. You forced me to tell you what I knew, and that wasn't very much."

"I mean for helping me find out what really happened in 1987." He held her hand in his. "I'm sure that with your help, I could go into the bank's computer and find out exactly what happened back then."

"Twenty-five thousand dollars for losing my job? No thanks." Alex pulled her hand back. "I happen to need my salary. I have student loans to pay off— and they're a lot more than twenty-five thousand dollars, I can assure you."

"But you wouldn't *have* to lose your job for helping me. We could work on this together—in secret. You could even do it in your spare time."

"I'm sorry. The answer's no."

"I'll pay you a fixed fee, then, for each hour you spend on my behalf. All you have to do is go in and look inside the bank's computer and see what happened to that account in 1987."

Alex shook her head. "You don't ever give up, do you?"

"I just want to know what happened. And without your help, I'm afraid I never will."

"Look," Alex spoke softly, "there's really nothing I can do for you. Even if I wanted to do research for you, I'm not allowed into the bank's records. All I have access to is the code."

"But what happened is certainly accounted for *somewhere* in the bank's computer, isn't it?"

"Ruedi, a computer's records are one thing; the code is another. The project I'm working on only deals with the part that tells the computer how to operate. It doesn't have anything to do with the bank itself, or with the accounts."

"But the code told you about my father's account *and* his company in 1987."

"That was a fluke. I have no idea why the code was put in there in the first place. It was a one-shot deal, an anomaly."

"But there may be more anomalies." His eyes widened. "Couldn't you just look? Simply to put my mind at rest?"

"Sorry." Alex shook her head. "If I got caught, I'd get fired. I'd probably never get another job in consulting again."

"Oh, come on." He stared at her. "Couldn't you just try?"

She shook her head. "The only reason I agreed to meet you today, to have lunch with you and Ochsner, was to make sure I got *out* of this. I want to protect my job, not to lose it."

"But with your share of the fee, you could quit your job."

"I told you, twenty-five thousand wouldn't even *begin* to pay off my debt."

"But what if there's *more* than a million dollars in the account?" Ruedi raised his eyebrows.

"Ruedi, *twice* that amount still wouldn't be enough. I'm sorry."

"I tell you what. Let me go in and check how much is in the account. Then you can decide."

Alex didn't answer.

"All I'm asking you to do is wait out here for five minutes. I'll go in and ask how much is in the account, then I'll come right back out. You don't have to risk anything. Okay?"

"It's late." Alex pointed to a clock hanging in the Bücherer watch store window across the street. "I have to be getting back to work."

"Come on." Ruedi smiled. "Live a little. It's only one fifty. I'm sure you don't have to be back at work until two. Come on. It's a beautiful Friday afternoon. You can certainly go in a few minutes late."

He was right. Even if Eric were back from lunch exactly at two, he wouldn't care if she were a just few minutes late.

"Okay. I'll wait for you over there." She pointed to the Bücherer shop. "But only for ten minutes."

"Thanks!" Ruedi got out the napkin Alex had written the code on. "This is the account number, right?" He pointed to the first line and read the number. "249588?"

"That's what it was back in 1987. But, as I told you, it's probably had numbers and letters added to it over the years."

"It doesn't matter. If I show them my ID, they have to tell me about *any* account in my name. I already have one here, one that my father left me. If there's another, and I ask for it, they *have* to tell me about it. That's the law."

"Do you always get everything you ask for?"

"*Almost* always." Ruedi smiled. He walked toward the door of the bank, then turned back to Alex and made a slight bow. "By the way. Thank you for your help today."

"You're welcome."

He held up his finger. "And think about this: by waiting out here for me, you can keep me honest."

"What do you mean?"

"Since the account's in my name, I *could* take *all* the money in the account, right?" He turned and jogged across the street, narrowly missing a passing tram.

While she waited, Alex watched the young Swiss bankers walking by. Many of the men had taken off their jackets. She grimaced when she saw how some of them wore pants that didn't match their jackets, and how many of them were wearing white socks, short-sleeved shirts, and oddly patterned ties. Any New York or London banker would be shot for wearing these clothes. Yet here in Zurich, they thought they were actually stylish.

She looked into the window of a travel bureau and read through the featured offers—romantic weekends for two in Paris, Amsterdam, or Prague. She had gotten about halfway through the details when Ruedi's reflection appeared in the window.

"Can you wait just a few more minutes?" He put his hand on her back. "They took my ID and said they had to check the computer to see if there were any other accounts with my name on them."

"That should take all of ten seconds."

"They said it would take a few minutes. When I showed them that account number, they said they would have to check with the private banking department.

It's in another part of the building apparently." He put his hand on her shoulder. "What were you looking at?" He pointed into the travel agency window. "See anything interesting?"

Alex nodded toward the Amsterdam flight offer. "My best friend from business school is living there now. Her partner just had a baby and I still haven't been there to—"

"Hey, look at that!" Ruedi moved over to the watch store window next to them. "That's exactly like my father's watch." He pointed to an antique gold Rolex in the back of the display case. "It's in my safe-deposit box at the moment. I've never been able to bring myself to wear it."

Alex looked at the price tag. The dollar value was almost half of her yearly salary.

"I tell you what." Ruedi took her arm in his. "I'll give you the watch. To thank you."

"For what?"

"I would never have known about this account if it wasn't for you."

"Ruedi, I could never accept your father's watch."

"Then I'll buy you one. Once I get my father's fees from that account, I'll buy you whichever watch you want." He pointed into the Bücherer window. "As a gesture of my appreciation."

"Have you forgotten that you only get your father's fee when the account is returned to its rightful owners? And there's no way of finding out who they are until Ochsner dies."

"Hey, there's no harm in dreaming, is there?" Ruedi walked back to the travel office window next door. "You never know what life's going to throw your way, do you?"

"Anyway," Alex stared at the beautiful watch in the display case, "no one knows how much is *in* the account. Five percent of fifty thousand dollars wouldn't even buy one of those."

She pointed to a silver Rolex in the middle of the case. "In fact, you'll probably end up buying me one of those." She pointed to a blue plastic Swatch in the front of the case.

"Hey," Ruedi turned back to Alex, "you heard what Ochsner said. There may be a *lot* of money in that account. I mean, think about it. Why would a

Jewish family go to all that trouble to put their account in someone else's name if they didn't have a lot of money to hide?"

"What makes you so sure the family was Jewish?"

"Come on." Ruedi walked back to Alex. "Why else would you put your account in someone else's name shortly before the outbreak of World War II?"

"Good point." Alex looked again at the watches. "I wonder why the European Jews decided to put so much of their money in Switzerland, right under the Nazis' noses. You'd think they'd want to get as far away from Hitler as they could."

"Where else could they have gone?" Ruedi asked.

"I don't know. America? Canada? Anywhere but Nazi-dominated Europe."

"Actually, you may not know this, but very few countries were willing to accept Jews in those days. Even America—despite what they want you to believe."

"I don't—"

"It's true." Ruedi shrugged. "I'm sure they don't tell you this in school, but the truth is, the Americans were just as anti-Semitic as everyone else. Sure, they let in a few Jews. Famous ones, like writers or scientists. But most countries had quotas on the number of Jews they would allow in. Even the U.S.," He held out his arms and shrugged. "The truth is that most of Europe's Jews had nowhere to go."

He walked closer. "Did you ever hear about the ship full of Jewish refugees that made it to Florida? The people on board could see the lights of Miami. But the U.S. authorities wouldn't let them dock. They sent the ship back to Europe."

"Is that true?"

"Of course it's true."

"And why didn't they go to Israel?"

"Don't you know that Israel only came into existence in 1948?"

Alex shook her head. "Not really."

"Well it's true." Ruedi nodded. "Before the war, Palestine was a British protectorate and the last thing they wanted was more Jews coming in. Didn't you ever see the movie *Exodus*?"

"No."

"Well, you certainly saw *Casablanca*. Remember how everyone there was desperate to get exit visas to Portugal? And even then it wasn't sure you'd get permission to go to America or another safe country." He paused. "For most Jews, there was no way to leave Europe.

"Fortunately, they had the option of putting their money in Switzerland."

"So Switzerland took their money but didn't give them a place to live?"

"Actually, Switzerland took in more Jewish refugees per capita than most other countries—including the United States. It's just that, being surrounded by Nazi-controlled Europe . . . there was a limit to what we could do. We couldn't have stood up to Hitler completely. He would have destroyed us." He shrugged. "And *then* what would have happened to all the Jewish assets in Swiss bank accounts? They would have lost everything, except what was in those trustee accounts, of course."

"Speaking of which," Alex pointed to the bank, "shouldn't they be ready for you by now?"

"You're right." He turned and walked across the street. He gave a little wave to Alex and walked into the bank.

Alex checked the time in the watch store window. It was past two. Just a few more minutes and she could go back to work.

Ruedi reappeared within minutes, holding out his empty hands.

"What happened?" Alex asked.

He walked up to her and shrugged. "The private banking department wants to see me in person before I'm given access to the account."

"So go see them."

"They made me make an appointment. And they said I have to show them my father's death certificate, a copy of his will, and *my* birth certificate to prove I'm really the heir to his estate. I'm supposed to go back Monday morning at nine." He put his hand on her shoulder. "Do you want to be here?"

"What for?"

"Don't you want to keep me honest? Keep me from stealing everything in the account?"

"It's really none of my business."

"Aren't those the words Ochsner used?" He cocked his head slightly. "Hey! I just thought of something. Don't move. Okay? I'll be right back." He disappeared into the travel office.

Minutes later he came out with a travel voucher in his hand. "A little present for you." He handed the voucher to Alex. She flipped it open and read quickly. It was a round-trip ticket to Amsterdam, business class. "What is this for?" she asked.

"It's my way of thanking you for helping me today."

"But I can't accept this, I didn't do anything."

"Come on. It's my way of apologizing for being such a jerk last night. And this morning. I know I can get a little crazy sometimes."

"Ruedi, you really didn't have to."

"Come on. You have to take it. It's nonrefundable. And it's only good for this month. Use it or lose it." He smiled. "Another great expression I picked up in Los Angeles."

She noticed that her name was printed at the top left: *Payton/Alex Ms.*

"How do you know my name?"

"It's on your baggage tag, on your laptop case. When I leaned down to pick up my pen cap this morning at Café Schober, I couldn't help noticing it. Sorry." He smiled innocently.

"So you knew all this time?"

He nodded. "But don't worry, I didn't tell Ochsner." He put his hand on her shoulder. "I told you that you could trust me to keep you out of this, remember? Just go."

CHAPTER 7

Zurich
Friday Evening

The Jumbolino AVRO RJ circled Zurich once, headed south toward the Alps, then banked sharply to the northwest, toward Amsterdam. Alex leaned back. She felt the power rising from underneath her. After two glasses of champagne while she waited for the plane to take off, she felt euphoric.

After takeoff, a flight attendant offered her more champagne. "Sure, why not?" Alex took a long sip, leaned back in the blue leather seat, and watched the sun set over the mountains.

The events of the last twenty-four hours flashed by: discovering the code, the stupid mistake with Eric's phone, meeting Ruedi at Café Schober, lunch with Ochsner, Ruedi offering her a Rolex, the ticket to Amsterdam. Life had suddenly become much more interesting.

She closed her eyes and drifted off to sleep.

"Look! Greenhouses. Thousands of them."

Alex woke up with a start.

"See? They're glowing!" The man next to her was leaning across her lap, trying to look out the window. "Down there." His breath reeked of garlic. "We grow everything here, you know, all year round. Tomatoes, asparagus, endives. Even tulips, believe it or not."

"Would you mind?" Alex asked politely. "You're pushing me against the window."

"Oh, I'm sorry. I just get so excited when I return home after a long trip." The man was wearing a suit and tie, but his long gray hair made him look like an aging hippie. "I've been on a concert tour in the Far East."

"See? We grow carnations, too," he continued. "And roses—millions of them. Did you know that? See how the greenhouses are glowing in the evening light?" He leaned over Alex again to look. "It's beautiful, no?"

She looked out the small window. "Yes, it is." The landscape was beautiful, and it was covered with countless greenhouses—long, slender fields of light, linked by lead-colored, ribbonlike canals.

"Look like giant solar panels, don't they?" The man touched her arm. "Only instead of absorbing energy, they're giving it off."

"Looks more like a circuit board to me."

"Do you work with computers?"

Alex nodded.

"So where do you work?" he asked.

"For a bank, actually."

"A Swiss bank? I'm angry with them. Ever since those scandals."

"We are about to land in Schiphol Airport. The temperature is 20 degrees Celsius, 68 degrees Fahrenheit. The local time, 7:42. Please make sure that your seatbelts are securely fastened and your tray tables are locked in their upright position . . ."

"Is this your first visit here?" the man asked.

Alex nodded.

"You're going to love Holland. It is so beautiful. And the food. *Lekker!* You must try the Indonesian food. It used to be a Dutch colony, you know. They have something called *Rijstafel*. It's out of this world."

The plane landed with a thud. Alex immediately unbuckled her seat belt and pulled her carry-on bag out from under the seat in front of her.

"But you have to promise me to be careful," the man said. "There's a lot of crime in Holland."

People started to move down the aisle. He stayed seated, blocking Alex's exit. "There are many things to see here. The museums especially, like the Rijksmuseum, the Stadelijk Museum, and the Van Gogh Museum. And the Anne Frank House, of course. I'm sure you've heard about that. You must go there."

"I'll try." The aisle had emptied. Alex stood up. "Shall we go now?"

Nan was waiting for Alex outside customs. She looked great: big, blond, and wholesome. "Welcome to Amsterdam, hon!" She gave Alex a strong hug. "It's so great to see you. But you look tired. Have you been sleeping okay?"

"Actually, last night I hardly—"

"Did you eat on the plane? We can make you something at home. Or, if you want, we can go out."

"I already had some champagne on the plane. But they didn't serve dinner."

"Great. We can meet Susan later. She's feeding Jannik right now, but she said she'd meet us for a drink at a bar on the Leidseplein if she can get a sitter. Is that okay with you? It's called the Palladium. You'll love it." She grabbed Alex's suitcase. "Let's take the train into town. It leaves from right under the terminal."

She led Alex through the crowded arrivals hall. "I can't believe you decided to come up like this, on the spur of the moment. It's not like you. You're going to love it here. Especially Jannik. He's so cute. A bit of a nightmare right now, though. He's got some sort of bug. You won't hurt our feelings if you want to stay at a hotel but—"

"I couldn't afford a hotel right now, even if I wanted to. I was lucky to get this ticket to come here."

"What did you do? Win the lottery?"

"Kind of."

"Lucky you!" Nan dropped several coins into the yellow and black machine. She headed for a waiting train marked CENTRAL STATION. "I hope you don't mind sleeping in the living room. It's much quieter in there, anyway. As far from Jannik's room as you can get."

"I don't mind."

"I can't wait for you to meet him. It'll have to be tomorrow, though. He'll be sleeping when we get in tonight. I love him so much—as if he were my own." She pulled Alex aboard a second-class car. Still the frugal Nebraska farm girl, Alex noticed, despite having a fancy job, no debts, and a partner whose father owned half of downtown Philadelphia.

Nan sat down and patted the seat next to her for Alex. "We've already done the adoption, you know. It's so easy here in Holland. Our little man now has two official mommies. It'll be interesting to see what difference there is when I have my baby."

"You're pregnant, too?" Alex asked.

"Next year." Nan smiled broadly. "We're going to use the same guy who donated the sperm for Jannik. That way, the kids'll be biological siblings. Cool, huh?"

When they pulled into Amsterdam's main station, Alex could smell the sea. Next to the platform was the harbor in full splendor, full of ferries, tugboats, and freighters. It reminded her of Seattle.

People crowded in around them to wait. They seemed happy. The Dutch, Alex noticed, seemed to have a freshness, a vitality, a cheerfulness that didn't exist in Zurich.

Alex took a deep breath. "It's great to be here."

"I think you're going to love it here." Nan pulled Alex through the crowded station. "They have so many bars and discos, great restaurants, and the museums are fabulous."

"So I've heard."

"From whom?"

"A *very* talkative guy on the plane. He also said I should go to the Anne Frank House."

"He's right. You should. We went there our first weekend here. It affected me even more than Susan, I think—and she had family in the Holocaust." Nan led Alex to a tram stop in front of the station. "I'd go with you again, but I don't think I could handle it a second time. Plus I have to work. Maybe Susan could go, but she's going to be busy with Jannik during the day. Tomorrow night I've promised her the night out, assuming we get a sitter. Just us girls. Is that okay with you?"

"Sure."

"Are you seeing anyone in Zurich, by the way?"

"Not really. There's this guy I work with, but—"

"Really! What's he look like?"

"Short blond hair. Nice body. Kind of looks like Sean Connery."

"A blond Sean Connery? Sounds gruesome." Nan smiled. "So, you having sex with this guy?"

"Not really."

"Is that a Clintonian answer?"

Alex laughed. "You should have seen me last night. I made a complete idiot of myself. I thought he was inviting me back to his room."

"And?"

"I felt like such a fool. He was only interested in drinking at the bar."

"Then he's a total fool. You're one of the most beautiful women I know. And believe me, I know women."

"Well, he's the senior on the project I'm working on. And according to Thompson rules, we're not supposed to have sex with—"

"Are you kidding?" Nan laughed loudly. "Susan used to work in consulting too, you know. And you should have heard the stories she told me. There was a *lot* of sex going on behind closed doors at her company. Rules or no rules."

A graffiti-covered tram pulled up next to them. "Anyway, I bet he was just leading you on. Men do that sometimes, you know. Just to get you to want them even more."

"And how is it that you, of all people, have become so knowledgeable about heterosexual romance?"

Nan laughed. "Hey, I grew up with three brothers, remember?" She led Alex onto the tram marked LEIDSEPLEIN.

Alex held on tight as the tram lurched forward. She could still see Nan and her family posing for the obligatory photos at the Yale School of Management graduation: her tall, handsome, farm-bred brothers, along with their beaming parents, standing proudly with their arms around Nan and a very pregnant Susan. They had all taken Alex to a night on the town in New York before putting her on the plane to Seattle to see her mother.

"You should listen to what I have to tell you." Nan spoke loudly as the tram sped down a cobblestone street running along a narrow canal. "No red-blooded male in his right mind would say no to you. You're in great shape, cute as a button. Okay, your tits are a little small, but that's from all the working out you do, which gives you the hottest hard-body around." She smiled broadly. "Anyway, it's going to be *easy* to find you a boyfriend here. Someone like him," Nan pointed to a handsome man with blond hair riding his bike alongside the tram, furiously pumping the pedals of an old rusted bicycle. As if on cue, he looked up at Alex and smiled. "I told you!" Nan laughed loudly.

The tram suddenly screeched to a stop. Nan picked up Alex's suitcase and was out the door before Alex could protest. "Come on, let's see if we can find Susan."

They plunged into the crowded square. To their right, a man was juggling flaming batons. The fumes from the burning batons drifted over the square, mixing with the smell of beer and roasted waffles. One of the buildings had the words Hirsch & Cie engraved onto the pediment. The old-fashioned abbreviation reminded Alex of the code.

"Hey, check that out." Nan pointed to a bearded man sitting cross-legged on the paving stones in front of them. He was blowing deep, hollow noises out of a long wooden tube. "It's a didgeridoo. Cool, isn't it?" She pulled Alex toward a crowded terrace lit up by a bright-red neon sign flashing Palladium — Palladium — Palladium. Through the crowd to their right, Alex noticed the man from the plane, talking to a small group of men. "Hey, I know him. He's the guy I told you about from the plane."

"Look! There she is!" Nan pointed to Susan sitting at one of the tables in the front. "Let's go." She pulled Alex up the steps to the terrace. "Isn't she beautiful?"

"Wow." Susan had always been good-looking, but now she looked stunning. She looked relaxed, content, at peace. She was wearing bright red lipstick and a sleek blue dress, and her dark hair was tied tightly in the back, making her delicate face even more striking.

"So?" Nan asked. "Am I a lucky woman or what?"

"Maybe *I* should become a lesbian and have a baby."

Nan let out a huge laugh. "I don't think you have to go that far, honey." She pulled Alex through the crowd. "But we can always get drunk tonight and talk it over."

Alex glanced around for the man from the plane, but he had disappeared into the crowd.

CHAPTER 8

Amsterdam
Saturday Morning

Earsplitting screams resounded through the apartment. The smell of diapers filled the air. Alex pulled a pillow over her throbbing head and tried to go back to sleep.

She suddenly remembered the dream she'd been having. She was in bed with someone. Eric? It was a tall man with a smooth muscular back. He was turned away from her, and every time she tried to get near to him, he'd move away. She wanted to be close to him, to feel his body against hers, but he wouldn't let her. Suddenly, he was standing in the corner of the room with his back to her, kissing someone else. The other person's hands gently caressed his back. She couldn't see who it was.

"Sorry for all the noise." Nan came into the living room and sat down next to Alex. "Hey, are you okay?"

"Not really."

Nan pulled the pillow from over Alex's head. "We think it's a problem with his digestion." She held up a bottle in one hand and a dirty diaper in the other. "We're going to try feeding him again, then try putting him back to sleep. I have to go in to work today, but I'll be back this evening."

She stood up. "Hey, why don't you go to work with me? The office isn't far from here. It's in Haarlem, a short train ride away."

"Thanks, but the last place I want to be right now is inside an office." Alex looked out the window. "I think I'll go out for a while."

"Sure. If you want, the Anne Frank House is near here, next to the Westerkerk, just around the corner. Or you may want to try the Van Gogh Museum. It's brilliant." Nan handed Alex a set of keys. "Just be back in time for dinner, okay honey?"

"Sure."

After a quick coffee and pastry in a café across the street, Alex walked along the canal until she came to the line in front of the Westerkerk. The church's carillon chimed the quarter hour. She got in line behind a French tour group that was talking loudly.

A young couple got in line behind her and immediately started kissing. "Who was she again?" the man asked in a thick Scottish accent.

"A girl who was *pair*secuted," the woman replied.

"Was she?" They went back to kissing.

Alex turned to face the strong, cool wind blowing in off the sea. Zurich seemed so far away, so different from this place. She felt strange being surrounded by all these people in such a festive mood.

The people coming out of the museum looked completely different from those waiting to go in. They seemed sad, sullen. Many were lingering around the entrance to the steel-and-glass museum bookshop—as if they didn't know where to go next.

Once she got her ticket, Alex climbed the steep stairs leading to the Frank family's spice shop. At the entrance to the first room was a large sign explaining how the Franks fled Germany after the Nazis came to power in 1933—when Anne was only five years old.

On the wall was a quote from Anne Frank's diary: "1940. After the German invasion of Holland, Jews are banned from trams, Jews are forced to wear a star." Farther along the wall was another entry: "1942. Every night people are being picked up without warning. This is awful. They treat them just like slaves in the olden days. I get frightened myself when I think of close friends who are now at the mercy of the cruelest monsters ever to stalk the earth."

Above the text was a photograph showing Nazi officers riding through Amsterdam in an open jeep. Swastika flags billowed behind them. Alex noticed that the church tower in the background was part of the Westerkerk, the church she had been standing next to outside.

The crowd moved into the next room, but Alex stayed behind, intrigued by an enlargement of a document entitled "Oproeping." It had been sent to the Frank family on the night of December 12, 1942, telling them to report to a "work camp" in Germany. Even though it had been written in Dutch, the order had been signed by someone from the Zentralstelle für jüdische Auswanderung, German for the Central Office for Jewish Emigration.

As she read the document, she imagined what the Franks must have thought—what Anne must have thought—when they received orders telling them to leave Amsterdam. At the bottom of the document was a list telling the Franks what they could bring with them.

Alex read the first entry: *1 koffer of rugzak*. One suitcase or backpack. Alex translated the list easily. The Dutch words were eerily similar to German. She was able to understand almost every word in the list.

> *2 paar sokken*—two pairs of socks
> *2 onderbroeken*—two sets of underwear
> *2 hemden*—two shirts

The list looked so ordinary, so innocent, as if the people receiving these marching orders were being sent off on vacation.

Alex heard a soft voice next to her. She turned her head slightly and saw a young man who was also whispering the words on the list. He looked good. He looked Latino, with jet-black hair and a goatee, but he was dressed like a classic Yalie—light brown slacks, long-sleeved oxford-blue shirt, dark leather loafers. His shirtsleeves were rolled up, revealing strong forearms with a dusting of fine dark hair.

On his left wrist, he was wearing a silver Rolex, just like the one Alex had been looking at in the Bücherer store window earlier.

"Amazing, isn't it?" He turned to Alex. "The words seem so mundane. But when you think about what they really mean . . ."

Alex nodded. "I was just thinking the same thing."

"Do you need any help translating?" he asked. His English had a slight accent, but Alex couldn't place it.

"I think I got the gist of it." Alex replied. "It's so similar to German."

"Oh, are you German?"

"No." She turned to him and smiled. "I'm American. But I live in Switzerland. And you? Are you Dutch?"

"With this face?" He smiled broadly. The white of his teeth contrasted sharply with his dark hair, his tanned skin. "I'm Brazilian, actually. But I used to live in the Hague. My father worked for the Itamaratí, the Brazilian Foreign Service. And I was lucky enough to have a Dutch girlfriend, for a few months anyway." He held out his hand. "My name's Marco, by the way."

"Hi. Mine's Alex."

His handshake was firm, yet gentle. His eyes were light blue, almost green.

"Can you believe how perverse they were?" He pointed to the blown-up photograph showing the Nazi troops entering Amsterdam. "They sent this letter to the all the Jews in Holland, acting as if they were going to send them away to the mountains for some sort of summer holiday." He nodded to the list. "They told them to bring all this stuff. But they were sending them away to die."

He read the rest of the list aloud, translating into English as he went.

1 werkpak—one work jacket.
2 wollen dekens—two wool blankets.
1 eetnap—a bowl.
1 drinkbeken—one drinking glass.
1 lepel—one spoon.

People began crowding in around them. "Let's go into the back."

"Why?" Alex asked.

"That's where the family hid for over two years. Anne called it her secret annex." Marco led Alex around a moveable bookcase filled with dusty tomes and into a narrow hall. "It's right through here."

"So you've been here before?" Alex asked.

"Yes, once as a kid. I never forgot it." He walked over to a panel on the far wall. "See?" He pointed to a line in the middle. "This describes their pretext for their disappearance—they said they were fleeing to Switzerland, that they had a Swiss bank account, which gave them the right to go there. The father sold his spice business to his Dutch partner, who promised to give the business back once the war was over."

Alex remembered her conversation with Ruedi yesterday in front of the bank in Zurich. How all those families had put their money in the hands of Swiss trustees thinking they would get everything back at the end of the war. And how trustworthy had the Swiss actually been?

They moved into the back room where Alex read how the Franks' Dutch trustee had not only risked his life by hiding the entire family, but insisted on returning everything to Mr. Frank after the war, including Anne's diary. If not for him, no one would ever have known what happened.

"This was her room." Marco led Alex into a small chamber in the back corner of the building. One wall was covered with magazine cutouts of famous movie stars. A faded map of Europe was pinned to the wall near the door.

"See? This is where they were keeping track of the Allied advance." Marco's finger traced a trail of small red pins leading from the French coast to Holland. "Look, the Allies had landed in Normandy. They had already made it to Belgium, in fact. Almost to the Dutch border, when the Franks were discovered by the Nazis. Apparently they were exposed by someone. No one ever found out who."

Alex read the quote from Anne's diary next to the map: "June 6, 1944. This is D-day. The invasion has begun! Great commotion in the secret annex. Would the long-awaited liberation ever come true?"

A bell chimed outside and the room began to fill with a large group of French tourists. They spoke loudly, pushing their way through the small room, taking Alex and Marco with them.

The next room was full of computer terminals. Alex stopped at a small video screen documenting the story of the ship Ruedi had told her about. It had, in fact, been just off the Florida coast. Thousands of Jewish refugees who had already been refused entry in Cuba had tried desperately to get permission to enter the United States, but the local authorities wouldn't let them in. After several days, the ship sailed back to Germany. Almost everyone on board, the documentary explained, ended up in Nazi concentration camps.

Alex felt people crowding in around her. She looked around for Marco. He was nowhere to be seen.

She moved on to the next screen showing an interview with a woman who was with Anne Frank and her sister at Buchenwald. The woman told how the Nazis treated the children—describing rape, torture, forced labor, and painful medical experiments. She described how Anne and her sister had "fortunately" died of typhoid fever before the torturers got to them.

The interview was illustrated with black-and-white footage showing life in the camps. In one scene the Nazi soldiers were herding prisoners down a muddy embankment. Most of the prisoners were naked. Barely more than skin and bones. The soldiers lined the frail men and women in rows on the edge of a deep pit and shot them, methodically. One of the women looked eerily like Alex's mother—at the end, after her body had been ravaged by the cancer.

She watched wave after wave of prisoners disposed of—their lifeless bodies pushed down into the pit and the next line of prisoners brought forward. Strangely, no one ran. No one screamed. No one reacted in any way to what was going on. They simply stepped up to the edge of the embankment to await their turn to be killed.

The air in the overcrowded room was getting hot and stuffy, and Alex began to perspire. She looked around again for Marco. He was nowhere to be seen. She squeezed through the crowd, toward the blue Exit sign at the far end of the room. He wasn't there either.

Maybe he's outside, she told herself.

She walked toward the exit, down a hallway lined with glass cases holding different editions of Anne's diary: Dutch, Hebrew, Arabic, Russian, Spanish, Italian, English, French—even German.

At the end of the hall, just before the exit door, was a quote from Anne Frank's father reproduced on the wall, something he said when he returned to Holland after the war, after surviving the camps and losing his family to the Nazis.

Despite her desire to get outside, Alex was drawn to the text. She read it carefully: "I've lost everything except my life," he wrote. "What happened cannot be changed anymore. The only thing that can be done is to learn from the past and to realize what discrimination and persecution of innocent people mean. To my opinion, everyone has the duty to help to overcome prejudice."

Alex pushed open the heavy metal door and stepped into the sunlight.

CHAPTER 9

Amsterdam
Saturday Evening

"What do you mean you lost him?" Nan took a gulp of her margarita. "Are you crazy?"

Blanca's Cantina—a Mexican restaurant transplanted to Holland, with ficus trees, fake adobe walls, and hundreds of tequila bottles in rows behind the bar—was filled with smoking, drinking, laughing revelers.

"So why didn't you go back inside and look for him?"

Alex shrugged. "They don't let you back in after you leave."

"Are you crazy? You should have paid for a new ticket if you had to. You're acting just like you did at Yale. Always so aloof. You've got to start being more assertive. Grab for all the—"

"But the line was halfway up the canal. It would have taken hours to get back inside." Alex took a long sip. "Actually, I waited outside for the longest time. I must have counted the bells chime the quarter-hour at least five times. There was nothing else I could do."

"So let's just drink and forget everything." Nan ordered another round of margaritas. "What do you say we go out tonight and kick up our heels a little? Stay out all night, if we want? Jannik's in good hands with the sitter."

"I don't know. After everything's that's happened today . . ."

"Let's ask Susan when she gets here—see what *she* wants to do." Her eyes lit up. "Hey, we could go to a disco! There's one right near here. It's huge. Everyone goes there. It's mixed, like most places here—gay *and* straight. I'm sure we'll find *someone* there for you to fall in love with."

"I'm not sure I'm up for it." Alex caught a glimpse of herself in the mirror behind the bar—she looked tired. "The Anne Frank House got me thinking today."

"About what?"

"A lot of things. About what happened to her. About what happened at work this week. About what happened to my mother."

"You still suspect that your mother's aide had something to do with her death?" Nan edged her chair closer. "You know, I once read a statistic that 35 percent of people think that someone else was responsible for their parents' death? Even if it happens in the hospital, they still think that someone was involved."

"Don't you think it's strange she died the night I got back from Yale? I didn't even have a chance to talk to her before she died."

"Maybe she asked Evelyn to do it? Did you ever think about that?"

"But why choose the night I got back from B-school?"

"Did you ask Evelyn about it?"

Alex nodded. "She denied it, of course. She said that my mother's cancer had simply metastasized much more quickly than they expected. That she was probably holding on until I got home." She shrugged. "But why not have me come home earlier? Why let me stay at Yale through graduation?"

"Maybe your mother didn't want to spoil it for you. Maybe she didn't want to be a burden. Which is also probably why she didn't name you executor of her estate."

"Did you know that I checked with a lawyer after the funeral? To see if everything was legal."

"And?"

"It was. The lawyer said it wasn't uncommon to name a friend the executor. That since there was nothing left in the estate, it wouldn't have made much sense to name a lawyer, or anyone else, executor."

Nan took a deep drink. "Didn't you tell me once that your mother got a lot of stocks from your father when they divorced?"

"They were mostly computer stocks. Apparently, the dot-com crash liquidated most of them."

"Did you ask your father about them?"

"You know we never talk much—just birthdays and Christmas." She took another sip. "Anyway, I already know what he would have said: that my mother was always a disaster with money and that it was no surprise that there was nothing left." She took another drink. "I had to use almost all of my signing bonus from Thompson to pay off my mother's medical bills."

"She didn't have any insurance?"

"Not enough, apparently." Alex began to peel off the top layer of the cardboard coaster. "I just wish I could have had a chance to talk to her before she died."

"To tell her you loved her?"

"Among other things . . ."

"Listen, honey." Nan put her arm around Alex. "Your mother knew you loved her. I'm sure of that. You were everything to her. She thought the world of you." She put her hand on Alex's. "And that's probably why she *wanted* it to end the way it did. She didn't want you to see her like that—the way she was at the end."

"Like those people in the videos at the Anne Frank House." Alex took a deep breath. "God, it was horrible."

"You can't forget—after being there, can you?"

"Especially after what happened this week in Zurich."

"Which was?"

"I don't know if I—"

A waitress wearing a tight black T-shirt with no bra came over and told them their table would be ready in a few minutes. Nan ordered another round of margaritas.

"So what *did* happen?" She turned back to Alex once the waitress had left.

"I'm not sure I can tell you. It's kind of a secret."

"Are you kidding?" She moved her stool closer. "Susan used to tell me about her projects all the time when she worked in consulting. She just never named names. It was fine."

Alex took a deep breath. "I also feel kind of stupid about what happened."

The waitress brought them their new drinks.

"So what happened?" Nan prodded.

Alex took a deep sip. "I inadvertently contacted a client of the bank where we have our project."

"So?"

"You know they could put me in jail for that in Switzerland?"

"Yeah, yeah, yeah. I know all about the Swiss paranoia for secrecy." She smiled. "So what happened?"

She took another drink. "We made this bet, my coworker and I, to see if this guy whose name we found in the code still existed. So I called directory assistance, and they connected me, automatically. I had no idea they did that."

"They do that in Holland, too." Nan took a deep drink. "But I still don't see what the problem is."

"Well, for one thing, I was using my coworker's phone."

"Ouch." Nan raised her eyebrows. "What did he say when he found out?"

"He didn't." Alex looked into Nan's eyes. "I made sure of that."

"How?"

"I met the guy."

"You *what?*" Nan almost shouted the question.

"I *had* to. He said he'd tell Eric if I didn't meet him. He heard Eric say something about the date—October 19, 1987. It made him crazy. He said he'd keep calling back—on Eric's phone—until he found out what it was all about."

"So? If it was your coworker who spilled the beans about the code, why were you the one who had to—?"

"Because *I* was the one who made the call. I would have lost my job if they'd found out. Eric too, probably." She took another drink. "So I met with him. To keep anything from happening. He gave me no other choice."

"Men. They're amazing."

"Actually, he wasn't all that bad. But then he insisted that I meet his father's old partner for lunch—to find out what happened to his father. The account I discovered was apparently set up before World War II, for a Jewish family, it seems. And the strange thing is, they set up something called a trustee account. That's where they put the assets in the name of—"

"I know what a trustee account is, hon. Susan's parents set up one for both of us. Mainly to avoid taxes on the inheritance."

"But this one was a *secret* trustee account. Even the bank didn't know who it really belonged to. Apparently, a lot of these accounts were set up in Switzerland before the war, and most of them have never been discovered."

"Look! There she is!" Nan stood up and waved. "Over here, honey."

Alex saw Susan easing her way around the heavyset woman who was playing a medley of Cole Porter songs on the piano. Susan gave both Nan and Alex a kiss on the lips, then Nan pulled Susan onto her lap. "Isn't she the most beautiful woman you ever saw?"

Susan blushed, then pointed to their half-empty margarita glasses. "Looks like you guys have wasted no time. I wish I could join you, but unfortunately I'm still nursing and will have to stick to orange juice."

"Alex was just telling me about how she single-handedly uncovered a secret Swiss bank account owned by a Jewish—"

"Keep it down," Alex grabbed Nan's arm. "I told you, if the bank finds out I'll lose my job."

"Don't worry." Nan put her hand on Alex's. "We'll be discreet. I promise." She took another drink and motioned for Alex to continue. "So, how does the story end?"

"Actually, okay. I got this trip to Amsterdam."

"Paid for by the guy whose father owned the account?" Nan asked. "What's he like? Good-looking?"

"You're incorrigible." Susan kissed Nan and turned to Alex. "Please forgive her."

"You got to hear the whole story." Nan sucked on the straw of her margarita and began to fill Susan in on the details. As she was describing the code Alex had found, Susan interrupted her.

"What was that date again?" she asked.

"October 19, 1987," Alex replied.

"That's it."

"What?" Nan asked.

"It sounds to me like someone was trying cover their losses from the '87 crash."

"Which crash?" Nan asked.

Susan smiled. "I always forget how young you girls are." She took Nan's hands in hers. "October 19, 1987—Black Monday—the biggest percentage drop in Dow Jones history. Even more than the crash in 1929. You don't remember that?"

Nan shook her head. "Not really. I was still in grade school."

"It doesn't matter. What's important is that the crash was huge. I remember: I was living with my father in Philadelphia at the time. He came this close to losing everything." She held up her thumb and forefinger, almost touching. "When his stocks tanked, the banks hit him with a margin call. He had to come up with the funds to cover it. Otherwise he would have lost all the money."

"Why?" Nan asked.

"In a margin account you buy stocks with borrowed money. Basically, you have to put up some of the money on your own, and the bank gives you the rest."

"Why would they do that?" Nan asked.

"So they can earn interest on the loan, big dummy. And they want you to be able to buy more stocks—that way they can collect more fees."

"Got it."

Susan took a drink of her orange juice. "Clients like margin accounts because they get more bang for their buck. When the market goes up, they earn a lot more than they normally would have."

"And what if the market goes down?" Nan asked.

"That's when the shit hits the fan, so to speak. In a falling market, the client can lose everything—quickly. That's why the bank gives you a margin call. It tells you to put up more money to cover your losses, or they sell everything right out from under you."

"So it's a bit like the bank foreclosing on your house when property prices start to go down?"

Susan nodded. "Exactly. I remember that during the '87 crash, my father had to put up some of his buildings as collateral. That way he was able to keep his stock portfolio intact. When the market came roaring back a few days later, he was fine. If he had been forced to sell at the bottom, he would have lost everything."

"And if you didn't have a spare building to put up as collateral?" Nan asked.

"You needed to find some other way to cover your losses."

"Like an unused trustee account sitting in your Zurich bank?" Alex asked.

"Exactly." Susan turned to her. "What better way to ride out a margin call than tapping funds in an unused bank account that you had control of? All you would have had to do was get the computer to print up a bogus sale statement." She turned back to Nan. "When I worked in investment banking, in a crunch, we'd sometimes let clients fax us a statement from their bank showing that they were selling us top-grade securities—like U.S. Treasury bonds—and that the money from the sale was being credited to us. That way, we knew that the collateral was on its way."

"Like the proverbial check in the mail." Alex summarized.

Susan nodded. "You got it. In this case, all you would have needed was some document showing that money was on the way. That you had the wherewithal to ride out the crash. If you had access to the computer, it would have been easy. All you would have had to do was print up a statement that made it look like you had the assets to cover your losses."

"Wait a minute." Nan shook her head. "Why go to all the trouble of creating fictitious bank statements when you could have just sent them the money?"

"What do you mean?" Susan asked.

"I mean if you had access to a secret Swiss bank account that no one was watching, why not just transfer the money you needed and forget the rest?"

"If this was like the trustee accounts my father set up, the fund managers *can't* access the funds." Susan turned to Alex. "Whoever was managing this account probably only had the right to instruct the bank on the securities to buy and sell."

"Sounds right." Alex nodded. "That's the way the guy at lunch yesterday described it."

"So there you have it." Susan turned back to Nan. "The only way to use the fund was to sell a big chunk of securities and then change the name on the sale statement to make it *look* like the securities were being transferred by someone else."

"And it would never have been noticed?" Nan asked Susan.

"If I remember right the Federal Reserve stepped in immediately and pumped up the money supply. Within days, the stock prices came back to where they were before the crash, which means that money for the margin call would no longer have been needed. Whoever falsified the statements could have just told the bank to cancel the bogus sale." Susan sat back. "And no one would have been the wiser."

"Until Alex came along." Nan held up her drink to toast. "Good job!"

The waitress came by to tell them that their table was ready.

"I'd still be careful if I were you," Susan told Alex as they stood up. "When I worked in consulting, one of the primary rules was never to go outside the limits of your mandate."

Alex finished off her drink. "It's not as if I did it on purpose."

CHAPTER 10

Amsterdam
Saturday Night

The line to the disco stretched haphazardly down the canal. As Nan had predicted, people of every imaginable gender and persuasion were waiting to get in. Men, women, drag queens, machos. Everyone seemed at ease, relaxed, and friendly. Alex heard at least five different languages being spoken around her.

It was half an hour before they made it to the entrance. They were just about to head in when Alex spotted him walking through the crowd toward them.

"So *there* you are!" Marco walked over to Alex and kissed her on both cheeks. "I was looking for you half the day."

"I was looking for you, too."

"She's being polite." Marco flashed a smile at Nan and Susan. "I was sure she tried to get rid of me at the Anne Frank House."

"I waited outside for you for over an hour."

"And I waited inside for you for almost two."

"Really? Where?"

"Inside." Marco nodded. "Are you going to introduce me to your friends?"

Alex introduced him to Nan and Susan. "He's gorgeous," Nan whispered to Alex as she moved forward to shake Marco's hand. He kissed both Susan and Nan on the cheek.

He looked great—his hair was perfectly combed, his skin glowing. He was wearing a dark sports jacket and a light blue shirt. It made him stand out in the crowd of disco aficionados. "I'm so glad I found you." He smiled at Alex warmly. "I was beginning to think I'd have to go to Zurich to track you down."

"Do you want to join us?" Nan moved aside to let Marco into the line next to them. "We were just about to go in."

"I'm not really into discos." Marco shrugged. "Actually, I was going to go for a walk along the canals. It's such a beautiful night." He turned to Alex and nodded slightly. "Would you like to join me?"

After three margaritas, she didn't hesitate.

She turned to Nan and Susan. "Do you mind? I can always meet you guys later."

"No problem." Susan pulled out her keys. "Just take these. In case you don't find us in there."

Marco gently rested his hand on Alex's back and started walking toward the flower market along the canal to their right. "What were you celebrating?" he asked. "It looks like you guys were having fun."

"We were just having a girls' night out." Alex moved in closer as he put his arm around her.

A group of drunk Dutch teenagers stumbled toward them, eating sausages, drinking beer, and laughing loudly. Marco—quietly, effortlessly—placed himself between them and Alex and steered her to safety. His hand felt strong, warm, secure.

"Thanks," Alex smiled. "You seem to know what you're doing."

"Actually, when I was in college, I used to be a karate instructor." He turned to her and smiled. "But now those days are over. I'm about to start working at Itamaratí."

"What's that?" Alex asked.

"The diplomatic corps—our version of the State Department. Hey, look at that." He pointed to an old art-deco cinema. "Hey, I bet it's where she went to see the movies."

"Who?"

"Anne Frank. Remember all those pictures of movie stars she had pinned to her wall?" He led Alex over to take a closer look. "It's amazing, isn't it? Another piece of her life right here in the middle of this city."

Marco reached down and touched the date etched into the concrete at the base of the front porch: 1931. "I bet she probably stood on these very steps." The colored lights from the Tuschinski Cinema marquee created a soft pastel glow on his face. "Just think, she and her sister probably came here on Saturday afternoons to see the moving pictures. Before the war, before the Nazis came marching in and deported everyone."

Is that what happened to those people who opened that account in Zurich? Alex asked herself. *Is that why they couldn't be found after the war?*

She thought of the flippant way Ochsner had talked about them. "It's *not the job* of Swiss bankers to go around the world sticking their noses into clients' private matters. It's their job to hold the clients' assets responsibly until they come . . . that's what Swiss banking is all about."

"Hey, let me show you something. You're going to love this." Marco led Alex slowly through the empty flower market. Thousands of discarded tulips and roses were piled beside the closed-up stands. Some had fallen into the canal. She breathed deeply, welcoming the scent of the flowers and the fresh salty air.

When they got to the end of the market, they walked over to the railing along the wide canal. Tiny yellow lights lining the arches of the bridges were reflected in the dark water below.

"You know, you were incredible in there today."

"Where?" Alex asked.

"The Anne Frank House. I was watching you. You looked so . . . moved."

"How could you not be?"

"Not everyone was." Marco slid his hand across the top of her back and rubbed gently. "You're different, you know. I'm just getting to know you, but I like what I see."

"Thanks. Me too." Alex looked up at Marco's face. His eyelashes cast long shadows down his cheeks. He seemed so calm and secure. She looked down at their joined silhouettes reflected in the water below along with hundreds of tiny lights from the bridge's arches.

"Have you ever been to Australia?" Marco asked.

"No. Have you?"

Marco nodded. "Did you know that the Australian aborigines believe that the world was created by dreams?"

"How so?"

"They believe that dreams bring the world into being, and that every time you dream you're creating more of the world we live in."

"Sounds good."

"What would *your* dream be?"

Alex didn't have to think long. "First I'd pay off my debts. And then I'd—"

"You could have anything in the world, and you'd ask for money?"

"You're right." She smiled. "I should come up with something more important. It's just that . . . the truth is . . . I'm not sure anymore *what* I'd ask for."

"How about an end to hate and prejudice? After what we saw today . . ."

"Sounds good."

"And *this*."

"What?"

"To be standing here, along the canals of Amsterdam—with you."

He leaned over and kissed her.

"Nice." He kissed her again.

Let yourself go, Alex told herself. *Don't hold back now.*

Marco took her arm in his and gently led her away from the market, down the narrow cobblestone streets, along the canals, through the deserted squares of Amsterdam.

Alex didn't say anything when they passed Nan and Susan's house. When they entered the Leidseplein, the square where she and Nan had met Susan the night before, Marco gestured to an ornate stone building on the far side of the square. "There's my hotel." He pointed out a corner window with a balcony. "See over there? That's my room."

"It looks huge."

"It is."

"You should see where *I'm* sleeping. I woke up this morning to the sound of a crying baby and the smell of dirty diapers."

CHAPTER 11

Amsterdam
Sunday, Late Afternoon

Alex watched a pair of rabbits scurry across the tarmac and hide in the tall grass along the runway. Wind socks blew furiously in the late-afternoon wind. In the distance, an El-Al jet took off. As her plane taxied for takeoff she leaned back and thought of the night she had just spent.

She closed her eyes, remembering being with Marco. His warmth, his smell, the way he'd made love to her.

They'd even decided to meet again next weekend. He was going to be in Paris, and Alex had said she'd join him there—without even thinking about how much it would cost. She'd worry about that later.

"*Cabin ready for takeoff.*" A flight attendant handed Alex a copy of the Swiss Sunday newspaper, the *Sonntags Zeitung*, then quickly moved on. Alex was about to shove it into the seat pocket in front of her when she noticed a small headline at the bottom of the front page: *Bankier Tod*—Banker Dead. *Suizid in Basel.*

Her heart froze when she saw the name on the first line: "Georg Ochsner fell from the Wettstein Bridge in Basel late Friday night . . . a 100-meter fall into the Rhine . . . instant death . . . body washed onto the riverbank in Klein Basel . . . retrieved by the police . . . no witnesses . . . no signs of foul play."

They used the words "suspected suicide" several times throughout the article, as if they were trying to convince everyone that nothing untoward had happened. But Georg Ochsner didn't seem the kind of person who would want to jump off of a bridge—at least not the Ochsner she'd met on Friday.

Call Ruedi, she told herself. *Now.*

She ran to the back of the plane. "I need to use the phone," she told the flight attendant. "I have to call someone in Zurich immediately."

"We're in the middle of the takeoff!" the flight attendant answered brusquely. "You have to return to your seat. Now!"

Alex stared out the window as the plane climbed over Amsterdam harbor, then out over the flat Dutch countryside. Ruedi's number kept going over and over in her head, just as it had Friday morning. *What happened to Ochsner? Would Ruedi know? Was he still alive?*

Finally, the seat-belt light turned off. *"Hier ist Ihr Kapitän. You are now free to move about the cabin."* Alex immediately returned to the phone at the back of the plane. She quickly ran her credit card through the magnetic reader, then dialed Ruedi's number. It rang several times before the answering machine picked up.

"Ruedi, it's Alex," she shouted. "If you're there, please answer."

Nothing. She then called the hotel switchboard. There were no messages for her.

Then she remembered that Ruedi didn't know where she was staying. He had no way of contacting her. In fact, the only phone number he had for her was Eric's. Would Ruedi have called *him*?

Alex called his cell phone, just to check. "Hi Eric, how's everything?"

"I'm fine. I'm in Geneva, visiting friends. Why do you ask?"

"No reason. I was just wondering. Will you be back in Zurich tonight?" It sounded like he was in a bar.

"Look, Alex. I think you should know something. The reason that I didn't . . . that I wasn't interested in you the other night is because I'm gay. I thought I should tell you. It's not that I don't like you, it's just that—"

"It doesn't matter."

"I just want you to know so there are no more misunderstandings. If I were straight, you'd be the first person I'd—"

"Eric, I said it doesn't matter. Really. I've got to go now." Alex hung up and tried calling Ruedi's office number, but there was no answer there either.

In the airport arrivals hall, she tried calling him again. Still no answer at either of his numbers. She called directory assistance and asked if she could get Ruedi's cell phone number. They gave it to her immediately.

He didn't answer that number either. But it didn't make sense. Ruedi seemed to always have his cell phone on. Where was he?

Or was he lying at the bottom of the Rhine, too?

Don't panic, she told herself. *It'll all be all right.* But the same thoughts kept coming back: *Georg Ochsner was not the kind of man to commit suicide. And if it wasn't suicide, then what was it? An accident? No chance. Murder? But who would have killed that pathetic old man? And why? Could Ruedi be involved in some way?* She got in line for passport control. Ruedi would have had no reason to kill Ochsner. He could have gotten access to that account by walking into HBZ and asking for it. Ochsner had said so himself.

So what happened?

She noticed a door with the word POLICE written on it. A man was just walking out. He wore a blue shirt with large epaulettes embroidered with small gold letters: "Kantonspolizei Zürich."

"Excuse me." Alex walked over to him.

"Ja?"

"If I think someone in Zurich may be in trouble, do I have to give you my name? Do I have to get involved if all I want is for you to check and see if he's okay?"

"You don't have to give your name, no." He looked surprised by Alex's question. "But who is this man? How do you know he's in trouble?"

"I don't know for sure, but if someone could go check . . ."

"You must go through there." He pointed to a sign marked Zollfrei — Nothing to Declare. "The Zurich police is *after* customs. In Parkhaus A. This is the airport police."

Alex got back in line to go through customs. *That's it. Get the Zurich police to look into it,* she told herself. *Don't give them any information about yourself. Just tell them Ruedi may be in trouble and let them do the rest.*

Outside customs she found the elevator for Parkhaus A. Next to the fourth-floor button was a little shield with the words Polizei — Police written on it.

She remembered Susan's words in Zurich: "Don't go outside the limits of your mandate."

She pushed the button and waited for the doors to close.

Maybe I should call the bank and tell them what happened. No. Keep them out of it, she told herself. *Keep everyone out of it. Everyone except the police. Let them take care of it.*

The elevator doors opened. She walked over to the glass door marked Polizei and rang the bell. She was buzzed in immediately.

She walked over to a man sitting behind a thick glass window. He was reading a newspaper. He had a scruffy three-day-old beard, and he was wearing jeans and a plaid shirt.

"Ja?" He looked up from his newspaper.

"Are you the police?" Alex spoke into a small microphone next to the window.

"Yes, what do you want?"

"I was just wondering . . . if you could check on someone I know. He lives in Zurich. I think he may be in trouble."

"What kind of trouble?"

"I don't know. He isn't answering his phone."

"What do you want *me* to do?" He stared at her blankly. He had no gun. No badge. Nothing to reassure her. Just a thick glass wall for protection—for *his* protection by the looks of it.

"Couldn't someone go to his house?"

"What is your relationship to him? Are you a family member?"

"No, I'm just a friend. I just want to make sure he's safe."

"Unless you're a family member, you can't—"

"Here." Alex took out a piece of paper and wrote down Ruedi's name and number. "Can't someone just check to see if he's all right?"

He shook his head. "Did you go there to check?"

"I don't *want* to go there. I just want to make sure he's okay." Alex pulled her hair behind her ears and leaned closer to the microphone. "Why can't *you* do something?"

He looked over the top of his reading glasses and said something Alex couldn't understand.

"Could you repeat that?" she asked.

"I said that you should try contacting the *Stadtpolizei*. They might be able to help you. We're the cantonal police—the regional police—and unless you're a relative there's nothing we can do."

"Where are they?" Alex asked angrily.

"At the Centrale Revier—FNZ."

"Where's that?"

"It's in downtown Zurich. But it's Sunday. I'm not sure anyone would be there now. They're only open in the morning on Sundays."

"There's no one at the Zurich Police Station on Sundays?"

"Not at the Centrale Revier, but maybe if you called them, someone could give you the office responsible for—"

"Why can't *you* call them?"

"Why?"

"Forget it." Alex walked quickly toward the taxi stand. On her way, she spotted a long row of telephone booths. She used one of the phones to double-check Ruedi's address.

Within minutes she was pulling up to a stately old three-story apartment house on the Zürichberg, an elegant residential neighborhood filled with old villas and apartment buildings, each one more opulent than the next.

In front of the house was a Stadtpolizei Zürich car with its lights flashing. Had the cantonal police contacted them after all?

Ruedi Tobler was standing next to the car. He looked angry. The police-woman next to him was writing something in a notebook.

Alex jumped out and ran over to Ruedi. "Thank God you're alive."

He just stared at her.

"Where have you been?" Alex asked him. "I thought something might have happened to you."

He continued staring at her angrily.

The police officer looked up from her notebook. "Are you the one who spoke to my colleagues at the airport?"

"Yes." Alex turned back to Ruedi. "Why didn't you answer your phone?"

"I had it turned off. I was with Mrs. Ochsner. She's in quite a state. As you can imagine, under the circumstances." He made it sound like it was her fault, as if Alex had done something wrong. "I was just walking in the door when the police pulled up. They said an American woman at the airport had told them to come here. I assumed it had to be you."

"I was worried about you."

"I was worried about you, too, but I didn't send the police to interrogate you." He turned to say something in Swiss German to the police officer. She shook Ruedi's hand once, and walked back to her car.

"What do we do now?" he asked Alex laconically.

"I don't know. I'm just happy to see you're all right."

"Well, as you can see, I'm alive and well." He still sounded angry.

Alex noticed that several of Ruedi's neighbors were watching from their windows.

"I'm sorry." She put her hand on his shoulder. "It's just that when I read about what happened to Georg Ochsner, and I couldn't reach you anywhere, I thought that the right thing to do would be to have the police check."

"I appreciate the thought. But ever since my father's death I've had a problem with the police. They're the ones who tried the hardest to convince me it was a suicide. They weren't interested at all in considering the possibility that someone had killed him. And now with Ochsner, it's the same thing." He motioned toward an upper floor of the apartment house behind him. "Come on, let's get out of my neighbors' prying eyes."

Ruedi had to undo two sets of locks to open the door to his second-floor apartment. Just inside was a large painting of Marilyn Monroe on a gold-leaf background. Alex walked over for a closer look.

"It's a Warhol. Do you like it?" Ruedi closed the door carefully behind them. "Here, follow me." He showed Alex into the living room. The walls were covered with paintings in all shapes and sizes.

"This one over here is my favorite." He led her around a low table covered with art books and framed photographs to a large, brightly colored canvas that covered almost an entire wall. "It's called *The Last Supper*. It was one of Andy's last works."

"You were on a first-name basis with Andy Warhol?"

"Actually, I did know him," he said casually. "Would you like a drink?" He walked over to an art deco bar in the corner and began opening a bottle of wine. "Is Bordeaux okay?"

"Sure." Alex sat down on the white, oversize sofa. On the table next to the books was a framed photograph of Elizabeth Taylor. It was signed, "Dear Ruedi, All my love. Elizabeth."

"Another friend." Ruedi handed Alex her glass of wine. "She used to come to Switzerland to spend Christmas with us—in Gstaad." He held out a silver cigarette box. "Do you smoke?"

"No thanks."

"Well, I definitely need one." Ruedi pulled out a long gold-tipped cigarette and lit it as he sat down next to Alex. "You can't imagine what the last two days have been like. Getting the call from Madame Ochsner yesterday telling me her husband had committed suicide. It brought back so many memories of what happened in 1987."

He took a long sip of wine. "On my way back from Basel, I drove over the Wettsteinbrücke, the bridge Ochsner fell or was pushed off of." He took another puff. "It was incredible—it was almost as high as the Golden Gate Bridge. Can you imagine anyone jumping from there? Especially Ochsner?"

"So why did the newspaper say it was a suicide?"

"Because that's what the police told them to say. They found a note on the bridge. His wife showed it to me." Ruedi set the wineglass down on one of the books and sat back. "It had almost exactly the same wording as the note my father left. He told his wife to take care of the children. And nothing more." He turned to Alex. "It was like he was trying to send *me* a message. I mean, why else use the same words my father used?"

"You think he was forced to write the note?"

"Could be."

"Or maybe in his distraught frame of mind, he used your father's words without thinking."

"Maybe," Ruedi answered. "But I can't help but think that maybe I should have told the police about our meeting with him."

"You didn't?"

"Of course not. Because then I would have had to tell them about you." He looked at her intently. "And I promised I'd keep your name out of it, remember?"

"Thanks." Alex looked outside. It was getting dark. "I guess there's no point of getting the police involved if all we're talking about is a hysterical old man."

"Do you mean me?"

"Of course not. I was thinking of Ochsner." Alex took another sip. "Did you think he might have killed himself . . . to cover something up?"

"Like what?"

She thought of Susan's theory about someone using the account to cover a margin call in 1987. "Remember, the code told the computer to change the name on the sale order from Rudolph Tobler to Tobler & Cie. And who was in charge of Tobler & Cie at the time? Ochsner." She sat back. "Or maybe it's none of our business."

"Could be." Ruedi got up and poured himself more wine. "In any event, we'll find out soon what happened to him. I asked Madame Ochsner to have the police do an autopsy." He came over and filled Alex's glass. She noticed the wine was a Lynch Bages, an expensive Bordeaux that her mother drank only on special occasions. Ruedi acted as if he drank it every day.

"In any event," he went over to the balcony and looked out, "I'm sure the police will try to close the case as soon as they can. Just like they did with my father. And everything will be peaceful again." He stared out the doors for several minutes.

Through the glass doors, Alex could see the lake. Hundreds of small boats were crisscrossing the Zürichsee. In the distance, the sun was setting over the Alps. "When do you think we'll get the results from the autopsy?" she asked.

"Tomorrow, they said. Mrs. Ochsner asked me to make the call to the Institut für Rechtsmedizin. What do you call it in English?"

"The coroner?"

"That's the word." Ruedi snuffed out his cigarette in one of the porcelain ashtrays on the coffee table. "Until then, we'll just have to wait."

"I should probably go." Alex stood up.

"Don't you want to stay for dinner?" Ruedi asked. "My cleaning woman prepares something for me every Sunday. There's usually enough for two."

Alex looked at her watch. It was almost nine. "I don't know. I should probably be getting back to the hotel. My friends are waiting there for me."

"Just let me go check in the kitchen and see what she made."

After he left, Alex walked over to the painting and examined it carefully. *Should I even be here?* she asked herself as she gazed at the Last Supper scene. *Can I trust this guy?*

Her gut told her yes. But, just in case, she should probably tell someone where she was. But who? She couldn't tell Eric. Then he'd know that not only had she contacted a client of the bank, but she was having dinner with him.

"We're in luck!" Ruedi walked over to her with an extra place setting and fresh wineglasses. "There's plenty of food. Enough for both of us."

He set the table for two. "Please say you'll stay. I don't want to eat alone tonight."

Alex hesitated.

"Are you nervous about being here?" Ruedi asked.

"Not really," she lied.

"You shouldn't be." He opened the new bottle of wine, a Chateau Lafitte, an even more expensive Bordeaux than the first.

"Don't worry." Ruedi handed her a full glass. "If I were going to hurt you, I wouldn't have invited you in, would I?" He smiled. "Thanks to you, the police know you're here with me."

CHAPTER 12

Zurich
Monday Morning

"Zurich isn't LA, you know. We don't have random killings here." Ruedi led Alex upriver from her hotel and over a wide pedestrian bridge across from the Storchen. "If Ochsner was killed, he was killed for a reason."

"You're sure about that?" Alex struggled to keep up with him.

"We'll know for sure once we look into that account." He pointed to the narrow pedestrian street leading to the Bahnhofstrasse. "And don't worry, all you have to do is wait outside, like you did last Friday. Once I see the account, I'm sure we'll know why Ochsner died." He took hold of her arm and pulled her forward. "It's impossible that he killed himself for no reason."

"Maybe there *was* a reason." Alex pulled to a halt.

"Like what?"

"Ruedi, there's something I should tell you. *Before* you go in there." Alex pointed to a low concrete bench on the side of the bridge looking out toward the lake. "Have a seat."

Alex sat next to Ruedi and began to explain Susan's theory about the margin call and how the trustee account could have been used to temporarily cover up losses during the October 1987 crash.

"So all we're talking about is an old man who got his fingers caught in the cookie jar?" Ruedi stared into Alex's eyes. "But I don't understand. If Ochsner *did* come up with a bogus sale order during that crash, wouldn't the bank have found out sooner or later?" His eyes narrowed. "Wouldn't *someone* have found out?"

"Not necessarily. The way the code was set up, the computer generated the sale order automatically. No one at the bank would ever have known about the change. All Ochsner would have had to do was show the falsified statement to his bank, to assure them that the money was available to cover his losses, and no one would have been the wiser."

"But the ruse couldn't have lasted. No matter what the sale statement said, the transaction was for my father's trustee account, not Ochsner's company. The bank loaning the money to Ochsner in his margin account would have found out, sooner or later, that the two sale orders had been switched, wouldn't they?"

"Yes, but the markets apparently rose during the days following the crash. Right back to where they were before, in fact. Which means there would no longer have been any *need* to cover the losses."

"Because?"

"Because there wouldn't have *been* any losses. The falsified sale order would no longer have been needed. The proceeds from the sale of the securities in the trustee account could have then been reinvested and no one would have been the wiser."

"But my father," Ruedi stared into the lime green water flowing beneath them, "how could he not have known what was going on?"

Alex shrugged.

Ruedi looked at her incredulously. "You think my father was in cahoots with Ochsner? You think that's why he killed himself in Tunisia? And *that's* why Ochsner killed himself on Friday?"

"Why not?"

"But my father knew *nothing* about computers. There's no way he could have manipulated that code—for any reason." Ruedi put his hand on Alex's shoulder. "Think about it. He was born in 1906. Do you know how old he was in 1987?"

"Eighty-one. But that doesn't mean he couldn't have found someone to do the work for him."

"But why would he use the trustee funds to cover a margin call for an account that didn't even belong to him? Ochsner told us himself that he was the owner of Tobler & Company at the time. And that he didn't even know about the trustee account until my father left for Tunisia, which was several days after the crash."

"Maybe Ochsner was lying."

"It still doesn't make sense. Why would Ochsner have told us about the trustee account if he had used it to cover his losses? Ochsner wasn't the type to forget something like that. He had a mind like a steel trap."

Alex shrugged. "So how would *you* explain it?"

"In the movies, the French would say, *cherchez la femme.* In Hollywood, they'd say, follow the money."

"And?"

"Basically, if you're looking for a motive, you should always try to figure out who would profit from the crime." His eyes widened. "With all that money sitting there, and with no one watching it . . ."

"But someone *was* watching it. Ochsner was. Your father, too."

"And look where they ended up!" Ruedi stood up. "That's why I want to see the account. That's the only way we'll know what really happened." He patted the side of his worn leather briefcase. "And now that I've got all the documents they asked for, there's nothing they can do to stop me from finding out."

Alex watched Ruedi walk through the revolving glass doors of HBZ and hand a teller his documents. After several minutes of discussion, the teller handed some pages to him. Ruedi looked through them carefully, then said something to the teller.

The teller shook her head no, several times.

Ruedi then turned away and walked out of the bank, passing directly in front of Alex without saying a word. He crossed the street and stopped in front of a Luis Vuitton boutique and waited.

Alex walked over to him. "What are you doing?" she asked.

"Don't let anyone see you talking to me," he whispered.

"Why so cloak-and-dagger?"

"Don't say anything. You'll understand when you see this." He set the documents on the ledge under the shop window and walked away.

Alex picked them up and started reading. At the top of the first page was a red HBZ logo with the words KONTOAUSZUG—ACCOUNT STATEMENT. Underneath was a blue subtitle: U.S. Dollar Account.

She glanced to the bottom of the page: Total: U.S. $12,104.65. The next page had the Euro balance. It wasn't much bigger. She flipped through the remaining pages, seventeen in all, and added up the other currencies: Japanese yen, Hong Kong dollars, Canadian dollars. It all came to approximately $32,400.

And this was an account that was supposed to have millions? It didn't make sense.

She looked up and saw Ruedi duck into an opening halfway down the block. She followed him.

It didn't make sense, she told herself. Why would Ochsner make such a big deal about how well he and Ruedi's father had managed the account, if they had been stealing the money all along? Why would Ochsner brag about exponential growth and appreciation if there hadn't been a lot of money involved?

She entered the courtyard and saw Ruedi head behind a large cast-iron fountain and disappear through a doorway on the other side.

She followed him out to the street and caught up with him as he crossed the bridge next to the Storchen. He was halfway across the bridge, almost to the stone Kriminalpolizei building, when he turned to her and said, "It was the perfect crime."

"What do you mean?" Alex asked.

"The perfect crime. The one in which no one even knows a crime's been committed." He motioned for her to join him on a bench, the same bench they had been sitting on before. "Think about it: all the money in this account has been sitting there, just waiting for someone to show up to claim it."

"And?" Alex asked.

"After my father died, Ochsner was the only one who knew about the account."

"Except the people who opened it."

"And they're probably all dead." Ruedi stared out into the water. "Just like Ochsner."

He turned to her. "Ochsner killed himself when he saw that his perfect crime was about to be uncovered." He shrugged. "It's obvious. *He's* the one who'd been stealing the money all these years."

Alex shook her head. "I don't buy it. When we had lunch with him last week, Ochsner didn't act the least bit bothered that you'd found out about the account."

"That's because he knew the game was up. Can't you see? Ochsner used the account to cover his losses in 1987 and then killed my father when he discovered what was going on. And when Ochsner saw that *we* were about to expose his crime, he had two choices: kill us or jump. He chose the easy way out."

"So that's it? Case closed?"

"Exactly."

Alex shook her head. "Last Friday, Ochsner didn't act at all like someone who'd been caught red-handed."

"Maybe it was just a ruse."

"So why agree to meet with us for lunch in the first place?" Alex asked.

"To find out what we knew."

"Then why go through all that song and dance about trustee accounts, Jewish owners, unopened letters? Why tell us about the account at all? If you remember correctly, *he* was the one who told you where the account was. Not me."

"Probably a death wish. Once he saw that we were on to him, he didn't want to live any more."

"Death wish? Perfect crime? You're starting to sound like a bad Hollywood movie."

"I'm sorry, but it's the only plausible explanation."

Alex shook her head. "Ochsner would never have indicated there were millions of dollars in the account if he was the one who'd plundered it. Someone else *has* to have stolen the money."

"Who?"

"I don't know." Alex's mind raced through the possibilities. The computer code was definitely put in there for a reason. No one would have gone to all that trouble to use that account to cover a margin call if it didn't have a lot of money in it, correct?"

"Let me see something." Ruedi grabbed the account statements and began adding up the cash positions. "Maybe there was money in the account at one time, but Ochsner stole it—*after* he used it for the margin call. *After* he killed my father."

"Then why would he tell you about the account now?"

"I don't know." Ruedi stared into her eyes. "But if Ochsner didn't steal the money, who did?"

"What about your father?"

"You think *he* stole the money? *After* it was used to cover the margin account during the crash?" Ruedi paused. "And the reason Ochsner didn't tell us about it last Friday was because he was trying to cover up? Keep me from finding out what a crook my father really was?"

"What other explanation is there?"

"But my father had absolutely no motive to steal. He had tons of money. Look how much he left me. All those paintings I bought with the money I inherited from him."

"How do you know that wasn't the money from the trustee account?"

"No way. That money was there from way back. My father always kept me informed of his financial situation, from the time I was a little boy. I can assure you, he had tons of money, from his father, and his father before him. From long before the trustee account ever existed." He paused. "And if he had stolen the money from the account, there wouldn't have been anything to use to cover the margin call during the 1987 crash, right? You said yourself that the trustee account would have had to have a lot of money in it, otherwise what would have been the purpose of the computer manipulation?"

"Good point."

"Your theory also doesn't explain why Ochsner committed suicide. He couldn't have done it to keep me from finding out what my father had done with the trustee account. His death put the account directly into my hands."

"That's true."

"So, computer genius, what do you think happened?"

Alex's brain filled with if/then heuristics: If Ruedi's father had stolen the money, then there would be no reason for Ochsner to commit suicide. If Ochsner had stolen the money from the account, then he wouldn't have told them about it in the first place. If neither Ruedi's father nor Ochsner stole the money, then where was it now?

Then she remembered the letter.

"Didn't Ochsner say that the letter disclosing the real owner of the account could only be opened after his death?"

Ruedi looked at her quizzically. "You think Ochsner killed himself so I could get access to that letter? Why didn't he just give it to me?"

Alex stood up and leaned over the railing to look into the river. The cold water rushed below her.

Then it hit her. What if Ruedi had stolen the money? He could have done it when he was in the bank this morning. It could have been transferred in a matter of minutes. From one HBZ account to another.

She looked over at him. Or maybe he did it last Friday, while she stood outside the bank waiting for him. Or after she left for Amsterdam. Is that why he bought her a ticket? To get her out of the way?

Is that why Ochsner was killed? To get *him* out of the way, too?

Alex glanced over at the police station on the far side of the bridge. The doors were hidden behind four gigantic stone columns. She calculated how long it would take to run over there.

She picked up her purse. "Well, whatever happened, it's over. It's no business of mine." She turned to go. "I'm going back to work now." She started to walk toward the police station.

Ruedi grabbed her arm. "Wait a minute. You think *I* may have killed Ochsner, don't you?"

She pulled back. "Let go of me!"

Ruedi refused to let go. "You think *I* killed him to get at that letter?" He pushed her to the edge of the bridge.

"Are you crazy? You're going to push me in too?" Alex looked down. It was only a few feet to the water. "This isn't Basel, you know. I could just swim away."

Ruedi let go of her arm. Alex started to run. "Before you go," he yelled after her. "There's one thing you should know. I could have gotten access to the account any time I wanted."

Alex stopped halfway across the bridge.

"Why would I kill Ochsner," Ruedi asked, "if the account was in my name?"

Alex turned back to him. "So he wouldn't report you."

"You're a naïve one, aren't you?" Ruedi walked toward her. "Then why didn't I kill you, too?"

"Because the police knew I was with you." She glanced over at the Kriminalpolizei building. "You wouldn't have been able to—"

"But the police didn't know your name. They didn't know *who* you were. They would never have connected your death with me."

"Once they found out I was missing, the officers I talked to yesterday at the airport would have been able to make the connection eventually."

"You don't get it, do you?" Ruedi walked up to her calmly. "The money was given to my father in *trust*. That means he—or I—could do whatever we wanted with it." He put his hand on her shoulder. "And where there's no motive, there's no crime."

Alex struggled to clear her mind. The events of the past four days flooded her brain. After three nights without much sleep it was hard to keep everything straight: three suspects, three time frames, two possible outcomes—good or bad—for each scenario. The permutations seemed almost limitless.

"Think about this." Ruedi handed her the bank statements. "If I wanted you out of the way, why would I insist on bringing you along with me to the bank this morning? Why would I show these account statements to you at all?"

He pushed them into her hand. "If you believe I'm the one behind it, why don't you take these to the police?"

Alex took hold of the statements.

"You want proof that I have nothing to hide?" Ruedi grabbed Alex's hand and pulled her toward the police station. "Let's tell them everything. Then there'll be no reason for you to be afraid, right? And once they know about the account, once they know about you, there's no reason to suspect me."

He rang the bell. The mirrored panels in the thick door reflected his angry face. "Let's go in."

Alex hesitated. Ruedi had to be the one behind it. It just didn't add up otherwise. He must be bluffing. "What's this going to prove?" Alex asked nervously. "What can they tell us in there?"

Ruedi rang the bell again.

But if he did tell the police about discovering the account, how long would it be before the bank found out what she had done last week?

He rang a third time, holding the ringer for several seconds.

Should I call his bluff? Alex looked up at a crumbling statue of an avenging angel over the station door. It was holding a sword in one hand. The stone sword was completely covered with pigeon excrement. The other hand was raised in a defiant gesture; the middle finger looked like it was sticking up.

The door buzzed. Ruedi pushed it open and walked inside.

Alex followed him in and watched as Ruedi got in line behind a Spanish couple. They were trying to get a parking permit. The policeman at the desk listened to them struggle in German, then told them to go to the Stadtpolizei.

He waved Ruedi to the front.

Ruedi walked forward. Alex held back.

The moment of truth.

"Ja?" the policeman asked in brusque Swiss-German. He had a scruffy, three-day-old beard, just like the policeman at the airport. "*Was wilsch?*"

He was sitting at a desk behind a high stone wall, like a judge ready to pass sentence on the poor supplicants below.

Ruedi handed him the HBZ documents. "Take a look at these," he told the policeman in English. "My name is Rudolph Tobler, and we suspect a crime has been committed."

He had said the magic word: *crime*. The policeman quickly took the documents and began reading.

"This is a trustee account from before World War II," Ruedi explained. "And it's at the Helvetia Bank of Zurich. In my name. And I think someone's stolen the money."

The policeman read through the pages carefully.

It was now clear that Ruedi wasn't bluffing. Alex touched his shoulder lightly. "I'm sorry. Maybe we should just leave."

Ruedi turned to her angrily. "You're amazing. You know that?" He spoke loudly enough for the policeman to hear. "You're the one who started this. Now you want me to stop! What can I do now? Tell them it was all a joke? You can't have your cake and eat it, too."

The policeman at the desk called in someone from the back room. He wore a business suit instead of a uniform, and he was clean shaven. He looked more like an accountant than a policeman. He began looking through the documents carefully.

The room was hot, stuffy. Alex noticed that there wasn't one window in the whole place. It was as if they were in a tomb, completely sealed off from the outside world.

The man in the suit began speaking to Ruedi in Swiss German. Alex leaned in to hear what they were saying. She couldn't understand a word of their guttural dialect. She was relatively sure of one thing, though. No one had mentioned her name.

"*Wo ist die Vermögensausweiss?*" the policeman asked.

"What is that?" Ruedi asked in English. "This is all the bank gave me."

"That is only the cash position." The policeman switched to English, too. "You need the other document." He spoke slowly, as if he were speaking to a child. "You need the Vermögensausweiss."

"What is he asking for?" Alex asked.

"I don't know. Some other document. Something about Vermögensausweiss, whatever that is."

Alex remembered reading something about the Vermögensausweiss in her training manual at HBZ. Then it hit her. "I think he wants the securities statement," she whispered to Ruedi.

"You mean, they didn't give it to me at the bank?"

"Apparently not." Alex remembered how HBZ carefully divided commercial and investment banking activities into two parts. Each account had two statements, a cash position and a securities position. "I think you have to ask."

Ruedi took Alex's arm and led her out of the station. "What a fool I was. I should have known to ask for other statements."

"Typical, isn't it?" Alex walked out into the bright midday sunshine. "Swiss bankers don't give you anything, don't tell you anything—unless you ask for it."

Ruedi Tobler walked out the front door of Helvetia Bank of Zurich holding a thick stack of papers. "Here they are." He handed them to Alex. "All the assets in my account listed in alphabetical order. Thirty-seven pages of them."

Alex immediately started reading as they walked down the busy street. "It's packed with blue chips. Triple A, top-of-the-line securities from every major market in the world." She flipped through the pages quickly and added up the various totals. "At least we know now that the account wasn't plundered."

"Incredible." Ruedi leaned over to look. "How much is there?"

"Three hundred and ninety-seven—by the looks of it."

"Three hundred and ninety-seven what?"

"Million, Ruedi." She handed him the documents. "This account is worth almost four hundred million dollars."

CHAPTER 13

Zurich
Monday, Noon

"*Merci vielmals!*" Ruedi slipped his cell phone back into his pocket. "That was Ochsner's wife. She said the coroner found no sign of foul play." He led Alex across the Bürkliplatz and over to a stone podium overlooking the lake. The snow-covered Alps covered the horizon.

"So I guess it's clear now." He stopped next to a statue of Ganymede with a large eagle on his shoulder. "Ochsner must have panicked when he saw we were about to uncover what he did in 1987." He put his hand on the boy's foot. "After I told him about the code, he probably figured I'd discover the account soon enough. And once he got back to Basel, he realized that sooner or later someone would figure out what he'd done." He paused to watch a lake steamer come in to dock on the quay beneath them. "I just wish he'd told me what happened to my father before he died."

"But he *did* tell you."

"Oh yeah? I still don't believe that my father committed suicide. And not until I have some reason to change my mind will I . . ." he turned to Alex, "I just want to know for sure what happened."

"Maybe you'll *never* know." Alex walked over to him. "Sometimes things are better off left as they are, aren't they?"

He stared out at the lake. "I always thought that one day I'd know for sure . . ." He turned to Alex. "Hey, I just thought of something! Doesn't HBZ keep a record of everything that happened in their computer? Could it go back as far as 1987?"

"They say they delete everything every few years."

"But the truth is?"

"I don't know. Knowing HBZ it's probably stored on disk somewhere." She shrugged. "They'd never admit it though. But I'm sure that any bank that would pay us a fortune to go through old code from back in the eighties would have kept—"

"Wait a minute! *You* have access to the bank's computer, don't you? You could get any information you wanted!"

"I'm not allowed into the bank's records. I'm only allowed into the code, the part of the computer that tells it what to do."

"So can't you get the computer to give me—the client—the information I'm asking for?"

"No can do. Sorry." She held out her hand. "I have to go now. I told my colleague that I'd be in late. I didn't say I'd be out all morning."

"You're going back to work? After what we've just been through?"

"Sorry. I have a job."

"Hold on." He looked at his watch. "You can't go back to work now anyway. It's noon."

He smiled. "Come on. Let me buy you lunch. I don't feel like eating alone—not today."

Ruedi pointed to an elegant old hotel on the lake's edge to their right. "That's the Baur au Lac. They have one of the best restaurants in Zurich. You can even eat outside, in the garden."

He took her arm. "What do you say? Let me treat you to lunch to thank you for helping me." He started walking. "Come on. After what I put you through this morning, it's the least I can do."

The price of Alex's appetizer, a salad with foie gras, was more than she spent on most meals. Ruedi insisted on ordering a Brunello di Montalcino dei Angeli, the most expensive wine on the menu.

"Lucky you." Alex watched as they poured the wine carefully. "You now have an account with more than a third of a billion dollars in it. You could eat like this for the rest of your life."

"But it's not my account, remember?"

"You're right, but you know you could take the money out anytime. Who's going to stop you?"

"You forget." He toasted to Alex and took a long sip. "The police know all about me now. *And* about the account."

"As if they care." Alex took a sip. The wine was excellent.

"I still can't get over how much money was—*is*—in there though." Ruedi held his wineglass up to the light. "I can't believe that someone would put so much money into someone else's hands."

"I'm sure there probably wasn't anything like that in the account when they opened it." Alex did a quick calculation. "Assuming the assets they put in your father's name grew at only 5 percent a year, which is less than Ochsner led us to believe, you still wouldn't have needed more than a few hundred thousand dollars in the 1930s to get to $397 million today, even with market crashes—as long as you kept reinvesting interest and dividends."

"Really?"

"It's the wonder of mathematics. Exponential growth, Ochsner called it. Remember? The growth compounds on itself. It's like starting with a penny and doubling the amount every day for a month. After thirty days you'd have more than a million dollars." She took a long sip. "What *I* can't believe is that no one from the bank ever contacted you. In the States you would have been bombarded with annual reports, proxy requests, tax forms. My mother always got tons of that stuff and she didn't own any stocks to speak of. Imagine having hundreds of millions of dollars invested in stocks and bonds. There's no way you wouldn't have been sent *something*."

"But this was a *secret* account." Ruedi said it as if those two words explained everything. "They never send you anything unless you ask for it. They never contact you at all unless you ask it."

"Even so. Don't you have to pay taxes on income in Switzerland? Capital gains? Why didn't they ever contact you?"

"If the tax authorities aren't told about an account, they have no way of knowing about it."

"How could they not know about an account with a third of a billion dollars in it?"

"You don't know much about Swiss banking, do you?" Ruedi smiled. "By law, Swiss banks can't tell *anyone* about an account—even the tax authorities." He poured more wine into their glasses. "In fact, Swiss banks will never contact a client unless the clients ask them to. The truth of the matter is that most foreign account holders don't receive any information by mail because they don't want to run the risk of the tax authorities at home finding out they have an account here. They usually come to Switzerland about once a year, just to see how their account's doing. They take a bit out to spend on shopping—in Paris or London or wherever—then they go home. That's it."

"And if they *never* show up?"

Ruedi shrugged. "The bank just waits. By law, they can't do anything else. The only way a Swiss bank can ever disclose an account—to anyone—is if it can be shown that a crime's been committed." He sat back and lit a cigarette. "And I'm talking about real crimes—not tax evasion, which by the way is only a civil offense in Switzerland, not a criminal offense. If you were Swiss and you were caught cheating on your taxes, they couldn't put you in jail. You would just have to pay what they say you owe."

His phone rang. He looked at the LCD display, then looked up at Alex. "That's weird. It says it's Ochsner."

Ruedi pushed the button to answer. "It must be his wife." He began speaking Swiss German.

"Poor woman." Ruedi hung up quickly. "She just wanted to make sure I'd be at the funeral on Tuesday." He set the phone back on the table. "She also told me a lawyer's been trying to contact me. Peter Koth, her husband's executor. I know him, actually. He used to work for my father."

"About the letter, probably." Alex took a sip.

"Peter told her he's been calling me all day at home. Mrs. Ochsner asked me if she could give him my cell phone number." He took another sip. "I told her yes."

"Maybe now you can find out who the account holder is."

"I'm sure that's what he wants to give us. Just think!" Ruedi put his hand on her arm. "If we were able to find that family . . . that would be super fantastic. Just imagine, handing over all that money to someone. Three hundred and how many millions?"

"Three hundred and ninety-seven. Minus what's owed to your father— what's owed to you, now that you're—"

"Exactly! And don't forget that we agreed to split everything fifty-fifty."

"Huh?" Alex did the calculation quickly. Five percent of $397 million was $19,850,000. "Do you realize that half of your father's management fee would be almost $10 million?"

"So? What makes you think my offer doesn't still hold?"

"Ruedi, you can't be serious."

He shrugged. "Why *wouldn't* I want to give you your share? If you helped me find the owners of the account, I'd be happy to—"

"You'd be willing to pay me almost $10 million to help you find a lost family?"

"Why not? I saw how you work. The other day with Ochsner, you didn't let him get away with anything. I saw how well you think. With your mind for numbers . . ." He smiled. "Why not? I need someone like you on my side."

"Why don't you go to the police?"

"The police wouldn't do shit. You saw how they are."

"But you don't need to pay me half your fee to find out what happened to the owners of that account. You could hire a detective. You could hire a *team* of detectives."

"According to Ochsner, my father already did that, but he wasn't able to find anything about this client, right?" His eyes widened. "But now we have computers to help us—the World Wide Web, databases, whatever. Come on, this is our chance to do what my father and Ochsner were never able to."

"But you could do it *yourself* and keep the whole twenty million."

Ruedi shook his head. "I'm sure that without someone helping, without someone like you helping me, I wouldn't get anywhere. I don't know the first thing about computers." He shrugged. "Didn't you notice in my apartment? I don't have one."

"I noticed."

"And with your skill with computers, we could go onto the Web and find tons of information that was never available before."

"There are a lot of people search engines out there. I even saw some Web sites at the Anne Frank House that can help you track down people who disappeared during the Holocaust."

"See? That's just what I'm saying. That's why I need your help."

"But you could get anyone to do a computer search for you. You could even give this information to one of those Holocaust groups. Let them do the search. I'm sure they'd be very interested."

"Which is precisely why I *don't* want to let them get involved. I'm sure they'd in all likelihood just try to give the money to Holocaust victims."

"What would be so bad about that?"

"First of all, we don't know for sure that this family perished in the Holocaust. In fact, we don't know anything about them. Just that they trusted my father to . . . take care of their assets." He put his hand on Alex's arm. "They may still be alive."

"True."

"*That's* why I want to see that letter. And that's why I want you to help me find them."

"I'd love to help you, Ruedi. How could I say no to ten million dollars?" Alex shook her head. "But if the bank ever heard about what I was doing, if they ever found out I was getting involved with one of their clients, they'd—"

"But you're *already* involved." Ruedi poured another glass of wine for both of them. "And don't forget, this client is asking for your help. There's nothing wrong in that, right?"

"You'd be willing to pay me $9.8 million for helping you? It doesn't make sense."

"It does make sense. If you get your money, that means I also get mine." He paused. "And in the process, I might be able to find out what happened in 1987."

"So that's what this is all about? You still want me to help you find out what happened to your father."

He paused. "I just want to be able to put it all behind me." He stared down at his hands. "And I'm not sure that I want anyone else finding out."

"Finding out what? That your father may have helped Ochsner use the trustee account during the crash?"

He shrugged. "I just want to know, one way or another." He finished off his glass. "Which is why I want to find out what happened to that account in 1987."

He immediately poured another glass. "And if along the way, I find the real owners of the account, so much the better."

He held up his glass for a toast. "To success. To *our* success." He smiled. "With both of us working on the same side, the odds are definitely in our favor."

He did have a point. Probability analysis had been one of Alex's best classes at business school. You multiplied a reward by the chance of attaining it to get a probable reward. Even with an infinitesimal chance of success, a path was always worth taking if the reward was high enough. And for $10 million, you didn't need extremely high odds to make the endeavor worthwhile.

"So?" he asked. "Do you accept?"

It was like spotting a lottery ticket on the sidewalk. The only way to find out if you were a winner was to reach down and pick it up.

"I accept."

"Wonderful." Ruedi smiled broadly. "There's only one condition."

"I should have known. What is it?"

"I'd like you to go with me—just once—to the bank."

Alex shook her head. "No."

"Hold on. Hear me out." He took a deep breath. "I just want to go in and talk to the people in charge of my account. Maybe they can help me find out what happened."

"Why do you need me to go with you?"

"I want you to help me ask the right questions. We don't have to tell them who you are. No one in the private banking department can say anything about you to anyone in the other parts of the bank anyway. That's what Swiss bank secrecy is all about, right?" He smiled. "Just say you'll do it. Then we can get started finding that family." He held up his glass for another toast.

"There really is no such thing as a free lunch, is there?" Alex toasted back.

Ruedi's cell phone rang. He answered it quickly and spoke for a moment in Swiss German, then set the phone down next to his wineglass. "That was Peter. He wants to bring us the letter. He said he'll be right over."

Ruedi moved his chair closer to hers. "Take a look at the letter. See what it says. Then you can decide if you'll help me. And don't worry about Peter. I promise I won't tell him who you are." He squeezed her arm lightly. "I kept my word with Ochsner, right?"

He pulled out a fountain pen and a piece of paper. "This might make you feel more comfortable." He read aloud as he wrote: "I, Rudolph Tobler, of Nägelistrasse 8, Zurich, Switzerland, nominal owner of an account at the Helvetia Bank of Zurich, account number—"

He looked to Alex for help. She told him the number without hesitation.

He smiled. "See what a great team we make?"

He then went back to his writing. "I hereby agree to pay one half of my share of the account—2.5 percent—to Alex Payton, U.S. citizen residing in Zurich."

He finished with, "This commitment is subject to the full authority of Swiss law and cannot be revoked under any circumstances." He handed the document to Alex for her approval.

She read through it carefully. As she finished, she looked up and saw a tall, well-dressed man with gray hair walking toward their table.

Ruedi stood to greet him. "Herr Koth, how nice to see you again."

Koth looked distinguished, like the quintessential Swiss businessman. He reeked of propriety and pipe tobacco.

He said a few words in Swiss German, then handed an envelope to Ruedi. He didn't once look at Alex.

Before Peter left, Ruedi asked him to witness his signature on the document he had prepared for Alex. He carefully folded over the top of the document so the lawyer could only see the signature. He then pulled out a notary seal he had in his briefcase and pressed it to the document to make it official.

Had Ruedi asked him to bring it? Alex wondered.

As soon as Koth was gone, Ruedi tore open the envelope and pulled out a smaller envelope with a wax seal on the back. On the front, it had several lines of handwritten text. "It's from my father."

Ruedi read aloud: "Dear Ruedi, please take care of this account for me. I'm sure I can trust you to do the right thing."

"Strange," Ruedi muttered, "it sounds eerily like his suicide note." He turned the envelope over and over in his hands. He then picked up a knife from the table and held it aloft, like a miniature Excalibur. "And the winner is . . ."

He slit open the envelope carefully, leaving the seal intact, and pulled out a single sheet of vellum. He held it up for Alex to see. One side was filled with typewritten text.

Ruedi held it up to the light and looked at it carefully. "It's in English. I guess it was easier for the client to understand."

At the bottom of the page, Alex could make out two signatures. One of them was clearly "Rudolph Tobler, Zürich." The other looked like "Aladár Kohen, Budapest."

Ruedi laid the faded letter on the table and began to read aloud.

> Declaration: Concerning account 2495 at the Helvetia Bank of Zurich-Hauptsitz, registered in the name of Rudolph Tobler, Spiegelgasse 26, Zurich, Switzerland

"That's our old address." Ruedi's eyes lit up. "That's the house where I grew up—before we moved to the Zurichberg." He continued reading.

> 1. The above-mentioned account is a trustee account, opened in the name of Rudolph Tobler, hereafter referred to as Trustee, for the benefit of Mr. and Mrs. Aladár Kohen, Andrássy út. 6, Budapest VI, Hungary, hereafter referred to as the Owners.

> 2. This account belongs in its entirety to Mr. and Mrs. Aladár Kohen. In the event of their death, the account is to be divided among all of their children.

> 3. In the event of the decease of the Trustee, nominal ownership of the account shall be transferred to his heirs and likewise in perpetuity until the Owners reclaim the account.

> 4. In remuneration for the careful and trustworthy management of this account, 5 percent of the account's total value will be paid to

the trustee or his heirs, at the time that possession of the account is duly transferred to the Owners and/or their heirs.

Signed in Zurich, Switzerland on the twenty-second day of May, 1938:

Rudolph Tobler, Zürich   Aladár Kohen, Budapest

Ruedi handed the letter to Alex. "It's definitely my father's signature. But what kind of account number is that?" He pointed to the top line. "It only has five digits."

"I'm sure it's the same account," Alex replied. "The core numbers are correct. The others have simply been added over the years." She picked up the document and read carefully. "So at least we know the owners' names: Mr. and Mrs. Aladár Kohen."

"Notice that it's a Jewish name?" Ruedi asked. "That explains why they had to open a trustee account. Why they had to put their money in my father's name in the first place."

"And did you notice how someone underlined the word *all*? Why would they do that?"

Ruedi leaned over to look. "It's the same ink Aladár Kohen used to sign his name, which means he's the one who did it." Ruedi took the letter out of Alex's hands. "Maybe he didn't trust one of the sons or daughters. Maybe he was afraid one of them would try to get all the money."

"In any event," Alex sat back, "it means he had more than one child, which means we have a better chance of finding someone."

Alex realized that she had begun using the word *we*.

"Let's call them!" Ruedi pulled out his phone and began dialing.

"But there isn't a phone number."

Ruedi smiled. "Yes, but there's a name. And you of all people should know about directory assistance." He dialed three fives and waited.

As Ruedi spoke, Alex recognized the word *Ungarn,* the German word for "Hungary." Ruedi then carefully spelled out the letters, "K-o-h-e-n." He held up his crossed fingers and sat back to wait.

A little too easy, isn't it? Alex asked herself. If Ruedi's father wasn't able to find the Kohens after the war, what chance did they have of finding them now, in the phone book?

She picked up the agreement giving her half of Ruedi's share. It looked official with the signature, seal, and notarization.

"*Sind Sie sicher?*" Ruedi set the phone on the table and shrugged. "Not one Kohen in Budapest. Which is strange, isn't it? I thought Kohen was a common Jewish name."

"Maybe not if it's spelled with a *K*."

"Could be." Ruedi sat back. "I have a friend from Budapest, Sándor Antal, a professor who was doing a sabbatical in Zurich a while ago. He told me once that most of the Jews in Budapest changed their names long before the war, at the beginning of the century in fact. Unfortunately, anti-Semitism wasn't invented by the Nazis." He put the envelope in his briefcase and stood up. "Are you ready to go to the bank now?"

"Sure. Just let me call my colleague and tell him I'm not going to be in this afternoon either."

"Don't worry." Ruedi led Alex toward the main entrance of HBZ. Sun was shining through the Linden trees lining the Bahnhofstrasse. "Even if the bank found out about you helping me, which they won't, you could resign."

Alex turned to Ruedi. "This might sound strange to you, but I happen to need my salary to live on."

"But now that we know the name of the account owners, you could earn way more money helping me."

"But I can't live without my job. I don't have million-dollar paintings. I have debt that I—"

"How much?"

Alex shook her head. "Lots."

"How much?"

"You don't want to know."

"Sure I do."

"I know this might sound crazy to you, but it's more than a hundred thousand dollars."

"Really?"

"That's what graduate school in America costs these days. Believe me."

"That's incredible."

"Incredible but true, which means I'm going to have to live like a pauper for the next five years or so."

"But you must be earning a *lot* of money working on the bank's computer."

"I am, but almost all of it goes toward paying off my loans." Alex walked over to the ATM in the entrance to HBZ. "You want to see something?"

She inserted her cash card and shielded her hand as she typed in the PIN. She printed out the account balance and handed the small slip of paper to Ruedi. "For your information, this is how much I've been able to save since I started working here in June."

He read the slip carefully. "That's less than a thousand dollars!"

"Exactly. Now you see how I can't risk losing my job to help you." She pushed Cancel and pulled out her card.

"Let me show *you* something." Ruedi walked over to the machine. "I happen to have an account here, too." He put in his card, punched in a few buttons, then looked carefully at the slip Alex had given him. "Let's see if this works . . ."

"What are you doing?" Alex asked.

"Hold on. How much is the dollar worth these days?"

Alex checked the currency rate display window to her right and gave Ruedi the exchange rate to the fourth decimal. "Why do you want to know?"

"You'll see." He pushed a few more buttons and then pulled out his card. "This should make you feel more comfortable about helping me."

"What are you talking about?"

He stood back from the ATM. "Check your account balance now."

Alex inserted her card into the automated teller, typed in her PIN, and called up the account balance. It was the Swiss Franc equivalent of $100,000.

"What the—" She pulled her hair behind her ears and leaned in closer, blocking the sun with her hand to see better. "Why did you do that?"

"A simple intrabank transfer. I got your account number off the slip and transferred some money into your account." He handed it back to Alex. "If two accounts are both at HBZ, you can transfer almost any amount you want between them. And it's effective immediately. I use it to pay bills sometimes. They call it intrabanking. All you do is—"

"I know how it works. I can't believe that you have so much cash in your account and that you'd—"

"I just sold one of my paintings, an Eric Fischl." He smiled. "And I haven't decided what to do with the money." He put his card back in his wallet and leaned against the display window next to Alex. "So, are you happy *now*?"

"Ruedi, there's no way I can accept this."

"Then think of it as a down payment." He shrugged.

"Still, I can't."

"Then try looking at it this way: I just gave you the first installment of the money we're *both* going to get. When we find the Aladár Kohen family of Budapest."

"And if we don't find the Kohens?"

"Then think of it as an insurance policy. In the remote case that you do lose your job, you keep the money."

"You can't be serious."

"Of course I am." He put his hand on her shoulder. "And don't worry. I'll make sure no one finds out about you. I promise. It's in my *own* interest, after all. I need you as much inside the bank as outside. Shall we go in?" He turned and walked through the door, beneath the two naked cupids.

The elevator door opened to the second floor and Ruedi escorted Alex into an elaborately furnished wood-paneled room. Light was streaming through windows facing onto a courtyard. The floor was covered with several old Oriental carpets.

A dark-suited concierge came over and greeted them. "*Gruëzi!*"

Ruedi immediately began speaking English. "We'd like to see the person responsible for overseeing my account. The number is . . ." He turned to Alex. The concierge carefully wrote the number as Alex recited it.

"Someone will be with you shortly." He motioned to a group of leather chairs in the far corner of the room. Ruedi sat down and began going through the documents.

"I still can't believe how much there is in this one account: IBM, Nestlé, Daimler-Benz, Google, Microsoft. I can't believe the bank didn't tell me about all this when I was in here earlier."

"Why should they?" Alex asked. "Didn't Ochsner say that the account was being managed by someone outside the bank?"

"Yeah, someone at a small investment company called FINACORP." He looked up. "But that doesn't mean there isn't someone inside the bank who's overseeing what goes on. That's who we're going to meet now, I hope."

He shook his head. "I still think he should have made sure I was given these statements when I was in here this morning. HBZ collects a lot of fees on these accounts, even if they *don't* manage the money. And on one *this* size, they must be making a fortune." He shrugged. "Or maybe he handles $400 million accounts all the time."

"Tell me something. Why does the bank allow outside fund managers to be involved at all?"

"Because many clients *want* to use outside fund managers to make investment decisions. They usually get better returns than the people inside the bank. And a few percentage points of higher returns easily cover the extra cost. My father, for example, was much better at choosing stocks than the bank. That's why people used him." He shrugged. "Also, clients like getting a more personal service."

"And the bank doesn't mind letting someone else manage their accounts?"

"What do they care? They get paid no matter what. Big banks like HBZ even give computer terminals to the outside fund managers so they can access their clients' accounts online. In the end, the banks get more business. And more fees."

"How much?"

"Who? The fund manager? About a half percent, I think. That's what my father charged anyway."

"And the bank?"

"They usually get about a half percent, too. If you include the commissions and things like that."

"Is that how much Ochsner was paying that man to manage your account?" Alex asked.

"Probably."

"Do you know how much a half percent per year is, on an account this size?"

"Who cares? Clients of Swiss banks don't really mind paying all the fees. They like the security of having their money here. It's so much safer than keeping their money at home—in Argentina or South Africa or wherever. Do you know how much they'd have to pay in taxes if they kept their money in their home countries?"

"But the bank and the fund managers are *each* making almost $2 million a year on this one account."

"So?" Ruedi asked. "Who cares?"

"So Ochsner was paying some guy $2 million a year just to tell the bank how to invest the money?"

"That's how it works here. But I'm sure that the guy who's managing the account doesn't get to keep all the money—they usually have to share the fees with all the other fund managers in the company." He looked out the window. "Don't forget that running a company in Switzerland isn't cheap. Life's expensive here. There are lots of bills to pay."

Alex took the account statements from Ruedi's hands and looked through them. "Do you realize that by accepting that 5 percent lump-sum fee back in 1938, your father gave up years of additional profit?" she asked.

"But $20 million is a lot of money." Ruedi's eyes widened. "What more could you ask for?"

"But think of all those other fund managers who took the usual half-percent annual commission on accounts like this, after all these years, with the accounts growing exponentially. They probably earned a hundred times that much."

"Who cares?" Ruedi answered blithely. "It still means ten million for each of us."

"You're right." Alex carefully scanned the account statements. "It's strange. There's no mention here of *any* management fees being paid out."

"It makes sense. Remember what the guy at the police station said? The Vermögensausweiss—the account statement—only shows what's in the account, not what's been coming in or going out."

"That's something else you should ask for." Alex handed back the papers.

"See how useful it is to have someone like you helping me?" Ruedi patted her on the back. "What would I do without you?"

A short, dark-haired man walked across the lobby. He was wearing a forest green suit jacket, brown pants, white socks, and black shoes. He held out his hand to Ruedi. "*Es freut mich nochmals.*"

"It's nice to see you, too, Mr. Versari." Ruedi answered, in English. "As you can see, I've brought a friend along this time. She's my private advisor, *à titre privé*, helping me with this account."

"Nice to meet you." Versari shook Alex's hand perfunctorily and turned back to Ruedi. "Shall we go?"

Alex noticed how he didn't ask for her name. He just pointed to the door at the far end of the room. "This way, please."

He led them down a long series of narrow corridors. Like a Chinese box, the private meeting rooms and interior courtyards of HBZ seemed to go on forever.

He took them into a small, elegantly appointed room facing another courtyard. The windows were covered with translucent white shades.

"Would you like some coffee?" he asked. "Mineral water?"

"Nothing. Thank you." Ruedi took the documents from Alex's hands and handed them to the banker. "We want some more statements from my account."

"Certainly." Versari motioned for them to sit down. "What can I do for you?"

Ruedi glanced at Alex and started in. "I want a log of *all* transactions for this account. Especially what occurred in October of 1987."

"1987?" Versari raised his eyebrows.

"Yes. I need them to put all the documents in my father's estate in order."

"But I don't think our files go back that far. A few years, yes, but not 1987."

"I'm sure you can find it." Ruedi glanced at Alex again. "It must be in your computer somewhere."

"I don't think that's possible." Versari shook his head slowly.

"Then, maybe my colleague could explain better." Ruedi glanced at Alex and sat back.

She cleared her throat. "Mr. Versari, I'm sure the records must be stored on disk somewhere." She glanced over to the computer terminal in the corner of the room. "All you have to do is have someone go into the computer archives."

"Let me see something." Versari opened his folder and read quickly. "It says that your account here is actually managed by someone at FINACORP—in

Zurich. I'm sure it would be easier to contact them to get the information you require. Their offices are not far from here—on Gartenstrasse, I believe. I don't have any direct contact with them, but the computer sends them a copy of every transaction. On their computers there are, I'm sure, copies of all the relevant information you are looking for."

"But I want the information *here*!" Ruedi's voice rose. "And if you're not willing to help me, I insist on speaking to a bank manager."

"I don't see what good that would do." Versari kept his hands folded in front of him. "I told you there is no way for the bank to access the information you are asking for."

"Look." Ruedi shouted. "I've come into this bank several times over the past few days, and every time I ask for something, I'm told to come back, to go somewhere else. I'm getting tired of this."

"But there's nothing I can do." Versari shrugged.

"You don't believe I have the right to this account either, do you?"

"That's not the point, Mr. Tobler. I'm only authorized to—"

"Take a look at this." Ruedi reached into his briefcase. "This letter proves beyond a shadow of a doubt my right to have any information I want concerning this account."

He pulled out his father's agreement with Aladár Kohen and started reading aloud. "If the trustee should die, the official ownership of the account will be transferred to his immediate heirs and likewise in perpetuity." Ruedi handed Versari the letter and sat back, folding his arms. Alex could see out of the corner of her eye that he was smiling. Once again, Ruedi Tobler was getting what he wanted.

Versari glanced at the document and reached over to pick up the phone. He dialed a four-digit number and waited.

"What are you doing?" Ruedi asked.

"I need to ask one of our jurists for an opinion."

"Why do you need to ask a lawyer's opinion?" Alex asked. "You know the account belongs to Mr. Tobler."

Versari held up his hand. "Don't worry. This will only take a moment. It's just a formality."

Several minutes later a tall, handsome woman with bright red hair walked into the room. "Reinbeck. Pleased to meet you." She shook Alex's hand first, then Ruedi's. "And the document?" She held out her hand to Versari, and he passed her the letter obsequiously. She read through it quickly.

Alex detected a faint odor of perfume in the air—lilies, or patchouli. Reinbeck was wearing a perfectly tailored business suit. She looked important.

"This seems to be a trustee account." Reinbeck sat down across the table from Ruedi and Alex. "Something I haven't seen in a long time."

"Yes, it was opened in my father's name, before World War II. But now it belongs to me," Ruedi answered. "And I simply want Mr. Versari here to show me the account transfers that took place in the past. Especially the ones for 1987. I have every right to ask for that, don't I?"

"But you're only the trustee."

"Exactly. And as you can see by the letter, I'm in charge now. I'm my father's sole heir. I can ask for any document I desire. Isn't that correct?"

"Not anymore."

"What do you mean? Until the family is found, *I'm* the one responsible for this account."

"That may have been the way it worked in 1938." Reinbeck handed the letter back to Ruedi. "However, in the meantime, the laws have changed."

"What are you talking about?" Alex asked. "Mr. Tobler has every right to see what's going on with his account."

"I'm sorry. I'm only following the rules, which were changed because of pressure from the American government." She held her eyes on Alex's.

"This account is in the name of Rudolph Tobler, and until the true owner is found—"

"But that's the problem." The lawyer put her hands flat on the table. "A few years ago, the U.S. government, among others, put pressure on us to prohibit anonymous accounts, ostensibly to stop the flow of drug money. And we did what they wanted. Reluctantly, I may add. Now all Swiss accounts have to disclose the beneficial owners."

"So?" Alex asked. "We know who the beneficial owner is. It's in the letter."

Reinbeck pulled a document off the top of a stack near the computer. "Do you see this?" She handed an account-opening packet to Alex. "Please look carefully at the form in the back."

Alex opened to the last page, saw a large black *A* at the top, followed by the words *Feststellung des wirtschaftlich Berechtigten.*

"That form, declaring who the beneficial owner is, is now required for every account at the bank," the lawyer explained. "Even the ones that were opened in the past. There is no grandfather clause."

"But now we *know* who the beneficial owner is." Alex motioned for Ruedi to give her the letter. She began reading. "His name is Aladár Kohen. And here's his address. Andrássy út. 6. Budapest."

Alex got out her pen and began filling in the form. "Then Mr. Tobler will have the right to access his account, correct?"

Reinbeck shook her head. "It's not that easy. We now need to know who the current beneficial owner is."

"With all due respect, this form only asks for the *name* of the beneficial owner—not whether they are still alive." Alex pushed the completed Formular A across the table.

Reinbeck pushed it back. "But the beneficial owner has to be a living person."

"But you don't know for a fact that this couple *isn't* living, do you?" Alex pushed the form back to Reinbeck. "So therefore, the form must be valid. At least until it can be proven that they're dead."

"Actually, it's the opposite. We need proof they're alive." Reinbeck stood up. "It's the law now. Exactly the way your government wanted it." She pointed to the document. "In order to get access to this account, you must provide us with some form of proof that these beneficial owners are still alive. Obviously, it would be best if they were to come into the bank themselves."

"Did you ask for proof they were alive when you opened this account?" Alex asked.

"We didn't even know they existed," the lawyer countered. "That's the whole point of these trustee accounts. The bank was never told about them." She turned to Ruedi. "And now that we know that it is a trustee account, there's nothing we can do until we have proof of beneficial ownership."

"In the past," Versari explained, "one *could* open an account here with simply a handshake and a signature. But now we absolutely need to know who the beneficial owner is. And if you can't prove to us that Mr. and Mrs. Kohen are alive, you need to prove to us that they are dead. And then give us the names of their heirs."

"And until we give you the information you require," Ruedi asked, "we aren't allowed to see anything?"

"Nothing." Versari sat back and folded his arms. "And that means the fund manager at FINACORP will *also* no longer have access to the account. Isn't that correct?" He turned to Reinbeck for her approval.

She nodded.

"Effective immediately?" he asked.

She nodded again. "Until they provide us with a living beneficiary, the account is blocked."

Ruedi stood up. "Considering that the family was Jewish, and that they lived in Nazi-occupied territory during World War II, how probable is that?"

CHAPTER 14

Zurich
Monday, Midafternoon

"I can't believe I was so stupid." Ruedi pushed through the midafternoon shoppers crowding the sidewalk in front of the bank. "Why did I have to show them the letter?"

"It wasn't your fault." Alex struggled to keep up with him. "You couldn't have known."

"I just wanted to drive home the point that I had every right to see the account, and it backfired. I'll *never* get the information now." He reminded Alex of the Tin Man from the *Wizard of Oz*, waiting to be allowed inside the Emerald City only to be told, "Don't you know? Nobody can see the wizard. Nobody."

"All I wanted," Ruedi turned to her with a pleading look in his eyes, "was to see what the computer did back in 1987. I just wanted to see the statement with my own eyes. But now, I'll never know."

"Can't you put that behind you?" Alex asked. "Why not concentrate on finding the family, getting the twenty million."

"That's it!" Ruedi's eyes widened. "All I need to do is find the family! And get *them* to fill out that Formular A. HBZ would *have* to let me see the statements then."

"Why are you worrying so much about that account statement?"

"Because it will tell me why my father died."

"I can tell you right now what it would have said." Alex pulled Ruedi to a stop. "It's just a matter of decoding the instructions that were put into the computer. The code told the computer that any sale statement that got printed on that day in October would have had the name of your father's company on the top, instead of the name from the trustee account. That's all. Nothing more."

"But we don't know what sale it applied to."

"What difference does it make?"

"It'll just help me know for sure."

"Forget it. It's not gonna happen."

"I just had an idea!" Ruedi's eyes lit up. "We could go to FINACORP. I'm sure they have all the old records. Remember? They're the ones who took over when Ochsner gave up managing the account. And as the official account holder, I have every right to make them show me everything." He pointed across a small canal. "Their offices are over there, I think. All we have to do is go in and ask."

"But Ochsner told us that the man at FINACORP only started managing the account in the early nineties. The manipulation on the code occurred in 1987."

"No problem." Ruedi pulled her ahead. "If I know Ochsner, he gave that man at FINACORP everything, including the bank statements from before he retired."

"And if he didn't?"

"There's no harm in asking, is there?" Ruedi tapped the side of his briefcase. "And these documents certify that I'm the official owner of the account. As account manager, FINACORP has to let me have access to the files, right?" Ruedi started crossing the bridge.

Alex held back. "But the bank just removed FINACORP as managers of the account."

"But FINACORP doesn't know that. Not yet." He turned back to Alex. "Remember what Versari said? He doesn't have any contact with them. He only sends them copies of the account transactions—after they've been executed. It'll be days before they find out."

"But if they try to use the computer to execute a trade, they'll know immediately."

"Which is why we have to go there now."

FINACORP—FINANCIAL ASSET MANAGEMENT CORPORATION was engraved on a gold plaque on the door. Ruedi pushed a small gold button to the right of the door and stood back. "Now remember," he whispered to Alex, "just act like nothing's wrong. It'll be fine. I'll do all the talking."

"I don't understand why you need me here at all."

"I need you to help me look through the file as quickly as possible. Then we get out before they find out I got them removed from the account." Ruedi rang the bell again.

The man who opened the door looked like he'd just stepped out of a Brooks Brothers catalogue. *Finally, a good-looking banker*, Alex thought. Tall, handsome, perfectly groomed, and impeccably dressed. A perfectly tailored gray suit and a white shirt. And a Hermès tie, just like Ochsner.

"Grüezi." Ruedi shook his hand and started speaking. "I'd like to see my account."

"Who are you?" The man switched effortlessly into English.

"Rudolph Tobler."

"Mr. Tobler!" He obviously recognized the name. "Please come in." He shook Alex's hand. "My name's Christoph Pechlaner, by the way." Just like the bankers at HBZ, he didn't even ask for Alex's name. Discretion oblige.

Pechlaner led them through a narrow hall into a large conference room looking out onto a tree-shaded courtyard. Modern art covered the walls.

"Thank you for meeting us on such short notice." Ruedi opened his briefcase and got out his documents. "I'm here to get some information related to my account."

He read the account number from the top of the HBZ statements he pulled out of his briefcase. "This should just take a few minutes."

He handed Pechlaner his passport and the other documents.

"I'm a bit confused." Pechlaner looked through Ruedi's passport carefully. "I thought this account was part of an estate managed by Georg Ochsner."

"It is," Ruedi answered quickly. "My father's estate." He pointed to his birth certificate and his father's death certificate. "And I'm his only heir."

"But I'm under the impression that when he gave my colleague the mandate to manage this account, Mr. Ochsner told us there was no heir. He said that he would inform us of the true owner when the time came. Until then, my partner, Max Schmid, was told to manage the account conservatively, which he's been doing for many years now."

"Well, as you can see by these documents, I'm the only heir there is. I'm now the person you have to deal with."

"I think you need to go over all this with Mr. Schmid. Especially considering Mr. Ochsner's death."

"Then tell Schmid that I'd like to see him immediately."

"I can't. He's on a business trip. He'll be back tomorrow, though. In time for Georg Ochsner's funeral."

"I'm sure I'll see him there, then." Ruedi took his passport back and put it into his briefcase. "But I'd still like to see my account statements."

Pechlaner looked through Ruedi's other documents. "Everything does seem to be in order." He stood up. "If you don't mind, can I make copies of these documents?"

"Whatever you need," Ruedi replied. "As long as I get access to my account."

As soon as Pechlaner was gone, Ruedi turned to Alex and smiled. "See? It's working." He stood up and began walking around the room. "In a few minutes we'll know everything."

He began examining a small, framed drawing next to the door. "That's Jean Cocteau." He then moved over to a lithograph of oversize brush strokes on the next wall. "A Lichtenstein. These guys have good taste."

The door opened and Pechlaner walked in, carrying two dark gray binders. He laid them down on the table with a thud. "These are everything that we have up here."

Alex noticed the numbers on the spine: HBZ KONTO: 230-SB2495.880-O1L. It had gained various numbers and letters over the years, but it was certainly the one Ruedi's father had opened in 1938.

She picked up the first folder and read the label: Kontozustand 1–3 Quartal. It contained the quarterly account balances for the past eight months. The other folder held all the transactions statements for the same period.

"I'm sure you'll find everything in order." Pechlaner sat down across from them. "I've also taken the liberty to print out a chart showing the account's performance over the last few years." He laid a computer-generated bar chart in the middle of the table.

Ruedi leaned down to look at it. "As you can see," Pechlaner explained, "the account's consistently gone up, despite all the market turbulence."

Ruedi pushed the chart back to Pechlaner. "That's nice, but what I'm really interested in are the account statements for 1987."

"Why?"

"Because I need to complete the files for my father's estate. And since this account is the last thing pending, I need to see how much it was worth at the time he died. Which was in October 1987."

Ruedi was turning into a good liar, Alex noticed. Or was he always like this?

"I'm not sure our archives go back that far." Pechlaner opened one of the folders and read through the account summary on the first page. "According to this, we only started managing this account in January, 1991."

"But Mr. Ochsner told me he gave you all the previous documents. Could you just go take a look?" Ruedi persisted. "You certainly have an archive somewhere, I'm sure."

"Downstairs, in the basement, actually." Pechlaner stood up. "But I can't promise you anything. As I said, this account isn't mine to manage."

"I'd appreciate it if you'd take a look."

"It may take a few minutes."

"No problem." Ruedi walked with Pechlaner to the door. "If you want, I'll help you."

"Nein!" Pechlaner answered quickly. "We don't allow *anyone* into the basement. I'm sure you can understand why. Our clients' files are strictly confidential." Pechlaner closed the door tightly behind him.

"Do you think he'll find it?" Alex asked. She picked up the account transactions folder and began flipping through the pages.

"I hope so." Ruedi got up and began pacing the room again. "I really want to know what happened."

"And if you don't find out?"

"Then no harm in trying, right?"

"Wow." Alex stopped at a page in the middle of the folder. "Look at this." She pointed to an entry in the middle of the page. "Did you know there was a safe connected to your account? Here's an automatic debit—for a safe-deposit box at HBZ Zurich." She held out the page for Ruedi to see: *Schliessfach 4483, Miete. HBZ HAUPTSITZ.*

"It must be huge. It's been costing you over four thousand francs a year."

Ruedi read the debit slip carefully. "It says it's in the vaults of the HBZ main building—where we were this afternoon. I wonder why HBZ didn't tell me about it when I was in there earlier. Or why there wasn't a key in the envelope my father left for me."

"Maybe the Kohens have the key."

"Or *had* it." He stared over at Alex. "I wonder why Ochsner never mentioned it."

"Maybe he didn't know about it."

"How could he not know?" Ruedi asked. "The debit got made every year, right?"

"But don't you remember what Ochsner told us? He only looked at the quarterly account balances." Alex pointed over to the other folder. "To see how the account was doing. He didn't know or care how much was being paid out in safe fees—or any fees for that matter—as long as the account was growing regularly."

"You're right." Ruedi came over and watched Alex flip through the remaining credit–debit slips. "It'd be fun to go in and see what's in that safe, wouldn't it?" He put his hand on her shoulder. "I *could,* you know. Even if you don't have a key for a safe at a Swiss bank, all you have to do is pay 500 francs to have someone come in and drill the lock open. As long as you have the right to access the safe. It's happened to me before."

"But you don't have the right to do that any more. You've been cut off from the account. Remember?" Alex studied an HBZ *Credit-Gutschrift* page. "What's this? It looks like someone sent $4.2 million into your account in January."

Ruedi leaned over and looked. "Why would they do that?"

Alex flipped through the next pages. "There are several more, in fact." She added them up quickly.

Numbers. You couldn't argue with them. Alex had loved them as a child because they were the one thing that wasn't affected by the chaos of the world around her. Numbers were forever—immutable. They never lied. Like when she was seven and found out she had a one-year-old half brother, she'd had irrefutable proof that her father had started his new family before he had left her and her mother.

"Where is BVI?" she asked. Alex pulled out another credit slip and held it to Ruedi: *Ueberweisung zu gunsten des Kontos* 230-SB2495.880-0L *von: Caribbean Trust Bank, BVI.*

"The British Virgin Islands, probably. I have some friends who have a house there, actually. But why would they send money to my account? They don't even know it exists. Nobody does."

"That's the whole point, isn't it?"

"What do you mean?"

"It was only a matter of time until it happened."

"What?"

"Think about it, Ruedi. A multimillion-dollar account with no one looking at what's going in or coming out. Just a doddering old man who religiously checks the account balance at the end of each quarter."

"Someone's been using this account for money laundering?"

"Of course. As long as they made sure the money came in and went out before the end of the quarter, Ochsner would never notice."

"Maybe he was in on it." Ruedi's eyes widened. "He was the only one who had the power to transfer money in and out. Since he was the executor of my father's estate, and since this account still belonged to the estate, he could have done anything he wanted."

"But why would he tell us about the account then? And don't start with your 'death wish' theories." Alex glanced toward the door.

"You think it was FINACORP doing it?" Ruedi asked. "But why would Pechlaner show us these if that were the case?" He pointed to the two account folders.

"Maybe he's not the one doing it. Maybe it's the other guy."

"Schmid?" Ruedi shook his head. "But how could he? How could the bank not have seen what was going on?"

"You said the bank doesn't care *what* happens to the account, as long as the outside fund managers didn't transfer any money out."

"You're right. They probably didn't care at all about money coming in—they must have loved it, in fact. It meant more fees for them. But they would never have let Schmid transfer money out. That's the one thing outside fund managers are never allowed to do."

"But Schmid wasn't transferring money out." Alex held up a page marked Aktenkaufvertrag—Stock Purchase. "He was investing it in a stock fund based in Cyprus."

Alex pointed to the bottom line of the statement. "See? Shortly before the end of the last quarter, Schmid told HBZ to make two separate investments from your account into these two Cyprus funds. And the amount invested was, coincidentally, the exact amount that had come in during the quarter from the British Virgin Islands."

She opened the other file. "And where did it go? Into these two investment funds, both based in Cyprus." She showed the relevant pages to Ruedi. "We studied these off-shore centers in business school. No one really oversees what happens in them. Once the money got transferred into them, it would have been easy to divert it back to whoever sent it to your account in the first place. That's what money laundering is all about, right? Erasing all traces of its illicit past. And what better way to do that than send it through a secret Swiss bank account and a couple of anonymous funds in Cyprus?"

"But why didn't any of this show up on the statements that Ochsner looked at?" Ruedi asked. "If they were investments, wouldn't they have appeared on the securities statement somewhere?"

"They *do*." Alex reached over and flipped through the statements Ruedi had brought in with him. She pointed to two small entries toward the middle. "Look how the number of shares you own in those Cyprus funds keeps going up, quarter after quarter, but the share price keeps going down, which means that the total amount of money in the funds never changes. These must be two of the worst-performing funds in the history of international finance." She sat back. "And I bet your account was the only one investing in them."

"But aren't the authorities supposed to oversee what goes on in funds like that?" Ruedi asked.

"Not in places like Cyprus, apparently. Caveat emptor. It's up to the investors to keep an eye on what's going on. In this case, it was up to Ochsner. But since he never looked at anything but the bottom line, he never knew what was going on."

"How could he *not* have known what was going on?" Ruedi whispered. "He told us he checked the account statements like clockwork."

"Precisely. He checked the account balances at the *end* of each quarter. And since the amount of money they lost in the Cyprus funds was exactly the same amount that came in during the quarter, he never noticed anything was wrong."

Alex reached over and put the transfer slip back exactly where she had found it. "All the money launderers had to do was make sure all the inflows and outflows got balanced out before the end of the quarter, and they could start doing it all over again."

"Let me check what happened this quarter." She opened the credit–debit folder again and flipped through the pages for the months of July, August, and September. "There've been three transfers into the account since the beginning of July. For a total of $21.3 million."

"Shit!" Ruedi muttered. "What are they going to do when they find out that they've been cut off from the account? That there's no way for them to get their money back?" He glanced toward the door.

"Wait a minute," Alex whispered. "There was hardly any cash in the account this morning, remember. Maybe it's already been transferred out. It *is* almost the end of September."

"Not necessarily," Ruedi answered. "A good fund manager would have put the money into time deposits. That's what my father would have done, anyway."

"Let me check." Alex opened to the section in the investment portfolio showing short-term investments. "You're right. Here it is. Exactly $21.3 million in a fiduciary deposit at UBS Luxembourg. And guess when the time deposit comes due?" She pointed to the end of the entry. "The last week of September. In three days' time."

"Which means the money hasn't gone out yet."

"But the investment order may have already been sent through." She flipped to a section in the end of the transactions file marked PENDENT — PENDING.

"Here it is." She pulled out the last page. "This investment order was sent in to HBZ at the middle of last week. Schmid told HBZ to make a new investment in those two Cyprus funds. And guess for how much? He told HBZ to invest $4 million in one fund and $17.3 million in the other. That makes a total of $21.3 million, the exact same amount that came in during the quarter."

"So everything's fine!" Ruedi took the investment order and put it back into the folder carefully. "They got their money back. And as long as we pretend not to know about what was going on, we're okay."

"But why is it still in the pending folder?" Alex asked. She read through the investment order carefully. "Uh-oh."

"What?"

She pointed to a small line at the bottom of the page. "They can't execute trades like this one online. Since the Cyprus funds are not listed on an automated exchange, it has to be done manually."

She pointed to three words at the end of the sentence: *per Hand, Börse.* "That means that the trade was given to the bank's stock market department to do manually. It's probably still in the pipeline."

"So how long will it take to be executed?" Ruedi asked excitedly. "How long until their money is transferred out of my account?"

"Let's check what happened before." Alex flipped to the March and June transactions summaries. "It looks like the other trades took from seven to ten days before the money was transferred to the funds' bank in Cyprus: the Mediterranean Credit Bank of Larnaca."

"So how do we make sure that—"

"Shhh!" Alex pointed toward the door. "I hear someone coming."

She closed the folder quickly and slid it back over to the middle of the table where Pechlaner had left it.

Ruedi walked over and pretended to be looking at the paintings as Pechlaner walked in, carrying several folders. "Sorry for the delay." He was breathing heavily. "It took me a while, but I think I found everything you wanted."

CHAPTER 15

Zurich
Monday, Late Afternoon

"We have to make sure they get their money." Ruedi walked quickly across the small pedestrian bridge leading over the canal. "We need to make sure the trade goes through . . . so they don't come after us—after me, I mean." He stopped suddenly and turned back to Alex. "Oh my God! I just thought of something. What if Versari stops the trade from being executed?"

"How could he? The trade was sent in by computer. Versari will only see it when it shows up on the client's account statement—*after* the trade's been executed. And by then, the money will be in Cyprus."

"But what if he goes looking through the account's pending trades?" Ruedi asked. "Just like we did back there?"

"Why would he do that?"

"I don't know. Because he has it in for us? You saw how he is." He nodded. "I'm telling you, we have to find a way to make sure the trade gets executed immediately—before they have a chance to cancel it."

"But there's nothing we can do. All we can do is wait for the trade to go through on its own, and then walk away as if we had no idea of—"

"But I want to make sure that it goes through. Now. Just to be sure."

"Making sure that everything's perfect is what got us into this." Alex shook her head slowly. "You just saw back there that the trade in 1987 was nothing more than a cancelled sale of random securities from your father's account. It didn't amount to anything. If we'd just left well enough alone—"

"But we didn't. Okay? And now we really are in trouble. If the money launderers find out that I know about the account—that I know what they've been doing—they'll come after me. They may even kill me, just like they did Ochsner."

"Ruedi, we don't know what happened to Ochsner. Maybe he did commit suicide. Maybe the money launderers didn't have anything to do with—"

"And what if they did?" He stared into Alex's eyes. "I'm not going to sit around and wait for a bunch of crazy drug dealers to come after me."

"You don't know that they're drug dealers. You don't know who they are. They could be anyone."

"You're right, it could be *anyone:* arms dealers, corrupt dictators, the Russian Mafia." Ruedi shook his head. "You think I'm just going to sit around and wait for them to come after me?"

"So why don't you go to the police?"

"And tell them what?"

"The truth."

"Yeah, right. You saw how they treated us before. Without proof they're not going to do anything. The only evidence we have," he pointed toward the FINACORP offices, "is in *there*. And in the bank."

He looked back at Alex. "And even if they do believe us, and start investigating, it's going to be obvious how they found out about it. The money launderers will know that I reported them." He shook his head slowly. "The only advantage I have right now is that nobody knows that I know. Nobody knows that *we* know. We have to find a way out to make sure that nobody knows what we discovered."

He leaned on the railing and stared into the canal. It was lined with boats, each one with a pristine white canvas cover. "I'm afraid, Alex."

He turned to her. "I mean, think about it: my name is on the account. How hard do you think it would be for them to find me? I'm right in the phone book, for God's sake. Even *you* were able to find me—and you weren't even trying."

He held out his hands. "We have to go back to the bank and convince them to put FINACORP back in charge of the account. That's the only way to make sure the trade goes through. The only way we can ensure that the money launderers don't find out that we know, that we're involved."

"And how do we do that?"

"I don't know."

"You saw how they were." She pointed toward the bank. "They're not going to let you touch that account without a valid Formular A that shows who the real owners are."

"So let's find out who they are."

"A-l-a-d-a-r K-o-h-e-n." Alex typed the eleven letters into the rectangular field at the top of the screen, and then clicked Search. She sat back and waited until the page filled with text.

"What does it say?" Ruedi peered over her shoulder.

"Look." Alex pointed to a line that appeared at the top of the page: *Resultate 1–10 von 126,860.* "There are more than a hundred thousand Web sites with either the name Kohen, Aladár, or both."

She moved her cursor over the first line. "See? Here's someone who's named Aladár Lilien who's the president of an orange juice company in Israel called Kohen Brothers. Could he be the one?" She moved the cursor down the page. "And here's another one: Aladár Faragó, the author of a book on a family named Kohen who lives in Buenos Aires." She skimmed down over the next twenty sites. "See? Every one has both names, but not together."

"How do you know? Shouldn't you have to go through them all?"

"You don't have to. The search engine does it for you. It puts the sites with both names together at the top of the list for you." She pulled her hair behind her ear. "But, just to make sure." She inserted quotation marks around the two names and clicked Search again. "I'll tell it to only look for those two words together."

The screen flashed a solitary line: *Es wurde keine mit ihren Suchanfragen gefunden.*

Alex twisted her head and looked up into Ruedi's eyes. "Understand all that?"

"It means there's nothing. Nil. Nicht." He pulled out the letter signed by his father and handed it to her. "Are you sure you used the correct spelling? There's an accent on the name Aladár."

"I'll put it in, but it won't make any difference." Alex moved back to the keyboard and tried every possible combination of accents. "It doesn't make any difference. There's no mention of those two names together. Anywhere."

"So what do we do now?" Ruedi asked.

"Try checking the other search engines." She went back to the URL window and called up a new search engine. "Let me try the others."

"Go ahead. Try everything." He placed his hand against Alex's shoulder to stand up. "While you're working, I'm going to make a couple copies of this letter—one for you and one for me. Then I can put the original in my safe-deposit box, in my bank. Just in case."

While he was gone, Alex tried the name in every search engine she could think of. With accents, without accents, with capitals, without capitals. Every time the same answer came up: nothing.

"Any luck?" Ruedi sat back down and handed her a copy of the letter.

"Not yet."

He also handed her the notarized agreement to split the 5 percent fee. "Just in case you find them."

Alex folded the document carefully and put it in her purse. "Let's hope."

She then turned back to the screen. "Let me try some of the Holocaust sites I saw at the Anne Frank House." She went through them all, but still found no mention of Aladár Kohen. "This site in Washington, DC says you have to go there in person if you want them to do a search."

"So go." Ruedi pulled out his credit card and laid it on the table next to her. "Book any flight you have to. Go wherever you want. Just find him."

"Even if I *did* find Aladár Kohen on one of those Holocaust lists, what good would it do? We need heirs to get back into the account. *Living* heirs."

"Well, find some. Go to Budapest if you have to. I don't care how much it costs." He pushed the credit card closer to her hand.

"Why don't *you* go to Budapest?" Alex didn't look up. "Didn't you say you had a friend there? Maybe he could help you."

"I can't go. Not right now. I have to go to Ochsner's funeral tomorrow. If Schmid doesn't see me there, he'll know something's up, for sure. I have to go there and pretend that nothing's wrong."

"Maybe it isn't."

"You want to take that chance? You want to wait and find out that the trade *didn't* go through? Then what? I don't want them coming after me." He patted her hand. "Come on. I'm sure you can find something."

"I don't know." Alex shook her head. "I'm tired, Ruedi. Do you realize that I've hardly slept for four days? Ever since I spoke to you on the phone? Why don't we get a good night's sleep and start again in the morning? You can go to the funeral tomorrow, and then we can—"

"But we need to do something today. Before they find us."

"Us?"

"Let's be realistic, Alex, if they come after me, how long do you think it will be until they come after you?" He took a deep breath. "No matter how brave I may seem, do you think I'd be able to resist?"

"Are you saying you'd tell them about me if I don't go?"

"I'm just being realistic. Who knows what they're capable of." He shook his head solemnly. "Anyway, even if *I* don't tell them anything, they may already know about you. What do you think Ochsner told them before he—imagine them holding him over that bridge in Basel, two hundred meters above the Rhine, what *wouldn't* he have said to . . . to save himself?"

"But he didn't even know my name."

Ruedi stared into her eyes.

"You didn't tell him my name, did you?" Alex asked.

"No." He put his hand on her shoulder. "But even without a name, how hard do you think it would be to find the young American woman working on the computers at the Helvetia Bank in Zurich?"

CHAPTER 16

Budapest
Monday, Early Evening

The plane landed with a thud, and an antiquated jitney came out to pick up the passengers. Suddenly, everyone began speaking loudly. Alex couldn't understand a word they were saying.

On the bus taking them to the arrivals hall, the same three words kept flashing over and over: *Üdvözöljuk Budapest Ferihegy*.

Alex looked up at the clock on the side of the steel-and-glass terminal. Eight p.m. It had been one of the longest days of her life: three visits to the bank, another to the police, one shady fund manager, two bottles of wine, one hundred thousand dollars in her bank account, and an international money-laundering operation waiting to blow everyone to smithereens.

It was like Time Bomb, the game they used to play in Seattle when she was a child. You wound up a small ersatz bomb and passed it from person to person. When the timer went off, the bomb exploded, and the person holding it got "killed."

Now Alex was playing a new version of the game. After Aladár Kohen and his wife opened a trustee account in Zurich in 1938, they disappeared, putting Rudolph Tobler, Sr., in charge. After holding the bomb for almost fifty years, he suddenly committed suicide. Or did he? Then it was Georg Ochsner's turn. He held the bomb until Rudolph Tobler's son found out about the account. But just as he was about to hand over the bomb, he died, too. And now Ruedi had the account. It was ticking, loudly. And Alex was standing right next to him.

After passing through customs, Alex went straight into the arrivals hall to look for the man Ruedi had told her to meet. "Trust me. You won't get far in Hungary without someone to help you," he'd said. "I'll call Sándor and arrange everything. He'll take good care of you. He's a good old friend."

Old seemed to be the operative word. Sándor must have been about seventy. Alex spotted him under the Találkozóhely—Meeting Point sign. He was waving to her excitedly. Even though it was a warm September evening, Sándor wore a long, flowing overcoat.

He had dark skin and bright, shining eyes. Everyone around him was pushing and shouting in Hungarian. The language sounded strange, like a code. It had no similarity to any language Alex had heard before.

Sándor pushed through the crowd toward her. He held a single red rose in his hand. "You must be Rudolph's friend." His voice was deep, melodic. He rolled his *r*'s heavily. "Here, I bought you a flower. It was very expensive. I hope you appreciate it."

He handed her the rose and made a slight bow. "Welcome to Budapest."

"Thank you, Professor Antal. I—"

"Please. Call me Sándor." He pronounced his name *SHAN-dor*.

With a graceful swoop, he took her hand in his and kissed it. "You are even more beautiful than Ruedi said." He stared at her for several seconds. His eyes were opaque, green gray with a light film on the surface, as if they were made of glass.

He took her arm and began walking. "I will take you to your hotel now. Then we can have dinner."

Alex accompanied him to the crowded exit door, her shoulder bag, purse, and roll-on suitcase in tow. "Thank you for meeting me, Professor Antal. I have a lot of questions to—"

"There will be plenty of time for that in town. I have arranged for you to stay at the Gellért, one of Budapest's oldest hotels. I hope you like it. It is directly on the bank of the Danube."

He led her outside. "We'll take a taxi, yes? That's the way we *do* things here.

"Whatever you say."

Something about Sándor's voice sounded familiar. Alex couldn't place it, but she was sure she'd heard it before.

As they exited the terminal, a man walked toward them quickly. Alex pulled back instinctively, holding tightly onto Sándor's arm. Sándor shooed him away forcefully. "Don't be afraid." He turned to Alex and smiled. "We have some customs here that you may find strange, but don't worry, all right?" She suddenly placed the voice: Dracula.

Sándor led her to a line of taxis waiting in front of the terminal and got in the first one, a white Opel. Alex had to put her bags into the trunk herself.

As the car sped off, she rolled open the window and let the fresh air blow in. It smelled of cut hay.

"That is Budapest." Sándor pointed a long, thin finger southward. Hundreds of domes, spires, and gothic rooftops filled the skyline. "Beautiful, no?"

"Yes it is."

"Budapest once rivaled Vienna, you know. It was once the most beautiful city in Europe." He pointed to the crumbling old buildings flashing by. "It even rivaled Paris and Berlin. We were always the crossroads between East and West, you know, populated by many races."

They came to a stop at a busy intersection. A crowd of people surged across the road. "Look into their eyes," Sándor said. "See how some are dark and some are light?"

The people here did have beautiful eyes, Alex noticed. Intense, alive, penetrating. She thought of Marco's eyes. Where was he now? In Paris already? Waiting for the weekend to arrive? Waiting for her to join him?

She suddenly realized it had been only yesterday that she left Marco in Amsterdam. In the meantime, she'd been in three countries.

She noticed Sándor staring at her legs. She pulled down her skirt, trying to make it look natural. "Have you lived in Budapest long?" she asked.

"My whole life. Except for a brief sabbatical at the university in Zurich. That's when I met Rudolph." The car slowed down. "See over there?" He pointed to a gold-domed structure. "When it was built, it was the biggest synagogue in the world. There was a huge Jewish population here before World War II. More than 20 percent, in fact."

"And now?"

"Look there." He pointed to a large suspension bridge up ahead. "That's the Danube. One of the four great rivers of the world."

As they crossed the wide bridge, a strong wind swept into the car. It felt hot, as if it were coming off the desert. Alex looked into the greenish brown water flowing below them.

"It's not blue," she muttered.

"It never was." Sándor smiled. "Perhaps Johann Strauss thought 'The Brown Danube' wouldn't sell his music as well. An early example of false advertising."

The taxi suddenly came to a stop. "Here you are." Sándor pointed to a large stone structure. GELLÉRT HOTEL was etched in stone above the massive doors. The building looked more like a wedding cake than a hotel.

"I've taken the liberty of reserving a table for us at the Kárpátia, on the other side of the Danube." Sándor held out his hand to say goodbye. "It's a *must* for all visitors. I will meet you there at 10 p.m. Yes?"

The first thing Alex did when she got into her room was check the Budapest phone book one last time. She found three Kohlbergs, one Kohnovitz, and several Kohlers. But not one single Kohen.

She decided to call Eric. He wasn't at the hotel. She tried his cell phone.

"Hello?" There was a lot of noise in the background, voices mostly. It sounded like he was in another bar.

"Hi, it's me. Can you talk?"

"Sure. Where are you?"

"I can't tell you right now. I just wanted to let you know that I won't be in the office tomorrow. In fact, I may have to take a leave of absence for a few days."

"What's going on, Alex? You can't just disappear like this, without a—"

"I'll call you tomorrow and explain."

"Crissier asked where you were. I said you were sick."

"That's right. I have the flu. Tell him that I'll be back to work in a few days."

"Okay, but . . . where are you? The readout on my cell phone doesn't show a number. You're not in Switzerland at all, are you?"

"I can't explain right now." Alex heard a noise and looked over to see a long, white envelope being slid under her door. "I've got to go. Sorry. I'll call you tomorrow."

"But why can't you tell me what's going on?"

"Gotta go. Bye."

She went over and opened the envelope. It was a fax, from Ruedi. The document had been written by hand.

Dear Alex,

Good luck finding the Kohens.

I hope you don't mind that I resort to this primitive means of communication. Can you believe it? I don't use e-mail.

I checked with that lawyer at the bank again, just to see what exactly we would need to do to get back into the account. She said someone from the family should appear in person. But, it would be possible for them to send a letter—or give us a power of attorney to have access to the account—as long as their signature and identity were certified in Budapest—by the Swiss consulate if possible.

If Aladár and his wife are dead, you have to find children—or grandchildren. And you'll need the same documentation from them. But in that case, you would also need to provide the bank with the parents' death certificates. She also said we would need a "proof of parenté," whatever that is, to show that the person you found really is the child or grandchild. I guess it's like a birth certificate—something that says who the parents were.

I hope this all makes sense to you.

I wish I could be there to do all this with you. I'll be in Basel all day tomorrow for the funeral. I'm not looking forward at all to meeting Schmid, but I have to. And I have to make it look like nothing's wrong.

I'll let you know what happens.

Good luck,

Ruedi

PS I hope Sándor isn't driving you crazy. Remember, dirty old men need love, too.

The vaulted ceiling of the Kárpátia was covered with frescos—intricate designs of grapes, vines, and birds. The restaurant looked like an old Transylvanian castle. The only thing missing was a vampire.

And there he was, sitting at a table in the far corner, still wearing his long, flowing overcoat. Sándor stood up to greet her. "Good evening."

He kissed her hand. "I've already ordered you an aperitif, a glass of Tokaji wine. You'll like it."

Alex sat down across from him. "I'm not sure I should be drinking any more wine today."

"But that is not the way we do things here, Alex." Sándor smiled as the waiter served them from a small cart nearby. "Welcome to Budapest." He held up his glass for a toast. "To success. To your success."

Alex took a small sip of the wine. It was dry, yet strangely sweet.

"What exactly are you looking for, by the way?" Sándor asked.

Before Alex could answer, a group of violinists came over and began to play next to them.

"Gypsies," Sándor explained, "a great tradition here." He sat back to listen.

How much should I tell him? Alex wondered. *He is Ruedi's friend, but how much can I trust him? How much can I trust anyone these days?*

"Lehar—one of my favorites." Sándor's head moved slightly to the music. "Those were the days, weren't they?"

When the piece ended he turned to Alex and said, "Ruedi told me you were looking for a man named Aladár Kohen or someone from his family."

"That's correct." Alex took another sip of wine. "Do you know how—"

"He said you want to find them as quickly as possible."

"That's right. Do you know of any way I can—"

Sándor held up his finger authoritatively as the waiter arrived. He ordered for both of them in Hungarian. "I ordered you the house specialty," he told her once the waiter was gone. "Goulash soup and roast duck. I'm sure you'll like it."

"So do you have any idea how I could find the Kohens?" Alex asked. "We tried calling information from Zurich. And I looked in the phone book at the hotel, but there's apparently not one Kohen in Budapest."

"In the whole country, in fact. I checked, too."

"Why not? I mean, isn't Kohen a common name?"

"Not really. Not with that spelling." Sándor took another drink and sat back. "Actually, there may have been Kohens at one time. But not anymore."

"Why not?"

"The sad truth is that there are not so many Jewish people left in Hungary anymore. And most who are still here don't have Jewish names. They changed them at the beginning of the century, the twentieth century. It made it easier to move up in the economic and social circles, you see." The appetizers arrived and Sándor began eating his immediately. "After the revolution," he continued speaking while he ate, "the revolution of 1956 I mean, many people left Hungary—especially the intelligentsia—or people who had the money or connections to get out."

He began spreading a thick chunk of bone marrow on a small piece of toast. "Like George Soros. He was a Hungarian, you know. And Jewish. From Budapest, in fact." Sándor shoved the concoction, whole, into his mouth. "He and his family survived the war by hiding out in the countryside. He ended up in America, and made a fortune speculating on currency fluctuations. And then there's Andrew Grove. He founded Intel, you know. It's a computer manufacturer."

"I know, Sándor. I work with computers."

"But did you know his family name was originally Graf? They changed it to Grove when they moved to the United States. Did you know that?" Sándor spoke through mouthfuls of toast and marrow. "And then there was Harry Houdini. He was Hungarian, too."

"Mr. Antal—Sándor." Alex took a deep breath. "This is all very interesting, but I've come here to find someone who—"

"Go see a lawyer then." He looked offended, as if Alex had broken an unspoken rule: Don't interrupt Sándor while he's pontificating. He looked around for the waiter. "I'm going to order a bottle of wine," he announced. "That is, if you don't mind."

"I'm sorry." Alex tried to speak calmly. "I didn't mean to—"

"I can even recommend a good one. Szabó Antónia. She's a friend of my cousin's." He turned to listen to the gypsy musicians.

Alex told herself to wait patiently until Sándor was ready to talk. Eventually he would tell her what she wanted to know. All in due time.

When the main course arrived, she watched him devour an entire calf's tongue between gulps of wine. Then, halfway through the meal, he began giving Alex a stream of advice, as if nothing had happened.

"The first thing you need to do is get death certificates," he said between mouthfuls. "Then you can find out where he lived and who his parents were. But each district of Budapest issues its own death certificates. And there are more than twenty districts."

"But I'm looking for a *living* family member."

He glanced at her angrily. "But of course, Alex."

Be careful, she told herself. *Let him talk.*

"Maybe you should look in the old telephone books." He took another bite of his calf's tongue. "In any event the lawyer I recommended can help you."

The gypsies began playing classical music to a French-speaking family sitting next to Alex and Sándor. The family looked picture-perfect. The parents were sitting across from their two well-dressed teenage daughters. Everyone sipped wine politely, naturally. The older daughter was wearing a beautiful gold chain around her neck. It had a single jeweled pendant.

She turned to Sándor and noticed him staring at the younger daughter.

When they brought the bill, he ignored it—he just continued telling about how each Budapest district kept its own records and how if you wanted to find information, you had to go to each one.

Alex quietly got out her wallet and paid with the money she had withdrawn from her recently augmented account. She used the HBZ ATM before she left Zurich to withdraw the equivalent of five thousand dollars in euros and Swiss francs—more money than she had ever had in her hand at any given time.

At the coat check stand Sándor wrote out the lawyer's name and address on a small piece of paper. "This may help you."

Alex read it carefully as they walked outside. *Dr. Szabó Antónia, Szentkiralyi utca 92–94.*

"Does this Dr. Antónia speak English?" Alex asked.

"Actually, Antónia is her given name." Sándor smiled. "Szabó is her family name. In Hungarian, names are written backwards."

"Why is that?"

He smiled. "Because that's just the way we do things here, Alex."

Back in her room, Alex plugged her laptop into the hotel phone and went online to check every search engine she could think of. Just as in Zurich, she found hundreds of thousands of pages with the name Kohen scattered all over the world and thousands with the name Aladár. But when she put both names in together, there was still nothing.

She sat back and stretched. Her whole body ached. She realized she'd been hunched over the computer for several hours without finding anything.

Don't despair, she told herself. *It's going to take work to find a family that no one's been able to find since World War II. Get some sleep. Then get up early and start again.*

Just before she logged off, she decided to check her e-mails. Hidden among a slew of e-mails from Thompson & Co. was one from Marco. It had been there since yesterday. Alex felt the blood rush through her body as she opened it.

"I'm just about to leave for Paris, the next stop on my tour. Why don't you call me?" he wrote. He gave her the Paris number, then added, "I miss you."

She looked over at the phone, then at the clock. It was almost three in the morning. She decided to send him an e-mail. "Marco, I miss you too. Alex."

Seconds after she clicked Send, an answer appeared.

Alex clicked on the tiny mailbox. It was from Marco.

"Can you send me your telephone number? I'll call you."

Alex imagined Marco's questions when he saw that her telephone number had a Budapest, Hungary prefix. "Can't we just talk online?" she wrote back.

"Of course." He gave her the URL of a private chat site on the Web. "I'll be there, under the name Frank. Why don't you log on as Anne?"

Within seconds, they were in their own chat room.

Frank: How are you?

Anne: Okay.

Frank: Just okay?

Anne: If you only knew what I've been through since Amsterdam. Was it just yesterday that I said goodbye to you?

Frank: It seems a lot longer, doesn't it? I've been missing you.

Anne: Me too.

Frank: I keep thinking about our night together.

Anne: Me too.

Frank: Holding you in my arms. Making love to you until the sun came up . . .

Anne: Marco, can I ask you a favor? Let's pick different names? It's kind of creepy seeing the name Anne Frank on this type of conversation.

Frank: You're right. It's no problem. All you have to do is click on Name Change at the bottom of the page. Like this!

Marco: See?

Alex: Wow! That's better.

Marco: We can talk, too, you know. Why don't you let me call you?

Alex: I'm not at my apartment. I'm not in Zurich.

Marco: Where are you?

Alex: I can't tell you. I'm working on a project. Something that came up at the last minute.

Marco: Sounds mysterious.

Alex: It is. I'm trying to find someone who doesn't seem to exist.

Marco: Maybe I could come and help you. Who are you looking for?

Alex: A man who probably died a long time ago.

Marco: Where are you going to look for him? In the cemetery?

Alex: Might not be a bad idea, but it's kind of late to head out there now in the middle of the night.

Marco: Maybe I should come there and help you. Be your bodyguard. I have a black belt, after all.

Alex: I know. You showed me some good moves in Amsterdam.

Marco: Where? On the street or in my room?

Alex: Both.

Marco: God, I wish I were with you.

Alex: Me too.

Marco: In Brazil, we have a word for what I'm feeling. It doesn't exist in English. *Saudades.*

Alex: Sounds beautiful. What does it mean?

Marco: It's impossible to translate it. It means something like longing. Like, I'm missing you right now.

Alex: I'm missing you too.

Marco: I'd love to be there with you right now. To look into your beautiful eyes. Touch your long, dark hair. Hold you in my arms.

Alex: Sounds good.

Marco: You know, you try to appear strong, but what I see inside is a tender, fragile young woman.

Alex: Really?

Marco: God, I wish I were there with you right now. I'd take you in my arms and caress you . . .

Alex: Where?

Marco: I'd start with your face, then your cheeks, then your ears, then your lips. Then I'd move down to your long, beautiful legs. Then slowly back up to your stomach, your breasts. I love that they're small. That's the way we LIKE them in Brazil.

Alex: Really?

Marco: Really. Did you know that plastic surgeons in Brazil do most of their business making women's breasts smaller?

Alex: I didn't know.

Marco: And yours are that way naturally, right?

Alex: Of course.

Marco: I'm getting excited, just thinking about . . . about you. Where are you now?

Alex: Sitting on my bed.

Marco: How?

Alex: Cross-legged. My laptop perched on my knees.

Marco: What I wouldn't give to be there. What are you wearing?

Alex: You really want to know?

Marco: I want to know everything about you.

Alex: Just my Yale sweatshirt.

Marco: Nothing else?

Alex: Why do you ask?

Marco: I'm curious.

Alex: I don't like cybersex, if that's what you're wanting.

Marco: So let's talk on the phone.

Alex glanced over at the old-style phone next to her bed.

Alex: I'd rather not use the hotel phone. Do you have VoiP?

Marco: What's that?

Alex: Web-based phone. You don't have it?

Marco: No, but why not let me call you? Where are you?

Alex: I can't tell you.

Marco: Why not?

Alex: I just can't. I'm sorry.

CHAPTER 17

Budapest
Tuesday Morning

Alex was awakened by pounding on her door.

It was Sándor, in full regalia: a new bright red pochette in the pocket of his double-breasted suit, a checkered shirt, and a paisley tie. A heavy umbrella with a wooden handle dangled from one arm.

"Oh, did I wake you?" he asked innocently.

"Actually, you did." Alex pulled her terry-cloth robe around her. "It's eight-thirty in the morning."

"Exactly."

"I was on the Web until late last night—doing some work."

"Well, we've got work to do of our own." He nodded energetically.

"Now?"

"Yes, now." His cloudy green eyes scanned her body. "We must leave soon. I don't have all day. Come on. Get dressed." He tried to come inside.

"I thought you weren't going to help me." Alex held onto the door firmly.

"Of course. I've already spoken to the records office for the Sixth Arrondissement. Andrássy út is where the Kohens lived, no? Isn't that what Ruedi said?"

"Yes, but—"

"Unfortunately, they have no record of Aladár Kohen's death. Nor for any other Kohens, for that matter. But I came up with an idea." He smiled slyly. "Unfortunately, for that you have to get dressed. We need to go to the Seventh Arrondissement. Do you want me to wait in here?" He started to walk inside.

"Can you wait for me downstairs? I'll be a few minutes."

"All right. I'll meet you in the breakfast room then. But hurry. I have a class to teach later on today."

When Alex closed the door, she noticed another envelope lying on the floor. She tore it open. It was another fax from Ruedi. Several printed pages were attached.

Dear Alex,

I went back to that Internet café, and they showed me how to use that search engine you showed me. Guess what I found out? That Cyprus has been for years a major money-laundering center—for the Russian Mafia, especially. Apparently there are more than twenty thousand offshore companies in Cyprus that are linked to just the Russians. But they're not alone. Everyone's in on it. Dictators, terrorists, Mafia. The list goes on and on. I even read that Slobodan Milošević, the Yugoslav dictator, apparently laundered more than four billion dollars through Cyprus banks and offshore companies.

It's extremely important you find that family immediately. We have to make sure that the money gets transferred out of my account as planned. Only then can we relax.

I'll be at Georg Ochsner's funeral all afternoon. Call me on my cell phone if you need me.

Ruedi

Alex glanced through several copies Ruedi had downloaded from the Web. They all came from reputable sources: CNN, the U.S. Department of State, OECD, the *New York Times*. They backed up what he was saying. Cyprus was full of illegal activities.

Maybe he's right, she whispered to herself as she headed into the bathroom. *Maybe he's been right all along.*

The phone rang just as she was stepping out of the shower. It was Sándor. "Where are you? I'm waiting for you downstairs in the restaurant."

"I'll be down in a few minutes."

"Hurry then. We have to be on our way."

But first Alex had to watch Sándor consume virtually everything the extensive buffet had to offer: cheeses, cold cuts, scrambled eggs, red and green peppers, coleslaw, cucumbers—even marinated fish.

All she could handle was a croissant and a cup of coffee.

"It's like this." Sándor spoke with his mouth half-full as he had last night. "Kohen Aladár is probably dead—even if he did survive the war, which is possible. Many Jews in Budapest survived, you know. The Germans only invaded Hungary at the end of the war, when the Soviets were on their way in. Before that they thought we were their allies, that we would solve the Jewish problem on our own." He shoved more food into his mouth and continued. "But even if he survived the war, he's probably dead now. Assuming he was forty or so in 1938 when he signed that document, he'd be . . . let's see . . ."

"Over a hundred today."

"Exactly." Sándor nodded. "Which means that the best way of finding out about him is to find when and where he died, which means finding his death certificate." He took another bite of toast smothered with liver pâté. "The problem is that in Budapest death certificates are issued in the arrondissement where you die. There's no central registry."

He took another sip of coffee. "I figure that someone of Aladár Kohen's means, if he died in a hospital, would have been taken to a private hospital. And the most elegant private hospital at the time was the Fasor Szanitórium, which means we have to go to the records office of the district where the Fasor was located."

Alex grabbed her purse. "So let's go."

"All right. Just let me finish these fish eggs." There was a cab waiting outside the hotel. They were at the door to the records office of the Seventh Arrondissement within minutes.

Inside, Sándor walked up to one of the teller-style windows in the inner courtyard and began speaking Hungarian to a dark-haired woman half-hidden behind a leafy fern. As Sándor spoke, she shook her head. Alex heard her say the word *nem* repeatedly.

Sándor turned to Alex and shrugged.

"What does *nem* mean?" she asked.

"It means no. She says they only issue *kivonats*—birth and death certificates—on Mondays and Thursdays, and today's Tuesday."

Sándor turned back to the woman and spoke for several minutes. Alex watched as the woman began nodding. She said the word *igen* several times, and picked up the phone. While she spoke Sándor turned to Alex. "*Igen* means yes."

"I figured that out."

"I was very clever. I told her you've come all the way from the United States, and that you have to get on a plane tonight, that you have to have the death certificate today." He smiled.

"Her sister works up in the death records office." He pointed to a narrow flight of stone stairs at the entrance to the room. "They're going to make an exception for me."

The woman who answered the door upstairs looked exactly like the woman downstairs, except she had blond hair—and plainly visible black roots.

Alex looked inside and saw several women sitting around a wooden table, playing cards. The woman at the door listened to what Sándor had to say, nodding continually, saying *nem* and *igen* several times. She pointed to a bench out in the hall and closed the door.

Sándor went over and sat down. "She said she's going to start looking at the beginning of the war, in 1939. But if he died during the war, I'm sure it would have been in 1944 at the earliest. That's when the Germans came marching into Hungary.

"It's strange. The Allies had already arrived in Amsterdam in 1944. Anne Frank had almost made it through the war when—"

"Actually, the Allies were arriving here in 1944, too. The only problem is that they were the Russians, not the British or the Americans." He took a deep breath. "In fact, it was only when the Russians were on our doorsteps that the Germans came in. That's when it all happened. In the winter of 1944–45. The sad part is the Hungarian Fascists were just as vicious as the Nazis. Worse, actually. When the Hungarian government fell, they went crazy. They didn't even wait for the trains to take the Jews to the Nazi camps. They started to kill them right here in Budapest. I heard many stories of Jews being pulled from their apartments in the middle of the night and herded down to the riverbanks and shot. They shoved the bodies into the freezing water. Many were still alive, apparently."

The door opened and the woman leaned out to hand Sándor a small green paper, folded in half. It had a seal on the front.

"*Köszönöm szépen!*" Sándor bowed to her repeatedly, as if he were a Japanese businessman. The woman smiled repeatedly, bowed several times, then went back inside, closing the door with a bang.

Sándor looked at the document then held it up triumphantly. "It's the kivonat. Aladár Kohen's death certificate." He unfolded it and began to translate. "It says he died in this arrondissement in 1945. On the twenty-second of January. It also says he was forty-six years old when he died."

He looked into Alex's eyes. "He was probably brought to the hospital here after the fascist attacks. January 1945 was the peak of the atrocities." He handed Alex the document. "So now we know." He turned and started walking down the stairs.

"Wait a minute." She scanned the death certificate quickly. She couldn't understand a word. Just *Kohen Aladár* and the date. "How do I find out if there are any heirs?" she asked.

Sándor had disappeared down the broad stairwell. She ran after him. "But I thought there would be more information here." She handed the death certificate back to him. "Doesn't it say anything about survivors? His wife? His children?"

"No. Just that he died in 1945. When he was forty-six years old." The wizard had spoken. Sándor pushed open the door to the street. Traffic noise flooded into the courtyard. "I have to go now."

"I'm sorry. Dr. Szabó can only see you next week. She has no time . . . for new client."

Alex strained to hear over the noise from the street. "But I need to see someone today. It's urgent."

"Please call back next week. Yes?"

"I can't wait until next week. Can't *anyone* see me?" Alex removed her earring and held the phone tightly to her ear. "I need to find out if someone from Budapest has any heirs. I have the death certificate, but that's all."

"When did he die?"

"In 1945."

"I am sorry."

"But can't *you* help me? I was recommended by Sándor Antal. Do you know him?"

"Nem."

Alex took a deep breath. "He's apparently a friend of Dr. Szabó's. And I've come all the way from the States. I have to get on a plane tonight."

"I'm sorry. You have to call back next week. Yes?"

Alex felt lost, angry, and confused. Why was everything here such a struggle?

She took a deep breath and tried again. "Look, I just arrived in Budapest. I don't speak a word of Hungarian. All I need is someone to help me get some information. Is there any way you can help me? I would pay you if necessary."

"I'm only lawyer's assistant. I am having only just finished law school."

"That doesn't matter. I don't need a lawyer per se. I just need someone to help me find a family who used to live in Budapest. They had a secret bank account in Switzerland."

Silence. At least the woman had stopped saying no.

"If we find a member of the Aladár Kohen family," Alex continued, "there's a multimillion-dollar account waiting for them in Zurich."

The woman waited a few seconds before responding. "Maybe you *can* come by."

"Thank you!"

"But be sure to ask for me. My name is Sára."

On the way to the lawyer's office, the taxi drove down a long, broad avenue lined with crumbling palatial buildings. The name, Alex noticed, was Andrássy út—the boulevard where the Kohens lived before the war. She got out the copy Ruedi had made of the trustee account agreement to confirm. She was right.

She asked the driver to stop for a minute in front of number six.

It was a huge neoclassical apartment building directly across from the opera house. There were twenty-seven doorbells. Not one of them had the name Kohen.

She tried ringing a few. Asking each time, "Do you know a family named Kohen? Aladár Kohen?"

"Nem. No Kohen."

She had the cabdriver ask in Hungarian. The answer was still the same: "Nem."

At the door to the lawyer's offices, Alex was stymied again. Everything on the gold-plated plaque next to the door was written in Hungarian. She tried pushing several of the buttons, but nothing worked. After a few minutes, a pregnant woman walked up to the door, punched in the code, and entered quickly. Alex grabbed the door just before it closed.

The young woman looked back at her and smiled. "Are you the woman I spoke to?"

"Are you Sára?" Alex asked.

"Igen." She held out her hand. "I am so sorry for being late. I had errand. My baby will be soon, and I have many things to prepare before it arrives."

"Congratulations. You must be very happy."

"Igen." She smiled. "I am." She led Alex down a dark hallway and then up a long flight of stairs to a large wooden door. Inside, it looked more like an apartment than an office. Armchairs and bookshelves filled the room.

Sára showed Alex to an overstuffed chair in the far corner and went over to talk to a woman seated at a large wooden desk next to a window overlooking the street.

Alex stared at the death certificate. She thought of Sándor's story, of how the Fascists were throwing wounded Jews into the river. Was that what had happened to Aladár Kohen? Was that how he had died? Was that how he ended up far from his home?

Sára came over and sat down beside her. "What exactly you need?"

Alex handed her the death certificate. "As I said on the phone, the Aladár Kohen family has a bank account in Switzerland. All they have to do is show up to claim it." Alex noticed the woman at the desk glance over when she said the words *bank account* and *Switzerland*.

Finally, she stood up and came over to where Alex was sitting. She sat down next to Sára and held out her hand. "Maybe I can help you. My name is Szabó Antónia."

Alex began the story again, but Antónia interrupted her almost immediately. "Now that you have a death certificate, it is clear what you need to do next. You need to get the birth certificate." She had obviously been listening the whole time. "In that way, you can find out more about his family. Since you don't know the names of his wife or his children, it's the only way." Her English, Alex noticed, was much better than Sára's.

Antónia asked for the death certificate and read through it carefully. "I see." She looked up and smiled. Her teeth were yellow, like Ochsner's. "This, of course, doesn't tell us when he was born, but you can figure that out by subtracting the two numbers. See how it says that he was forty-six years old when he died in 1945?"

Alex nodded.

"By subtracting the two numbers you can deduce the year he was born."

"And?" Alex asked.

"Take that information to the Jewish Center. That's where all the records are kept for Jewish citizens from before the Communist era." She handed Alex the kivonat. "Ask for the birth certificate."

"And once I get the birth certificate?" Alex asked. "What do I do then?"

"The birth registry can then be used to help you find out where the family lived, what their profession was, even how many children they had. But you first have to find the entry for Kohen Aladár's birth.

"It won't be easy." She smiled condescendingly. "The Jewish Center's system is—how do you say?—a bit antiquated." She stood up. "But fortunately you have Sára here to help you. She's an expert at the Jewish Center." She held out her hand to say goodbye. "I must be going now. I'm expected at court."

Alex shook her hand. It was hard and calloused.

"Be persistent," Antónia admonished. "If you can't get the information you want at the Jewish Center, you won't get it anywhere. The city archives have no information on Jewish citizens, at least not from before the socialist time."

"Why not?" Alex asked.

"Because that's the way they did things here—before the war at least."

"We're lucky. I know the Rabbi here." Sára led Alex to the entrance of the Jewish Center. "That is how I was able to get them to agree to meet us so quickly. He helped with my marriage in March."

"So you're Jewish?" Alex asked.

"Yes." Sára pointed to the large synagogue to their right. "That's why I decided to meet you. When you mentioned the name Kohen, I knew it had to be a Jewish family." She led Alex to a metal detector at the main entrance. The guards asked Alex to put everything she had through the machine, including her shoes.

"Unfortunately, we must do this all the time now. Ever since September 11. A sign of the times we live in."

Alex looked into the courtyard and noticed that the Star of David had been used for every decorative detail, including the design on the ceiling of the neo-Gothic arcade. A small mound of rocks was piled in the center of the courtyard.

"That is memorial to the dead," Sára explained.

"And this," she pointed to a weathered bronze plaque to their left, "this is memorial plaque." She ran her fingers over the words: *E HÁZ MÁRTÍRJAI— 1941–1945, EMLÉKEZZÜNK.*

"See?" Sára touched her fingers to the letters *EMLÉK*. "That means 'memory.'" She glanced at Alex. Her eyes looked sad. "This memorial is dedicated to memory of the martyrs of this house, it says."

Sára pointed to the list of names on the bottom half of the plaque. "It tells us we should never forget."

Alex scanned the list of names: Grün János, Horowitz Ferenc, Malesch Simon. Not one Kohen.

They were given clearance to enter, and Sára led Alex up a long flight of stairs and into a large wood-paneled room overlooking an inner courtyard. She told Alex to wait at a desk by the entrance and walked over to present their "case" to a man seated at a table next to the window. He must have been about eighty, and he was wearing a faded blue cardigan sweater. His tie, Alex noted, had a series of strange symbols: a triangle with the letter *H* at the pinnacle, and two *E*'s underneath. The triangle looked just like the pyramid on the U.S. one-dollar bill. It even had a human eye at the apex.

Alex stood patiently as Sára spoke to the man for several minutes. Light poured in from the window behind the man to light up their faces. Sára spoke slowly, clearly enunciating the words *Kohen* and *Aladár* several times.

Alex remembered Antónia's words: "If you can't find the information at the Jewish Center, you won't find it anywhere."

The man began searching through the mountain of papers on his desk. After several minutes, Sára came over to explain what was going on. "He told me he would make exception for me and try to find the information today. But he only works until lunchtime. After that, they stop for the day. And tomorrow the office is closed." Alex looked at her watch. It was already eleven.

Sára took the death certificate and went back to the old man's desk. He looked at the document carefully, as if this were the first time he'd ever seen one. After several minutes, he reached over and pulled out a leather-bound book from a wooden shelf next to the window and began poring over the entries, one by one. Sára leaned over his shoulder, helping him search through the handwritten text.

An older woman with thick glasses and a long black dress came over and placed several folders on the table, then went back to her desk. The click of her hard-soled shoes on the wooden floor was the only sound in the room.

The system they were using, Alex noticed, hadn't changed since the nineteenth century. No computer, no database, no central list, no cross-referencing, not even an index. Just an oversize handwritten book with chronological entries—one book for each year and a separate section for each letter of the alphabet.

Alex watched and waited nervously as the old man personally looked through every page. Every once in a while he would look up and lose his concentration. Sára would then have to gently guide him back to where he had left off.

After about an hour of work, Sára walked back to Alex and shrugged. "We're up to April. Unfortunately, since we do not know which month Mr. Kohen has been born in, it is taking long time. It seems the year 1899 was big year for births in the Budapest Jewish community."

"Why are you looking in the book for 1899?" Alex asked.

Sára looked surprised. "Because the birth certificate says he was forty-six years old when he died in 1945." She squinted her eyes. "Forty-six from 1945 is 1899. Yes?"

"No. Not necessarily." Alex shook her head vehemently. "Aladár Kohen died in January. The kivonat says he was forty-six years old when he died, but there's almost no chance he was born in 1899—unless he was born before January twenty-second. And you've already checked the entries for January."

Sára nodded hesitantly.

"It's like this." Alex stood up. "If he wasn't born before January twenty-second, he hadn't had his birthday yet. Right? Which means that when he *did* have it, he would have turned forty-seven. He would have been forty-seven years old in 1945, not forty-six. And 1945 minus forty-seven is 1898." Alex pointed over to the old man poring over the 1899 birth registry. "He's looking in the wrong book!" Alex realized she was almost shouting.

She looked over and saw the old man and his assistant staring at her in shock. She had obviously broken another unspoken rule: Don't criticize the system. Had they even understood her? She repeated what she said. They just stared.

She knew she was right. Numbers didn't lie.

Alex got up. Sitting quietly and waiting patiently wasn't going to do any good.

She walked over to a calendar hanging on the wall next to the old man's desk. He stared at her incredulously.

Underneath a photograph of a menorah was a line of each month of the year—with their names written in Hungarian. Alex pointed to the first one, Január. "This is the month he died. Right?"

He didn't answer.

She then pointed to the other months. "Aladár Kohen was certainly born in one of *these* months. Which means he is not in that book." She pointed to the book in the old man's hands. "If you'll allow me . . ." She walked over to the bookshelf and pulled out the 1898 volume.

She brought it back over to the man and laid it front of him. "This is the one you should be looking in."

He didn't move.

"Do you mind if I take a look?"

Alex opened the book and began looking down the lists, slowly flipping through the pages, one by one. All of the entries had been put in by hand, Alex noticed, with a quill, apparently.

Several names caught her eye: Kohnowitz, Kravitz, Kronenberg—but there was not one single Kohen.

Sára volunteered to help Alex with the search. When they were about a third of the way through the book, Sára said, *"Itt van!"* Sára pointed to a name at the bottom of the page. Alex leaned over and saw the name *Kohen Aladár* scribbled in black ink.

Her heart leaped. The entry was followed by several Hungarian words in handwritten text and two small Stars of David. Next to each star was a number. "And what does it say?" she asked Sára.

"It says here that his father was professor and that his father was named Rihárd. The mother was named Patricia."

"And what are those two little stars for?" Alex asked.

"I don't know."

Sára brought the book over to the old man and spent several precious minutes soothing his ruffled feathers. Finally, the old man sat back down at his desk to read the entry. After several seconds, he muttered something to Sára.

She turned to Alex to translate. "The first star means his mother was member of Jewish faith. That is important as it is the mother who determines whether you are considered Jewish."

"And the second star? Is that for his father?"

"No. The father's religion is not so important. It says that Kohen Aladár married a Jewish woman. That's important because the children would then be considered Jewish."

"So he had children?"

"I don't know. Let me ask." Sára relayed Alex's question to the old man. "He says the only way to find out if there were children would be to look through the birth registries one by one. But since we don't know which years they were born in, it would take days. He said that if you give him the family names you want them to look for, they do a search at the end of each month, with all the names that people have requested."

"But I can't wait until the end of the month. Can't you ask him to make an exception? Do a search *today?*" Alex glanced over at the shelves full of birth registry books. There must have been several hundred. "Or maybe *I* could look through them. I'll sit here all afternoon if I have to."

Sára relayed Alex's request to the old man, then turned back to Alex and said, "He says that they don't let *anyone* go through the books."

"Can't you ask him to make an exception? Tell him that I've come all the way from the U.S.? That I have to go back tomorrow? That I'll pay him whatever it takes."

"I doubt that will work, but I'll try."

Alex waited while Sára spoke for several more minutes to the old man. The word *nem* was used far too often to presage a positive outcome. While she waited, Alex read through Aladár Kohen's birth entry several times. She was intrigued by the number next to the stars.

"What does this mean?" she asked Sára when she came back. The old man was already putting on his cardigan sweater, getting ready to leave.

"Let me find out," Sára replied.

She went over to the assistant, who, after listening to the question, walked over and got down the birth registry for 1903.

"What's going on?" Alex asked Sára.

"Apparently, the number next to the second star, the one certifying that his wife was Jewish," Sára explained, "tells where to find her birth register."

The assistant quickly turned to a page near the end of the book. She moved her finger down the page slowly, then stopped at an entry near the bottom. She started speaking Hungarian to Sára.

Alex went over and looked at the entry: *Blauer Katalin. 18. I. 1903.* The entry was followed by several lines of text.

Sára translated for her: "It says, 'Blauer Katalin was born on January eighteenth, 1903, and her parents were Blauer Jacob and Strauss Júlia. There are two addresses. One is their home on Andrássy út 6.'"

"That's where the *Kohens* were living in 1938!"

Sára turned to the assistant and spoke for several minutes. Alex listened to the bells outside. They sounded like the ones next to the Anne Frank House. She listened to them chime twelve times.

Sára came over and tapped Alex on the shoulder. "She thinks the Kohens must have inherited the flat after the parents died. She said they could do another search at the end of the month to find out when Katalin Blauer's parents died."

"I don't need to know about people who died," Alex replied. "I need to know about people who are still *alive*."

"Then why don't we try the telephone book?" Sára said. "Maybe there's someone left from the Blauer family."

"Great idea!" Alex spotted a telephone book on the old man's desk and went over to open it. Sára helped her look through the listings.

"I'm sorry," Sára said after a few minutes. "There is no mention of any Blauers at all." She put her hand on Alex's arm. "At least we tried."

Alex looked across the room and saw the assistant putting the 1903 birth registry back on the shelf. "Wait a minute!" She turned back to Sára. "Didn't you say there were *two* addresses in there?"

"You're right." Sára asked the assistant to take the book down. They reopened it to the entry for Katalin Blauer. Sára read the entry carefully. "It's a factory." She looked up at Alex and shrugged. "A leather factory."

"And where is it?"

"Újpest. Just a few kilometers up the Danube."

The road was full of potholes and the taxi shook and rattled. Alex watched Sára grimace with each bump. "Are you all right?" she asked. "Should we tell him to slow down?"

"Is all right." Sára smiled. "Will be in Újpest soon. Is not far."

"How soon will you be having your baby?" Alex asked.

"Just a few more weeks." Sára sat back and closed her eyes. "They tell me it will be a boy."

Alex remembered holding Jannik in Amsterdam. She remembered his smile, his warmth, his smell—almonds and baby oil.

The landscape gradually changed from nineteenth-century urban decay to crumbling Soviet-style apartment houses and rubble-littered fields.

Suddenly, the driver pulled into an open field and turned off the engine. He muttered something in Hungarian, then got out of the car and lit a cigarette.

"He said that this is the address." Sára pointed out the window. "But there's nothing here."

Alex got out and scanned the empty horizon. The only thing she could see was a large suburban shopping mall in the distance and the word *Duna* spelled out in large red letters.

"Are you certain this is it?" Alex climbed back in next to Sára. "Can you ask him again? Just to make sure?"

Sára spoke with the driver for several minutes, then turned to Alex. "He says maybe the factory was destroyed in the war."

"Isn't there anyone around we could ask?" Alex asked.

"Not that I know of." Sára looked at Alex sadly. "I'm sorry."

Alex walked through the streets of downtown Budapest. She felt completely frustrated. After everything she had been able to accomplish, she wasn't any closer than when she arrived.

She saw an Internet café and went in. She tried every search engine she knew, including all the Holocaust Web sites. There were hundreds of Kohens, many Blauers, thousands of Aladárs and Katalins, but not one single mention of Aladár Kohen, Katalin Kohen, or Katalin Blauer. What had happened to them? Had they all disappeared into thin air?

Alex walked outside in a daze. She slowly walked through the narrow pedestrian streets of Vaci utca, wondering what she was going to do next. Go back to Zurich? What would she tell Ruedi?

She heard an old disco song, "I Will Survive," rifting out of a narrow alley. She followed the music to a small pub called The Amstel River Café. She went inside.

It was crowded and noisy. She took a seat at the bar. The Dutch beer posters covering the walls reminded her of Holland and of Nan and Susan and Marco.

Behind the bar, she noticed several rows of strange-looking bottles of liqueur called Unicum. She decided to order one. Or two or three. Why not?

Why not just sit here all afternoon and get drunk? she asked herself. *Why go back to Zurich at all? Why not take Ruedi's hundred thousand dollars and never go back?*

She watched the bartender pour the syrupy liquid into a miniature martini glass and set it on the bar in front of her. Alex reached for it. *Bottoms up!*

"Don't do it." The voice sounded American. "You're gonna hate it."

She turned to see a young man with dark crew-cut hair standing at the bar next to her, a bottle of Amstel in his hand.

"Why not?" Alex asked. "It's a local specialty, isn't it? It can't be that bad."

"You'll see."

She took a sip. She almost spit it out. It was worse than cough medicine. She handed the glass back to the bartender.

"Don't say I didn't warn you." The young man smiled and held out his hand. "My name is Panos, by the way."

"Nice to meet you." Alex ordered an Amstel.

"Are you from the States?" he asked. "I went to college there."

"Where?"

"Brown. It's in Rhode Island."

"I know where it is. I went to graduate school at Yale."

"Wow!" He sat down next to her. "Two Ivy Leaguers. What a coincidence."

Her beer arrived. Panos toasted with his. "Welcome to Hungary." He smiled. "Although I'm not Hungarian, in case you could tell by my accent. I'm Greek, actually."

"So what are you doing in Budapest?" Alex asked.

"Medical school. I did premed at Brown. I wish I could have gone to medical school in the States, too, but it was too expensive. And as a foreigner, I couldn't get any student loans. So I settled for Hungary. It's better than in Greece and cheaper, too. Fortunately, the courses at the medical school are all in English."

"Hungarian is an incredibly difficult language, isn't it?"

Panos nodded. "Impossible."

"I even needed help to read the phone book today."

"What were you looking for in the phone book?"

Alex took a sip of her beer. It was ice cold. "Not a what. A who."

"Who then?"

"A family that used to live here." Alex took another sip. "Unfortunately, they seem to have disappeared."

Should I be telling him all this? Alex asked herself.

"Did you try looking in the old phone books?" Panos asked.

"What good would that do?"

"Hey, this was a Soviet country for fifty years. You learn to appreciate anything that wasn't censored. You'd be surprised what you can learn." Panos took another sip. "Up at the library, sometimes I look through the old telephone books and newspapers, just for fun. Especially those from the time before the Russians arrived. You should never ignore the past, as Mnemosyne would say."

"Who?"

"Mnemosyne." He pronounced it: *ne-MAH-zee-nee*. "The Greek Goddess of Memory."

He pulled his stool closer. "Mnemosyne's job was to remind the mortals not to forget. Actually, there's a whole science named after her. The science of memory. It's called mnemonics."

"Actually, I *do* know about that. We use mnemonics in the computer world all the time. Like, how to remember passwords or long strings of digits. Fortunately, I have no difficulty remembering numbers."

"Really?" Panos pulled his stool up a little closer. "I had a friend once at Brown who could never remember anything. She had the worst memory in the world. She was the wife of one of my classmates. Her name was Thalia. She was a very beautiful woman. Just like you." He smiled at her.

Alex wondered why she was suddenly meeting all of these smart, good-looking, young men wherever she went.

Her night with Marco in Amsterdam flashed through her mind—followed by last night's marathon session on the Web.

"The thing is," Panos continued, "Thalia would never be able to tell a story without turning to her husband and asking, 'Honey, what was that person's name?' or, 'When were we there?'" He smiled. "You know how that works."

Alex nodded.

"But then they got divorced. And my friend realized she had no memory at all. It was as if she hadn't lived all those years. She couldn't remember anything." He finished off his beer and ordered another. "So you know what she did? She went up to Cape Cod, rented a house, and spent a whole week writing about everything she had lived through with her husband. Just to get her memory back."

"Did it work?" Alex asked. The bartender replaced both their bottles with fresh ones.

"She's a totally different person today." Panos smiled. "She remembers everything. Even her old telephone numbers. As if anyone would want to do that!"

"Good point." Alex suddenly remembered Sándor's remark about old telephone books. Then it hit her. Old telephone numbers were just like old bank accounts: they may get longer over the years, but often the core digits remain the same.

Then she remembered Eric telling her the same thing: they had kept adding numbers and prefixes to his number in Copenhagen, but the original number was still there—somewhere.

Just like at the bank. The Kohen account at HBZ had started out in 1938 as a five-digit number. She remembered it perfectly from the letter signed by Kohen and Tobler: 24958. But over time, it gradually evolved into a twelve-digit behemoth: 230-SB2495.880-O1L. The current number might appear to be totally different, but the original number was always there, buried—just waiting for someone to discover it.

"Where did you say I could find the old telephone books?" She got out her wallet to pay.

"They have 'em at the library I go to—the National Library. It's up on Castle Hill, in Buda." His eyes widened. "But the telephone company headquarters is nearby." He finished off his beer. "I bet they have 'em, too. Do you want me to go with you and show you?"

"Sorry, Panos. But this is something I have to do myself."

It was just around the corner: a drab concrete building with the word Telefony written in bright green letters above the entrance. Alex pushed open the thick glass doors and walked over to a desk marked Információ.

"Do you have old telephone books here?" she asked.

The woman at the desk stared at her for several seconds. She must have understood the question, because she slowly pointed up a long flight of stairs at the far end of the lobby and muttered something in Hungarian. One of the words Alex recognized: igen.

As she climbed the stairs, Alex noticed that a wall next to the wide, circular stairway was covered with a large Plexiglas map of Budapest that showed the different districts marked with large roman numerals. Just as Sándor had said, each section of the city had a name: Erzsébet, Teréz, Ferenc József.

As Alex reached the top of the stairs, her heart soared. The long room was filled with computer workstations. She walked up to a young man seated at the reception desk. He was wearing a white cotton shirt with no collar. He looked like a hospital orderly.

"Do you speak English?" Alex asked.

"A little."

"Are these computers connected to the telephone company's database?" Alex asked. "I need to see what the number was for a factory in Újpest. It belonged to a family named Kohen." She wrote out the name and handed it to the man. "And then I'd like to search for the same string of numbers in any company that—"

"That is for Internet." The man shrugged. "It is for surfing."

"Great. But I need to first find an old number, for a leather factory named Blauer, then I need to look through all the numbers that may have that string embedded in them."

"Old numbers are over there." The young man pointed to a low, metal file cabinet at the far end of the room. "Those are old telephone books. You can look yourself."

"Thanks." Alex went over and knelt down at the first cabinet and slid the door open.

The narrow shelves were full of old telephone books, haphazardly stacked. She pulled one out. The title was completely incomprehensible—*Távbeszélő, Betűrendes és Szaknévsora*—but the year was clearly visible: *1936*.

She opened it to the *K*'s and felt a rush of adrenalin as she saw the name in print: Kohen, Aladár. And the address checked out, too.

She went back to the desk and asked the young man if there were yellow pages from that time. "No yellow pages for those—not before World War II." He pointed to the *Távbeszélő* book she still held in her hand. "Companies are in there. All together with names of people."

She flipped to the *B*'s and found an entry for Blauer.

"Is this a company or a family?" she asked.

The man leaned over to read. "Is company. Leather factory. Is in Újpest." It had the same string of names that Sára had written down at the Jewish Center. Alex pointed to 43632, the number that followed the entry. "Is this number still in existence?" she asked. "I know that the family and the factory may no longer be around, but if this number is still in existence—in one form or another—it may be possible to find *someone* who knew what happened to them. Whoever ended up with the number may be able to tell me."

"Nem. No number like that any more."

"I know," Alex persisted, "but even if this string of numbers has had new numbers added to it, like a new prefix." She pointed to the computer on the desk between them. "Couldn't you put this into your computer and check? All you would have to do is run a regression analysis, I'm sure you could—"

The clerk started to shake his head before Alex had finished speaking.

"But if you ran this number through your database, you could cross-reference it against the list of companies that have anything to do with leather. Companies that may still exist today."

"Nem." He shook his head.

"No that you can't do it? Or no that you don't want to do it?"

He looked into Alex's eyes and shrugged.

She took a deep breath. "Look, all I'm asking you to do is check—"

He started shaking his head again before she had a chance to finish her sentence. He turned his back to her and started shuffling some papers on the shelf behind him. It was obvious he wasn't going to lift a finger to help her.

"Then let *me* do it." Alex patted the monitor. "In five minutes, I would be able to find what I need."

"No." He didn't even look up.

"Then sell me the CD-ROM of all your numbers. I'll take it over there," she pointed to the Internet terminals. "I can do the regression analysis on my own."

"Nem CD-ROM." He looked up and shrugged.

"You don't have a digitized list of your numbers?" Alex's voice rose. "We're in the twenty-first century, for Christ's sake." She grabbed the monitor and twisted it slightly. She recognized the software program immediately. It was one that she'd used in college.

"Easy." She twisted the monitor toward her. "Just give me five minutes and I'll be able to—"

"Nem!" A hand came down and grabbed her wrist. An older man wearing a suit and tie had come out of the back room, probably alerted by Alex's shouting. He held onto Alex's wrist tightly and said something in Hungarian. His grip hurt.

Alex pulled back. "Let go of me!"

"You have no right to touch our computers," he shouted. He had the same smell Crissier had, a mixture of perspiration and old garlic.

"All I want to do is check to see if there are any numbers in use today that have this string of digits." Alex pointed to the entry in the book for Blauer. "Please, can you help me? All I want to do is—"

"This is all I can give you." He handed her a telephone book. "There is no way I will allow you to see our computer files."

"Why not?"

"For security reasons, we can't allow anyone into our computer files."

"And you don't have a CD-ROM? Nothing on the Web with a database?"

"This is all we provide to the public." He pointed to the thick book.

"But how can I use this?" Alex flipped to the first page of numbers. "This'll take forever." She ran her finger down the first column. The numbers flashed by. There wasn't one single case of 43632 in any of the three columns. She had just begun on the second page when she felt the man's hand on her shoulder.

"Are you really serious?" he asked. His voice had calmed considerably. "You are really going to look through the entire book?"

"If I have to." Alex looked up. "I'll do whatever's necessary."

He sat down next to her. "Tell me what are you looking for exactly?"

"I want to see if this number," she wrote out the five-digit string on a piece of paper lying on the desk, "may still exist. It could be that whoever has it today, has some connection to the original family who had the number back in the 1930s."

"But when people get a new number, it has no relation to any previous one."

"But not if it's a company." Alex tried to speak calmly. "If a company changes names, or owners, or was moved to a different site, they would still keep the old number, wouldn't they? To have continuity, for the customers to stay in touch."

"This is possible, yes." The man nodded.

Alex went back to the list. "So even if it had prefixes added to it over the years, the original number would still be in here." She ran her long fingernail down the third column. "It must be in here somewhere."

"But this is the white pages." The man reached around the corner and pulled out the yellow pages. "You need these." He opened to the index. "What kind of company did you say it was?"

"It was a leather factory." She showed him the paper Sára had written down at the Jewish Center. "The name was originally Blauer, but the owner was a family named Kohen."

"Let's see." He ran his finger down the list of categories. "Here it is." He turned to a page in the middle of the book and showed it to Alex. "These are all companies dealing with leather. But there are none with the name Blauer or Kohen."

Alex quickly scanned the list. There were about thirty entries. Not one of the numbers had the five-digit string she was looking for. She turned to hand the book back to the man but he had disappeared.

The young man at the desk pointed over to the file cabinets of the old books. "Over there."

Alex walked over to him. He was sitting on the floor, going through a dusty old tome. Once again, the only thing Alex could decipher on the cover was the date: 1947.

"No mention of the leather factory in here." He didn't look up. "It would have been in here, though. There were no yellow pages then." He quickly flipped to the *K*'s. "No mention of them here either. With a name like Kohen, it is no surprise they didn't survive."

"Aladár Kohen died in January 1945."

He looked up at her. "From what I hear, it was all chaos then. What the Nazis didn't blow up, the Soviets did. I don't think they even published telephone books during those—" He stopped.

"What is it?" Alex asked.

"If I remember right . . ." He leaned over and examined the war-year books carefully. "Yes, that's it. They end with 1943 and begin only again in 1947. This is what you need." He reached in and pulled out a thick, paper-bound pamphlet. The title page read: *Pótfüzet—Magyar Postavezérigazgatosag—1945*. It was written by hand.

"Is that the telephone book from 1945?" Alex asked.

"Not really. It's the book of changes." He flipped through the flimsy pages quickly. "Since they didn't publish any telephone book in 1945, all they published was a list of the changes to the previous phone book. That way, they could avoid printing a whole new book. People only had to look in here to see if someone had a new number." He flipped through the *B*'s and the *K*'s. "No mention of them here either . . . but if I remember right . . ." He flipped to a handwritten list on the back cover. "These were added later. After the book was published. It is from the time at the very end of the war, when the Nazis came marching in."

"So if a company had been seized by the Nazis," Alex asked. "If they discovered that the owners of a factory were Jewish—"

"Exactly." The man ran his finger down the two-column list. "If the factory had been confiscated—or sold to an Aryan family."

Alex leaned over his shoulder to read down the list with him. Everything had been written in by hand, but the numbers were legible. Halfway down the page, she saw it: 43632. The sequence from the old Blauer factory was barely legible, but it was there. It was followed by several words in Hungarian.

"What does it say?" Alex asked.

"It says to see a listing of Vilmos. There's another company, apparently." He reached over and pulled out the 1943 telephone book again. "*Gumi* means 'rubber,' but they probably did leather work, too. Maybe the Nazis allowed them to take over the factory.

He looked up. "Itt van!" He nodded. "That means 'eureka,' you know." He handed the book to Alex and showed her the entry for Vilmos Gumi.

"I wonder if this factory is still around. If so, they may know what happened to the Blauers, or the Kohens. If they were the ones who acquired the old Blauer factory."

The man went back to the desk and looked through the current yellow pages carefully. He started shaking his head. "There's nothing. No mention of any Vilmos factory at all. I checked everywhere. Under rubber. Under leather. Under anything remotely connected to that kind of business."

"But what about the residential numbers?" Alex grabbed the white pages and flipped to the *V*'s. "Look! It's here." She pointed to a lone entry.

The man read it aloud. "Vilmos Zsuzsi, Közraktár utca 22 Tel. 2174801." He looked up at her and smiled. "Zsuzsi is her first name. I think it means Susan, yes?"

The wind blew fiercely as Alex headed down the Danube, the paper with Mrs. Vilmos's address clenched firmly in her hand.

She glanced up the hill to her right and saw a gigantic statue of a woman, her arms up in the air, holding what looked like a feather the size of a house. Or maybe it was an olive branch, or a laurel wreath—the sign of victory.

She rang the buzzer marked VILMOS and stood back to wait.

"Hallo?" It was the same voice Alex had heard on the phone.

"Mrs. Vilmos, it's Alex Payton, the woman who called you." Before Alex could say anything more, the door began buzzing and kept buzzing until she reached the landing on the third floor.

The old woman was standing in the doorway wearing slippers and a house-coat. She held the door open with one hand and motioned Alex in with the other. She had dark rings under her eyes. She looked tired. But her voice was strong. "Hallo! Hallo! Come in."

"Thank you so much." Alex shook her hand. It was tiny. Her handshake was weak. "Do you mind if we speak English?" Alex asked.

"Oh, you are American!" The woman's eyes brightened. "Yes, of course English. That makes things better. Please. Come in." Her English had a strong accent. "Please sit down. Make yourself at home." She waved her hand noncha-lantly as she lowered herself into the decrepit armchair.

The small studio apartment smelled of mildew. The only furniture was the faded armchair and a bed. The floor was covered with worn-out Oriental carpets.

Alex sat on the narrow bed. It was covered with a worn crocheted spread.

"Please, excuse this place." Mrs. Vilmos shrugged slightly. "It's nothing like what I used to have before. Before the Communists took everything away." She made a slight wave of her hand.

This woman had an elegance about her, Alex noted, despite her modest sur-roundings, despite her poverty. She sat erect, regal, self-assured. And her hair was sparkling. Alex looked closely and saw that she was wearing a thin hairnet woven with tiny colored jewels.

"That is my mother." She pointed to a framed black-and-white photograph on the table to Alex's right. "She was beautiful, no?" The woman in the photo-graph was dressed in a flowing nineteenth-century gown and a sparkling tiara. She was surrounded by Greek pillars and several potted plants.

"That was taken at our country house, in Miskolc," Zsuzsi explained. "It is old, of course, like everything here. Including me." She smiled.

"It's beautiful." Alex handed the picture back. "Mrs. Vilmos, I need to ask you some questions."

"Please. Call me Zsuzsi." She pronounced it *SHOO-Shee*.

Alex took a deep breath. "Zsuzsi, I'm looking for the family of Aladár Kohen. I understand he died in Budapest in 1945 but—"

"Yes, during the war."

Alex nodded. "I need to find out if his wife or his children are still alive."

Zsuzsi leaned forward. "The Blauer family was actually quite close to my husband. I didn't know them very well. But I do know—through my husband—that Kohen Aladár married Mr. Blauer's only daughter. Katalin was her name, I think. Anyway, he took over the Blauer leather factory when Mr. Blauer and Mrs. Blauer died. And I think they had two children, a son and a daughter."

Finally. Alex had finally found someone who knew the Kohens. They were no longer an illusion. They were real.

"The Blauers' leather factory was the biggest in Hungary. It used to be the biggest in the Austro-Hungarian Empire. During the war, they were forced to sell it. They were Jewish, you see."

Alex nodded. "I know."

"They asked my husband, Karl, to buy it from them to keep the Nazis from getting it. My husband was a good man. He was always helping people. That's why when the Russians came that day, asking for him to help—"

"Mrs. Vilmos. Zsuzsi. I need to know. What happened to the Kohens?"

"It was terrible." Zsuzsi's eyes flashed with anger. "I learned all about it in the *Konzentrationslager.*"

"So you were you with the Kohens in the concentration camps?" Alex asked excitedly.

"No. I told you. I lived in Miskolc. In the north. They deported us long before they started deporting the Budapest Jews. I was sent to Auschwitz early. In 1944. But I was transferred to a work camp, because I was strong in those days."

Zsuzsi took a deep breath. "It was in Allendorf. In Germany. They put me to work making bombs—Nazi bombs. I was there for a year, but that was more than enough." She lapsed again into silence, her hands folded quietly in her lap.

The ticking of a clock filled the room—interrupted occasionally by a siren from the busy street outside. The smell in the apartment was the same as in Alex's mother's room at the end—the smell of a sick, old woman.

"In 1945, the Americans liberated us," Zsuzsi continued. "They treated us wonderfully, I must say. I'll never forget them. The American soldiers, they gave us everything we could want—chocolate, cigarettes, stockings. I hadn't seen things like that since before the war." She leaned back and closed her eyes. "They even put me in a *Spital*, a convalescence home, I think you call it. They fed me so well that when I returned to Hungary, I weighed over 100 kilograms."

Over 220 pounds, Alex calculated. This tiny, frail woman was once over twice her present size. "When exactly did you find out what happened to the Kohens?" she asked.

"When I left Germany, my suitcase was full of gifts from the American soldiers." She sighed. "But when I arrived in Soviet-occupied Czechoslovakia, the soldiers, the Russian soldiers, they took everything, including the suitcase itself. All the chocolates, the food, the stockings . . . everything."

"And the Kohens?"

"When I got back to Hungary, I had nothing. And my family was gone. They had all been killed. That's when I decided to move to Budapest. That's when I met my husband, Karl." Zsuzsi dabbed her eyes with her handkerchief.

Alex waited a moment, then asked, "So when did you meet the Kohen family?"

"I *never* met the Kohens." Zsuzsi looked angry at the question.

"But I thought you said you knew them?" *Was this going to be another wild-goose chase?*

She shook her head, no. "I was in the Konzentrationslager, how could I have known them?"

"Zsuzsi, listen. It's extremely important I know what happened to them. There's a bank account in Switzerland that belongs to them."

"In fact, the Blauers were friends of my husband's. He, not being Jewish, was able to buy their factory from them when the Nazis came in at the end of the war. Then when the Soviets came in the factory was damaged—pretty badly, in fact. But my husband worked hard to get it up and running again. I married him a year after I got back. He was a good man. Then, one day, I think it was in 1947, some Russian soldiers came to the door and told my husband that they needed his help. *'Malinki robot,'* they said. Do you know what that means?"

Alex decided to just let her continue speaking, just as she had with Sándor.

"It means 'come help us with some work.' That's what they said to him that day. Come help us. That's all. We need you. Just for today. So he went." Zsuzsi paused. "I never saw him again."

She started crying.

Alex got up and knelt by her side. She took Zsuzsi's tiny hands in hers. "That's okay. It'll be all right."

"They took him away to Siberia," Zsuzsi blurted. "Someone found a note he dropped from the train and brought it to me. I still have it." She looked around the room desperately. "I know it's here somewhere."

"It's okay." Alex told her. "It doesn't matter."

"He told whoever found the note to go to me and tell me what had happened—that he was being sent away. He told them to tell me he loved me." Zsuzsi pulled out her handkerchief and wiped away her tears. "I never heard from him again. Never." She leaned back in her chair.

Alex went into the alcove kitchen and got Zsuzsi a glass of water. She gave it to her and stayed by her side, waiting for her to regain her composure.

"I hoped he might be allowed to come back," Zsuzsi continued. "But he didn't come. And then the Communists took the factory away from me. They took everything, in fact. I was lucky to be able to get this apartment. This is all I have now."

The phone rang and Zsuzsi got up with great difficulty to answer it. "See what the Nazis did to me?" She limped to the phone.

While Zsuzsi talked Alex thought of how she must have suffered at the hands of the Nazis, of how much she must have left out of her story. She remembered the video at the Anne Frank House chronicling the suffering and the torture, the starvation, and the macabre Nazi experiments.

Zsuzsi said *Servus* several times before hanging up.

Alex helped her back to her chair. If you ever get the money, she told herself, make sure this woman gets something, too, to have a home and the medical care she deserves.

"It was a terrible thing what they did," Zsuzsi said as she sat down.

"What who did?"

"The Nazis. Isn't that why you're here? To find out what they did to the Kohens?"

"Yes, of course." Alex's heart sank. "I was just wondering what—"

"It was at the end of the war, just before the Russians came into Budapest. Aladár Kohen was among the first wave of men killed. They pulled them out of their homes in the middle of the night, took them down to the river and shot them.

"His wife, Katalin, I heard, was able to pay a lot of money to some Nazi officer who promised them safe passage to Romania. You see, it was safe for Jews there at that time." Zsuzsi leaned forward and stared into Alex's eyes. "But she was betrayed."

"How?"

"Several families were. They paid the Nazis to let them go to Romania. The Soviets had almost arrived, so everyone wanted money—even the German soldiers." She took a deep breath. "The Blauers got on a train, a normal train apparently. The Nazis told them they were all going to be taken to Bucharest. That they would be there within twelve hours." Zsuzsi paused. "But do you know what they did, the Nazi *Schweine*? The officers took all that money, promising to help them escape. But, they sent the train to a forest in the eastern part of Hungary and they . . ." Zsuzsi's voice cracked. "They killed everyone."

"Oh my God."

Zsuzsi sat back. "Fortunately, the daughter was already there."

"What daughter?" Alex almost shouted. "Where?"

"The young one. She was already in Romania."

"A daughter survived the war?"

"Magda. A wonderful young woman. I met her once. In this very apartment. It was after the Soviets took my husband's factory away, after they took him to Russia." Zsuzsi got out her handkerchief. "I never heard from him again."

"Is Magda still alive? Do you know where I can find her?"

"The last I heard, she was on her way to America. She came here, saying she wanted to speak to my husband. She needed money for her escape, she said.

But Karl had already been taken away by the Russians. There was nothing I could do for her. The Communists had already stolen everything."

Alex leaned forward. "So did she make it to the U.S.?"

Zsuzsi shook her head. "I don't know. That is the last I heard from her."

"Isn't there anyone else who might know? Another friend of the family?"

She gave a little wave of her hand. "I'm sure there is no one else." Her eyes started filling with tears again.

CHAPTER 18

The sun was setting as Alex's plane landed in Zurich. It felt as if it had been the longest day of her life—and it wasn't over yet.

She tried calling Ruedi from the airport. Just as before, there was no answer on any of his numbers. She decided not to leave a message. This information was too important.

As soon as she got to her room at the Wellenberg, she plugged in her laptop. Just as she had booted up, there was a knock at the door. "Open up. It's me, Ruedi."

"You're never going to believe what I found out," she told him as she opened the door. "There's a daughter who's—"

"Wait." Ruedi pushed inside. "You never know who may be listening."

He closed the door carefully behind him. "What did you find out?"

"The Kohens had a daughter named Magda. And apparently she survived the war. She was in Romania. But I'm not sure if—"

"Did you get her to sign the form? Do we have access to the account now?"

"Not so fast." Alex sat back down at her laptop. "I haven't found her yet. She was last seen heading to America."

"Well we've got to find her." Ruedi followed her to the desk. "We need someone to give us authorization to get back into the account."

"I already searched the name Magda Kohen before I left Budapest, but just like with Aladár Kohen, there was no mention anywhere on the Web."

"Well, keep looking." He ran his hands through his hair. "You should have seen me at the funeral. I was a nervous wreck, having to make small talk with Max Schmid. You can't imagine what it was like. Talking to him like that, knowing what I know."

Alex typed "Magda Kohen" into a new search engine and pushed Go. "Still nothing."

"He acted as if nothing was wrong." Ruedi sat up. "You know what he asked me? If the beautiful woman with me yesterday was my wife. Pechlaner must have told him about our visit." He went over and stood by Alex. "I don't think they know anything about what we discovered, though. Schmid told me he was looking forward to continuing to work as my fund manager. That he'd try to do just as good a job as he did for Ochsner. He acted as if nothing was wrong—as if everything was going to continue as before."

"Of course. Why kill the goose that laid the golden egg?" Alex tried another search engine. Still nothing. She wondered where Magda was now. Had she made it to America? Was she married? Was that why there was no mention of her maiden name? Did she have any children? Was Magda even alive?

"Moreover," Ruedi continued, "he kept bragging about what great returns they'd gotten over the years. Can you imagine? Right there at the funeral, in front of the body. He was disgusting. Fat. Huge. Like you only see in America."

"Not just in America." Alex kept working at the computer while she talked. "You should see the consultant overseeing my project at the bank. He's gigantic. And he's Swiss. Then there was that guy today at the telephone company in Budapest."

"Okay, but none of them are money launderers."

"That's true." Alex turned and looked up at Ruedi. "Did you ever stop to think that maybe Schmid really doesn't know anything about the money laundering? That maybe it was Ochsner who was working with them the whole time? That Ochsner was the one who told Schmid to invest in the bogus funds in Cyprus and Schmid was just doing what the client told him to?" She paused. "Maybe *that's* why Ochsner killed himself when he saw that you were asking questions about the account, that you were going to go into the bank and—"

"Then why did he tell me about the account in the first place?"

"When he saw that you'd learned about if from me, maybe he thought it was just a matter of time until—"

"Could be." Ruedi shook his head. "But what difference does it make? If the money isn't sent to Cyprus, the money launderers *themselves*—whoever they are—are going to come looking for me, looking for their money. They're not going to let $20 million just disappear into my account. That's why we have to find that daughter."

"And then what? We can't bring her into it, just to . . . to throw her to the wolves."

"Of course not." Ruedi put his hand on Alex's right shoulder. "Once the account is transferred into her name, or the name of the heirs, the account starts a new life. As long as they let us make sure the previous trades go through. Then they can take their money and walk off into the sunset." He squeezed her shoulder gently. "But we have to find someone to sign the Formular A to allow us to make sure that nothing happens—to us or to anyone."

Alex turned back to the computer. "I'm trying. But no matter how often I put in the words 'Magda Kohen,' I'm told that my search doesn't match any documents and I should be sure all of my words are spelled correctly."

"Did you try putting in accents?" he asked. "Are you sure the spelling is correct."

"Her name doesn't have accents." Alex leaned back. "And I'm sure the spelling is correct. I checked with the lawyer before I left Budapest." She went back to the computer. "It's just like with her father. There are thousands of Magdas out there, hundreds of thousands of Kohens, but not one single entry with the whole name 'Magda Kohen.' I know because I put the name in quotation marks like before and—"

"Maybe she got married." Ruedi leaned in to look. "But still, you'd think her maiden name would appear *somewhere*."

"Actually, that's the one thing that computers never seem to know about. That's why they always ask you to give your mother's maiden name when they want to verify your identity. It's the one bit of information that's kept secret."

"That and your social security number. They always seem to ask you that in the U.S. when they want to make sure you are who you say you are. Unfortunately, we Swiss don't have a social security number. It drives the Americans crazy."

"That gives me an idea." Alex pulled back her hair, tucked it behind her ears and moved back to the keyboard. "There's a social security Web site in the U.S." Alex did a quick search then sat back shaking her head. "Fortunately, there's nothing."

"Why fortunately?"

She looked up at Ruedi. "Apparently they only list people who've died."

"And dead people don't do us any good." Ruedi shook his head. "To get back into that account, we need to find a *living* heir."

"I've checked all the Holocaust sites, too. But she's not there either. None of the Kohens are, which makes sense. If they were killed by rogue Nazis on their way to Romania, it's clear that their names wouldn't have been on any official list."

Ruedi put his hands on her shoulders. "Well, you've got to find her. And quickly. Who knows *when* Versari is going to decide to discover the unexecuted trade."

"For the life of me, Ruedi, I can't find her." Alex went back to work on the computer. "I've tried every search engine I know. Plus I've tried all the sites for family trees, genealogical databases, even telephone listings across America. I always get the same answer. No. Magda Kohen has disappeared, just like the rest of her family."

"Except we know she wasn't killed by the Nazis."

"And that she was heading to America after the war. But after that there's no trace of her."

"Can you try just typing in the word *Magda*?" Ruedi asked.

"I've already tried that." She typed "Magda" into the search engine and pushed Go. "See?" She pointed to the number flashing at the bottom of the screen. "There are over 3,240,000 Magdas out there, but not one of them appears to be ours."

"Shouldn't you scroll down and look through the list?"

"I don't have to. That's why I put the words *Magda Kohen* in quotation marks. And there isn't one single mention of her anywhere—at least not with the name Kohen." She sat back. "Although, one of these Magdas could be her, but there's no way of knowing."

She reached over and clicked on one of the Magda entries in the middle of the page: `100 ans de cinéma sous la direction de Magda Wassef` (Editions Plume); `www.france2.fr/`

"See? This one's in France. It's Magda Wassef. Maybe our Magda moved to France after the war, met a nice man named Wassef, got married, and settled down." Alex sat back again. "But there's no way of knowing."

"Maybe we could call her? There's a telephone number at the bottom of the page."

"Sure," Alex answered sarcastically. "Why not contact every one of them? All three million two hundred and forty thousand."

"Like her." She clicked on another entry. "Magda Weiher. It says she's a food consultant in Germany. Do you think *she's* the one we're looking for?"

She clicked on another. "Or how about this one: Dr. Magda Campbell, in Minneapolis—a urologist."

Alex moved the cursor down to the bottom of the first page. "Look, there's even one in Hungarian. Maybe we should call her. But what would we say? Were you once Magda Kohen?" She moved the little hand back and forth over the entry: Tartalom Elõzõ Következõ Kósáné Dr. Kovács Magda munkaügyi miniszter: Elnök . . .

Alex sat back. "It's hopeless."

Ruedi leaned over to look, putting put both hands on Alex's shoulders. "I don't understand a word of it. Except the name. It's all gibberish to me."

"Tell me about it. I just lived through that nightmare for the last twenty-four hours."

"I've never been. It's apparently a fantastic place to visit."

"And then there was your friend Sándor. What a strange man."

"I warned you."

"You did." Alex moved the cursor back and forth over the name *Kovács Magda*. "But I swear, if he'd said the words 'But you know, Alex, that's the way we do things here' one more time, I—"

She froze the cursor over the word *Kovács*.

"Oh my God."

"What? Do you think that's her?"

"Not at all. But remembering Sándor's words . . ." She scrolled quickly back to the search engine's home page. "I can't believe how stupid I was."

"What are you talking about?"

Alex clicked on the name and switched the words inside the quotation marks. "*This* is the way we *do* things here."

"Magda Kohen" became "Kohen Magda."

"What are you doing?" Ruedi asked excitedly.

"In Hungary, last names come first." Alex clicked the Search button. "Sándor told me that about a hundred times. If I only hadn't tried to save time by using quotation marks, by insisting on the name the way *I* thought it should have been written, the computer would have found her for me. What a fool I am."

The computer suddenly began flashing: "1 match found."

"Itt van!" Alex shouted.

"What does that mean?" Ruedi asked.

"Eureka." Alex smiled. "It means we've found her." Alex scrolled down to the lone entry that had appeared on her computer screen:

```
1. Microform Collections - Columbia University
Oral History Collection [URL:www.lib.umd.edu/
UMCP/MICROFORMS/columbia_oral.html] Microform
Collections. Columbia University Oral History
Collection: International Affairs/Diplomacy.
Held In: Lawrence Library. Location Code &
Call. Archive Manager: Pablo Fuentes Loyola.
Page size 5K - in English [ Translate ]
```

"But I don't see her name anywhere in there." Ruedi leaned over Alex to read through the entry. "How do you know it's her? Does it say where she lives? Does it say how we can contact her?" He was leaning on her shoulders so hard it was starting to hurt.

"Just hold on." Alex clicked on the entry and waited. "Let's look at the entire page."

"If she's the one," Ruedi whispered, "you have to go to New York immediately. Get her to fill out that form. I'll stay here so I can go into the bank as soon as you get it and tell them, all right? Then I'll tell Versari to make sure that all trades are executed. Before we hand the account over to her."

"Wait a minute." The page had turned blank. "We're not there yet."

"What happened?" Ruedi squeezed tighter. "Did you lose her?"

"I'm waiting for the page with her name to download from the Columbia University server, but . . ." She leaned closer. "Wait, here it comes now."

A line in large, dark blue letters appeared in the middle of the page: `Columbia University. Lawrence Library—Oral History Research Office. The Oral History Collection of Columbia University. Edited by Sonja Kilian and Sebastian Triska.`

It was followed by a list, arranged in numerical order. Alex scrolled down through the list quickly. "Here it is!" She reached out and touched her fingertip to a line at the bottom of the page: `Oral History 0341: The Kohen Magda Story—Or, How a Hyphen Allowed Me to Cross the Iron Curtain.`

"That's *got* to be her." Ruedi patted her on the back. "Let's open it and let's see."

Alex had already clicked the cursor on the underlined title.

They waited several seconds. Nothing happened.

"Where is it?" Ruedi asked.

"I don't know. There's no hyperlink." Alex flipped back to the Oral History Project home page. "There's a telephone number."

She looked at the clock at the bottom of the screen: 8 p.m. "That means it's two in the afternoon, New York time." She reached for the phone.

"Use this." Ruedi handed her his cellular. "You never know who may be listening in at the hotel."

"You may be right."

Alex had to speak to three different people before she could find someone who could tell her that the oral histories were not yet available in digitized form. Most of them were handwritten or typed on a typewriter. If you wanted to read them, you had to go there in person.

CHAPTER 19

New York
Wednesday Morning

"Remember, honey," the librarian spoke with a light Southern accent, "you're not allowed to take this out of here. Or copy it. It's still protected by copyright." She handed Alex a thick manila envelope and pointed to an empty desk in the corner of the office. "You can sit down over there to read it if you'd like."

Alex immediately opened the envelope. She started reading before she even reached the desk.

Oral History 0341: The Kohen Magda Story—Or, How a Hyphen Allowed Me to Cross the Iron Curtain. This oral history is based on a tape-recorded interview with Magda Kohen conducted by Kathryn Straton on April 17, 1977, at Columbia University as part of the ongoing Oral History Project. Mrs. Kohen has read the manuscript and made minor corrections and emendations. The reader should bear in mind that he or she is reading a verbatim transcript of spoken rather than written words.

Question: Mrs. Kohen, let's begin by having you tell us a bit about your childhood.

Answer: Well, I was born on July 1, 1928, in Budapest. We had a large apartment on the Andrássy út in addition to our country house. I had a wonderful childhood, actually. We traveled often— to Switzerland, to France. To England, I think we went twice. And we went to the mountains, of course. Often. My father loved the mountains. He could name every peak by heart, you know. He could give the exact altitude of every peak in Europe. It was quite amazing.

Q: Where were you when World War II began?

A: Just before the war, we went to Venice for a holiday. That was the first time I heard about the so-called Jewish laws. We were there with a cousin of ours who told us about it—because you could read about those things in the newspapers there. That was the last time we traveled.

Q: So you were in Italy at the outbreak of the war?

A: No. We had gone home to Budapest. During the first years of the war, things were relatively normal. The Hungarians were more or less allowed to run everything their own way. No anti-Jewish laws were passed, for example. Not until the Germans arrived. It was only when the Soviet troops were approaching that the Nazis decided to take things into their own hands. That's when they invaded Hungary. I think it was March 1944.

Q: And what happened then?

A: I don't really know. My father decided to send me to Romania. He said the rest of the family would follow in a few months. But I never saw him or any of my family again.

[Mrs. Kohen requested a pause.]

Q: Would you like to continue?

A: Yes. At the beginning, I stayed with a family in Timisoara. They were not Jewish, you see. They were friends of my parents. And they accepted me as one of their own.

   I quickly got a small job, as a nurse's assistant, even though I was only fifteen. Probably because I spoke so many languages. Anyway, I was given a red cross on my uniform because I was working in a laboratory. It was funny, the German soldiers used to ask me for directions in the street—because of my uniform, yes?

   I often sent them in the opposite direction. For fun. I was afraid they were going to catch me one day, but they never did.

   They liked me, you see, because I spoke perfect German, and I looked German with my blond hair and blue eyes. They wanted to go out with me too, but I said, "No, I'm sorry, I'm too young."

Q: So Romania was occupied by the Nazis?

A: Yes. Occupied, so to say—until the Russians came to chase them away. But we had already left by then. What happened is that there was a Romanian general who was the head of the police in Timisoara. He was married to a cousin of the family I was staying with. Anyway, one morning, he called the family and said, "You better leave because the Germans are going to come and take you away." Someone must have told the Germans about me not being their daughter—that I came from a Jewish family. We never knew who.

   We all got on a truck that was already full of a lot of other people and went to Caransebes—in the east.

   While we were there, we learned the Russians were getting closer. We thought they would save us.

Q: What was life like in Caransebes?

A: We stayed with a very nice family there. I remember, there weren't enough beds, there wasn't enough water—we all washed in a little basin. But compared to what other people were going through, this was nothing.

When the Russians arrived, we went back to Timisoara. We thought everything was going to be okay. We were happy that the Russians came to liberate us from the Germans. Who knew that the Russians would be just as bad—or worse?

Q: What was life like under the Soviets?

A: A nightmare. As you can imagine.

Q: What can you tell us?

A: The Soviets did terrible things. The first army that came to liberate was General Tolbuchin's army; they were from Siberia, I think. They never saw a toilet in their life, I'm sure. They had never seen a bidet, either—they drank water from it. I mean they were really primitive—they were the ones who raped girls and so on. But I was spared—maybe because an officer lived in our house.

They had funny tricks, those Russians. You weren't supposed to have any foreign money in the house, you know like dollars and things like that, and they would come to search the house. They actually occupied our house. We were allowed to sleep in the living room, and a Russian officer took the main bedroom. His aide de camp took the other bedroom, my bedroom.

It was a Russian soldier who helped us get news of my family in Budapest. He was a gentleman, one of the only ones.

Q: How did you find out about your family?

A: It happened like this. We had a very nice dog, a dachshund named Alpha. This Russian came to our house one day and started playing with Alpha in the garden. We weren't able to speak Russian, but using our hands and feet or whatever, we somehow were able to communicate with him. We found out that he went to Budapest every week, with some kind of merchandise, back and forth. So once we gave him the address of my family and one of our neighbors and asked him to deliver a letter.

After his next trip, he came back with a little note from the neighbors telling what had really happened. That my mother and brother had been tricked by the Nazis into giving them all their money—telling them that they would be given safe passage to Romania, where they thought they were going to join me. Of course, they were betrayed. The train took them to a forest, and they were shot. It was horrible.

My brother could have been in the Olympics you know. He was a fencing champion. A great one. Then the Fascists came and removed him from the university—for being Jewish. They told him he had to go to a work camp, but he stayed in Budapest to be with my mother. He had to go into hiding, though. Then my mother got the idea to come to Timisoara, where it was relatively safe for Jews. She paid an enormous amount of money to some Nazi officers who agreed to help them get to Romania. Only they were betrayed. They were killed by the Nazis on their way to join me.

[Mrs. Kohen requested a pause.]

After hearing after the war what had happened to my family, I decided that I had to get out of Romania. That I had to get to the West, somehow. But I had no money. My family's leather factory had long ceased to exist. It had been sold at the end of the war to a man named Vilmos. He had been a friend of my father's and was quite fair about it, apparently. Because the Nazis were going to take the factory anyway, as part of an Arisierung campaign, where they put all Jewish property in the hands of Aryans.

So Vilmos Karl bought the factory from my father—for a quite fair price apparently. But then it got destroyed when the Soviets came into Budapest at the end of the war. And then he got taken away by the Russians. I spoke to his wife later, on my way to the West. Her name was Zsuzsi, I think. She told me what had happened—that her husband had been taken away by the Russians and that the factory had been destroyed. So she didn't have any money to give me.

Q: So how did you get out?

A: It wasn't easy. First, I needed a passport. And that was almost impossible. I could have tried to cross the border clandestinely, but the Romanian family would have gotten into trouble if I were caught. So I tried to do something, invent something so that I could get a passport. The situation was getting desperate. Churchill had not yet coined the phrase Iron Curtain, but we knew exactly what was going on—those of us who lived there.

At the time, you couldn't even leave Timisoara without permission. I invented a story that I was getting married in Budapest. I asked a friend from Budapest, his name was Elemér, if he would play along with the charade. And he sent me letters saying he wanted to marry me, which I took to the authorities as proof.

In the meantime, I was able to get a letter from a cousin of my mother's who was living in America. It was an affidavit of sorts saying that he would support me once I got there. But I still needed to get out from the Soviet zone, and for that I needed a passport. So for two years I had to go back and forth to Bucharest to get my passport. You needed ten different papers. By the time you got one paper, the previous one was no longer valid.

You had to stand in line for hours, for six or seven hours sometimes. And when you got to the front of the line they said you had to come back tomorrow.

But I was insistent. They started calling me little lovebird, or something like that: "La Mica Inamorată" in Romanian.

The interesting part of the story is that I had a very nice friend named Daniel who became an important Communist in Bucharest. He was part of the police. Actually he was the head of a department. He invited me many times to go to Communist reunions for young people, et cetera.

Anyway, one day, I met him on the street in Bucharest. I already had my petition that had been running for over a year and I was still waiting for an answer. I don't know how he knew, but he said to me: "I hear you're waiting for a passport."

I said, "Yes, I want to get married in Budapest."

Daniel said, "Do you have the petition number?" I always carried it in my bag, you see. So I gave him the petition number. He said he would do what he could to help me.

In the meantime I went to the American diplomatic mission in Bucharest and showed them the letter from my mother's cousin who lived in Pennsylvania. The man who worked there told me I would be better off going to Budapest—that the American Embassy there could help me more. But for that, I still needed a passport. I asked them to hold the letter for me because I was afraid to be carrying it around. If the Romanian authorities had found out that I wanted to go to America instead of Hungary, they would never have given me a passport.

And so, after weeks and weeks, I was finally given an interview with Madame Ana Pauker, who was the head of the Romanian Communist party. I will never forget her face. The door was opened for me. I stood in the doorway and her eyes pierced through my head, and she was maybe four meters away. She didn't even let me come inside her office. She said, "You don't even have to tell me anything. I know everything. It's all been taken care of. You can go."

Q: So, you got your passport?

A: Yes, but only later. First, I had to go to the police department on a certain day. When I went there, I was given another paper. Actually they wrote it on the other side of the same paper, saying to come at 5:30 p.m., after the offices were closed.

I was quite afraid because people were being arrested—all the time. And no one ever heard from them again. So I told my friends, "Look, I have to go after the offices are closed, and I don't know what is going to happen to me. But, if I do not come back, you know where to come and look for me. Right?"

I went to the police department. It was 5:30 p.m. I was taken to see the head of the office, who was a woman. I could see a blue passport lying next to her on the table. She told me to sit down. She picked up the passport and gave it to me, asking me to sign a paper—a sort of a receipt. And just at that moment, my friend Daniel came in through the door in his uniform and said, "I would like you to sign it with my pen."

Actually, it's clear that he helped. And then I promised myself that if ever I had a son, I would name him Daniel.

Q: And then you returned to Budapest?

A: Yes, and now comes the part where I explain why my story should be called "How a Hyphen Allowed Me to Cross the Iron Curtain." You see, the passport was only supposed to be good for travel inside the Soviet Bloc. It came with the following comment: "Valid for Hungary" and there was a little hyphen, followed by "Czechoslovakia." Don't ask me why; I never asked to go to Czechoslovakia.

Do you know what I did? I used the passport to first go to Hungary. But before I left, I went to see the man at the American Mission, his name was Greg something or other. I asked him to see if he could send my letter to the American Embassy in Budapest. He said he would see what he could do. So as soon as I got to Budapest, I went in and they told me, "We have your letter. It was sent to us from Bucharest. If you give us your passport, we can put your visa for the United States in it."

I said, "But my passport is only valid for Hungary and Czechoslovakia. Even if I had the U.S. visa, how would I get out of Hungary?"

"Is there any way you can get to France?" they asked. Because, you see, in France, things could be arranged more easily—it was out of the Soviet sphere of influence.

So I went to a friend who was a lawyer in Budapest and he told me, "It is very simple. You have a passport that says 'valid for: Hungary-Czechoslovakia' with a hyphen between. You just add another country!"

Q: What do you mean?

A: In Romanian, you see, you can use a hyphen in place of a comma. It means the same thing. So all I had to do was find a way to add another country to the end of "Hungary-Czechoslovakia" by adding another hyphen.

For days, I had to mix the ink. Then I learned to imitate the writing. After a few days of practice, I added the word *France*. Then the passport read: "valid for Hungary-Czechoslovakia-France." Just think, if they had put "Hungary and Czechoslovakia" in the original passport, I couldn't have added anything. That is why I say my life was saved by a hyphen.

Q: And when did you leave Hungary?

A: I left two days later. I couldn't wait. I didn't contact anyone who knew me from before. I heard everyone thought I had died during the war, so I just let them think that. I decided it was better that no one knew what I was up to. Anyway, the day I left, the first of July, 1947, was my birthday. Can you believe it? I took the Arlberg Express, the one my father loved so much because it crossed the Alps.

I traveled from Budapest to Vienna, Buchs, Zurich, Basel, and Paris. The trip took two days and two nights. On the train, I met a Swiss journalist coming from the Balkans who had written articles about the situation there. He knew how poor life was in Romania and Hungary—I'm telling you, I hadn't seen an orange since before the war.

When the Austrian border guard noticed in my passport that it was my birthday, the journalist said, "We should go into Vienna and celebrate." You see, there was a stopover in Vienna of about four hours, so he took me to a Heuriger—a sort of wine tavern— and we celebrated my birthday and my "escape" from Hungary and Romania. And from then on, every time the train stopped for longer than an hour—in Innsbruck, in Salzburg, in Zell am See— we would hire a fiacre and make a tour of the city.

When our train left Vienna there were two American soldiers in my compartment. They were from the Philippines, which was part of the United States in those days. I still remember one of the soldiers' names: It was Elmer Forte. Just like my friend from Budapest: Elemér, the one I was supposed to marry.

Everyone in our compartment—we all became great friends. It was a very tense journey. Don't forget, at that time Austria was still partly occupied by Russian soldiers, so I wasn't out of danger yet.

When we got to the border with Switzerland, at Buchs, we all had to get off the train to be inspected. We were in the last compartment, and by the time the border police got to me, everyone else had already gone across the border, including the two soldiers. I was extremely frightened. This was my last barrier to cross. But somehow the forgery worked.

When I finally crossed the border, I was greeted by the following picture: the two Americans had gone ahead to the Swiss side of the station and were bringing me a huge basket full of fruit and chocolates. I never saw anything like it. They started to sing "Happy Birthday" to me. I began crying like a "madeleine." I was so happy.

Q: How did you get to the United States?

A: As soon as I arrived in Paris, I went to the American Embassy. But it ended up taking me almost a year to get all my papers in order. In the meantime, the French gave me a "Titre d'Identité et de Voyage" allowing me to stay in Paris as long as I had to. They were marvelous about it.

While I waited, I supported myself by giving French lessons— usually to children of foreigners who were there, like me. My cousin sent me some money from America. I was also able to retrieve some money from a Swiss bank account that my parents had in Zurich. The French authorities helped me get death certificates for my father, mother, and brother. It wasn't easy, considering how they died, but I needed these documents so the bank in Switzerland would give me access to my parents' account in Zurich.

Unfortunately, there wasn't much in there. Only some cash and a bit of gold. All in all, there was about two thousand dollars in total. It was enough to pay for my passage to New York, however. And to get me started in America.

See, here on my passport? There is an entry stamp, from when I went back into Switzerland to liquidate the account. It was at the Helvetia Bank of Zurich. They were all very correct about it, actually. Considering how little was in the account.

Q: When did you leave France?

A: In 1948. That's when I got my visa to travel to America. The day I received it, I booked passage on the *Mauritania*. I arrived on August 16. I'll never forget it. We arrived during the day. We sailed into New York Harbor. It was morning, the sun was shining.

Q: Could you see the Statue of Liberty?

A: Of course.

Alex rubbed her eyes as she slid the twelve-page document back into the envelope.

She felt exhausted, but somehow, after reading this woman's adventure, her marathon of the past few days seemed like nothing.

And where was she now? Magda Kohen had obviously made it to the United States. But then what happened?

Alex checked the date of the interview on the envelope. It had taken place more than twenty years ago.

Was she still alive? Married? Living on a farm in Pennsylvania with her uncle?

Alex asked the librarian. "Where can I make a copy of this? I need to save—"

"I told you, no one can make copies of the oral histories." The woman walked over to where Alex was sitting. "Because of the right-to-privacy laws."

"But why take someone's oral history if you're not going publish them?" Alex stood up. "Why not let people have access to them?"

"Actually, we *do* want to publish them. We just have to get them in digital form. And we're a bit short of funds right now."

"If I can find Mrs. Kohen, I'm sure there'll be enough money for digitizing."

"Oh, I don't think so. If you saw how Mrs. Kohen lives, you'd know that—"

"You've actually been to her home?"

"Yes, I went there to help take the oral history. I was the one who took the notes." The librarian smiled broadly. "She's quite a firecracker. It's amazing how she's able to live so well on so little money."

"So she's still alive?" Alex's heart was pounding. "How can I contact her? It's extremely important for me to—"

"Not so fast. The Federal Right to Privacy Act forbids us to give out any information about participants in the Oral History Project."

"But if she's still alive I have to meet her."

"I'm sorry." The librarian put the original back in the file cabinet and sat back down at her desk. "I'm not allowed to give out *any* more information. I'd lose my job."

"Look . . ." Alex noticed the librarian's name on the plaque on her desk. She decided to use Sándor's trick. "Do you realize how important this is Mrs. Ragsdale? As soon as I found this woman's name on your list, I got on the first plane out of Zurich. I actually spent the night at the airport in London just to be on the first plane out, to be here as early as possible. I have to meet her—as soon as possible."

"I suppose I could tell her that you're looking for her and see if—"

"Please tell her that it concerns a bank account in Switzerland. That it's imperative to meet with me as soon as possible. It's extremely important."

"I'll see what I can do."

"Thank you!" Alex grabbed a slip of paper and began writing. "Here's my number. It's the Yale Club. That's where I'm staying while I'm in New York. I checked in on my way here." Fortunately Nan and Susan, both members, had authorized Alex to stay there whenever she was in New York.

"Tell her to call me as soon as she can, okay?" Alex handed the number to the librarian. "I'll be waiting."

CHAPTER 20

New York
Wednesday, Late Morning

The red message light was blinking as Alex walked into her room. She immediately dialed the operator. "Yale Club, Marie speaking."

"Do I have a message?" Alex asked. "I see my light's on and—"

"Oh, yeah. A Mrs. Rimer called."

"Rimer?"

"Yeah. And she's left a number. 212-989-8453."

"Was there a message?"

"No. Just that Magda Rimer called. That's all."

Within ten minutes, Alex was at the address Magda gave her on the phone—a crumbling old behemoth of a building in Chelsea, a brick-clad cruise ship run aground on West 24th Street. Magda had apparently notified the doorman. He waved Alex up as soon as she gave him her name. "8-H. You can go right up."

After ringing the bell, Alex stood back and took a deep breath. I'm about to hand this sweet old woman the key to almost unlimited wealth, she told herself. A chance to get back the life she lost.

She saw a flash in the peephole above the faded golden *H*. A voice called out from inside. "Are you Alex Payton?"

"Yes."

Alex heard several locks being undone.

"Just a moment." The door opened, but only a bit. It was held in place by a thick brass chain. Eyes peered out from halfway down the door, and at the woman's feet, four more eyes.

"Please come in!" Magda slammed the door and undid the chain. When she opened the door again, the two cats ran out, then stopped just past the broken marble sill.

"Don't worry about them." She waved Alex in, just as Zsuzsi had done, with a small movement of her hand. "They won't go anywhere. They're just curious, but not enough to do anything about it. They've never been out, you see."

Magda was elegantly dressed in a tweed suit, red silk blouse, and heavy shoes. She was beautiful, vivacious, smiling. Not at all the humble shell of a woman Zsuzsi was. Magda was glowing, in fact. Her hair was perfectly coiffed, her cheeks covered with rouge. She had a bright red jewel broach in her lapel.

Once Alex was inside, Magda carefully locked the door behind her. "I always lock all three, you see—two dead bolts and the chain. Three is my lucky number, you know."

"Yes, I know. I just read your oral history."

"Really." Magda's accent was definitely Hungarian, especially the way she rolled her *r*'s—just like Sándor.

She took Alex's hand in hers and led her to a couch along the far wall. "Make yourself at home. And please excuse the mess." She cleared a spot for herself on the couch and sat down next to Alex. "I don't get many visitors these days." The air in the apartment was hot and muggy and it smelled of cats.

"I have some important news for you, Mrs. Rimer. Or should I call you Kohen?"

"It doesn't matter what you call me. My marriage to Ritchie didn't last very long, you see. Even though I'm still in the phone book under his name." She smiled. "Why don't you just call me Magda?"

"Well, Magda, I've got some good news for you." Alex reached into her purse. "I flew over from Zurich just this morning—hoping to find you."

"Oh, yes. That nice woman at the Oral History Project told me you had something for me. She's so sweet. Calls me all the time to check on me. Is her project finally completed?"

"Not really." Alex got out her copy of the agreement between Magda's father and Mr. Tobler. "Actually, I think they've run out of money."

"Oh, really? You'd think they'd have bundles of it."

"Well, apparently they don't." Alex handed the letter to Magda. "Maybe you could give them a donation."

Magda smiled sweetly. "Oh, a donation would be out of the question." She glanced around the cluttered room. "You see? This is everything I have in the world. And the only way I can afford this apartment at all is because it's rent-controlled. Chelsea has become such a trendy neighborhood."

She picked up one of the long-haired cats and began stroking it; the letter fell to her lap. "And I'm leaving everything to you when I die, aren't I, my darling?" She nuzzled the cat's fur with her nose.

"I think you may want to reconsider." Alex picked up the letter and handed it back to Magda. "When you read this, you'll see."

"Why reconsider? These are my closest friends in the world. When I die, my few possessions are going to be sold to pay for their upkeep."

"You don't have any children? Grandchildren?"

"No." Magda made a little wave of her hand. "My husband was sick when we got married. We'd been friends for many years. We got married just before he died, in fact. More to make things official than anything else. He kept his own apartment though, even *after* we got married. How Woody Allen, n'est-ce pas?"

Magda patted Alex's hand. "He was a musician, you see. A jazz musician."

"The reason I ask about heirs is because—"

"Why would I worry about heirs? What you see here is all I have." Magda pointed to the stacks of old newspapers and magazines covering the floor of her apartment. The bookshelves were jammed to overflowing with old books and phonograph records. "I've become a *Lebenskünstler*—someone who can make do with almost nothing. It's an art, my friends tell me—an art I'm very good at." She smiled. "My family used to be quite wealthy, actually. But we lost everything in the war. Even the apartment. When I went back to Budapest . . . was it 1945? Maybe it was '46." Evidently Magda's memory had declined since she had given her oral history.

Alex took Magda's hand in hers. "Magda, I have some good news for you."

"So you said. But first, let me put on some tea." Magda stood up, and the cats flew to the floor. "It's been such a long time since I've had good news. Or any news, for that matter. I want to savor this." She walked into the kitchen, humming.

Alex noticed an old phonograph on the table next to the couch. She picked up the record on the turntable: *Ray Charles: The Golden Years.* It was covered with cat hair.

"So you like jazz!" Magda peered around the corner. "It's my passion, you know. When I moved to Chelsea in the summer of '55 . . . I think that's when it was . . . maybe it was '56. Anyway, I don't remember so well anymore. New York was *the* place to be then. Jazz was in its glory. You could go anywhere, Harlem, the Village. I used to go to all the clubs. I knew Herbie Hancock personally. He introduced me to Ritchie Rimer, my husband." Magda eyes sparkled. "He played keyboard for Wayne Shorter. Then he played for Miles Davis."

Magda came over and picked up an old album cover from a stack of albums next to the record player: *Miles Davis: Quiet Nights.* She held it up proudly. "See? It's signed. By Miles himself." Her memory had returned with a vengeance.

"I also have all the original Shirley Horn recordings, too." Magda walked back to the kitchen singing, "But don't change a hair for me, not if you care for me." Several minutes later, she brought a tray into the living room covered with cups, saucers, and two plates of cookies. "Shirley played her own piano, you know. And Oscar Peterson. He used to call me his little songbird—that's what they used to call me in Romania."

"I know. I read that in your oral history, too. Which brings me to why I came here."

"You've got to hear this." Magda set the tray on top of the books and papers on the coffee table in front of them and started searching for another record.

"Magda. I have something to tell you. It's extremely important. For you *and* for me."

Magda turned back to Alex with a worried look in her eyes. "What is it?"

Alex handed her the copy of the trustee agreement again. "Please read this—it explains everything."

"You're sure you don't want me to hold your passport for you?" Alex had watched Magda drop it twice since they left her apartment.

"Don't worry. I always carry it with me. And I've never lost it once." Magda held the passport proudly as Alex led her to the front door of the Helvetia Bank of Zurich's U.S. headquarters, on the corner of Madison Avenue and 55th Street.

"But take it if it would make you feel more comfortable." She handed it to Alex. "But don't lose it! You can imagine how important it is to me to have a U.S. passport. Even though I swore I would never go back to Europe, I want to know I *could* leave, at any time, if I wanted. After what I went through in World War II, I'm sure you understand."

"I do."

Magda looked into Alex's eyes. "You look nervous."

"I am a bit. We have to be very careful in there." Alex led her to the elevator. "Just do everything I tell you in there, okay? And everything will be fine."

"Come on, how difficult can it be to inherit a big, fat Swiss bank account?"

Inside the elevator, Magda pulled out several crumpled documents from her purse. "I brought everything they could possibly ask for. Birth certificates, death certificates, my husband's will. I have a certain experience in having the right documents, you know." She smiled. "Did you know that it was a hyphen that saved my life?"

"Yes, I know." The door opened and Alex walked over to a beautiful black woman sitting at a desk. There were no papers anywhere—just a telephone and a large vase filled with red orchids.

Alex wrote out the account number and asked to see an account manager.

"Please have a seat," the woman told them. "Someone will be right with you."

As soon as she was seated, Magda began reading the letter again. She rubbed her fingertip over her father's signature as she read. "I wonder why they never told me about this." She looked up with tears in her eyes. "If I had known . . .

everything would have been so easy for me." She wiped away a small tear that fell to her cheek.

"Maybe they thought you were too young. You were only ten years old when they opened the account in Zurich."

"How did you know that?" Magda's eye's widened.

"Your birthday was in the oral history. I just did the calculation."

"Aren't you the whiz?" Magda wiped her eyes with a hankie. "I wouldn't know how to calculate for the life of me. That's one thing I didn't inherit from my father. He could tell you the altitude of almost every mountain in Europe. The Mont-Blanc, the Eiger, the Jungfrau, most of the Carpathian peaks."

"Magda, when we get in there, could you do me a favor?"

"Of course, anything." Magda finished wiping her eyes and put her hankie back in her purse.

"In order to make sure that there is no unfinished business in your account, we're going to have to make sure HBZ executes all previous trade orders. That way, you'll have a clean slate when you—"

"Why should I let them do *anything* to my account? After what they did to me in Zurich, after the war . . . they could have told me . . . they *should* have told me about this account." Her eyes looked angry. "I went in there, you know, after the war, to the Helvetia Bank of Zurich."

"Yes, I read about that, too."

"I told them who I was. They told me all my documents were in order. But the account they gave me had almost nothing in it. If they knew I was the heir to my parents' estate, why didn't they tell me about *this* account as well? How could they?" She shook her head slowly. "I read through all those lists of dormant accounts. And there was no mention of this account, no mention of my name. Neither Kohen nor Blauer appeared anywhere. How can that be?"

"Actually, this account wasn't a dormant account. It was a trustee account. That's why it never appeared."

"What's the difference?"

Alex took a deep breath. "Your father apparently opened this account in the name of Rudolph Tobler, the father of the man who—"

"Then why didn't he contact me?" Magda asked angrily. "And why didn't the bank tell me about the account when I went in there after the war."

"It seems the bank didn't know that it was a trustee account. That was the whole point of this type of account. In the event that Hitler came into Switzerland, the Nazis would never know—"

"Then why didn't this Rudolph Tobler contact me after the war?"

"Apparently, Swiss bankers don't go around the world looking for clients."

"He knew whom the account belonged to. He should have come looking for me."

"It seems he did. That's what his executor said. He even sent people to look for the family in Budapest."

"Well, they didn't look very hard. I mean, even *you* were able to find me, right?"

"I was lucky. Without the Web, I'm not sure it would have been possible."

"Well, in any event, thank God you came along." Magda took Alex's hand and held it tightly between hers. "How can I ever reward you? How much can I pay you?"

"Actually," Alex pulled out Ruedi's contract, "Mr. Tobler's son has agreed to split his father's 5 percent fee with me if that's all right with you."

Magda read the agreement carefully and handed it back. "Of course it's all right with me. In my opinion, you should be getting it all."

"Since Ruedi Tobler's father never received anything for his work, it's probably only fair to—"

"Are you sure 5 percent for you is enough?" Magda asked. "I could give you some more."

She reached into her purse and pulled out her checkbook. "As an added bonus. For everything you've done."

"This will be fine, really."

"Are you sure?"

"Are you aware of how much 5 percent of this account is?" Alex asked.

Magda looked at her blankly.

"My half of the 5 percent fee is almost $10 million."

"My God." Magda shook her head. "Is that true?"

"It is."

"I wonder where my father got all that money? I knew my mother's family had a lot, but nothing like that. I just assumed it got stolen by the Nazis."

"Actually, it's been growing exponentially all these years. Unlike those dormant accounts, this one's been collecting interest and dividends that were consistently reinvested. Your third of a billion dollars probably started out at less than a million. Several hundred thousand would have been enough, with exponential growth, to reach the level it's worth today."

"It's more money than *I* could ever spend, that's for sure." Her eyes began to fill with tears. "Thank you."

"You're welcome." Alex felt a surge of pride. Her efforts, however reluctant, had brought joy to this poor, sweet woman. Magda was happy, and alive. *Just make sure she stays that way*, Alex told herself.

"You know what I thought happened to the money?" Magda dabbed her eyes. "I thought my mother used it all to pay her way to Romania. I thought she had given it all to the Nazis. The ones who betrayed her." She put her hankie back in her purse. "My worst nightmare was that my mother's favorite diamond necklace ended up in the hands of a Nazi. I kept imagining that some German soldier had given my mother's favorite diamond collier to his wife . . . or his girlfriend."

"Actually, it may be in Zurich."

"What do you mean?" Magda's eyes widened.

"It seems there's a safe connected to your account."

"You don't say!"

"Actually, it's in the basement of the main branch of HBZ. In Zurich. All you have to do is go in there and ask."

"Really?"

"Even if you don't have a key, apparently they'll drill it open for you . . . if you pay them a small fee to pay for a new lock."

"Oh, that would be marvelous. Could you help me?"

"Of course, but first we have to certify to HBZ that you're the account owner. Then you can do whatever you want."

A tall, well-dressed man came out of a side door and held out his hand to Magda. "Hello. I'm Michael Neumann, the assistant manager here." His English had a slight Swiss German accent.

He shook Magda's hand, then turned to Alex. "You must be Rudolph Tobler's friend from Zurich."

Alex shook the man's hand hesitantly. "How do *you* know that?"

"I was just on the telephone to my colleagues in Zurich. Believe me, it wasn't easy reaching them. It's the end of the day there." He turned to Alex. "Mr. Versari told me about the account and your visit there on Monday."

"Really?" She took a deep breath. "So, they probably also told you that they promised us that as soon as we found the beneficial owner of this account, Mr. Tobler would be reinstated as trustee."

"If that's what the owner wants." The banker looked at Magda. "Is that all right with you?"

"Actually, I'd like to put *this* woman in charge of the account." Magda smiled at Alex.

"Really?"

"Well, we can decide all that inside." The banker took Magda's hand and helped her up. "I assume you have identification?" he asked nonchalantly.

"Of course. I always carry this with me." Magda handed over her birth certificate and her passport. Neumann read them carefully and made a slight bow.

"Would you like to come with me, Mrs. Kohen? You may be more comfortable inside."

"*We'll* be more comfortable inside." Magda took Alex's arm and brought her along. "She's my personal advisor, you know."

Neumann led them into an elegantly appointed conference room filled with antique furniture and old paintings. Neumann left them for a moment to make copies of Magda's documents.

"This is so exciting." Magda patted Alex's hand tenderly. "I just wish my father and mother were here to enjoy this."

"I'm sure they'd be very proud of you."

"Where do your parents live?" Magda asked.

"My father lives in California. My mother lived in Seattle. She just died a few months ago."

"Oh, I'm so sorry." Magda continued holding Alex's hand. "I'm sure she must have been very proud of you."

"Maybe." Alex took a deep breath. "Magda, please don't forget that when the banker comes back, you instruct him to process all pending orders."

"But I don't want to let HBZ have anything to do with this account. After what they did to me." She shook her head. "The first thing I'm going to do is transfer everything to my account in New York."

"Magda, I'm not asking you to let HBZ manage your account forever. Just tell them to make sure that all the previous trades are allowed to go through."

"Whatever you say."

"It's just for a few days. Then you can do whatever you want with the money."

"Fine." Magda nodded. "But could I make a small withdrawal?"

"Of course." Alex patted her arm. "Take out as much as you want. It's your money now."

"And I'd like to pay you and Mr. Tobler's son what I owe you."

"Excellent. I'm sure you can arrange that with Mr. Neumann. All they'd have to do is take money from one of the fiduciary deposits. There are several in your account, if I remember correctly."

"And they'll make the transfer for me?"

"They'll do whatever you tell them. You're the client now." Alex wrote down her account number at HBZ and Ruedi's account number at his local Zurich bank. "Just show them this and the transfer will be taken care of automatically. And since all three banks are in Switzerland, it should happen instantaneously."

"Fine." Magda took the paper and held tightly onto Alex's hand. "And just in case there's a problem, I'll tell them that you are my advisor, that as long as I live they have to do whatever you say. Can I do that?"

"If you sign a power of attorney, yes."

"Then I'll do that. I'll tell them to let you execute whatever trades you see fit. But when everything is settled, I'm going to transfer everything to my own bank in New York."

"Fine."

"I'll show them. You'll see." She reached over and picked up several cookies from a small silver tray in the middle of the table.

The door opened and Magda slipped the cookies surreptitiously into her pocket.

"Mrs. Kohen?" Neumann asked.

"Yes?" Magda looked up at him guiltily.

"You are now the certified owner of account 230-SB2495.880-O1L." He handed Magda her documents. "You can dispose of it as you wish."

As they walked out the door of the bank, Alex offered to take Magda to lunch. For the first time in days, she was hungry. "Wonderful!" Magda clapped her hands gleefully. "Let's go to my favorite vest-pocket park. It's just around the corner from here."

She hooked her arm under Alex's and started walking. "It's on 53rd Street. Or is it 54th? Or maybe 55th. I know it's around here somewhere. It's not hard to find, it has a section of the Berlin Wall and the loveliest little fountain. And the best hot dogs in New York City."

"Aren't we a pair?" Alex held Magda's arm closely. "Two millionaires out for lunch in the most sophisticated city in the world, and where do we go? A park. And what do we eat? Hot dogs."

"You got to go with the flow, honey." At the entrance to the park, next to a gushing waterfall, Magda found a Sabrett's cart. She ordered two hot dogs.

"You want everything on it?" Magda shouted, trying to make herself heard over the sound of the water.

"Sure."

"Why not?" Magda smiled. "We're wealthy women now. We can afford it." Alex watched as Magda loaded on the sauerkraut, onions, relish, and extra mustard. What a wonderful woman, she told herself. Despite her age, she was fresh, so full of life and energy.

Magda handed Alex her hot dog and sat down next to her. "Isn't it beautiful here?" She reached over and touched a piece of the graffiti-covered slab next to Alex. "They brought this to New York, you know. It once divided East from West, you see. Notice how the side that used to face east is gray and lifeless? And the side that faced west is covered in beautiful colors? Now, you know why I didn't ever go back to Europe."

"You can now. If you want." Alex took a big bite of her hot dog. It was delicious. "You can afford to do whatever you want to do."

"We both can." Magda daintily licked the mustard and relish off her fingers. "We *both* can do whatever we want. We're millionaires!" She smiled gaily at Alex.

It was finally starting to sink in. Her bank account had probably already been credited with the $10 million from Magda's HBZ account. Since both accounts were in the same bank, it would have been done instantaneously. She was now a wealthy woman. She could now do whatever she wanted.

"You know what I'd like to do?" she asked Magda. "Take you out to dinner tonight, an expensive dinner at the best restaurant in New York. It'll be my treat."

"Oh, I don't know." Magda took a small bite and nodded. "I'm sure you have better things to do—with people your own age. I'm old enough to be your mother." She paused. "What am I saying? I'm old enough to be your *grandmother*. In any event, you're part of my family now."

She slipped off her shoes and stepped into the water. "Why don't you come in and join me? The water's fine!"

"As soon as I finish my hot dog." Alex watched Magda wading through the pool at the base of the waterfall. She looked so happy. After everything this woman had been through, after everything she'd suffered, she didn't stop enjoying life for one minute. She looked like she was going to enjoy her life fully, to the end. No matter what.

Alex thought of her own mother, how she'd died so young.

"You know what?" Magda turned to Alex and with a little wave with her right hand shouted something like, "She moans family too."

"What did you say?" Alex shouted back.

"Never mind." Magda smiled. "Why don't you come over and join me? You don't have anything else to do today, do you?"

"Actually, I *don't* have anything to do." She suddenly thought of Ruedi, waiting for her to call. "Wait a second." She looked at her watch. It was early evening in Zurich. Knowing Ruedi, he was going crazy waiting to hear from her.

"I've just got to make a quick phone call," she called over to Magda. "Then I'll come in and join you."

Alex spotted a pay phone near the entrance to the park and used a credit card to pay for the call. It's time to buy a cell phone, she told herself as she dialed Ruedi's cell phone number. You have $10 million in your bank account. You can now get all the phones you could ever use. You can do now whatever you want, in fact. Meet Marco in Paris. Travel with him wherever you want, wherever he wants. Stay in the best hotels.

"Tobler."

"Ruedi, I found her." Alex shouted to make herself heard over the roar of the fountain. "Everything's settled. We just left HBZ in New York and it's over, we—"

"Wait. There's something I have to tell you."

"We've taken care of everything. Magda signed the Formular A. The account is hers. And she gave me a power of attorney, which allowed me to instruct HBZ to let all of FINACORP's trades go through. Everything's been settled."

"No, it's not."

"Yes, it is. They even credited your account and mine with our share of the money that was owed to your father. We're both rich. We each have $9.925 million."

"Why haven't you answered my calls?" he asked. "Where have you been all day? I've left several messages at your hotel for you to—"

"I just told you: I've been busy finding Magda Kohen—or Magda Rimer as she's now called. I'm with her now as a matter of fact, and guess what we're eating for—"

"He called me." Ruedi sounded angry.

"*Who* called you?"

"Schmid. He tried to disguise his voice, but I know it was him."

"And?"

"He threatened me. He said I had to transfer—"

"Let me guess, $21.3 million."

"Did he call you, too?" Ruedi asked excitedly.

"No. But it's obvious what happened. He found out the account's been blocked." She pulled her hair behind her ear and held the phone tightly to her ear. "But it doesn't matter. Now that the account is in Magda's hands, the investment order will go through. FINACORP isn't going to be told why, but their trade will be executed as planned. Everything will be okay."

"But he said I had to send the money immediately. To an account at a broker-age house in New York called Malley Brothers. He even gave me the number." Ruedi read her the number quickly. "He said I had to make the transfer today."

"I can't believe he gave you his client's bank account number in the U.S. He must have really panicked when he saw that the money had been blocked."

"Wouldn't you? Knowing the money launderers were probably going to kill him, too!"

"Don't worry. Now that Magda's taken over the account, the transfer will be allowed to go through. It'll take two days—three days at most. It's all been taken care of."

"But he said I had to transfer the money today." Ruedi paused. "He said to send it immediately, or there would be *Konsequenzen*."

"Ruedi, I just told you, it's been taken care of it. Magda's account will make the transfer without her even knowing about it. She'll never miss the money."

"But I'm worried."

"Trust me. It'll be okay."

"I told him I'd get the money somehow, even if I had to sell some more of my paintings."

"You told him *what?*"

"I told him not to panic, that I'd send him the—"

"Are you crazy?"

"If I sell my Warhols I should have enough . . . it's just that it'll take several weeks to get the—"

"Don't you realize? By telling him you'll send the money, you admitted that you knew what was going on. That *we* knew what was going on."

"I didn't know what else to say."

"Why couldn't you just wait?"

"Don't worry, I'll get the money. I don't care if I have to sell everything."

"It's not an issue of money, Ruedi. If you'd just waited, the transfer would have gone through automatically. We could have acted as if we had no idea what was—"

"How was *I* supposed to know you'd found Magda?"

"So now it's my fault?"

"Why didn't you call me earlier?" Ruedi asked. "If I'd known you'd transferred the account to Magda, I wouldn't have—"

"I just found her two hours ago." Alex looked over at Magda standing in the fountain. She was feeding the cookies she'd taken from the bank to a small flock of sparrows perched on the edge of the fountain. "I took her immediately to the New York branch of HBZ to take care of the paperwork and she did everything I asked her to. Even giving us a power of attorney over the account that's good for as long as she's alive. Even paying us our share of the management fee."

"So let's use *that* to pay them."

"Are you crazy?"

"If you paid ten and I paid ten, I'm sure I could come up with the difference, somehow."

"What are you talking about?"

"If you go into HBZ in New York and transfer your money today . . . it's too late for me to transfer my money from here today, but I'll do it first thing in the morning. Then we can—"

"I'm not transferring anything to anyone. There's no reason to panic."

"We're talking about international criminals here, Alex. You have no idea of what they're capable of—"

"We have no idea who's behind the money laundering. It could be someone totally innocuous."

"Is that what you think?"

"Yes, I do."

"Then you have to find a way to prove it."

CHAPTER 21

New York
Wednesday, Late Afternoon

American bank secrecy. Was it an oxymoron as Ochsner said? Like random order? Irrational logic? Silent alarm?

Alex pulled out her checkbook as she walked through the main door of Malley Brothers at 200 Park Avenue. Her heart was pounding.

She walked up to the receptionist as if she'd been there a thousand times. "Hello. I need to make a deposit into one of your accounts."

"The cashier's office's in the back."

Alex opened her checkbook as she walked around the desks to a windowed office in the back of the room.

"Yes?" A heavyset woman sitting behind a thick pane of glass looked up lazily.

"I'd like to deposit a check into one of your accounts. It's for ten thousand dollars."

"Is the account in this branch?" the woman asked lazily.

"I don't know. All I have is an account number. It's a rent deposit, for a new apartment. And I have to make sure it's credited to the account today." Alex looked behind her. "There are other people who want the apartment, and I have to act fast. The owner told me to come in here. That you'd know everything."

The woman looked up at Alex. "What's the name on the account?"

"That's the problem. I have the name of the man who's renting me the apartment but I think the account's under a different name."

"You're supposed to have the account name."

"I know, but can't you help me? He has so many accounts here. But this is the number." Alex held up her check. After "Pay to the Order of:" she had written the account number Ruedi gave her on the phone.

The cashier typed in the nine-digit number. "You're in luck." She smiled. "The account's at our Tribeca branch."

"So I should go over there and . . ."

"You can make the deposit here. I'll make sure it gets sent over today." The woman held out her hand again for the check.

"Whom do I make it payable to?" Alex asked. "I have to make it out to someone."

"It says here Vortex Partners. Would that work?" the woman replied.

After dealing with the excruciating mania for secrecy in Swiss banks, Alex felt ecstatic. This was almost too easy.

She filled in the name on the check and began to hand it over, then pulled it back. "Actually, he told me he needed to get a confirmation, to make sure that the check really got deposited today."

"It'll be sent over there today. I promise. You can trust me."

"But I need a confirmation. Maybe I should just go over there myself. Just to be sure."

"Why? I can give you a deposit slip here." The cashier held out her hand for the check.

Alex decided to press her luck. "But I need to know that the money is actually credited to the account today." Alex looked around. More good news: a line had started to form behind her.

"I'd actually like to talk to the person in charge of the account. Just to confirm that the check has been deposited properly." She looked around again. "I'm sorry to put you through all this bother."

The cashier sighed. "I don't know why you can't just deposit it here." She typed a command into her computer. "The account manager's name is Jeff Norton. But I can assure you, if you deposit the check here—"

"That's okay. I'll just go over there myself and deposit it personally. Just to make sure." Alex folded up the check and put it back into her purse. "What did you say the address was?"

It was easy to get in to see him. Alex simply had to say she had several million dollars to invest. And she wasn't lying.

Norton was on the phone when Alex walked into his cubicle. He motioned for her to sit down and went on talking. "All right. You're done. You've just bought two thousand shares of IBM and a thousand shares of Unibanco."

Alex watched him type the orders into his computer. "You want to book them to the Miami account? No problem." He spoke loudly. "No, I don't need the number. I can get it through my Alpha Search." Alex watched his fingers carefully as he typed in a password to log onto the bank's database. It was easy to remember, it consisted almost entirely of numbers.

Within seconds, the monitor was flashing a long list of numbers and account details. Norton looked over at her and smiled as he continued speaking on the phone. He lifted his eyebrows, as if to say, "What can I do? I'm such a busy man." She had the impression he was putting on a show—a busy-broker act, just for her benefit.

Alex noticed a shelf of folders on the wall. Each one had a different account number printed on the spine. Many of them had the clients' names. Anyone who walked into his cubicle could see them.

American bank secrecy. It was just as Ochsner had said—an oxymoron.

Norton put his hand over the phone and whispered, "I'll be right with you."

Alex picked up a laminated chart lying among the papers on his desk. At the bottom of the chart was a sticker: "Property of J. Norton. Do Not Remove."

It was a proprietary data analysis of the Standard & Poor's 500 Stock Index performance during the twentieth century.

It showed the S&P 500 had risen exponentially, just as Ochsner had said, from a base of 100 in 1945 to over 60,000 by the end of the twentieth century. If all you did was re-invest interest and dividends, all you would have needed was several hundred thousand dollars in 1938 to turn it into more than a billion dollars by the end of the century.

Norton put down his phone with a bang. "So." He turned to her and smiled. "What can I do for you?"

"I'd . . . I'd like to open a brokerage account. I have several million dollars to invest. I just inherited it." Alex forced a smile. "I heard you were one of the best brokers around."

"I *am* pretty successful in picking the winners." He shrugged shyly.

"Like this." Alex held up the S&P graph. "Do you think you could do this well for me?"

"Oh, I like to think I can do much better than that." He took the chart from her and put it back on his desk. "My clients are very happy with my performance." He winked.

"It looks like you have a lot of clients." Alex pointed to the shelf of folders behind him. "How do you keep track of them all?"

"It's not easy. Foreigners like to set up a lot of companies. It's good for them, but a pain for us."

"It must be hard to remember all those account numbers." She looked at him adoringly. "How do you do it?"

"It's easy. The computer does the work for us. We just household them."

"What's that?" she asked.

Norton smiled condescendingly. "It's the system that links all the different accounts for each client."

"Really?"

"By the way, I see you don't have an accent. Are you a nonresident alien?"

"Actually, I live in Switzerland. Zurich, in fact."

"But are you a Swiss citizen?"

"No. American."

He paused. "Then someone's sent you to the wrong place. I only work with foreign accounts."

He leaned back in his chair and folded his hands behind his head. "Unfortunately, I can't take you on. As much as I'd like to." He reached over and started digging through the papers on his desk. "I'll find you a good account manager, though."

"But couldn't you make an exception?" Alex asked. "I have several million dollars to invest, and I'd really like you to be the one to—"

"I'm sorry." he shrugged. "Internal rules prohibit it." He looked through the Malley Brothers telephone directory for a few seconds, then wrote out a name and telephone number on a small piece of paper. "Unfortunately, this man is the one you have to go see." He handed her the paper and looked into her eyes longingly. "I'm really sorry. I wish I could work with you."

"Me too." Alex took the paper but didn't move. "I was really excited about working with you." She picked up the S&P chart again. "This is very interesting. Do you think you could make me a copy?"

Norton shook his head. "Sorry. The company that makes them doesn't allow us to copy them. We're supposed to order them, and this is the last one I have."

"Oh, come on. One little copy isn't going to hurt, is it?" On her way in, Alex had noticed there were no secretaries on this floor and no copy machines by the work stations. The Achilles' heel of the twenty-first-century office: computers could do almost everything—except make copies.

"Well," he smiled conspiratorially, "I suppose I could . . ."

He stood up. "I'll be back in just a minute."

Before leaving his cubicle, Norton reached over and hit the Escape key several times, bringing his computer screen back to the secure Malley Brothers main page. The tiny field for the password flashed inconspicuously at the bottom of the screen.

As soon as he was gone, Alex reached over and quickly typed in Norton's twelve-digit password. She then hit Enter and the screen flashed a menu of options. At the prompt Search For, Alex quickly typed in the account number for Vortex Partners. For several long seconds, the screen flashed "Search on: 066-198038." Then the account statement appeared. It had only a few thousand dollars in cash. The real money obviously got transferred to other accounts— accounts the guy at FINACORP probably wasn't even aware of. She spotted an Attached Accounts icon at the bottom of the screen and clicked once, repeating the exact sequence Norton had followed to initiate an Alpha Search.

Within seconds, she had a screen full of account names and addresses. Most of them were companies like ABC Trading and Vortex Partners—offshore companies probably. Only one had a name, but that was all she needed: Zinner, Miguel.

She quickly wrote it down, then clicked on the account number and an address appeared: Monte Verde Farm, Rodovia Juscelino Kubischeck, Km. 255, Catanduva, S.P., Brazil.

She glanced around the corner. Norton was nowhere to be seen. No one else was watching.

She clicked on the account icon again. This time, it gave her the account's portfolio, arrayed in spreadsheet format: approximately $160 million in stocks and bonds—in just this one account. And all of them were U.S. and European securities. Blue chips, every one of them. This was his official account, Alex realized. The one where the dirty money ended up, washed spic-and-span, cleansed of its illegal past.

She heard footsteps. She punched the Escape button several times, bringing the screen back to the main page and sat back down quickly.

Norton walked back into the cubicle smiling.

The entry field for "Password" on his computer over in the corner flashed innocently.

"What do you mean you don't want to wait?" Alex shouted into the phone. "You told me that if I found out who the account belonged to, you'd agree to let the transfer go through as planned."

"But now that I've found out we're dealing with a terrorist. I'm not about to sit around and wait for—"

"What are you talking about?" Alex screamed. A siren blared in the distance. "I just told you the account belonged to a man from some town in Brazil called Catanduva."

"That's why! While I was waiting for you to call back, I went to that Internet café and found out that the bank in Cyprus used for the funds transfer is in fact a front for the Hezbollah. You know who they are, don't you? One of the biggest terrorist organizations in the world. I read—I think it was CNN.com—that before September 11, Hezbollah was responsible for murdering more Americans than any other terrorist group, including Al-Qaeda."

"Fine, but this account belongs to someone in Brazil. What reason is there to think that—"

"The article I read said the Hezbollah was very active in Brazil." The siren was getting louder. "They apparently have huge smuggling operations on the border among Brazil, Paraguay, and Argentina. And the money the Hezbollah launders in Brazil is used to fund terrorist activities all over the world. There's no way I'm going to get involved with them."

"So why transfer your money—*our* money—to them?"

"It's the only way to get them off our backs."

"Ruedi, stop and think. If international terrorists really *are* involved in this account, you think that you can just pay them their money and they'll say, 'Thank you, Ruedi and Alex, for paying us what you owed us'? And then they'll just walk off into the sunset?" Horns were now blaring in all directions.

"But we have no other choice. Schmid said that we had to pay them immediately."

"Schmid probably panicked. And he's probably just trying to save himself." She took a deep breath and continued. "Think a minute. What if the Brazilian who owns the account has nothing to do with the terrorists? What if he has no problem waiting until the money comes in the normal way—via Cyprus?"

Ruedi didn't answer. "Why should we pay $20 million of our money to someone who's going to get it anyway? Magda won't ever notice what happened to her investment in Cyprus. Actually, it isn't her money anyway."

"Exactly!" Ruedi shouted. "Actually Magda should be the one to transfer the money to that account. All you have to do is give her the number of the account at Malley Brothers in New York and tell her—"

"I'm not going to get Magda involved."

"Then let me talk to her. I'll explain."

"There's no way I'm going to let you bring her into this."

"I'll call her if I have to. You said her name was Rimer, right? I bet her number's in the New York telephone directory."

Alex didn't answer. Ruedi was probably right.

"If *you* don't tell her to transfer the money," Ruedi continued, "I will."

"But why get that sweet, innocent woman involved if all we have to do is sit tight and wait for the transfer to go through?"

"I'm innocent, too. So are you. So why should we be the ones to suffer?"

"Look, Ruedi. Nobody has to suffer. If the trade goes through, no one will have to know we're involved or that we know anything about it." She took a deep breath. "I'm sure this guy in Brazil is just some sleazy businessman who wants his money to be safely laundered through an innocuous Swiss bank account."

"How do we know that for sure?"

CHAPTER 22

Rio de Janeiro
Thursday Morning

A wave of warm, humid air hit Alex as she left the arrivals hall. It was polluted sea air, not at all like the fresh, invigorating air in Amsterdam.

She got into a waiting taxi. "Take me to the best hotel in town."

"The Copacabana Palace?"

"Sure." She looked at her watch. Eleven hours left.

She'd already used up eleven of the twenty-four hours Ruedi had given her to find out enough about Miguel Zinner to show he wasn't a threat—or at least not enough to drag Magda into it.

She'd found out a lot from going on the Web in New York. But he wanted real proof that Zinner was just an innocuous, if corrupt, businessman.

The car sped off. Alex leaned back in her seat. She was exhausted. At JFK she had to fight to get on the first flight out. And despite being in business class she had slept in fits and starts, wondering what she was going to do when she got to Brazil.

Do what you have to, she'd told herself as she flew over the dark Amazon. *You have $10 million at your disposal. You can pay for the best lawyer in town, or hire a private detective—a team of them if you want.*

She'd even called Marco in Paris—and woken him up in the middle of the night—to ask his advice.

"Have you ever heard of Miguel Zinner?"

"Of course. He's one of the richest men in Brazil. He has one of the biggest farms in the interior. Why do you want to know?"

"I'm doing a report on him. On Brazil, in fact. For work. I thought you might know."

"Of course I do. Everyone knows him. Zinner's in the news all the time."

"Why would a farmer be in the news all the time?"

"His farm is probably bigger than some American states. It's certainly bigger than most Swiss cantons. He must be a billionaire by now."

"Could he be involved in anything illegal?"

"I don't know. Why do you want to know?"

"No reason."

"What's this all about, Alex?"

"Nothing. Go back to sleep. I'm sorry to have bothered you."

Traffic slowed to a crawl. Alex stared out the window. The highway was bordered on both sides by vast stretches of slums. Hundreds of thousands of small, dirty shacks covered the verdant landscape. The smell of raw sewage filled the car.

Alex thought of Magda sitting in her stuffy apartment in New York and how she'd be able to buy a new place now, a mansion, just like the one where she'd grown up in Budapest. What was she doing now? Sleeping, probably. Dreaming—of her new life to come, of her life of riches. *Until Ruedi gets hold of her. Then he'll pull her into this nightmare just like he's done with everyone else.*

It was like in *Brer Rabbit*, which her father used to read her when she was a little girl. Brer Rabbit got his paw stuck on the tar baby, and the more he pushed and pulled to get away, the more he got stuck. In the end, he was completely trapped.

She thought of how her first contact with Ruedi had been an innocent phone call. How he wouldn't give up until he met her, until he got her to meet Ochsner, until she was completely drawn in. The more she tried to get away, the worse it got.

They turned a corner and the azure Atlantic stretched out before them. The cab pulled up to the main entrance of the Copacabana Palace—it was stunning.

The driver turned to her. "Here it is, the best hotel in Rio. Is it good enough for you?"

In her room, a suite overlooking the sea, she got out the yellow pages and flipped through them until she found a section with the heading *Detectives Particulares*. She had to call more than a dozen before she found one who was open. She had to call several more to find one who spoke English. He said he could see her at noon.

Alex sat on the bed and tried reading through the articles she'd downloaded from the Web before she left New York. Unfortunately, almost all were in Portuguese. Several, however, had pictures. In one of them, Miguel Zinner was shaking hands with the *prefeito*, in another he was shaking hands with the *governador*.

There was no mention of Hezbollah, no mention of terrorism anywhere.

Alex looked at her watch. There were two more hours until her meeting with the detective. After five days of constant travel and hardly any sleep, it was starting to catch up with her. She closed her eyes and felt herself start to fade. There wasn't enough time for a nap. Besides, she didn't want to take a chance on missing the appointment. She decided to take a quick swim to help herself wake up.

The water was cool. Not as cold as the Pacific near Seattle, but cold enough to keep most Brazilians out.

Alex plunged right in. It almost took her breath away, but before long she was out beyond the waves. Here, on the nice side of town, the water was crystal clear.

As she knifed through the water, her mind started to clear. *It'll work out*, she told herself. *Everything will be fine.*

She noticed a man swimming next to her. He was wearing long trunks, the kind surfers wear. He was swimming fast, just as she was. She watched his lean, muscular torso cut through the waves. Tiny bubbles attached themselves to his smooth stomach as he slid through the water. She raised her head to get a better look, but a wave washed over her and he was gone.

Suddenly, she felt arms around her. She screamed and kicked furiously, then breathed in a mouthful of seawater and started choking, coughing.

Then she was being held up, out of the water. "It's all right. I'm here." He held her tightly.

"Marco!" Alex gasped for air. "What are you doing here?"

"I wanted to surprise you." He helped her through the waves and back onto the beach. He took her into his arms and rubbed her back softly. She was shivering, but Marco's hands were warm. His body was warm. He held her closely. "I'm sorry. I didn't mean to scare you. I just wanted to help."

"Why are you here?"

"I flew down to meet you."

"But I just called you last night. And you were in Paris."

"And you were in New York. I saw your number on my caller ID. Aren't you glad I came?"

"Sure, but—"

"No buts." He held her closer.

"It's just . . . I wasn't expecting it."

"It sounded like you needed me. Like you were going to go to Brazil without anyone to help you. I figured there were only two places you would have gone, Rio or São Paulo. I decided to try here first."

"You flew halfway around the world just to meet me?"

"Of course." His hands felt good. She was starting to warm up.

"How did you find me?" she asked.

"It wasn't hard. I called all the big hotels. There aren't that many. Yours was the third one I checked." He gestured toward the Copacabana Palace glowing white in the midday sun.

"When I got there, they told me you'd gone out for a swim, so I thought I'd join you." He smiled. "It was easy to spot you. You were the only one swimming besides the surfers. And it's not easy to forget what your beautiful body looks like. It's only been five days." He pulled her tightly against him. His hands continued rubbing her back. She felt him starting to get aroused.

"Do you want to go inside?" she asked.

As he led her toward the hotel, three teenage boys came walking directly toward them. They were barefoot, wearing tattered street clothes. Marco gently steered her away from them, just as he had that night in Amsterdam.

"You have to be careful," he said as he led her across the busy street. "It's not as safe as Zurich here. By the way, what did you find out about Miguel Zinner?"

"Not much. Not yet. I'm meeting someone at noon to go over it."

"Actually, I may be able to help you." He led her down a broad sidewalk covered with swirling black-and-white mosaics. "I have a friend who works for a big agro-industrial company in Catanduva, the same place where Miguel Zinner has his farm."

Marco held the door for her as they walked into the air-conditioned lobby. "He said he could even meet us this afternoon. If you'd like."

"Sure."

"There's only one problem. He lives in São Paulo, and he's leaving tonight for the U.S. He said we could go there and meet him before he gets on his plane—all the flights for North America leave in the evening there."

Alex looked at her watch. "Isn't there any way to delay it?"

"Unfortunately not. If we want to meet him, we'll have to go now. We can take a plane from Santos Dumont, but with all the traffic—"

"I don't know. Maybe I should stay here."

"Why? What's wrong?"

She looked at her watch. "I don't really have time."

"What do you mean? You just got here."

"It's just that I've been on so many planes in the last five days. Isn't there any way we could get him to come here? I'd be happy to pay for his flight."

Marco laughed. "He's a wealthy man. Money isn't going to make him change his plans. Not Digo Braga."

The traffic in São Paulo was even worse than Rio. It was stop-and-go all the way from the airport into the city. And to make matters worse, it was much cooler than Rio. The gigantic metropolis looked more like New York in winter than a balmy Latin American city. Skyscrapers filled the horizon.

Alex was getting sleepy. "Is traffic always this bad?" she asked Marco.

"Usually." Marco put his arm around her gently. "And it's no surprise either. Half the money they're supposed to spend on roads and tunnels in this city ends up in the politicians' pockets. The builders charge double what the projects really cost. And then they split the money with the politicians. It's a real racket."

"And people let them get away with it?" Alex asked.

"What can you do?"

"Put them in jail, perhaps?" They pulled to a stop. The trucks and busses around them were spewing exhaust.

Marco pulled her toward him. "You don't know much about Latin America, do you?"

She snuggled into his arms. "Hey, I was a computer science major in college."

"Sorry." Marco held her tightly. "It's just that politicians in South America are always getting caught with their hands in the till. It's a kind of sport, actually. Everyone does it. All the politicians. Even the president. Haven't you heard about all the recent scandals?"

Alex shook her head.

"And the sad thing is no one ever has to pay for what they've done. *Bicho ruim não morre.*"

"What does that mean?" Alex asked.

"Just an expression they use here. It means something like: bad beasts never die."

When they checked into the hotel in São Paulo, Marco insisted on putting the room on his credit card.

They barely had time to put their bags in the suite when Marco's cell phone rang.

"It's Digo," Marco said with a shrug. "He's early. Should I tell him to wait?"

"No." Alex grabbed her purse. "Let's get this over with."

Marco's friend was waiting for them at a small table in the bar. He was drinking a Coke and smoking a cigarette. He was partially bald, but very athletic looking. He wore small, wire-rimmed glasses, just like Ruedi's.

"Digo *bonitão*!" Marco shouted. "Thanks for meeting us."

He gave Digo a big hug and sat down next to him. "Digo's one of my oldest and best friends." Marco motioned for Alex to sit across from them. "He and I went to grade school *and* high school together. Then he went off to study in the States. At Penn."

"Really?" Alex asked.

Digo nodded.

"And Alex went to Yale." Marco said.

"How did you know that?" She asked.

"Your sweatshirt." Marco smiled. "Remember our cyber chat last Monday? You told me what you were wearing."

Alex felt herself blush.

"So," Digo took another sip of his Coke and set it back on the small table between him and Alex, "apparently you're interested in Miguel Zinner?"

"Yes, I am. Do you know him?" Alex asked.

"Quite well, actually. What do you want to know about him?"

"Everything. I'm writing a report for—"

"She's a consultant." Marco interjected. "Don't worry. She's a good friend. You can tell her everything."

"Okay." Digo took another puff on his cigarette and leaned closer to Alex. "Miguel Zinner's one of the biggest farmers in the country. His farm is called Monte Verde. It's in the interior. It's so big that you'd need a plane to see it all. He produces more coffee, oranges, hogs, and cattle than almost anyone around." He took another puff. "I've been there several times, on business. The farm is surrounded by wire fences, guard dogs, armed guards—the whole bit."

"Why would a farmer need armed guards?" Alex asked.

"That's normal in Brazil." Digo took another drink. "And Zinner must be worth billions. Although he's probably not the one who ordered the high-tech security. He's not the kind of guy to be afraid—of anyone." He shrugged. "He's a big man, in every sense of the word. He must weigh a hundred and fifty kilos. You should see his Rolex. They had to make it special for him. In pure gold, of course."

"The person behind the security is his right-hand man, José De Souza. He's a real *filho da puta,* if you pardon my expression—a real little shit. I used to have to do business with him. He's an asshole. He runs everything for Zinner on the international side. And just because he speaks English and French—and Zinner doesn't—De Souza acts like he runs the place."

He turned to Marco. "To give you an idea of the type of guy he is, whenever he's in São Paulo, he spends his time at Café Photo."

"What's that?" Alex asked.

"You don't want to know." Marco put his hand on her arm and smiled. "It's not for you."

"Why not?"

"It's a very expensive bar, frequented by wealthy men and a few selected women. Most of them are . . . how do I say, high-class hookers? Very beautiful. Very expensive."

"I bet that's where he'll be tonight," Digo added. "I heard he's in town this weekend."

"Do you think they may be involved in something illegal?" Alex asked Digo.

"*Everyone* in Brazil is involved in something illegal." He sat back and took a puff. "Let me give you an example. A while back, we were thinking of raising hogs on my farm. Everyone else seemed to be making a lot of money at it. So I made a spreadsheet showing the profit and loss figures. And for the life of me, no matter how I adjusted the figures, it just didn't come out. There was no way I could make money at it."

He rubbed out his cigarette in the crystal ashtray in the middle of the table. "So I took the figures to an accountant who specialized in farming and asked him what was wrong. He looked at my spreadsheet, then pointed to the amount I had budgeted for taxes. 'That's where you have your problem,' he said. 'You've based your taxes on 100 percent of your income.'" Digo shrugged. "So you know what he did? He took out his pencil and changed the tax payment to half of what I had budgeted. '*Now* you have a profit,' he told me."

"So?" Alex rubbed her eyes. It was getting smoky in the hotel bar, and she was tired. "What are you saying?"

"That everyone here cheats on their taxes." He finished off his Coke. "And if you're exporting several hundred million dollars' worth of goods a year, it really starts to add up. All you have to do is falsify your export documents by paying off people at the port. That way, no one knows how much you're really selling. And you book all your profits offshore—through companies set up just for that purpose, in the Caribbean, usually."

"Like the British Virgin Islands?" Alex asked.

"Exactly. Or Cayman. Or any one of the others. Everyone does it. The Brazilian government knows about it. But they don't do anything. They realize there's nothing they can do about it."

"So, all that unreported income, where does it end up?"

"It stays offshore, usually. It would be hard to justify bringing it back into the country officially." Digo lit another cigarette. "However, if you wanted to use it in a Puritan country like the United States, a country that doesn't turn a blind eye to tax evasion, you'd probably want to have it somewhere else."

"Like Switzerland?"

"Exactly. That way, you can bring it into the U.S. and it looks legit. You can use it to buy your fancy apartment on Central Park, or your house in Florida, or your kid's college education. Whatever."

So that was it? Alex asked herself. *Unreported profit? Tax evasion?* Zinner was laundering his money in Switzerland just to give it a patina of legitimacy—nothing more. And his fund managers in Switzerland probably just overreacted when they saw that the money was trapped in Magda's account. Typically Swiss, they tried to make everything perfect.

"Have you ever heard of the Hezbollah?" she asked Digo.

"Sure." He took a long puff. " Who hasn't?" Marco looked at Alex intensely. "Why are you asking that?"

"I read somewhere that Zinner had some connection with them."

"Where did you read *that*?" Digo asked.

"I don't know. It seems the Hezbollah has extensive operations in Brazil. In the no-man's-land on the border with Paraguay and Argentina apparently. They're involved in money laundering there."

"That may be true." Digo sat back. "But Zinner wouldn't have anything to do with them. He's Jewish."

"Really?" Alex asked. "How do you know that?"

"Zinner is a Jewish name. I'm surprised you didn't know."

Alex shrugged. "Sorry."

"I've heard that Miguel Zinner is one of Israel's biggest financial supporters in Brazil. In the United States, too. He's quite religious, in fact."

Digo snuffed out his cigarette. "There's no way he'd have anything to do with one of the most anti-Semitic organizations in the world."

The first thing Alex did when she got back to the suite was call Ruedi to tell him that there was no reason to panic—that all they had to do was wait and that as soon as Magda's money got sent to Cyprus, it would all be over.

Strangely, he didn't answer any of his numbers. She left a message outlining what she'd found out.

She then decided to call Magda, to make sure she was all right—that Ruedi hadn't gone back on his word to wait to contact her until he heard back from Alex.

"I'm having the time of my life," Magda gushed. "Thanks to you."

She sounded ecstatic. "We're having a little party in my apartment right now, with some of my friends from the old days—the few who haven't kicked the bucket." Alex recognized the music in the background: Shirley Horn.

"I haven't had this much fun in years." Magda had to shout to make herself heard over the background noise. "Too bad you can't be here to join me."

Alex looked over and watched Marco get undressed. He smiled back at her as he stepped out of his slacks.

"We're all going out tonight." Magda continued. "I'm taking all my old friends to the Blue Note. We're going to party like there's no tomorrow."

"Well, have fun. And be careful."

"I will. By the way, do you have Mr. Tobler's phone number? I'd like to thank him for everything he did for me, for handing over the account."

"Actually, why don't you send him a letter?" Alex watched Marco slip off his shirt. His torso was stunning. "Ruedi is very busy these days. We probably shouldn't bother him."

"Fine. Could you give me his address? I'll send him a letter."

"Excellent idea. The number is eight, but the street is . . . just a second." Alex got out her laptop and opened it to check Ruedi's address. "It's Nägelistrasse. Do you want me to spell it?"

"No need," Magda interrupted her. "I speak German, you know."

"Of course. I forgot." While she spoke Alex began closing the documents that were still open on her screen, including the articles on Miguel Zinner that she'd downloaded earlier that morning.

"I'd like to invite him to New York," Magda continued. "You, too. To celebrate. Do you like that idea? I'll take you out to the best restaurant in town. No hot dogs this time, I promise!"

"Thank you, Magda. That's an excellent idea. And remember, that no matter what happens, you can call and leave a message for me any time." She gave Magda her Thompson number. "It's an 800 number," she added. "You can call toll-free."

"Don't worry, honey." Magda giggled. "I have no problem with long-distance calls anymore. I'm a millionaire now, remember?"

"I know. Isn't it great?" Alex enlarged one of the photos on her desktop. Miguel Zinner was exactly as Digo had described him, big as a house and wearing the largest Rolex she had ever seen. He was standing next to a short, dark man with a three-day-old beard. The caption listed him as José De Souza. They were both standing in a small crowd and many of the men next to them were wearing military uniforms. A white poster above them carried the word *Inauguração*.

Alex hung up, and stared at the picture for several seconds. These were the men Ruedi was so afraid of—an overweight farmer and his two-bit sidekick.

Marco came over and wrapped his arms around her. He was wearing nothing but his white boxer shorts. "Are you going to play with your computer all night?" He bit her ear gently as he spoke. "Or are you going to come to bed with me?"

"Of course. Let me just close this last picture." She felt Marco's hands move over her breasts. De Souza's eyes stared at her from the photograph. "He looks mean, doesn't he?" she whispered.

"Who? De Souza?"

"Yeah. It's creepy, isn't it? It's as if he's watching us."

"So make him go away," Marco whispered. "Make it *all* go away."

As Alex moved the cursor across the photo to close it, it scrolled slightly to the right, showing several more people standing off to the edge of the podium. One of the faces was only partially displayed on her screen, but she recognized it immediately.

She scrolled the photo further and the complete face came into view.

"Come on. Let's go." Marco tried to lift her up. "We have more important things to do."

"Just a second." Alex pulled her hair behind her ears and leaned in to look. The man in the crowd was Jean-Jacques Crissier. What was the chief computer consultant of HBZ, her boss, doing in Brazil in the same crowd as a two-bit money launderer?

"What's the matter?" Marco asked.

"I don't know. Maybe nothing." Alex picked up the phone. "But I'm going to find out." She dialed Eric's number quickly.

"But—"

"Eric, it's me, Alex."

"Where are you?" he sounded panicked. "There's no number for you on my caller ID. Are you still outside the country?"

"Yes. I—"

"I haven't heard from you at all today—or yesterday for that matter. I left several messages for you on your Thompson voicemail."

"Has Crissier said anything?"

"Yes! He wants to know when you're coming back."

"Anything else?"

"He wants to know where you are."

"And what did you tell him?"

"That you had the flu. Like you told me." He paused. "But he said he wants to see you immediately. No matter how sick you are. What's going on, Alex?"

"I don't know." She took a deep breath. "But I'm going to find out."

"Are you in trouble?"

"There's only one way to find out." She grabbed her purse.

"Tell me where you are. Tell me how I can help—"

"I've got to go." She hung up and grabbed her purse. She pulled out her lipstick and started applying it in the mirror next to the door.

"What's going on?" Marco asked.

"I have to find out something. It may be nothing, but I need to be sure that Miguel Zinner is as innocuous as your friend says he is."

He stood up. "What are you talking about? Why can't we go to bed? I thought you were tired."

"I have to do this now. Tonight."

"But why?" He walked over to her. "Why can't we go to bed? Get a good night's sleep? We can learn all about Miguel Zinner tomorrow. What's the hurry?"

"You don't want to know."

"But I do. I'm in this now with you, Alex." He took her in his arms. "I want to help you. Let me. Please?"

"Then come with me now. I have to put something to rest. A crazy idea I have." She threw the lipstick back into her purse and clicked it closed. "*Then* we can relax. We can go back to Rio. Go wherever you want. Just help me make sure that no one can ever hurt me—hurt us. Ever."

Café Photo was full of men of every race and nationality imaginable. Many were young. Some of them couldn't have been more than twenty. The women were uniformly beautiful—and thin. They didn't fit the stereotype of prostitutes at all. Each one, without exception, had a small purse hanging from her shoulder—for the money, certainly.

Alex recognized De Souza immediately. He was sitting at the bar drinking whiskey, haranguing a man sitting next to him, talking loudly in English.

"The twelve-year stuff, you can drink it every day, you know. And not feel anything the next day." She could hear his voice distinctly over the noise in the room. "You feel it go down your throat like it's made of velvet. My favorite is Royal Salut. It takes twenty-one years to age. It's the crème de la crème." De Souza pronounced the French words with a thick, guttural accent. As he spoke, he took greedy little sips from his glass.

Alex moved closer.

"What are you going to do?" Marco whispered.

"Just wait for me here, okay?" She squeezed his arm gently. "This should only take a couple minutes."

Alex walked over and sat at the bar, across from De Souza. He glanced over at her immediately. Alex smiled. He lit up a cigar, keeping his eyes fixed on her. She looked away, deciding it might be more effective to play hard to get. When she looked back, he was gone.

Suddenly, she heard his voice next to her. "*Oi meu bem.*"

"Sorry. What did you say?" Alex asked. "I don't speak Portuguese."

"No problem. I speak everything." De Souza smiled. He had a mouthful of yellow, irregular teeth. "Can I buy you a glass of champagne?"

"Sure. Thank you."

He ordered two glasses. "Dom Perignon, is that all right?" He smiled again. "Nothing but the best for you." He sat down next to her. "You know what I'd like? To take you home with me. Show you a good time. Would you like that?"

"I don't know."

He leaned closer. "You're a very beautiful woman, do you know that?" His breath reeked of alcohol.

Alex could see Marco out of the corner of her eyes—discreetly watching them at the other end of the bar.

"You have beautiful eyes." De Souza glanced at her breasts. "A beautiful body, too."

"Thank you."

"They obviously think so too." He pointed a finger at two men standing across the room, talking to two thin, blond women. "They work for the governor, you know."

He put his hand on Alex's shoulder. "I know them. I know a lot of people here. They're all my friends."

"How did you get so many important friends?" she asked nonchalantly.

"I'm an important man, you know." Alex noticed that he was slurring his words slightly. "Important people trust me." He then mumbled something about "cash register" while he finished off his champagne.

"You can trust me, too." He took a puff from his cigar. The smoke went right into Alex's face. "I have connections, to people in high places. The highest." He took another drink.

"Actually, I may have heard of you. Didn't I see your picture in the newspaper a while back?" Alex asked.

"Could be." He put his hand on her leg. "Where was it?"

"I don't know. You were in a crowd of officials. I think you were with someone named Miguel Zinner."

"That's my boss." De Souza took another puff. "He's in Paris right now. At the Ritz. Maybe we should go there. I'd show you the town. You'd love it."

"And you were with someone else, too. Jean-Jacques Crissier, no?"

"Who?" He squeezed her thigh.

She repeated the name. "I think he's from Switzerland . . ."

"Never heard of him." He moved his hand down between her legs. "What do you say we get out of here? My car's waiting outside."

"I don't think so. I can't really—"

"What do mean you can't? No one says no to me."

"Actually." She looked around for Marco. He was no longer sitting across from them. "I'm supposed to meet a friend here."

"But you're with *me* now." He squeezed the inside of her thigh. "I'll take care of you tonight. You don't need anyone else."

Alex pushed his hand away. "Sorry. Maybe another time."

"What's the matter?" He put his other hand on her neck and squeezed tighter. "Don't you like me?"

"It's not that. I just can't leave right now." She tried standing up. De Souza's hand tightened on her neck.

"Not so fast. No one ever walks away from me."

"I'm sorry, but I have to go now." She tried removing his hand from her thigh. "You're hurting me."

"Then do as I tell you and you won't get hurt."

Suddenly, Marco appeared by her side, as if by magic.

"What's happening here?" he asked.

"Nothing. I was just leaving." Alex stood up and walked toward the door. She looked back to see what De Souza was doing. He was staring at her with his cigar in one hand and his drink in the other.

Marco walked up and escorted her past the phalanx of men in dark suits standing at the door. He calmly led her outside. He didn't seem afraid at all. He didn't even look back to see if De Souza was following.

"Hold on." Marco pulled Alex back as they reached the street. "There aren't going to be any cabs out here this time of night." He pulled her back toward the club. "Let's go back in and have them order one for us."

"No." Alex pulled him forward. "I just want to get out of here. Now!"

He held onto her arm firmly. "Alex, it's not safe here. Not at night. We'd be much better off waiting inside."

"There's no way I'll go back in there. Not with him in there."

Marco put his arm around her and walked alongside. "Then let's walk down to the Rebouças. We can probably get a cab there."

They walked for several blocks. Marco carefully kept himself between Alex and the road. The perfect gentleman.

Alex saw a well-lighted street up ahead. "Thanks Marco," she whispered, "for being there tonight. For being there for me."

"No problem." He held her closer. "Did you find out what you wanted from De Souza?"

"Yes I did, actually."

"Good." He leaned down and kissed her on her forehead. "You reek of cigar smoke."

"I know. He was disgusting, wasn't he? The first thing I want to do when we get back to the room is take a shower and wash off every trace of José De Souza."

"What do you say we take one together?"

"Sounds good."

"We could continue what we started back in the—"

Alex heard a loud thud. Marco was ripped from her arms, ending up on the pavement in front of her—a crumpled, motionless heap in the darkness.

The large, black Mercedes that had hit Marco squealed to a stop and José De Souza jumped out. He grabbed Alex before she could run and jammed his hand over her mouth. He began to push her into the backseat of the car. "You're coming with me, bitch."

Alex struggled more. He held on tight. She felt one of her high heels snap and she tumbled to the ground. She then felt De Souza trying to pull her up and push her onto the back seat of the car.

"No one *ever* walks away from me," he shouted into her ear. "Ever."

She tried to face him, to defend herself, but he held her face down on the back seat of the car, onto a coat reeking of stale cigar smoke. Something hard under the coat was cutting into her cheek.

She felt De Souza reach inside her dress and rip down her panties. She kicked harder, but he held her down even more forcefully. Her face was pushed down so hard that she could barely breathe.

"Be a good little girl and do exactly as I say." He pulled her legs open. "Daddy's going to teach you a little lesson."

Alex kicked. He pulled harder.

She screamed and squirmed, but the more she struggled, the harder he pushed her down onto the coat. She wasn't able to breathe at all now. Her head began to spin. She panicked. She tried kicking, twisting, turning in every direction, but he just pushed down harder. She could feel herself start to lose consciousness.

Alex bucked with all of her strength and was able to slip her hand under her head, creating a small space for air. The hard object under the coat was now cutting into the back of her hand. Was it a gun?

She felt a surge of energy as the air entered her lungs, and she gave another kick. De Souza pushed down further. She could feel him trying to push himself in between her legs. "You're going to get what you want now. What you've wanted all along."

Alex heard a buckle being undone. Then she felt her panties rip.

With his one free hand, he began fumbling down between his legs. "Come on. Just a little more. I'm almost ready." She felt the rhythmic motions of his hand brushing against her.

"Almost there." She felt his mouth close around her ear. He was breathing hard. "I'm almost ready now."

She grabbed onto the edge of the hard object under the coat and tried pulling it out. Kicking and squirming further, she was able slide it out. It was a small laptop. She swung it up over her head to try to hit De Souza's head.

He just laughed as he moved to one side. "It's no good, my *petite mouche*. There's nothing you can do to stop me now." She felt him pushing in harder. "Hold on tight, your Daddy's getting ready to come on home."

She swung the laptop again. This time, the corner hit him on the side of his face.

He screamed. "*Puta que pariú!*"

He used both hands now to pin her down, to immobilize her arms. But without a hand to help him, he was unable to penetrate her.

He moved up, using his body's weight to hold her down—her face pushed onto the coat. It was starting to cut off her air supply. She struggled to breathe, but hardly anything could come in—or go out. Her lungs started to burn.

She had a flash of her mother with her pillow held over her face, struggling. *Is this how she died, too?*

Alex's head started to spin.

In a last attempt to free herself, she kicked wildly, but without any air left, her strength started to ebb. Everything started to turn red.

Then she heard a thud. De Souza screamed into her ear. "*Merda!*" Then another thud.

This time, she felt the blow vibrate through her body. Suddenly, De Souza let go of her wrists and began to slide off of her body.

Alex twisted around and took in several quick breaths of fresh air.

Above her, Marco was standing by the side of the car, supporting himself with one hand on the open door. Blood was streaming down his face. He leaned down toward De Souza, who had curled up on the ground. With his free hand, Marco made a quick jab to De Souza's face, and Alex heard a pop, like a champagne cork going off. Blood began to shoot out of De Souza's nose. He screamed like a wild man. "*Para! Por favor!* Stop!"

De Souza rolled under the car to escape Marco's blows. Marco turned back to Alex. "Come on, let's go." He lifted her from the seat, gently sliding her skirt down from around her waist. "Let's get out of here. Before the police get here. With De Souza's connections, it's better to not get involved." He led her away from the car, limping badly, with one arm hanging by his side.

Alex followed blindly, not noticing that the small laptop was still firmly gripped in her hand.

CHAPTER 23

São Paulo
Late Thursday Night

Alex clicked the chain in place and pushed a heavy armchair against the hotel
room door.

"Don't worry. He's not coming after us." Marco came out of the bathroom
wiping the water off his face and torso. Alex could see several scratches along
his side and back. "In addition to breaking his nose, I also fractured several ribs
and his right arm. He's not going anywhere for the next few days."

"How can you be so sure?"

"I'm a karate teacher, remember? I know about these things."

"But if De Souza's a friend of the governor's, couldn't he send the police to
get us?"

"Don't worry." Marco walked over to her and took her in his arms. "He doesn't know where we are. He doesn't know our names. He doesn't know anything about us."

He moved her toward the bed. "Let's just go to sleep."

Alex pulled back. "I'm sorry," she whispered. "I want to take a shower first. I want to wash off every trace of that guy."

"Fine. I'll be out here if you need me." He limped over to the bed and lay down, face first.

Alex closed the door to the bathroom and turned on the shower. She let the steaming hot water pour over her for several minutes, then slid down and wrapped her arms around her knees. She started to cry. She cried until she couldn't cry any more, until the pain in her eyes and cheeks equaled the pain in the rest of her body.

When she came out, Marco was asleep. His pants and bloodstained shirt lay in a crumpled heap on the floor.

Alex sat down on the bed next to him. For several minutes, she watched his back move rhythmically with his breathing. The deep scratches glistened in the soft light of the room. This man, this handsome man, had saved her. And he had almost died in the process. She knew so little about him, yet after what they'd just been through, it felt as if she'd known him forever. She slid in next to him. He hardly stirred.

She lay there for several hours, wondering what she had done to deserve this. She had only tried to do the right thing, to find the best way out. And she had almost died in the process. So had Marco.

As she lay there in the dark, she kept flashing back to the moment when her air ran out—how she had come so close to dying in De Souza's hands—helpless, suffocating.

Was that how her mother had died? Held powerless under the pillow until there was no more air for her, no life left? How could anyone choose that way to go?

But her mother was in so much pain—and she hated pain. But to suffer through the horror of suffocation—it must have been hell for her.

And what if she had changed her mind halfway through? How could she have told Evelyn to stop?

Or what if it had been her aide's idea from the start?

But why? Evelyn had a good job with Mrs. Payton. Why would she want to end it?

Alex flashed on Ruedi's words: follow the money. But her mother had no money. What would have been the point of ending her life early?

If there's no gain, there's no motive. If there's no motive, there's no crime.

It made no sense.

It was just getting light when Alex finally felt herself start to drift off. She pulled in next to Marco and held him tight against her body. She began to fall into a deep sleep. The sleep of the dead, wasn't that what they called it? *Stop worrying about what may have happened*, she told herself as she drifted off. *Concentrate on the present, on finding a way to out of this nightmare.*

Alex was awakened by a call from the front desk, asking when they were going to check out—it was already afternoon.

Marco was still asleep. She got up to call Ruedi. There was still no answer.

What was going on? It had been more than twenty-four hours since they'd spoken. Hadn't he gotten her messages? Had he decided to go to New York to meet Magda and get her involved, too?

She dialed Magda's number. There was no answer and no answering machine either.

She calculated the time zones. It was late morning in New York. Magda should have been awake by now.

She checked her Thompson voicemail again. Strangely, there were no messages at all—not from Ruedi, not even anything work-related. Hadn't Eric said he'd left several messages for her? She walked back to the bed and gently shook Marco awake.

"Come on. Let's get out of here. Let's go to the airport. I want to go back to New York and check on someone. Then I want to go to Seattle. There's something I have to do."

Marco turned to her sleepily. "We can't leave. Not yet."

"Why not?" Alex began filling her carry-on.

He rubbed his eyes. "I told you. All the planes to the U.S. leave in the evening."

"So let's go the airport and wait." She threw in everything she had and closed the lid tightly. "Let's get on the first plane out."

"I don't think this is such a good idea." Marco wrapped the sheet around his waist and stood up, shakily.

"Why not?" Alex asked.

"Because as wounded as De Souza is, he's still capable of getting his thugs or the police to go to the airport and look for us. He could invent any number of excuses to have us arrested."

"But he doesn't know our names, right? And no one but him knows what we look like."

"I still think it would be wiser to wait until the last minute. You never know."

Alex picked up the phone and asked for the concierge. "Then I'm going to reserve a seat on the first plane out. I'll reserve one for you, too, okay?"

"Sure."

They put her on hold.

While she waited, she noticed De Souza's laptop sitting on the desk. "What is *this* doing here?" she asked Marco.

"You brought it here with you last night, don't you remember?"

"Unfortunately, that's the only thing I *don't* remember." She opened the lid. It sprang to life. The icon reading Dial-up Networking in the middle of the screen automatically clicked on and the screen began flashing: Monte Verde Intranet.

She noticed that the words *José De Souza* were already entered in the field for Name. A string of asterisks filled the Password field. She hung up, plugged the phone line into her computer, pushed Enter. The screen began to flash "Password Accepted."

"What's that?" Marco walked over and put his hands on Alex's shoulders.

"It's the farm's intranet, just for the company's use." She moved the cursor down to the prompts for Name and Password. "Like a lot of people, De Souza keeps his info filled in ahead of time." She thought of Panos's mention of mnemonics in Budapest. "Maybe he can't remember it."

The words *Connecting to Monte Verde Intranet* suddenly appeared on the screen. Then the words: *Bem Vindo.*

"Looks like you're in," Marco spoke softly into her ear. "That means 'welcome' in Portuguese."

At the bottom of the page was another field: *Monte Verde Farms—Operações Internacionais. Accesso: José De Souza.*

"The computer must think you're him," Marco massaged Alex's shoulders gently. "They've giving you access to the company's internal accounts."

Alex clicked Enter and two buttons appeared on the screen: Stockes and Vendas.

"The first one is 'stock,'" Marco translated. "Like what you have stored up in warehouses."

"You mean inventory?"

"That's it. And *Vendas* means 'sales.' See how they both have the word *Interna* written on them? It must be their internal *Caixa Dois* figures, the ones they don't report to the government—just like Digo told us."

"We should give this to the police." Alex got a diskette out of her laptop and inserted it into De Souza's computer. "Although, if what Digo says is true, they're not going to do anything about it."

Within minutes, she had Monte Verde's sales and inventory figures from the last five years—both the real and the reported figures.

Suddenly, a small line of text began flashing on the screen: Dial-up networking failed. Outside line disconnected.

"Strange. They don't want to let us log on again." Alex clicked the icon for *Log on*. Nothing happened.

"Maybe they figured out you weren't José De Souza."

"How could they know that?" She sat back to wait. "If they let us on once, they should let us on again."

"Or maybe they knew that you weren't De Souza all along."

"What do you mean?"

"Maybe they let you online on purpose."

"Why would they do that?"

Marco pointed to the phone line.

Alex felt a surge of blood rush through her body. "You think they were tracing our call to find out where we were?" She unplugged the laptop and threw it into the wastebasket. "Let's get out of here. Now!"

They were down in the lobby within minutes. Marco insisted on hailing a cab on the street instead of using the one provided by the hotel.

"If they come here looking for us," Marco explained, "we don't want them to know for sure where we've gone."

They climbed into a broken-down Volkswagen taxi. Marco muttered something to the driver and then turned to Alex. "Fortunately there are three airports in São Paulo—and De Souza can't be in all of them at once. And he's the only one who knows what we look like. Also, the main airport in São Paulo, the one with most of the flights to North America, has several different terminals. That's one of the advantages of being in a city with 20 million inhabitants." He pointed out the open window. "And this is the main disadvantage."

Cars, buses, and trucks blocked the streets in every direction. "Everyone's trying to get out of town for the weekend. And I can't say I blame them."

For a long time, traffic hardly moved. Fumes from the cars and buses stopped around them were pouring in through the cab's open windows.

Alex's eyes began to sting. "How long will it take to get to the airport?" she asked.

"Your guess is as good as mine."

It seemed to take forever. By the time they pulled up in front of the international departures terminal, the sun had become a faded orange ball in the heavily polluted late-afternoon sky.

Alex jumped out and got their bags from the trunk while Marco paid the driver. She saw him wince as he climbed out. "Are you sure you're okay?" she asked.

"I'm fine. Let's go."

He grabbed his bag from Alex's hand and headed inside. They ran toward the check-in desk but a woman in an official-looking dark blue uniform stopped them before they could get there. "You have to go through a security check first." She spoke a heavily accented English. "And I need to see your passports and tickets."

Alex handed over her ticket. "I need to change it—to fly to New York from São Paulo instead of from Rio. Since it's a full-fare ticket, that shouldn't be a problem, right?"

The security officer looked at Alex's ticket carefully. "You want to fly to New York now?"

"Yes. And we'd like to change my friend's ticket as well."

"Well, you better hurry." The officer stamped a little red seal on Alex's ticket. "The plane for New York is just about to leave."

Alex ran over to the check-in. "You've got to get both of us on the New York flight." She pointed back toward Marco, who was still at the security check. "I'll pay whatever it takes."

The woman read Alex's ticket carefully. "We normally require rerouting changes to be made in advance, but since this is a full-fare business class ticket . . . do you have any baggage to check?"

"No. I just have a shoulder bag and a carry-on."

"That's good. The flight is just about to close."

"Can we also change my friend's ticket?" Alex pointed to Marco. "We're flying together."

"Is his ticket for New York, too?"

"I don't think so. He flew in from Paris yesterday."

"Then he'll have to get a new ticket. Or have his reissued. I'm sorry, but that would take too long." She handed Alex a boarding pass with the word *Provisional* written across the front. "You're going to have to run as it is. Your plane has almost finished boarding."

"But he's got to come with me." Alex gestured toward Marco, who was walking up behind her. "Can't you do something? He has a first-class ticket. Can't it just be reissued?"

"That will take time. He can get on another flight to New York." She pointed to the Saídas—Departures screen on the wall behind Alex. "Now go. Or you'll miss your flight."

"But—"

"What's going on?" asked Marco. "Is there a problem?"

"They're refusing to put you on my flight." Alex was almost shouting. "Show them your ticket, maybe they can change it."

The agent shook her head no without even looking at Marco's ticket. "At this point even if he *were* able to change it, it would be too late. This flight's closed."

"Then put us both on a later flight." She pointed to the Saídas—Departure display. "There's another flight to New York with another airline that leaves in just over an hour. Let's take that."

"No way." Marco led Alex over to the passport check. "Get on this flight. Get out of São Paulo now. I'll join you in New York."

"How will you find me?"

"Wait for me at the airport—outside customs. If there's any problem, call me on my cell phone. It should work in the U.S., but just in case . . ." He pulled the hotel bill out of his pocket and scribbled a number on the back. "This is my answering service in Brasilia. You can always leave a message there."

He handed her the bill. "And how can I reach you?"

"I don't know. My Thompson voicemail doesn't seem to be working. I'll get a cell phone in the U.S., as soon as I get there—at the airport if possible. But just in case, try this number." She wrote Ruedi's cell phone number on the top of his ticket and handed it back to him. "He's a friend of mine. And I have a suspicion he may be in New York, too." As she handed him the ticket, she couldn't help noticing that it was first class. "Get there as soon as you can, okay?"

"I will." He kissed her quickly. "Now get going—or you'll miss your plane."

CHAPTER 24

New York City
Saturday, Early Morning

Alex waited for Marco at the airport for three hours. His flight from São Paulo arrived at JFK right on time. But he never appeared.

She called his cell phone from a pay phone outside customs, but there was no answer. She left a message on his answering machine as well.

There was no place to rent a cell phone nearby. *Better wait*, she told herself. *You don't want to miss him when he comes out.*

As she waited, she got out the hotel bill to check if she'd dialed the right number. She had.

While she waited, she read through the bill. Marco had given his real name when he checked in, she noticed. Marco Ferreira.

He had to give it. They'd asked for identification. But the address he was allowed to write in himself. And he'd chosen a winner: 263 Prinsengracht, Amsterdam, Netherlands, the address of the Anne Frank House.

She noticed that Marco had paid for her telephone calls as well. And the one she'd made to Magda had cost more than forty dollars, even though it had lasted for less than five minutes.

Her anger at the exorbitant bill turned to panic as she realized that if *she* could see Magda's number on the bill, then so could José De Souza and his men. By trying to make sure Magda was safe, Alex had put her life in even greater danger.

She ran over to a pay phone and called her. There was no answer.

No answer at any of Ruedi's numbers either.

And no messages at all on Alex's Thompson voicemail.

What the hell is going on? she asked herself as she headed toward the taxi stand. Whatever it was, Magda must be kept safe.

The taxi took less than a half an hour to get to Magda's building in Chelsea. Of course, Alex had told the driver she'd give him a hundred-dollar tip to get her there as quickly as possible.

"I'm sorry, you can't go up there right now," the doorman told her.

"Why not?"

"Mrs. Rimer's had an accident."

Alex let her carry-on fall to the floor. "What kind of accident?"

"We don't know. They're up there taking care of it now."

"Can I go up? I need to see her."

"I'm sorry. They said not to let anyone up. They're afraid that the press will want to—"

Alex left her carry-on and was through the door to the stairs before the doorman could stop her.

Her laptop case and purse banged against her legs as she climbed. She took two, sometimes three stairs at a time. "Don't let her be dead. Don't let her be dead." She repeated the words as she climbed. "Magda, if something's happened to you because of me, I'll never forgive myself."

At the eighth-floor landing, she spotted one of Magda's cats hiding behind the door. Alex reached down to pick it up, but the cat slipped away and darted up the stairs. It had blood on its back.

Alex ran down the hall to Magda's apartment. A yellow plastic NYPD ribbon had been stretched across the open doorway. A man in uniform was standing outside. "Can I help you?" he asked.

"I'm a friend of Mrs. Rimer's." Alex was completely out of breath. "Is she all right?"

"No, she's not. She had a heart attack." Alex noticed from the badge that he was the apartment building's security guard, not a police officer. "And she musta hit her head as she fell."

"How is she? Is she all right?"

"She's dead."

"No!" Alex held onto the doorjamb for support. "It can't be."

"Sure it can. She was really living it up these last days," the guard said laconically. "That must've been what killed her. The neighbors were even complaining about the noise. No wonder the old ticker went out on her."

Alex leaned over the NYPD ribbon and looked inside. The apartment still smelled of cats—and of Magda. She noticed the police chalk line outlining Magda's body on the floor next to the fireplace. One arm was at her side, the other stretched out toward the door.

It smelled like her mother's room, at the end, when she was dying.

She imagined Magda lying there dying, alone, with no one around to help. A woman who'd survived Nazi concentration camps, Soviet occupation, a flight across war-torn Europe. But she hadn't been able to survive this.

Alex looked over and saw Magda's other cat peering out from behind the piles of records next to the bookcase. The guard got down on his knees and held out a half-opened tin of cat food. "They told me to try and coax it out. But every time he gets close to coming out, someone like you comes by. They said if I don't get him out soon, they're going to have to put him to sleep. They don't want him disturbing the crime scene."

"Crime scene? I thought you said it was a heart attack?"

"Hey, lady. Don't get excited. This is New York City. They treat everything as a crime scene. Here, kitty, kitty."

"So they're doing an autopsy?"

"Of course. But I'm sure it'll come up negative. We know she was alone when she died. I had to use my keys to open her door this morning. After the neighbors called and said they heard moaning." He held up his set of keys. "And I had to open every lock."

"Not every one." Alex reached over and lifted up the chain. It was perfectly intact. "If she had used this, you would have had to cut it, right?"

The guard nodded.

"So this one wasn't locked."

"And?"

"She told me she always used three locks. I remember it perfectly. Three was her lucky number."

The guard shrugged. "I wouldn't know."

"Someone could have locked the door from the outside, couldn't they? To make it look like nothing happened. Except they couldn't have attached the third lock. Do you know if they found her keys on her? Anywhere in the apartment?"

"Look, lady, I'm just the security guard. You'll have to go tell your theories to the police."

"It's not a theory." Alex looked over at the panicked cat. "If you knew Magda, you'd know that she'd never leave her door unlocked."

"Whatever you say." The guard got down on one knee and pushed the tin of cat food inside the door. "Here, kitty, kitty."

Alex walked back down the hall in a daze. She felt dizzy, weak, tired—and angry.

She took the elevator back to the lobby. "You shouldn't have done that," the doorman sneered. "I told you not to go up there."

Alex walked over to her carry-on in the corner of the lobby.

"Are all these for Magda?" An old man was bent over, reading the note on a large bouquet of flowers next to Alex's carry-on. There were several others lined up along the wall.

"Strange, isn't it?" the doorman answered laconically. "The obituary will only come out in tomorrow's papers, but they've already started sending this stuff. Word gets around fast in this place, I guess."

Outside, Alex spotted a pay phone on the corner of 9th Avenue and 24th Street. She walked over and picked up the receiver. She paused a few seconds, then started dialing. Nine-One-One. *The police will listen to me here*, she told herself as she waited for an answer. *This isn't Switzerland—or Brazil. They're not going to be stopped by bank secrecy rules or powerful politicians.*

"Emergency. How can I help you?"

"I'd like to report a murder," Alex said.

"Where? Do we need to send an ambulance?"

"No, but I need to talk to the police. Now!"

"Just a moment. I'll connect you."

Within seconds a man answered. "Homicide. Can I help you?"

"I think someone's been murdered."

"What's the name?"

"I'd rather not give my name."

"What's the *person's* name then?"

"Magda Kohen. Rimer, actually." Alex spelled out both names.

"Address?"

"465 West 24th Street, Apartment 8-H."

"I'll connect you with that precinct. Hold on."

Alex prepared what she was going to tell them: that Magda always used three locks and that her chain wasn't attached when the super came in this morning. So? Was that going to convince them?

She could tell them about the $21.3 million from Magda's account on its way to Cyprus. What then? They'll want to see proof. Something that shows that her account was being used for money laundering. For that she needed account statements. She needed access to Magda's account at HBZ.

Then she remembered. On Wednesday, Magda had signed a power of attorney giving Alex full access to the account.

She hung up and dialed Michael Neumann's number at the HBZ New York branch. They had to give her anything she asked for. She could get every document she needed. *Then* she could go to the police. She'd show them everything. And let *them* take care of it.

"Hello, this is Michael Neumann, I'm away from my desk right now or on the other line . . ."

"Pick up!" Alex muttered. "Pick up, now!"

A heavyset woman walking by looked over and stared.

The HBZ recording went on to give her the option of speaking to the operator or leaving a message. She punched zero.

Still no answer.

"Goddamn it," she shouted. "It's 9:30 in the morning. Where is everyone?"

Not even the operator was picking up.

Then she remembered. It was Saturday. The reason she had almost missed her plane in São Paulo last night was because of the weekend traffic.

She slammed down the receiver.

Shit! The HBZ office in New York wouldn't be open for another forty-eight hours.

She started walking. *Don't panic*, she told herself. *You can go in first thing Monday morning. The information will still be there. Then you can take it to the police. It'll still be all right. Just wait patiently. Everything will be okay.*

She looked back and saw a van pull up to the front door of Magda's building. A man got out and brought in another large bouquet of flowers. *Buy the largest bouquet of roses you can find*, Alex told herself. She had time. The doorman said the obituary would only come out in tomorrow's papers.

Then it hit her: when HBZ opened on Monday morning, they'd find out that Magda was dead. And Neumann had made it very clear that the power of attorney Magda had signed last week was only valid as long as she was alive.

Alex's mind raced. There was a six-hour time difference between Zurich and New York. First thing Monday morning in New York meant early afternoon in Switzerland. That left a window of opportunity of six hours. If she could get to HBZ-Zurich on Monday before New York opened—before they informed the head office that Magda had died—Alex could go in and make them give her copies of everything—everything she needed to take to the police in New York. But that meant going back to Zurich immediately.

On her way to the airport, she stopped at an ATM and got as much cash as she was allowed. The first thing she did was buy a cell phone—the most expensive one they had—with fully functional voicemail.

She called Marco again, but there was no answer. She left a message at his answering service with her new number, asking him to call her as soon as possible.

Where was Marco? Was he in New York already? Looking for her?

She checked her Thompson voicemail again, but there was still nothing. Hadn't Eric said he'd left several messages? She called and left a message for herself, then called back to hear it. Still nothing.

It had definitely been disconnected. But by whom? Had Crissier found out what she was doing? Who else knew?

She tried calling Ruedi, but there was still no answer there either. She left a message telling him about Magda—and saying she'd be on the next flight to Zurich.

When she boarded the plane at JFK, she realized that despite all the security checks, the U.S. border police didn't have anyone to control people leaving the country. The only people who asked for her passport were the airline employees at check-in and boarding.

It wasn't at all like that in Brazil, where the border police checked everyone's passport carefully before they were allowed to the gates.

She then realized with horror that De Souza, with his connections to the governor, could easily have used the border police in the São Paulo Airport to find anyone he wanted. All he had to do was give them the name. And if they'd traced her call from the hotel, they would have found Marco's name.

CHAPTER 25

Zurich
Sunday, Early Morning

The plane was making its final approach to Zurich's airport. Alex woke up in a sweat.

She'd been dreaming that she was in a cataclysmic mudslide. Hundreds of people were dying all around her. The rocky hillside had come pouring down in a muddy tidal wave. Everyone was fighting to keep from being sucked into the raging torrent of mud and debris from the slums built on the escarpment above. In the middle of the river below, there was a wooden raft packed with people. Everyone was struggling to hold on, trying to keep from being swept under. A beautiful woman with dark, curly hair was trying to pull someone out of the water. "She's family, too," she shouted. She pulled a small child up onto the raft. The child was screaming frantically.

Alex woke up just as the plane was coming in for a landing.

She tried calling Ruedi from the airport in Zurich. There was still no answer—at either of his numbers.

She took a cab to her room to pack her stuff and be ready to leave as soon as she got what she needed at HBZ. Then she could go back to New York and take everything to the police, and finally put an end to this nightmare.

She inserted her card key into the front door of the Wellenberg Hotel Dependence. She glanced up at Eric's window. It was completely dark. Of course. It was early Sunday morning. He was probably still asleep.

Strangely, her key didn't work. She tried several times, then dragged her bags over to the hotel's main entrance. "What's going on?" she asked the receptionist. "I can't get into my apartment."

"Of course not," the receptionist replied abruptly. "Thompson's not renting the room to you any longer." She took Alex's magnetic key and dropped it into the wastebasket. "We stored your things in the back. Do you want them now?"

"What's going on?" Alex asked.

"You'll have to ask your manager at HBZ, Herr Crissier. He's the one who told us to—"

"What happened to my colleague, from apartment 32?"

"Oh, he left yesterday." The receptionist reached under the desk and handed Alex a sealed envelope. "He said to give you this."

Alex tore open the envelope quickly. "Hi Alex. I'm staying at the hotel just across the street from where we had dinner last week. You know where it is. Come there as soon as you get this message. Eric."

The Hotel Savoy Baur en Ville, one of the best hotels in downtown Zurich, didn't allow anyone to go up to a guest's room unaccompanied. A concierge had to escort Alex to the elevator and use a special key to get access to Eric's floor.

Eric greeted her in the doorway of his suite wearing a rugby shirt and a pair of white boxer shorts. "I'm so glad to see you." He pulled her bags into the room, shut the door, and gave her a hug. "I've been so worried about you. Are you all right?"

"I'm not, actually." She closed the door carefully behind her.

"What is it?" He moved toward her. "You look terrible. What's happened?"

"Why weren't you at the Wellenberg?" Alex asked.

"It's okay." Eric placed Alex's bags next to a room service tray outside the bedroom door. "Ruedi is taking care of everything."

"Ruedi? Tobler?"

"Yeah. He said we'd be safer here. He's paying for everything. At least until—"

"You're here with Ruedi Tobler?"

"Yeah." He gestured toward the bedroom door and blushed slightly. "We've been staying here."

"For how long?"

"Since last week. He called to see if I'd heard from you and—"

"Ruedi called you?"

"Yeah, last Friday." Eric pulled on a pair of faded jeans. "He was worried about you, Alex. He said he hadn't talked to you since you found Magda in New York."

"He told you about Magda, too?"

"Yes. *And* about the trustee account. He told me everything, in fact."

"I don't believe it."

"It's okay, Alex. He did the right thing in contacting me. He cares about you. He was worried about you. You have no idea. He's had to take pills every night to get to sleep—last night he took a lot. He's been out cold since early evening."

"So that's why he didn't answer his cell phone."

Eric stared into her eyes. "Alex, why didn't you tell me about the trustee account?"

"I didn't want to get you involved. I didn't want you to know what I did that night."

"Were you afraid I'd report you to Crissier?" He shook his head. "What a joke. He fired me, too, you know? He said he didn't need our 'services' any more."

"I'm sorry, Eric. Maybe I should have told you." She sat down on the couch. "I tried to solve everything myself. And look what happened."

A cell phone rang in the bedroom several times. Alex thought of Marco. She'd given him Ruedi's number.

"Why doesn't he answer it?" she asked Eric.

"I told you. He's been out cold, since last night."

"But it may be for me. Could you go in and answer it?"

Eric walked over to the door and opened it slightly. The phone suddenly stopped ringing.

Alex leaned back on the couch. "What a nightmare."

"Alex," Eric sat down next to her, "what's happened to you? You look terrible."

She closed her eyes. "You don't want to know."

"Come on, talk to me." He put his arm around her. "I'm in this now, you know. You can tell me."

He held her as she spoke. She was able to keep from crying while she told him about the attempted rape, about her escape from São Paulo, about getting the information on De Souza. But when she told him about Magda, it was too much. She broke down.

"Such a sweet old woman," Alex sobbed. "If it hadn't been for me, she'd be alive right now."

"It's not your fault. It's the fault of those—"

Suddenly the door to the bedroom opened. Ruedi walked out rubbing his eyes. "What's going on out here?"

"Alex?" He walked over to Alex. "God, am I glad to see you. I've been trying to call you for days, but your voicemail's not working." He tried to hug her.

She pulled back.

"What's the matter?" Ruedi asked.

"How could you?"

"What?"

"Bring Eric into this? You want another dead person on your hands?"

"What are you talking about?"

"First Ochsner. Then Magda. Who's going to be next?"

"Magda?"

"You better sit down, Ruedi." Eric pointed toward the couch. "We've got something to tell you." As Eric filled him in on the details, Ruedi sat silently. Suddenly, he got up and went over to the mini bar. "It's my fault. I should have left my father's death *ungeklärt*." He washed down two white pills with a small bottle of vodka. "If I'd just left well enough alone." He looked into Alex's eyes—his eyes were glassy and the pupils were dilated. "And you, how have you been able to get to all those places in such a short time? New York, Brazil, New York again, here?"

"Night flights, Ruedi."

He crossed the room and sat down next to her. "And after all that, all we can do is what I've said all along—we just have to wait for those transfers to go through."

Alex shook her head. "You don't get it, do you?"

"What else can we do?" Ruedi asked.

"Go to the police. In New York, at least. I'm sure they'll listen to us there."

"And you think *that's* going to end it?" Ruedi's voice rose.

"It's what we should have done from the beginning," Alex insisted. "It's the only way we can—"

"It's not the only way. It's the worst way." Ruedi stood up and walked over to Eric. "We go to the police now and you know the first thing the money launderers do? They'll come after us, that's what." He turned back to Alex. "You saw what they did to Magda. Is that what you want to happen to us?"

He went back to the minibar and got out another bottle of vodka. "We have to make sure that what happened to Magda doesn't happen again. To me and to you." He glanced toward Eric. "And to him, as well."

"And how do you propose doing that?" Eric asked.

"First we make sure they get their money. And then we—"

"They probably already have their money," Alex interrupted. "The Cyprus investment was cleared to go through last week. But that doesn't change the fact that they know about us now."

"Not for sure. That guy in Brazil never knew who you were, right?" Ruedi asked. "How will he ever be able to find you?"

"They found Magda," Alex replied. "A woman who's been lost for decades. How hard do you think it will be to find us?"

"Then let's find a way to make sure they can't—or won't—touch us," Ruedi replied firmly.

"How do you propose we do that?" Alex asked.

Ruedi replied in a low voice. "MAD. We get enough information on them to make sure they'll never harm us. It was in *Dr. Strangelove*—Mutually Assured

Destruction. All you have to do is convince your adversaries that if you're attacked, *everyone* gets hurt."

"This isn't a movie we're talking about here, Ruedi. Our lives are at stake."

"That's why we have to do something! We can't just sit here and wait for them to come after us."

"I still think we should go to the police." Alex replied obstinately.

"And then what do we do?" Ruedi asked. "I don't want to sit around the rest of my life waiting for the money launderers to come after me."

"What else can we do?" She looked over at Eric. "What do *you* think we should do?"

"Well, first I'd wait to find out what happened to Magda," he replied calmly.

"But it's clear she was killed," Alex rubbed her eyes. "I know it."

"You said they were doing an autopsy, right?" Eric put his hand on her shoulder. "Why don't you at least wait until—"

"We have to do something now!" Ruedi shouted. "We need to get as much information as we can so we can prepare for whatever's going to happen."

"He may be right." Eric turned to Alex and pointed to her laptop case. "Are those files you downloaded in Brazil in there?"

"Sure. But they're all in Portuguese."

"No problem." He opened the lid and the laptop sprang to life. He set it on the ornate desk and went to work. "I lived in Málaga for a year when I was in college. It shouldn't be hard—Portuguese isn't all that different from Spanish."

"Too bad Marco isn't here to help you." Alex came over and watched Eric open one file after another, creating a complex mosaic of spreadsheets on her screen. "He'd be able to—"

Suddenly she remembered: the call to Ruedi's phone. "Can you check your messages?" she asked. "Maybe it was Marco who called just now."

"Be my guest." Ruedi pulled his cell phone from his bathrobe pocket and handed it to Alex. "Push one and then put in my access code. It's 2505."

"Easy." Alex started dialing. "It's the first four digits of your office number."

"Exactly." Ruedi headed toward the bathroom. "If no one minds, I'm going to take a shower."

"*Sie haben vier neue Nachrichten.*" Alex pressed the phone to her ear and listened. There were four messages. The first one was from her. So was the second. Her voice sounded panicked, confused.

Then she heard Marco's voice: "Hi, this is Marco Ferreira, a friend of Alex's. Could you give her the message that I'm at Guarulhos airport in São Paulo, getting ready to fly out. Tell her everything's fine. Tell her I just bought a little present for her at the jewelry shop in duty-free. Tell her that I'm missing her already. Even though I just said goodbye to her."

Thank God! Alex sat back down on the couch. He had made it through the passport check. Or had he? She tried frantically to remember the sequence: security check, check-in, border control, duty-free, boarding. She called out to Eric, "Is duty-free before or after the passport check?"

"After. Always."

"Thank God."

Alex listened carefully to the message date and time. The call had been made two days ago. But where was he now?

She skipped ahead to hear the last message, left after this morning's unanswered call. Just a phone hanging up. Then a dial tone.

She skipped back and listened to Marco's message again. And again. She listened to it several times before Ruedi walked out of the bathroom drying his hair with a thick white terry-cloth towel. "Was it him?" he asked.

"There was no message from this morning's call." She handed him the phone. "I can't find one, at least."

"Let me check." Ruedi punched some buttons, looked up, and smiled. "This is how I found you, remember?" He held up the phone's LCD for Alex to see. It was a Brazilian phone number. But not the one Marco had given her.

"If you want to call . . ." Ruedi handed the phone back to Alex. "Just push the green button."

She tried, but there was no answer.

She left a message. "Marco, if this is you, please call back. I'm waiting to hear from you. Love, Alex." She handed the phone back to Ruedi.

He made a little bow. "You keep it. If your boyfriend calls you, you should be the one to answer it."

He walked over to where Eric was working and put his hands on his shoulders. "Well, young man?" He leaned down to look. "Did you find anything interesting?"

"Nothing so far. I'm correlating the information from all of the spreadsheets. It's kind of a mess, but I'm making sense of it."

"What we really need is to get the statements from the account." Alex went over to check Eric's progress. "But for that we have to wait until HBZ opens on Monday. Then we have a six-hour window of opportunity, before the New York branch opens. That's when they'll find out Magda's dead."

"What makes you think they don't already know?" Eric muttered.

"How *could* they know?" Alex asked. "Magda was killed on Friday night, after the New York office closed. The obituary will only come out in today's papers. And by the time the New York office sees it, it'll be Monday afternoon in Zurich."

"They could look on the Web." Eric kept typing as he spoke.

"But they'd still only know on Monday morning when they come in to work in New York, which would be early afternoon here."

"What about in Zurich?" Eric turned to her and raised his eyebrows.

"Why would they be looking through the Web?"

"Didn't you know? They have an office here that does precisely that. It's right in the basement, not far from our office. I went in there last week. I didn't have anything else to do at lunchtime with you gone."

"What do they do?"

"Look through Web sites—newspaper sites especially—searching for any mention of a client's death anywhere in the world. They do it in case a greedy heir tries to come into the bank and get access to an account before the other relatives have a chance. All the banks do it now. With modern technology, you can find out instantaneously when someone dies."

"And how would they know to look for Magda's name? Isn't that supposed to be a secret? Isn't that what Swiss bank secrecy is all about?"

"For every account at HBZ there's always someone at headquarters who knows who the owner is. Didn't you know that? They have this thing called a Formular A."

Ruedi turned to Alex. "We've heard of it."

"We had to fill one out in New York, giving Magda's name and address." Alex slumped down to a stuffed armchair next to Eric. "So now there's no way they'll allow me into her account. No way for us to get the documents we need."

"Sure there is." Eric turned to her and smiled. "Ruedi told me FINACORP has all the account documents. All we have to do is—"

"He's right!" Ruedi reached over and patted Eric's back. "And as far as they're concerned, I'm still the official owner of the account. All we have to do is go in there."

"Hold on." Alex interrupted. "There's no way Schmid would give us anything. If he's the one who's been arranging the money laundering, we're the *last* people he'll give information to."

"But what about his partner?" Ruedi smiled slyly. "I bet handsome young Herr Pechlaner would be more than happy to let us have a look at their files . . . if he's given the right incentive." He began dialing directory assistance. Alex recognized the numbers immediately. Three fives.

"I'll try him at home first." Ruedi whispered while he waited for the operator. "I'm sure he's going to be happy to hear from me." He smiled. "After all, as far as he knows, I'm the owner of a $400 million account, and I'm thinking of putting it all into his hands—and his hands alone."

CHAPTER 26

Zurich
Sunday, Late Morning

The street outside FINACORP was completely deserted. Ruedi rang the bell and turned back to Alex and Eric. He smiled. "You should have heard his reaction when I told him that I was fed up with Schmid and wanted to bypass FINACORP, to give him my money to manage personally, which meant putting *all* the fees from my account into his pocket." He rang again and waited. "Who would say no to $2 million a year for life?"

Pechlaner opened the door and stepped back in surprise. He obviously wasn't expecting three people.

"Don't worry, they're with me." Ruedi walked inside and motioned for Alex and Eric to join him. "These are my assistants. I'm sure you have no problem if they join us, yes?"

"Whatever you say, Mr. Tobler." Pechlaner let them in and closed the door carefully behind them. Alex noticed him lock the door twice.

"Thank you for meeting us so early." Ruedi led the way to the conference room. "But, as I said, I have to leave for a business trip this afternoon . . ."

Ruedi was back in form—getting what he wanted, one way or another. "Before I make you my sole fund manager," he told Pechlaner, "I need a little bit of information to put my account in order—before I transfer it into your care."

Alex glanced into the trading room as they walked by. Several computer monitors hung from the ceiling. She recognized the one on the left immediately; it was the online link to the Helvetia Bank of Zurich. She also noticed how the trading room was lined with thick folders. Just like Jeff Norton's office at Malley Brothers, each one had an account number printed on the spine. Only here, none of them had names.

"The first thing I want," Ruedi pointed into the trading room, "is to look at those documents you showed us last week. You remember, the account statements and transfer information for the past year? I just want to see exactly how much is in the account before I transfer it all into your hands."

"Of course." Pechlaner quickly went to the far wall of the trading room and started looking.

"That's strange." He put his hand on an empty shelf. "They're not here."

Alex walked over and looked. All the account numbers were in sequence, but the place where Ruedi's HBZ account folders should have been was empty.

"He must have taken them with him." Pechlaner looked through the files on Schmid's desk. "Although I don't know why. We *never* take these files out of the office."

"What about the documents in the basement?" Ruedi asked. "Maybe you could show us the most recent ones from down there."

This time, Pechlaner let them accompany him to the cellar. Apparently when $2 million was on the line, the normal rules for office security were quickly discarded. He searched everywhere, but the Tobler account folders were nowhere to be found. None of them. There was no longer any trace of the account anywhere.

"I can't understand it." Pechlaner shook his head slowly as he led them back upstairs. "Why would Max take everything with him? Do you think he knew you intended to transfer the management of the account to me?"

"I'm sure not." Ruedi frowned. "How would he have known?"

When they reached the top of the stairs, he put his arm around Alex. "So, what do we do now?"

"I have no idea."

"We always have the computer." Eric pointed into the trading room. "It's online twenty-four hours a day, isn't it? Even weekends."

"Well, yes. I suppose it is." Pechlaner answered hesitantly.

Eric walked over and sat down at the computer. He moved the mouse and the screen switched on, then moved the cursor to the field marked HBZ Access. He clicked twice.

A new screen flashed on with a small field in the middle. Above it was written the word *Password*. Eric turned to Pechlaner. "What's your access code?"

"Um . . . the bank said we were not to give it to anyone. That it was just for our use, to check the account balances and transactions only for the accounts we manage."

"That's fine." Eric sat aside. "*You* put in the code. I promise not to look."

"I'm not sure if I should be doing this." He sat down at the computer.

"Of course you should." Ruedi walked over and put his hand on Pechlaner's shoulder. "I'm the account owner, after all. And I'm instructing you to show me everything that's been going on in my account. Surely I have the right to do that, don't I?"

"I suppose so." Pechlaner typed in the code. A new field suddenly appeared: Kontonumber—Account Number.

Eric moved back over to the keyboard and typed in the number Alex gave him: 230-SB2495.880-O1L.

Suddenly the computer came to life. A long list of transactions and balances filled the screen. "That's it. We're in."

"Um . . . would it be possible to get us some coffee?" Ruedi asked.

Pechlaner stood up. "I suppose so."

"Do you have espresso?" Ruedi asked.

"Yes, but it may take a while. I'll have to turn on the machine."

"No problem. We have time. Does anyone else want some?" Ruedi asked.

As soon as Pechlaner was gone, Ruedi put his hand on Eric's shoulder and peered into the computer. "Can we get what we need?"

"Of course." Eric began typing. "I'm printing out all of the account transfers over the last six months." His fingers moved with lightning speed. "It'll come out in reverse order, but you'll have what you wanted." He pushed a button and the printer over in the corner came stirring to life.

"You did it." Ruedi patted Eric on his back. "Our hero."

"No problem." Eric shrugged. "Any computer novice could do it."

Alex walked over to the printer and picked up the first page. "Why are you printing them one by one?" she asked.

"It was the fastest way. Otherwise, I would have had to go through the FINACORP bookkeeping system, and that would have sent Pechlaner into a frenzy." He glanced toward the door. "Don't worry. It won't take long. Almost all the transfers we want are at the end of July. I saw them on the screen. We'll get them in a minute. There's only been a few since then—mainly wire transfers that Magda made last week."

"Well, here's the last one." Alex held up the transfer statement. "She made it last Friday, just before closing time in New York."

"Who to?" Ruedi asked.

"To herself. She transferred five thousand dollars to her local checking account."

"That's all?" Ruedi asked. "What can you do with five thousand dollars?"

"A lot—if you've been used to living on almost nothing for most of your life. You'd be surprised." Alex picked up the next page and started reading.

"Can't you go any faster?" Ruedi asked. "What if Pechlaner comes back and sees what we're doing?"

"Don't worry." Eric began playing with the speed-dial buttons on the phone beside him. "We're doing exactly what we said we would—we're getting all the information concerning your account."

"You mean Magda's account. Or it *was* until she died . . . I wonder who it belongs to now."

Alex didn't look up from the page. "She told me her cats were going to get it all."

"You're kidding!" Ruedi shouted.

"She didn't think she had any money."

"Only in America." Eric continued playing with the phone. "In Europe, that would never hold up in court. And now, since the account's in Switzerland, European law would apply: her family would have to get the money."

"But she doesn't have any family." Alex started reading the next transfer slip. "Unless—"

"Hey, check this out." Eric pointed to one of the buttons on Schmid's phone. "It says Miguel Zinner—Ritz Paris."

"That's where he is now, apparently." Alex kept reading the transfer statement. "Where's Nyon?"

"It's near Geneva. Why?" Ruedi went over to look.

"This says that on last Friday, Magda sent twenty thousand dollars to an account at Credit Suisse in Nyon."

"It's a little town along the lake." Ruedi leaned over Alex's shoulder to read. "Who's the lucky person?"

Alex read the two-line text: "'Wire Transfer from Magda Rimer, New York to Simon Aladár, Nyon.' The account number is even longer than the ones at HBZ."

"Simon Aladár?" Ruedi took the document out of Alex's hand and read carefully. "That's a Hungarian name, isn't it? Aren't they always written backwards?" Ruedi began imitating Sándor's voice, rolling his r's heavily. "But you know Alex, that's not the way we do things here. In Hungary the last name goes first and the first name last. By the way, you should pronounce his name SHEE-moan all-a-DAR, not Aladár Simon."

Ruedi's pronunciation sent a shiver down Alex's spine. Magda's words flashed into her mind. "She moans family, too." Isn't that what she said when she was walking through the fountain in New York?

"I just thought of something." Alex turned to Eric. "Aladár was Magda's father's name, right?"

"So?"

"Maybe Magda isn't the last living heir to this account."

"Really?" Ruedi shouted. "You think you might have found the new owner of my account? That's fantastic! We could go back to HBZ and—"

Just then, Pechlaner walked in, holding a tray of coffees. "What did you say about a new owner?" he asked.

Ruedi's face went white. "We were just talking about who'd inherit my account—after I die."

"You said there might be a new owner of the account." Pechlaner walked over and took the transfer document out of Ruedi's hand.

"I want to know what this is all about." He read through the document quickly. "Who's Magda Rimer?" he asked angrily.

"No one." Ruedi replied. "Just an old woman. It's none of your business, actually."

"You lied to me." He turned to Alex. "All of you." He walked over and grabbed the computer printout out of her hand. As he did, she caught a glimpse of the name at the top of the page: Magda Rimer.

Alex suddenly realized with horror that the name Magda had put on her transfer order to Aladár Simon in Nyon was her married name—the name that was registered in the New York phone book. Anyone who had access to the computer—even Schmid—would have been able to discover who she was. Would have been able to find her.

"Get out!" Pechlaner shouted. "I want you all out of my office. Now!"

CHAPTER 27

Nyon
Sunday Afternoon

The silver cell phone vibrated quietly in Alex's hand. She glanced at the LCD display. It was Eric.

"What's up?" Eric asked. "Where are you now?"

"Still on the train. I'm just about to arrive in Nyon."

"You sure you don't want us to come and help you?"

"I'm sure." Alex told him the same thing she had told Ruedi several times in Zurich. "This is something I have to do myself." She didn't want anyone else at this meeting. Especially when it might involve yet another member of the Kohen family.

As promised, Aladár was waiting for her at the station. He looked excited. It was easy to get him to agree to meet her. All she had to do was mention Magda.

He smiled shyly as he walked up to her and held out his hand. He was wearing the same type of suit Sándor wore in Budapest, but his was completely wrinkled—as if he had slept in it. In addition, two of the buttons of his shirt were put into the wrong holes. His tie was spotted with food stains.

"What do you say we take the boat? We can talk better out there." He pointed to one of the old steamers about to head across Lake Geneva. "And on a day like today, we'll be able to see every one of the Alps."

They walked to the landing and boarded the first boat leaving.

"See? That's Mont Blanc." Aladár pointed across the bow as the paddle-wheel steamer left the Swiss shore and headed toward Evian, on the French side. "It's 4,807 meters. Western Europe's highest peak."

"Mr. Simon, I have something to tell you."

"You can call me Aladár."

"The same name as your father?" Alex asked.

He nodded. "Who told you about me? Magda?"

"She tried. I just didn't understand what she was saying at the time."

"It was always difficult for them, you know. My father's family, his official family, never acknowledged me. His wife was high-society, you know—a Blauer. Someone like me, I'm sure you can understand, was a bit of a thorn in their sides." He pointed to the towering peaks as they approached the French shore. "My father was very kind to me and my mother, though. He gave me everything I could have wanted—everything except the Kohen name."

"But he *did* give you his first name."

"Yes. Even though my mother didn't want him to."

"Why not?"

"One doesn't name children after living relatives. Not in the Jewish religion anyway. It's considered bad luck." He turned to her and smiled. "But my father made an exception for me. He told me I was his favorite. Even though I knew he preferred Magda. She was his little princess."

He looked back to the mountains. The peaks were sparkling in the early-afternoon sun. "It's strange. I'll never understand how he could let me go off to the work camps and kept his one legitimate son with him in Budapest. It doesn't make sense. I wonder if he knew that by keeping his legitimate son behind, he was condemning him to death. And by letting the Fascists take me away, he was allowing me to live." The wind blew his long gray hair in every direction.

"Actually, the work camps in Yugoslavia were a blessing in disguise—many of those who stayed in Budapest ended up in concentration camps." He took a long breath. "Of course, the guards treated us horribly. But it was so late in the war, we knew it was just a matter of time until the Allies arrived."

The boat let out a blast as it approached the French side of the lake.

"It always amused me," Aladár continued, "how Goebbels would twist the news around to make things sound better for them. He described D-day as 'the last desperate measure of the defeated allies.' But everyone knew that the Nazis were losing. That it was only a matter of time. We saw the American and British bombers flying high in the sky over Yugoslavia, on their way to bomb the oil fields in Romania. Just seeing them gave us hope. We knew that help was on the way."

Alex remembered Anne Frank's joy at seeing the D-day invasion finally take place. *June 6, 1944. D-day. The invasion has begun.* She remembered reading that date with Marco in the Anne Frank House exactly eight days ago. Where was he now?

"Aladár, there's something I need to tell you."

He continued speaking. "The Russian liberators were almost as bad as the Germans. Wherever they went—in the small towns, especially—they began by raping all the young women. When they passed through Hungary on their way to Germany—it was the fall of 1944, I think—that's when I started my long trek back. Thank God, the Swiss gave me refugee status. That's how I was able to live here all these years. I get a monthly payment from the German government, too." He paused. "As an indemnity, you see. For what they did to me."

When do you tell him? Alex asked herself. *When do you tell him that he's lost his only remaining relative in the world?*

"See that?" He pointed to one of the snow-covered peaks coming into view above the port of Evian. "Those are the Dents du Midi. They're 3,257 meters high. And over there is the Dent Blanche, 4,356 meters."

"Your father knew the altitudes of all the Alps, too. Didn't he?"

"Yes. He was the one who taught me." His eyes turned sad. "How did you know?"

"Magda mentioned it in her oral history. Have you ever seen it?"

"Where is it?"

"In New York. At Columbia University."

"I never made it to America." He shook his head softly. "And she never came back to Europe. She did send me some money, though. I was never able to work, you see. After the work camps, I had to walk all the way back to Budapest. I still didn't know if my mother and father were alive or dead. When I finally got there, I went immediately to my mother's apartment. The neighbors told me she had been taken away, to Auschwitz. She never returned." He took a deep breath. "Then I went to my father's apartment, on Andrássy út. It had been taken over by squatters. The neighbors told me that he'd died at the hands of the Fascists—Hungarian Fascists—and that his wife and children had died in the concentration camps. No one knew, I guess, that Magda had survived. I only found out later, when she called me from New York. She found out from some common friends that I was alive—that I had survived the war. We were the only family either of us ever had."

"You never had a family of your own?"

"I know why you're asking." Aladár turned to Alex. "Magda told me about the trustee account." He shook his head slowly. "I can't believe it's been sitting there, all this time, less than three hours away from where I live. If I'd known . . . I could have claimed my share. I *am* Aladár Kohen's son, after all. He named me an equal heir—along with Magda and István—in his will. Unfortunately, after he died, after his wife died, there was such chaos. We never imagined there was so much left, so much that the Nazis never got their hands on."

"This may be of interest to you." Alex pulled out the agreement between Aladár's father and Rudolph Tobler. She showed Aladár the line at the end of the second paragraph: "In the event of their death, the account is to be divided among <u>all</u> of their children."

She handed him the letter. "I'm sure he meant you."

"I'm sure he did, too." Aladár stared at the letter. "My father was a good man. I'm sure he would approve of what we're doing with the money. It may be too late to change *our* lives, but there's something we should do, to make sure that what happened to us will never happen again to anyone."

"What are you talking about?"

"Didn't Magda tell you? We're going to use the money to set up a foundation to help educate children throughout the world. In an effort to put an end to discrimination."

"Magda changed her will?" Alex asked excitedly.

"Of course." Aladár sat down next to her. "You don't think she would leave almost $400 million to her cats, do you?"

He smiled. "She also told me that if something were to happen to her, I was to make sure I gave her mother's collier to the woman who found us. I guess that means you."

"What collier?"

"Her mother's favorite piece of jewelry, it seems. She wore it to the ball the first night she went out with my father in Budapest. It had several large diamonds. Magda wanted you to have it, apparently."

"Could you do me a favor?" Alex asked. She got out a piece of paper and wrote down Zsuzsi's name and address in Budapest. "Let's give it to her. She's the one who really needs it. I'm going to send her some money as well. For medical expenses and whatever else she might need."

"But shouldn't Magda be the one to give it to her?" He stared into Alex's eyes.

She didn't answer.

"What is it?"

Alex took his hand in hers. "Aladár, there's something I have to tell you."

His eyes filled with tears. "She's gone. Is that it?"

Alex nodded. "I'm so sorry."

He didn't move.

"It happened over the weekend. She was . . . we don't know for sure what happened. They said it was an accident. But if it wasn't, I promise you, I'm going to make sure that whoever was responsible—"

"Why didn't that man help her? Wasn't that what he was supposed to do?"

"What man?"

"That man from Switzerland—her banker. He told her he'd take care of everything."

"What banker?"

"She told me his name. What was it? Schmid, I think."

"Max Schmid? From FINACORP? He met with Magda on Saturday? Schmid was in New York?"

Aladár nodded. "He said he went there to help her. Magda said she first tried to contact the woman who—" He blinked. "I guess it was you. But she said she couldn't find you. That you'd checked out."

"Oh my God."

"I never heard from her after that."

The boat pulled into Evian Harbor and let out three strong blasts. Just then, Alex's phone began to vibrate. She glanced at the LCD. The number coming in had a Brazilian prefix. Alex answered immediately.

"Marco?"

"No, it's Digo. I just got your number from Tobler, the guy you told Marco to call?"

"What's happened? Is Marco all right?"

"No he isn't. He was arrested two days ago. I flew back immediately when I heard. They caught him at the airport with several kilograms of cocaine."

"That's crazy."

"Of course it's crazy. It's the pretext they're using until they can decide how to proceed."

"How is he?"

"He's alive, but just barely. They roughed him up pretty badly." He paused. "I'm not sure how long he's going to survive in there, Alex. You have no idea what it's like. I just went in to see him. It's a nightmare."

"What did he say?"

"Nothing. He wouldn't tell me anything. He just said to call you. That you'd know what to do."

CHAPTER 28

The high-speed train journey from Evian to Paris was the longest four hours of Alex's life. She spent most of the time going over the documents Eric had created on her laptop. Somehow he'd been able to organize the plethora of information she'd downloaded from De Souza's computer in Brazil.

Gradually, she began to understand what was going on. What had started out as a simple tax evasion scheme for Miguel Zinner's farm had eventually developed into a lucrative venture. The governor had a lot of money to launder, too—and what better way to do it than through an enormous Swiss bank account that no one was watching?

For a small percentage of the proceeds, Max Schmid had agreed to turn a blind eye as De Souza regularly sent Zinner's and the governor's money through the Tobler account. What did Schmid care? Tax evasion wasn't a criminal offense in Switzerland. Even if he did lose his job, he had built up a multimillion-dollar offshore account in the Cayman Islands.

With several hundred million dollars and no one overseeing it but an old man oblivious to everything but the bottom line, the Kohen trustee account had been the perfect vehicle. As long as De Souza had the money out before the end of the quarter, no one knew what he was doing.

The money got sent out to the Cyprus funds in the form of investments in bogus funds that were used to launder the money and get it back into the hands of the original owners. Counterfeit trades, phony investments, sham losses—whatever it took. They always found a way to get the dirty money clean and back into the pockets of Miguel Zinner and the governor. They even found ways to get the money into the hands of some of the governor's major supporters, who, in turn, were exceedingly generous to his campaigns. They also created a second Cyprus fund just to handle the additional expenses of running a successful money-laundering operation.

Every quarter several million dollars were sent through the two funds—80 percent into the main fund, 20 percent into the small one. Quarter after quarter, year after year. More than $100 million was being sent through the account annually.

But it still didn't add up. Why would they be willing to kill just to cover up a simple tax-evasion scheme? As Digo said, corrupt businessmen and corrupt politicians were a dime a dozen in Brazil. There had to be something else. But what was it? For the life of her, Alex couldn't figure it out.

The train slowed as it entered Gare de Lyon station. Alex got off as soon as it stopped and began running to the door marked Exit—Sortie.

What was she was going to tell them? All she had was a bunch of numbers. How could she force Zinner to let Marco go free if she didn't have anything else to fight with? But if she didn't do something now, Marco would die.

At the taxi stand, there was a long queue—and it wasn't moving at all. Alex walked to the front and saw that people were cheating, climbing through a small metal gate to cut ahead of the others. The people standing in line said nothing. Apparently in France, as in Brazil, cheating was a fact of life.

She lifted up the gate and got in the first cab, a Mercedes. "Ritz Hotel," she shouted. "As fast as you can."

The driver squealed off and headed across the river—to avoid the traffic, he told her. Then he was back on the right bank and began careening down a dark tunnel. "That is the Ritz just ahead."

Alex noticed a small mound of flowers by the side of the road. The driver said something that sounded like "lay-dee-dee." Then he tipped his hat.

Only when they were almost to the Ritz, did Alex realize what he had been pointing at: the spot where Princess Diana—Lady Dee, as he called her—had died.

As they sped around the square in front of the hotel, the tires rattled against the cobblestones. Alex thought of Lady Diana being driven through this same square that night, driven to her death by a drunk, drugged employee—someone she trusted would get her home safely. Even with all the power and money in the world, an irresponsible employee had brought her down.

Then it hit her. The same thing had been happening to Zinner. The information was all there in her laptop. All she had to do was listen to the story the numbers were telling.

The driver pulled to a stop in front of the hotel, but Alex made him wait while she got out her laptop and quickly ran through the spreadsheets and examined the numbers again. This time, she knew what she was looking for.

She walked up to the front desk with brio. "I'm here to see Miguel Zinner," she told the concierge confidently.

"Who may I tell is here?"

"Tell him it's Magda Kohen."

The concierge made a quick call in French, then turned to Alex. "He said to send you up. But you need to take one of the private elevators." He pointed down a long corridor to her left that headed toward the back of the hotel. "It's beyond the Hemingway Bar."

As the creaky gilded-wood elevator took her to Zinner's floor, Alex studied her face in the cloudy antique mirror. She looked thin, tired, and afraid, not at all like someone criminals would listen to.

She walked down a narrow hall to a small, dimly lit alcove. The walls on both sides of the door at the far end were covered with frescos showing a landscape with green fields, cows, and sheep in a peaceful bucolic setting.

She took several deep breaths, rang the bell, stood back, and waited. She could feel her heart pounding. *Be strong*, she told herself.

A huge bald man opened the door. Alex immediately recognized him from the photographs she'd downloaded from the Web. Miguel Zinner was just as Digo had described him—big. When he held out his hand to her, his gigantic gold watch sparkled in the dim light of the alcove.

"*Bom Dia, Senhora*." He shook her hand firmly. "It is big surprise to see you." His hand enveloped hers completely. "I thought you had bad accident in New York."

"Can I come in? I have a proposition for you."

"Please." He showed Alex into the suite and locked the door behind her. "I *am* businessman, after all." His English was bad, but it was good enough, Alex decided, to understand what she had to tell him.

She sat down on an antique sofa in front of a gilded coffee table and got out her laptop. "My name's not Magda Kohen, by the way."

"I was thinking not—"

"My name's Alex Payton." She opened the laptop. "And I have some figures here I think you might want to see." She clicked open a spreadsheet. Zinner sat down next to her and pulled out a long cigar.

"I assume you'll be able to understand most of this." Alex clicked open the second. "We've prepared an Excel summary to make it easier for you. Here, take a look."

Zinner puffed his cigar rhythmically as she walked him though the documents Eric had created. After several minutes, he stood up and walked over to a glass door leading to a large balcony. Alex could see the Eiffel Tower in the background. Without saying a word, he opened the door and went out to the terrace. He stood out there for several minutes, silently smoking his cigar, looking over the rooftops of Paris.

Why doesn't he say something? Alex wondered. *Doesn't he understand what I told him? Haven't I made it clear that he* has *to listen to me now?*

Suddenly, Zinner walked back in, took her hand and pulled her up, away from the laptop, over to a small door built into the living room wall. "There's someone I'd like you to meet." He opened the door and showed her in. "Go ahead."

She balked. "I want you to know, I've made copies of everything I've just shown you. If anything should happen to me, my associates will—"

"Don't worry." He smiled as he showed her through the doorway. "You can trust me." He led her into a suite almost identical to his own—antique furniture, soft lighting, tapestries covering the paneled walls.

A dark-haired man was sitting on the sofa with his back to her. He was talking to a beautiful young woman who was sitting across from him, wearing bright red lipstick. A bottle of champagne rested in a silver ice bucket on the table between them.

"I have friend who wants to meet you." Zinner's voice boomed.

He pushed Alex forward and closed the door behind them. The man on the sofa turned around. Even with the steel-and-gauze bandage covering his nose, Alex recognized him easily. It was José De Souza.

"What the fuck are *you* doing here?" he shouted. He struggled to stand up. His right arm, Alex noticed, was in a sling, his left leg in a brace.

She tried to move back through the door, but Zinner blocked her way. He clenched her hands tightly in his and twisted them behind her back. "Inside, now!"

"How the hell did you find her?" De Souza's half-opened shirt revealed a thick white bandage across his chest.

"Actually, she found *me*. And has been telling me some very interesting stories." Zinner's English, Alex noticed, had suddenly gotten better.

De Souza reached inside his shirt and pulled out a revolver. Alex tried to pull back as De Souza pointed the gun at her.

"No need for that." Zinner pulled out a small pistol of his own and pushed it to Alex's temple. "I'm running this show now." With one hand, he gripped both of Alex's hands behind her back.

"Fine." De Souza slipped his gun back inside his shirt.

Alex struggled to break free from Zinner's grip. "You told me I could trust you," she screamed.

"I lied."

Zinner pushed her to the other side of the table.

"But after everything I've shown you, how could you—"

"You really think you can walk into my life, my world, and tell *me* what to do?" Zinner spat at her.

"But I told you, if anything happens to me, my friends have the same information I do, and I'm warning you, they'll use it."

"Shut up." Zinner cocked the gun. "I don't give a shit about your information. And I don't give a shit about your friends."

De Souza sat down on the edge of the couch. "Kind of got in over your head, didn't you, *chérie*?" He smiled menacingly at Alex. "Like going to Café Photo that night." His teeth glowed yellow in the dim light.

"Speaking of which . . ." He turned to the woman sitting across from him and threw several hundred-euro bills onto the table "*Va t'en!*" he shouted.

She grabbed the money and walked out the front door, closing it carefully behind her.

"Ah, the wonders of Paris." De Souza sat back and smiled. "You know what Hemingway said about this place? 'When I dream of an afterlife in heaven, the action always takes place at the Paris Ritz.'" He ran his hand down between his legs. "What do you say we finish what we started in São Paulo, *ma chérie*?" He started rubbing his crotch. "Only this time you won't have your little friend to stop me."

Alex struggled to escape, but Zinner's viselike grip kept her from moving. The cold barrel of his gun was pressing hard against the right side of her head.

"Look what that little shit did to me." De Souza held up his broken arm with his good hand. "What was his name again? Marco Ferreira?" He reached for one of the newspapers lying next to the champagne bucket. "A nice name. It sounds Italian, doesn't it? Which made things easier for us. Precisely the kind of name people associate with the Mafia—*and* drug smuggling." He held up the newspaper for Alex to read.

The paper was in Portuguese. The only thing she could understand was the date. It was from Saturday, the day after she left São Paulo.

"Thank God, the Polícia Federal were more than willing to spot the asshole as he tried to flee." He turned over the newspaper and showed her the picture at the bottom of the front page. "Look at him. Isn't he beautiful?"

Marco was being led away by several policemen. His face was bruised, bleeding. One of the police officers was carrying a pile of small white packages. They might as well have had the word *cocaine* written right on them.

"One thing is sure. Our little drug bust really helped the governor's campaign." De Souza threw the newspaper back on the table. "Catching a cocaine smuggler right in São Paulo airport. The press had a field day. The governor was *very* pleased."

"A propos governor," Zinner pushed Alex forward, "our young friend here has been telling me an interesting story about what's been happening to the governor's money in Switzerland."

"So?" De Souza looked uninterested.

"She has an interesting theory. I think we should hear it."

De Souza's phone rang. He pulled it out, looked at the LCD display, smiled slyly, then looked at Alex. "It seems like one of your *friends* wants to talk to me."

He spoke for a moment in heavily accented French.

While they waited, Zinner pushed Alex down into the chair where the prostitute had been sitting. He gripped her neck in one hand and kept the barrel of the gun pressed against her temple with the other.

Her heart was pounding. She wondered why he was treating her like this, especially after all the information she'd just given him.

De Souza hung up. "I hear you've been trying to visit our friend Max Schmid in Zurich." He shoved the phone into his pocket. "Well, it looks like you finally get to meet him. He's on his way up now. Who knows, maybe we'll let *him* be the one to kill you."

Alex struggled to escape Zinner's grip. "You hurt me, and I promise you, my friends will go to the police. They'll tell everyone—the Brazilian papers, CNN, the police in Brazil, New York, Switzerland—"

He laughed. "You naïve little woman. Do you think we care *what* the police do? *What* the newspapers say? Brazil is full of corruption—it happens all the time. You think anyone will do anything to us? Do you think anyone really cares?" He gripped her neck tightly. "How could you think you could ever threaten *us*?"

"We don't even care about losing that account," De Souza added. "As long as we get our money back. And then we'll find another one. We always do."

"If you didn't care about losing that account, then why did you kill Ochsner?" Alex asked. "And why did you have to kill Magda?"

De Souza shook his head and smiled. "You may not believe this, but she really did die of a heart attack. Of course, our friend Monsieur Schmid paid her a little visit last Friday. Maybe he did get a little rough, but why would we kill her?" He paused. "He only wanted to make sure she signed the payment order. Which she did. After that, we didn't care *what* happened to her."

"And what about Ochsner?" Zinner asked.

De Souza looked surprised by his question.

"What do you mean?"

"Why did you have to kill him?"

"To protect you!" De Souza shouted. "We had to."

There was a knock at the door. "Entrez!" Zinner said. "Ah! Bonjour, Monsieur Schmid. Nice of you to join us." Alex turned to the open door and saw Jean-Jacques Crissier walk in boldly.

"My, my. Alex Payton. What a surprise." He closed the door carefully behind him and walked over to her. "It looks like you finally found what you were looking for, doesn't it?"

Alex's heart raced.

"She was just about to tell us why Georg Ochsner was killed." Zinner's fingers gripped Alex's neck tightly. "Why don't you repeat to Monsieur Schmid what you told me in the other room?"

"His name's not Schmid, it's *Crissier*," Alex mumbled.

"Actually, my name *is* Schmid." He walked closer, until his stomach was just inches from her face. "I only used the name Crissier to get my job at HBZ. I—"

"You don't have to tell her anything." De Souza shouted.

"Then, tell *me*!" Zinner sounded angry. "We're not doing this for her, we're doing it for *me*!"

"Go ahead," he turned back to Schmid, "Tell us what you were doing working on the Helvetia Bank of Zurich's computers when you were supposed to be looking after our money."

"I did it for you and the governor. When I heard they were going to debug the computers, I had to make sure they didn't discover what happened in 1987. To keep it from compromising our operation."

"Why do *I* care about what you did in 1987?" Zinner asked.

"Actually, I didn't do anything. I was simply executing orders for Ruedi Tobler's father. I was his IT consultant at the time, helping him install the HBZ system on his computers. He got burned on stock investments during the crash and needed a quick way to bail himself out. All his other money was tied up in real estate and art and—"

"What does this have to do with me?" Zinner interrupted. Strangely, his grip on Alex's neck had loosened slightly. He was now using his thumb to massage the base of her skull. "I want to know."

"When I heard that HBZ was going to clean out the bugs in their computers, I had to make sure no one discovered what I'd done in 1987."

"Is that why you killed Ruedi's father?" Alex asked.

"I didn't kill him. I didn't have to. He was going out of his mind. When they started investigating the manipulation of his account during the crash, he panicked. He got on a plane to Tunisia, saying Zurich wasn't safe any more. He said people were after him. He was crazy. I didn't *have* to push him. He jumped all by himself. All I did was watch."

"Did you watch Georg Ochsner commit suicide, too?" Zinner asked.

"No." De Souza answered quickly, authoritatively. "We helped him. We did it for *you*. And the governor. To protect the integrity of the account. To protect your money."

He pointed to Alex. "We even got the old man to tell us about her before he died."

"He didn't give us your name, but I knew it was you he was talking about." Schmid glared at Alex. "But I had to make sure. That's why I told a couple of the governor's men to follow you to Amsterdam."

"You what?" De Souza shouted.

Schmid looked surprised. "Why not? He told me to use them, to use anyone I saw fit to make sure nothing happened to him. To make sure nothing happened to the money in his account. How would I know the one who was working at the embassy would end up falling in love with her?"

"Marco Ferreira was working for you?" De Souza shouted. "Why the fuck didn't you tell me?" He pointed to the scars on his face. "Look what he *did* to me!"

"I had to know," Schmid answered calmly. "I had to know what she knew. When Ochsner called me after meeting with her, saying he wanted to make some changes to the account, saying he wanted to see *all* the old documents, I had to do something."

"So you killed him?" Zinner asked.

"Of course. He was going to find out what we had been doing with the account." Schmid answered matter-of-factly. "What else could we do?"

"But why kill someone who was on our payroll?" Zinner asked. "Someone who was working for us?"

"Ochsner?" Schmid asked incredulously. "He didn't have a clue what we were doing."

"You don't know anything." De Souza struggled to sit up on the edge of the sofa. "So why don't you just shut up?"

"Because I don't want him to shut up." Zinner insisted. "I want to know why we would kill someone who we were paying several million dollars a year to help us—"

"Several million dollars a year?" Schmid looked skeptical. "For *that* fool?"

"But José told me we *had* to pay Ochsner to grease the wheels in Switzerland. Five percent of the total. Every year. Just like what we paid you?"

"Is that what he told you?" Schmid glanced at De Souza. "You weren't paying me anything close to—"

"I told you to shut up." De Souza stood up on his one good leg. "You don't know what you're talking about." He reached inside his shirt and pulled out his gun. "I told you to always let *me* do the talking."

As he spoke, De Souza slowly screwed a black cylinder onto the end of the barrel. "You have no idea what was going on. You never did."

"Well, *I* have an idea of what was going on," Zinner shouted. "And I want to know why we were paying 20 percent of the money to people who had no idea about the account's existence."

"We were paying 20 percent?" Schmid asked.

"Exactly." Zinner replied. "The 20 percent in the small Cyprus fund was supposed to be divided four ways: 5 percent for you, 5 percent for my trusted assistant, 5 percent to Ochsner, and 5 percent to Rudolph Tobler."

"Rudolph Tobler? Are you crazy?" Schmid began backing up. Away from De Souza. Away from Zinner. "Why would we pay 5 percent of the money to someone who's been dead since 1987?"

"Not the father. The son." Zinner let go of Alex's neck and moved across the room toward Schmid. "José told me we needed to pay him, to keep him quiet. So we could use his father's old account to launder our money."

"That's absurd. Tobler didn't know *anything* about the account. Whoever told you that was—" A small hole suddenly appeared in the middle of Schmid's forehead.

Alex realized what happened only when he slumped to the ground, only when she saw the thin film of blood and brains on the tapestry behind him.

She glanced at De Souza. A small plume of smoke was coming out of his gun. He pointed it at her. Suddenly, Zinner ran toward De Souza.

Alex watched his right shoulder explode. His gun fell to the floor. Alex dove to get it.

De Souza pointed his gun at her again and was just about to pull the trigger when Zinner slammed him against the wall with the full weight of his body. With his one good hand, he grabbed the barrel of the gun and twisted it toward De Souza's face.

De Souza held onto the handle tightly. They both began shouting in Portuguese. Alex picked up Zinner's gun and stood up.

"Kill him!" Zinner shouted. With his one good hand, he kept the barrel of De Souza's gun stuck into his mouth. But De Souza kept his hand on the handle—and on the trigger.

"Do something!" Zinner yelled to Alex. "I need your help. Kill him or he'll kill us both."

She didn't move.

"Kill him and it will all be over—for both of us." He struggled to keep De Souza pinned against the wall with his body.

Alex stared at the gun in her hands. Several bound arrows were engraved on the handle. She lifted it and pointed it at De Souza. She had to use both hands to keep it steady.

"No. Not like that," Zinner shouted. "You have to use *his* gun. Get *him* to pull the trigger. We'll make it look like he killed himself. After killing Schmid."

Alex didn't move.

"Get over here." Zinner struggled to keep De Souza pinned against the wall. "I need you."

Alex wondered if she could just walk out and let them fight it out. One of them would survive. What would stop him from coming after her? After Ruedi? Eric? Or Aladár?

"Come over here," Zinner shouted. Blood was pouring out of his shoulder, onto De Souza's chest. "You have to help me. I can't do this alone."

Alex put down the gun and took a step forward.

"Just push his finger onto the trigger," Zinner shouted. "And I promise you I'll make sure the governor lets your friend go. Just promise that you'll never tell anyone what happened here."

De Souza tried to say something, but with the barrel shoved into his mouth, it was impossible to understand what it was.

"We only have this one chance." Zinner said calmly, determinedly. "But if you're going to do it, you have to do it now."

She could see that his strength was fading.

Alex walked up and stared into De Souza's eyes. She saw fear. She saw panic. The same panic Magda must have felt when they broke into her apartment. The same fear Ochsner must have felt when Schmid and De Souza were pushing him over the bridge. The same panic Alex felt when he was trying to rape her. She reached out and touched her finger to De Souza's blood-soaked hand.

"Do it, now!" Zinner shouted. "And you'll be free. All of you. I promise."

"How can I trust you?" Alex asked.

"You have my word."

"After you just betrayed me?"

"I didn't betray you. I needed to find out from De Souza himself what he'd done. How he betrayed *me*. I was never going to hurt you. I promise you, I'll make sure everyone is safe. Just help me take care of this."

She reached over and put her hand on De Souza's.

"Please," Zinner whispered. "You're the only one who can do it."

He was right. Even if Zinner could get his one good hand free, his finger was too big to fit around the trigger with De Souza's. Alex slipped her finger over De Souza's and squeezed slightly. He struggled desperately. Zinner held him tighter. "Do it now!" he shouted. "I can't hold him much longer."

She squeezed tighter.

"Please," Zinner pleaded. "It's the only way we can make it look like a suicide. The only way for us to get out of this alive—to make it end."

EPILOGUE

Dear Alex,

It's 4:30 in the morning and I'm sitting here drinking a Manhattan in a sippy cup. I'm so rummy I was afraid I'd break the crystal. And the scary thing is it seems like a perfectly logical thing to do.

It's just starting to get light—early winter means long nights and very short days here in Amsterdam. And it seems all my e-mails these days are written just around the crack of dawn.

Jannik is getting his first teeth, and I haven't really slept since you were here in September. The poor thing cries so much I hear him even when he's stopped. There must be a name for that. Something like, you know, the constant ringing in your ears thing after you've been too long in a disco. You know what I'm talking about. Or maybe you don't.

Last night was so desperate with his crying that I got out the bourbon and stuck my finger in the bottle and rubbed his gums with it generously. It actually seemed to help. Can't you just see me at the pediatrician's office explaining my practice of coating the inside of Jannik's mouth with booze?

I'm sorry to go on like this, it must sound like my mind is going to mush. Maybe it is.

Where the hell are you anyway? You must be eating in great restaurants and wearing beautiful clothes that don't smell like sour milk and aren't covered in spit-up stains. You get to read the paper in bed, sip orange juice, and snuggle up to a hot cup of coffee with Marco by your side. And you can drink Manhattans out of a real glass.

I just got up to check on Jannik. He's awake for the third time during this writing. Thank God for e-mail—we'd never be able to have a decent phone conversation.

And THANK YOU SO MUCH for all those goodies and toys you sent Jannik! They just arrived this morning. He's in heaven. You are way too generous, you know that?

By the way, when are you ever going to tell me how much money you found in your mother's estate? It must have been a lot—to allow you to quit your job at Thompson like that. I still can't believe you had the idea to go back and find out what that horrible aide of hers was up to. I hope she rots in hell for what she did. But I'm glad you've decided to put it all behind you—and that you've forgiven Marco for whatever it was he did. He's such a sweetheart. We're so looking forward to seeing you guys for Christmas (is it only three weeks away?). Jannik's first Christmas and Chanukah with you here with us. It'll be fantastic. Too bad you can't stay longer. When are you starting in New York, by the way? January? I'm so glad you accepted the offer to run that foundation—it'll give you something to take your mind off your mother and what happened to her. And it's awesome that your ex-partner from Zurich said he'd help you run it. Thompson must be really pissed off at losing both of you like that, but hey, you gotta do what you gotta do, right?

I better go now. You-know-who is crying again.

Love,
Nan

PS You never told me what happened with that account you found in Zurich? Did you leave the bank before you had a chance to find out? I found some stuff on the Web the other day that may interest you. Another sleepless night, what else was I going to do? Were you aware that they found more than 50,000 Swiss accounts that belonged to Holocaust victims? Most of them were dormant accounts, though. I found very little mention of trustee accounts. Strangely, the most revealing information was on the site of the Swiss Banking Consortium—go figure. There were two questions (and answers) that I thought you'd find interesting. I saved them for you:

Question: What exactly is Swiss banking secrecy?

Answer: Under Swiss law, the individual's right to freedom and to hold property is fully protected. The same legislation applies regardless of whether the assets entrusted to a Swiss bank for management belong to a Swiss citizen or to a foreigner. Switzerland's celebrated insistence on banking secrecy protects all customers and their assets against access by unauthorized persons or official bodies, on the condition that the assets deposited do not originate from activities defined under Swiss law as being of a criminal nature.

Question: I have heard that the list of Swiss accounts contains many dormant accounts opened by Swiss fiduciaries on behalf of victims of the Holocaust. Is that true?

Answer: Actually, there is no certain way for a bank to know whether a dormant account was opened by a fiduciary. Before and during World War II there was no requirement that a person opening a Swiss bank account on behalf of another disclose that information to the bank. However, it is very unlikely that the list of Swiss accounts includes a significant number of dormant accounts that were opened by fiduciaries for victims of Nazi persecution. If a fiduciary had acted properly, he or she would have returned the assets to their rightful owner.

Don't you just love their answer to that last question? It makes you wonder just how many of those trustee accounts are still out there, doesn't it?